A
BEAUTY

A
BEAUTY

CONNIE GAULT

McCLELLAND & STEWART

Library and Archives of Canada Cataloguing in Publication is available upon request.

ISBN: 978-0-7710-3655-2
ebook ISBN: 978-0-7710-3656-9

Typeset in Granjon by Erin Cooper
Frontispiece image: © Taiga | Dreamstime.com
Cover design: Kelly Hill
Cover image: © Jean-Marc Valladier | Moment | Getty Images
Printed and bound in the USA

The characters and events in this novel are fictitious. Any resemblance they have to people and events in life is purely coincidental.

McClelland & Stewart,
a division of Random House of Canada Limited,
a Penguin Random House Company
www.penguinrandomhouse.ca

1   2   3   4   5   19   18   17   16   15

Penguin
Random
House

For B. T. Hatley

A
BEAUTY

TREVNA

On the Saturday evening, the Gustafsons, Mr. and Mrs. and the two children, set out for the dance at Trevna. Mr. Gustafson wore a benevolent beard and Mrs. Gustafson wore a tight, shiny dress. The children had bathed. They weren't talking. They had hurried to get ready once it had been decided they wouldn't take the car, and after that fuss they were content to sit and let their bodies get accustomed to the rhythm of the wagon. All around them, land-scape of the sort they were used to rolled out to the edges of the sky. The axle creaked, the horses' hooves clopped, the sun sat in their faces. The children, behind their parents, got locked in a battle involving all four of their hands in a knot. Up front, Henrik scowled for several reasons that must have seemed important at the time, and Maria's bland countenance reflected nothing.

After a while Maria said to her husband, "All this sun in our faces. Soon you'll be sneezing." A little later she said, "I am happy with my cake. Lemons are expensive, but it's so much better with the lemon filling than the vanilla, it's like ice on the edges of your tongue. You must get a piece tonight, my dear. Children!" she called. "Be sure you get a piece of my cake at the supper." She swung her head back to be certain they were listening. "Stop that," she said. "Peter, you're to look out for your sister tonight."

The children took their hands back and sat on them, looking out in opposite directions. They had travelled only a short distance and were still crossing their father's land, so there was nothing to see.

Maria began to whistle. She often whistled. She felt herself to be purposefully alive. Henrik mumbled something that sounded like an admonition into his beard, but she wasn't listening; she was whistling "All of Me," which she'd only recently learned, and she was tapping on the side of the tin cake-taker she held on her lap. She always had something in her hands. Maybe a broom, maybe a rolling pin. On this Saturday evening she was holding her triple-layer cake with lemon filling and glossy, seven-minute frosting, from an old recipe of her mother's.

"I take after my mother," she said.

"Boundless," Henrik said, making the word sound gloomy.

"Boundless? What does that mean?"

"It's what sprang to mind when you mentioned your mother."

"Fat was what I meant. She was fat, too." Maria lived in an age when it wasn't a sin to be overweight, it wasn't even unfashionable for a married woman nearing forty, and she ate as much every day as she wanted. "And she always got her own way," she said of her mother. "It's good, isn't it? That we're taking the wagon to Trevna? Gas is such an extravagance. We don't want to rub our prosperity in others' noses. And what could be grander than this?" Her hand swept out over the hot August evening and the land they'd bought and paid for and the twin rumps of Bess and Basket and came back to drum again on the fancy tin cake-taker on her lap. It had been her favourite wedding gift. It was whimsically embossed with a formal Italian garden in contrast to the fields that lay around them, as dry and browned as the word *forsaken*, where cultivation had produced ruin, where dust rose from the earth the way mist would have risen from water in some other place. (But it didn't matter as much to them as to others, since Henrik was too smart to think he could farm it.) "And there's room in the wagon for an extra person," Maria added.

"I am sure you thought of that. But you don't think of everything," Henrik said.

"Look," she said.

They had finally passed the boundary of their land. He followed her pointing finger to the lonely farm buildings of their nearest neighbour and saw something similar to what she saw, although not exactly the same thing, because she saw Elena Huhtala sitting motionless on a swing with a cascading sunset behind her, and he saw Youth and Beauty. He had a poetic temperament that even life with Maria hadn't dampened.

"What did I tell you?" Maria said. "Oh, Lord. You're going to tell me people are complicated. Sometimes, you know, you're a trial to live with."

"You called on her yesterday and she said no."

"But Henrik, we have to turn in. We can't leave her sitting there like that."

Henrik didn't know why they couldn't leave Elena Huhtala sitting there like that, still as a silhouette on the swing her father had hung from the clothesline post like a gibbet. If it had been up to him, he'd have left her there, looking Symbolic.

"There is so much dust in the air," Maria said. "That is why we have such good sunsets."

⟨⟩⟨⟩⟨⟩

Elena was not moving at all; she was studying her awareness of suspension. The wooden board underneath her supported her weight as it had since she was a little girl, and the ropes, oily from years of being held in her own two hands, felt sturdy, but it was the lowered sun, warm on her back, that held her hanging in its horizontal rays. All around her, as far as she could see, the fields floated in the tricky light. She didn't think of moving; if she did, the entire world would rock.

Her father's land hadn't been planted in the spring. He'd given up. It wasn't farmland; everybody had told him that. You couldn't grow a decent potato on it. Forget about wheat. Instead of crops, now, or the prairie wool that might have sustained animals, there was only stubble, beaten down by the weather (that is to say, the wind) and lying uneven, like a brush cut on a kid with too many cowlicks. It was dull, dry straw but it gleamed like gold in this light. Maybe it had got to him, maybe looking at that gold one deceiving evening had been his last straw. It was the kind of thing he might have said, if he'd said anything, but she didn't want to be thinking his kind of thoughts. So she sat on the swing, clearing her mind. This wasn't difficult since an empty stomach tends to make the mind porous, and she couldn't remember when she'd last eaten. There was no food in the house, and the garden had given up the last of its pale, hairy carrots and wizened cucumbers. Once in a while as she sat there, a grasshopper looped through her vision, and tiny sounds infiltrated her consciousness, flowing in and out again. These were the familiar summer sounds of a fly buzzing, crickets creaking, and mice or garter snakes – or maybe just the earth's breath – rustling the grass. A cow lowed way down the road at the Svensons' place. The past crept into her mind, then, as it does when you're quiet: the long summer days she'd spent swinging on this swing, as if they still existed, as if they silently existed, alongside her, and if she swung forward, they'd swing back. Then came a rattling of wheels and a clopping of horses' hooves. She hadn't gone inside in time. Or the Gustafsons were heading out early for the dance. No, she'd dawdled, lost track of the hours. The sun was setting, for heaven's sake.

"Don't," she said out loud, but they did; they drove their team into the long driveway, the wagon wheels spinning the turn, all four Gustafsons waving as if they'd just discovered electricity and thought she should know about it. She started swinging, pumping hard, holding tight (she felt so light with the sudden motion). The ropes strained and squawked against the wooden crossbar above. At the top of the swoop, she lifted off the seat. If only, she thought – and she wasn't given to if-only thinking. But if only she could. Fly off into nowhere while the Gustafsons watched. They would be the perfect witnesses, able to attest to all and sundry that she'd gone, she'd gone so thoroughly she'd never return.

She didn't go anywhere, naturally; she plopped down on the seat again and swung back, and the Gustafsons waved some more from the wagon, and the Clydesdales set their relentless hooves down, the white hair on their fetlocks fluttering. Such a romantic picture, as if Time itself was lolloping through a veil of dust to pluck her up and take her with it. The dance was at Liberty Hall. Liquorty Hall, the young people called it, since high spirits were expected in those days.

She couldn't go on swinging once the wagon stopped or Mrs. Gustafson would be obliged to heave herself down and make the trek across the yard. She had to hop off in a jaunty, two-footed manner to show she wasn't sad and then she had to walk sedately over to the wagon to show she wasn't happy. It was her fate. Only eighteen, and everything she did had to be done in order to prevent something else having to be done.

With four pairs of eyes on her, it must have been difficult to know how to compose her face as she approached the wagon. The children didn't count, they were eight and ten, too young to have opinions anyone would listen to, but they might see through whatever expression she put on. In spite of all their parents' efforts to teach them complacency, they might still be capable of looking beyond the obvious. Luckily for Elena, although Henrik drove the horses, Maria Gustafson drove the family, and Maria's ego eclipsed anything resembling a nuance. Heartiness carried her over the roughest terrain; she hardly saw or felt the bumps.

"Come to the dance," Mrs. Gustafson said and beamed down from the wagon until her cheeks rose up and obliterated her eyes. She might have been praying, or more likely – seeing how pleased she was looking – overhearing a prayer that was being said especially for her. Mr. Gustafson might have been the one saying it; his long, corn-coloured beard trembled on his chest and his moustache quivered as if he had been speaking or was about to speak. You couldn't tell which it was, if either – the hair curled over his lips. Only his eyes were on display and they said very little. He had practised making them beatific. He gazed down at Elena Huhtala until she looked right at him, and then he shifted his attention to his placid horses, as if it was momentous when one lifted its foot and the other whisked its tail.

The children's mouths fell open. It was odd how it happened. They knew what the strange Finnish girl was going to do as soon as she knew it herself. Their surprise was over by the time she'd climbed up and settled in between them and put an arm around each of them for balance.

As soon as Mr. Gustafson turned the Clydes towards the sunset again, Mrs. Gustafson twisted halfway round in her seat (careful with the layer cake), so she could peer at Elena Huhtala. "Any news?" she asked, just as she had asked the day before.

Elena shook her head. She lowered her eyes, but Mrs. Gustafson didn't take that to signify anything. "You'll hear one of these days," she said. "He's likely written and his letter's gone astray. You know how the post is, it's not reliable at all, and men – well, you know what men are."

Elena did not raise her eyes to admit to any knowledge of men.

"He wouldn't think you'd be worrying," Mrs. Gustafson said, explaining.

"I'm not worrying, Mrs. Gustafson," Elena said. The horses picked up speed and the wagon lurched, but nothing changed her calm demeanour.

"Of course you are," Maria said. "What are you supposed to do with yourself, left like this on your own? You know you can stay with us. We'd be more than happy to have you. I hate to think of you out here all by yourself. We have an extra bedroom, you know, especially set aside for guests."

"I'm fine, really."

"At your age. What was your father thinking?"

"He's gone to look for work," Mr. Gustafson said. His wife went on regardless. The cake rocked on her lap. She had several theories to explore. She'd heard of a note left for the girl on the kitchen table. The Mounties had begun an investigation. Everyone had questions, no one knew the answers, unless the daughter did.

Elena squeezed the children's waists and watched the orange sinking sun to avoid looking into Mrs. Gustafson's pale, peering, guileless eyes. As for the children, they leaned into her on either side and seldom spoke except once in a while in a furious, whispered code behind her back. They giggled whenever one of the horses passed gas, and their mother shook her head each time and glanced indulgently at her husband. He ignored them as he did most of the time, since they provided him with as little opportunity for wit as for poetry. He was fond of being witty.

"I realize people are different," Maria said to Elena Huhtala. "Henrik often reminds me of it. Life would be so much easier if they weren't. Then they wouldn't be doing things you couldn't imagine."

"Your Clydes are beauties, Mr. Gustafson," the girl said. Her voice was low and she spoke with a slowness that made those few words sound earnest.

"They're only workhorses," Henrik said, trying for a modesty to suit his beard.

"But they're standouts," she said, looking down at their braided, beribboned tails and their shifting haunches and their deep, dark, leathery sheen, knowing that Mr. Gustafson bred them and would talk about them for a long time if ever allowed. He raised Aberdeen Angus cattle as well as Clydesdales. "My animals have made a Scotsman out of me," he liked to say. He appreciated the chuckle he sometimes got in response. Clydesdales were generally not as big in those days as they are now, and he liked their friendly height, but he bred them to be taller, as everyone did, because otherwise what was the point?

As for bigness, all around them the glowing sky was as huge as it could possibly have been if they'd been any place else, and it went on forever, as it does if you really look at it. But they didn't look; they were used to it and they had other matters on their minds, Maria in particular, who was going to have to answer to the ladies of her community when she got to Liberty Hall. How could she drive all the way to Trevna with Elena Huhtala wedged in between her offspring, and gather such a pitiful dribble to tell them? How could she let talk of the horses interrupt a full discussion of the possibility of an act she couldn't imagine? They'd be more annoyed with her than if she hadn't persuaded the girl to come. There was no excuse for it, so she patiently went at her from a creative variety of angles, while Henrik clucked at Bess and Basket until he heard himself and denied himself that comfort.

Behind them, the children swayed with the wagon's movement, either side of the strange Finnish girl, and fell almost into a trance. So forgetfully comfortable had Ingrid become that she tucked her cheek in along the plushy side of Elena Huhtala's breast and brought her hands up almost to her chin and whispered to her thumbs. Sometimes she made them whisper to one another, and they always said compelling things. Peter squirmed, on the other side, but didn't extricate himself from the arm that lay warm and lightly supportive and uniquely feminine along his back, even though it gave him the occasional shiver as he delved further into a story he was telling himself, a story in which old Mr. Huhtala's skeleton was discovered in a shallow grave in his own cellar. For a little while even Maria stopped talking, but she was only thinking what to say next, she was only moving from her inquest into the past to her advice for the future. "Now, Elena, you must make some plans," she said. "You can't go on like this. How will you support yourself? One good thing is you've got your grade twelve, now that's something most girls don't have, and you can thank your father for that. He was a man who valued education."

"Is," Henrik muttered.

"Oh. Yes, I meant that, Henrik, for heaven's sake. Although I don't know what good it does you to have your grade twelve out here in the middle of nowhere. He likely hoped you could go to college. In better times. Being an educated man, himself. But you'll probably marry soon, anyway, won't you? I don't like you on your own in the meantime. People talk, you know. It's not meanness, it's only natural, they wonder, and they talk."

"Look," Peter said, behind Elena Huhtala's back. He pointed up. It was a hawk, flashing light from its wings. "Seen something." Peter turned to watch it. "There," he said, satisfied, when it dove, beak down, to the earth.

"As I was saying," Mrs. Gustafson continued, but Mr. Gustafson started talking, too, and stopped her.

"What do you call those pictures on our bedroom wall?" he wanted to know. "Sentimental things. Pretty couples painted in black on glass, with a paper landscape behind them."

"I don't know that they have a name," Maria said. "Why do you ask?"

He shook his head; he didn't know. He reached over and patted her wide knee and she, ever generous, shifted the cake. "Oh, I can taste this cake," she said. "It is so good, my mother's recipe, so moist and substantial. But the cost of lemons! Oh, yes, I know, Henrik, why you're thinking of them. It's our pretty Elena Huhtala, sitting on the swing. You were a picture, my dear," she said, rearing back again to peer into Elena's eyes. "Your hair all lit up like a halo." She laughed as if she'd made a joke. "But this cake," she went on. "Wait till you taste it. You can make it with vanilla filling but it's not as good. The lemon filling is so cool in your mouth. I can feel it on the edges of my tongue when I say it. And with three layers, you put it twice so it soaks all through the cake. Now Henrik is going to tease me and say, 'What about the frosting, Maria? You haven't said a word about the frosting.' Oh, look, here is Liberty Hall. And half the district's arrived already."

They pulled into the yard in front of the country hall and Henrik stopped the team near the door to let them step down.

"I'll hand you the cake," Maria said to the girl.

When her feet hit the dirt, Elena turned and put her hands up for the cake. It dipped when she took hold of it, being heavier than she expected. Seeing that, Maria didn't leave her in charge of it for long. As soon as Arnie Lindquist had given her a hand down, she took it back and sailed it past the group congregated around the hot dog stand, towards the open door and the crowd inside. It was almost as if she was carrying Elena Huhtala to them on a platter.

Maria set her cake down beside the other offerings and faced the women who'd trailed behind her. She threw up her hands and admitted defeat – not that defeat ever cowed her. "It's true," she said. "I drove all the way to Trevna with the girl and I didn't learn a thing. Good heavens, ladies, it wasn't from lack of trying."

"She doesn't know any more than we do, poor kid," Hilda Lindquist said. "How long's he been gone now?"

They decided it had been about five weeks since any of them had set eyes on Mr. Huhtala, although that didn't mean he'd been gone so long. Sometimes ages passed without any of them seeing him. He was an outsider, they'd always said, and it was only the truth, a Red Finn in a community of Swedes, who'd refused to live among his own, who'd turned his back on his own. It was said he refused to speak Finnish and hadn't let his daughter speak it since they'd arrived in Canada, although this wasn't anything his neighbours could corroborate. Many of them had never spoken to him. They'd seldom seen him up close; from the road as they'd passed his farm he'd looked tall and gaunt, his clothes flapping about as if the wind had intended from the day it saw him to blow him off his own fields. And now, "They say he left a note for her, on the kitchen table."

"The Mounties came to the house to ask if we knew anything," Thelma Svenson said.

"They were at the Huhtala place an hour at least. Searching for him."

"Do you know, I'm not sure I'd recognize Matti Huhtala if he walked in the door," Britte Anderson said.

"Oh you would if you'd ever spoken to him, yeah," Maria said. "You wouldn't forget him if you'd ever been face to face."

The ladies looked expectant – Maria had blushed, as if the thought of Matti Huhtala had aroused a memory best kept private – but she bustled off across the hall, her dress shining particularly brightly across her broad backside where the wagon seat had polished it.

"Well," Thelma said. "What does that mean?"

"Peter's pulling Ingrid's braids," Britte said. "We'll never know."

Aggie Lindquist brought her *Photoplay* magazine with her for the times no one asked her to dance. The one she had was the one with Garbo on the cover and afterwards she never could believe she'd lost it. No, it was stolen and she knew who stole it even if she couldn't do a thing about it. Garbo had a deep, pale fur collar like a cloud around her neck and face and she had her proud look on, as if to say she'd endured a lot of cloudiness and could withstand more. Aggie could put that look on her own face – chin up, eyes down, as if your own cheeks are more interesting than anything out there beyond you. As long as she owned the magazine she had that look down pat, but it didn't come naturally to her, and once the thing was gone she could tell in the mirror she couldn't get the right droop. The piece inside was "The High Price of Screen Love-making." She'd read it to gauze. It didn't help. She waved her hair every Saturday morning and she gazed into the distance a lot with a soulful expression that seemed to say surely, somewhere, there was a better world, and that didn't help, either.

She saw Elena Huhtala walk in with Peter and Ingrid Gustafson on either side of her. Before the other girls noticed her, Aggie saw her and kept the secret for the few minutes it took until they cottoned to her being there. Aggie was the one who'd first said Elena looked like Garbo, and you might as well say she looked like the queen, because Garbo was a Swede. But Elena Huhtala was a Finn. Maybe there were Swedes in her family somewhere, Aggie didn't know. None of the girls had liked *Anna Christie* much. Garbo wasn't even pretty sometimes in it, and they hadn't liked her voice, hearing it for the first time. It was disturbingly husky and she had an accent too similar to their parents'. But she was great at the end. She won them over in the end. Elena Huhtala was the same. You couldn't say she was always pretty, but she was always great. Grand, that was the word. And she was prettier than Greta Garbo, maybe, to start with; Aggie thought she was.

Aggie liked to watch people when they were on their own, that is, on their own in a crowd; she'd discovered that an individual's particularity stood out against a background of other people. Garbo was who she was partly because of all the movie stars she wasn't, and Elena Huhtala was special because she was different from the rest of them. For the little time she had before the other girls would rush over, Aggie watched Elena standing alone by the door, kind of floating there as if she'd forgotten anyone could see her. In that old, faded, limp brown dress. The girl was dirt poor. She had only the one dress and when she washed it, God knew what she did to be decent in front of her father. She had no mother and she didn't pretend otherwise. Maybe that was the very thing that made her so grand – she didn't pretend about anything. They say actresses pretend, but Aggie said you watch Garbo. That was acting, not pretending, and Aggie had seen a number of her pictures. Elena Huhtala had never seen one, not one. Once or twice the girls had said they should pool their money and take her along to the Odeon, pick her up on the way to Trevna, but they never had. She wouldn't have gone with them anyway, Aggie could have told them that, they'd only have made her feel even poorer.

As soon as they saw her inside the hall, the girls went to her, and Aggie tagged along behind them. She was there to see when Nils Larson caught Elena's eye from across the floor, and there to hear when Doris Knutson said, "Somebody's happy," rolling her eyes his way, and all of them giggled. Nils was twenty-one and had a solid job with the Sask Western grain elevator company. Lillian Larson, his sister, was among the girls gathered around Elena, and nudged her with her elbow as if she was already in their family. "Maybe tonight's the night," she said. Aggie kept it to herself, but she thought it would be a pity, even if he was the best catch around. Elena should have something better than marriage and staying here and turning into a farmwife. "Oh, sure," Elena said when Lillian said maybe tonight would be the night. She went through the gestures any of them would have used, a shrug, a toss of the head, and they giggled some more, but they all knew no matter how much she tried, she'd never be one of them.

And that was the way she was really like Garbo. Nothing that happened to her or around her really affected her. In the middle of that circle of girls, she stood apart. It was a kind of sadness! Aggie hadn't seen that before. Maybe it was clearer tonight because of her dad. Or maybe she generally hid it more than Garbo. After all, she wasn't trying to portray a whole life in a couple of hours, the way you had to in a movie. Aggie kept her eye on Elena and what she saw was that even when she'd kid around, even when she was laughing out loud, there would be a shadow to the laugh. Aggie wasn't going to talk about it with the others. They might not have noticed it. Aggie might be the only one seeing it flicker in her eyes and cling to her mouth at the end of a smile, as if she only ever expected disappointment and she could see it coming a mile away.

Doris Knutson had green eyes so maybe it was natural that among the girls she was the one most jealous. She'd stand back sometimes at gatherings, putting a curse on Elena Huhtala that would have her dead or at least ugly by the next morning. They all respected her so much. You had to pretend to like her as much as they did. Just try being catty about her and you'd catch sight of someone's lifted eyebrow. The momentary pleasure of giving in to temptation would be swamped by the extra sympathy Elena would get just because of it. Still, when old Mrs. Sundstrom came over and drew Elena aside to complain to her about her arthritis and her husband, Doris saw a chance and started talking out of the side of her mouth. "Did you hear what Peter Gustafon's going around saying?"

It made them into a clique, her talking like that; it made a tight little fist of them. The girls leaned their heads in, all except Aggie Lindquist.

"Peter Gustafson," Aggie said, snorting.

Doris ignored Aggie and cleared the frown off her forehead that came with the desire to murder her, and waited until every one of the girls looked right at her. She was going to get her money's worth out of this one. She was going to see it on their faces – that they wanted to hear what Peter Gustafson had said. It was a triumph for her to make them do that. "He says she sent her dad to the cellar for a jar of pickles and while he was down there," she took the time to look into their eyes, "she pulled the chesterfield over the trap door!" She had a few seconds to enjoy the girls' reaction and then they all looked away; every one of them looked some place else, at the floor or at the ceiling or at somebody over by the door. Doris was no dummy; she knew what she'd find when she turned around. And there was Elena, staring at her with that puzzled look she got on her face when she wanted people to feel sorry for her. Right away she lowered her eyes as if she might hurt Doris if she went on looking at her, or embarrass her even more than she already had. Doris knew that she'd begun discreetly, and she also knew she'd ended up quite loud. The quietness was awful, now. But it was thrilling, too. It was a moment of realness, at least. Doris threw back her head. Why shouldn't Elena know what people were saying about her?

Somebody had to say something. Lillian coughed and they thought she was going to speak, but she only got red in the face. Finally Aggie said, "Peter Gustafson," again, with another snort. Then even she started searching the hall for someone to save them. It was a relief when the music started up. It was like they all sighed. The Harmonics. A group from Charlesville, a couple of towns away, that hadn't played at Liberty Hall before. Usually they had accordions at dances, but this band had a piano, a cornet, drums, a sax, and a violin. And wouldn't you know it, the first song they swung into was "Bill Bailey, Won't You Please Come Home?"

"Golly," Aggie said right out loud, and they all knew what she meant. They all stared hard at the lady sitting at the piano who was wagging her whole thick body, revving up the energy to belt out the words. The song wasn't about a father, but even so.

"She seems very composed," one of the women said.

"She's a strange one," Thelma Svenson said. "Maria told me she called on her yesterday and she looked as if she didn't recognize her at first. She'd seen her sitting on that swing the way she has every day all summer, and turned in to invite her to the dance tonight."

"I heard she said no."

"She was very close to her father, was she?" one of the women murmured.

"Maybe too close," another said. "Just the two of them there on that lonely farm."

Thelma cleared her throat. As the Huhtalas' nearest neighbours, the Svensons might have been thought to know them best, even to have some responsibility for the girl, but Thelma pointedly had nothing to add to the conversation. She was well aware of the resentment in the community that led to this kind of gossip. Just because Matti Huhtala was aloof. To some that meant arrogant. It was said he'd taught at the university in Helsinki, and to those same people, this was grounds for believing he thought himself superior to mere farmers. The failure of his farm would have seemed like justice to them if it hadn't been that most of the farms across the west were failing.

They were all trying to look at Elena Huhtala without seeming to look at her. They didn't realize it didn't matter if they looked. They would see her dress, her figure, her hair, her face; they wouldn't see *her*, not the way Aggie saw her. They didn't know how. She was invisible to them. It didn't matter if they were shocked, if they gossiped, if they worried about her. All they wanted was an answer; they wanted an ending, and whatever it was they'd bring meatballs and stew, they'd bring pies and cakes and platitudes.

"It's the not knowing that's hard," the women said.

It was Aggie's opinion it was the not knowing they liked.

Elena was standing apart from the other girls now, nearer to the little kids, who were chasing one another, bumping into people and getting told off. Aggie thought she looked tired. She thought about going over and showing her Garbo's picture. "You can't tell what she's thinking, can you?" she could say when they put their heads together, studying the photograph. "But you can see her whole life in her face." This was a contradiction that Aggie had mulled over. Elena would understand, but it would embarrass her, especially tonight.

Doris's green eyes darted around the dance hall, searching for someone who could compensate her for not being Elena Huhtala. Then she saw the stranger. "Who's *that*?" she said. All the girls gawked and then pretended not to gawk, and wondered about their hair.

The stranger waited near the door for a while, lounging against the wall with a friendly expression on a face that looked as if it naturally fell into friendly lines. He wasn't in a hurry. He waited there until people got used to the idea of him. He'd obviously come to country dances before. He was good-looking without being handsome, which in that community meant he looked clean and respectable and quite a lot like one of them. He had his red hair slicked back, his shirt pressed. His suit had a drape to it that must have cost money. He chatted in a low-key, laconic way with the men who went by on their way in or out of the hall. It was the same way they talked to one another. Before long, word got around he was the owner of the flashy Lincoln roadster parked down the road, and the men started trooping out in twos and threes to inspect it, and then returned, eager to ask him about it and privately wondering if he might be a gangster.

Elena wasn't the first girl he asked to dance, but he'd had his eye on her, even when he was dancing with somebody else. Nobody had asked Elena onto the floor. They were waiting for Nils Larson to claim her. Then the stranger walked up, and without a word or a moment's hesitation, she stepped into his arms.

Before they'd turned twice, Nils was crossing his arms and Lillian was frowning so hard she looked just like him.

Mrs. Gustafson came over to the wall where Aggie was standing and said nice things to her about her magazine and then gave that up when she saw Aggie only wanted to watch the stranger dance with Elena Huhtala.

"That girl is getting too thin," Mrs. Gustafson said.

The band was playing "Always." Aggie couldn't for a minute take her eyes off the two of them as they travelled along the outside of the crowd, as swoopy and swoony as the music. Mrs. Gustafson started whistling along with the song. It was funny to hear the skinny little trills come out of her thick-packed body. The lady at the piano sang, and Mrs. Gustafson trilled along, and Aggie, smitten with the mystery of everything to do with the mingling of men and women, remembered with a quiver down her spine that where Elena Huhtala came from, nothing was for always. Her mother had died when she was barely two.

When the song was over and his hand was no longer firm on the small of her back but only lingering two-fingered on her shoulder, the stranger returned Elena to the place he'd found her beside Doris and Lillian. He knew enough to seek out other partners. "Thanks," he said as if it was anybody he'd just danced with. Aggie expected him to ask Doris or Lillian next, but he looked past them. He came right up and stood in front of her, smiling on her as if she'd magically turned into a door prize. She let the *Photoplay* fall to the floor. The nicest frilly tremble zipped through her entire body before he even put his arm around her.

Over by the open door, a group of men who'd just come in from visiting a whisky jug set up near the livery barn were discussing

Matti Huhtala's disappearance and agreeing that the conclusion they'd come to was unanimous. The RCMP were pretty sure, weren't they? The man had tried to sell his farm and failed. His machinery, the little he'd owned, was long gone. He'd killed the last of his chickens, one of the men said, and another joked that even his dog had died. So one day he went off with nothing but his rifle. What did that lead you to think?

"The daughter says no," Arnie Lindquist spoke up.

"Well," another drawled.

She wouldn't want to think it, would she?

The Mounties had asked Elena about the note, if she thought it was a suicide note. "I don't know," she said. That was only a few days after he'd left and she didn't want to prejudice them against him in case he was still alive. It was a crime to attempt to commit suicide, they told her. They watched her for a reaction, but she didn't have one. The idea didn't shock her; she'd already considered it a possibility.

"What do you think?" they asked.

"I don't think anything," she said. And it was almost true. She'd come home tired after a long, restless walk to nowhere, and found both yard and house deserted. And the note on the table, nothing else. She hadn't done any real thinking or feeling (which was what they really meant) since. If she thought about him, she stopped herself before she got all the way to "How could you do this to me?" She didn't know that most people feel numb when they've had a shock, or that most find anger easier than grief, if they can see a choice.

You must make some plans, Mrs. Gustafson had said.

In all the time since he'd left, all the days she'd sat out in the yard on the swing, not moving, at first waiting and then not waiting any more, she hadn't considered what to do next.

Nils was looking at her from across the hall. She supposed he'd earned the right.

You can't go on like this, was what Mrs. Gustafson said.

The stranger hadn't asked Doris to dance with him yet, and she was trying to pretend she didn't care. She was trying to pretend he wasn't a person you wanted to smile on you, or a person you watched after he'd turned away from you. And now here was Nils, making a beeline for Elena through the crowd, his face stern above the other heads. "Look out," Doris said, without thinking. He was stiff when he reached Elena, too. He didn't speak, just stuck his arm out to indicate his need to take her out on the floor in front of everyone. She looked up at him and smiled the thin, shadowy smile that Doris thought she must have rehearsed in her mirror.

Doris caught Aggie Lindquist watching her. You never knew what Aggie was thinking; she acted so dumb at times you could see why some people said she was half-witted. She made Doris wonder what kind of expression she'd had on her face that Aggie had picked up on. And then Aggie started laughing. Doris glared at her, but Aggie just threw back her head and growled, "I'm loving nobody," and Doris had to laugh with her. It was a line from *Anna Christie* that the girls had been repeating ever since they'd seen the movie. They could all picture the haughty, defiant, pathetic expression on Garbo's face when she said it, her eyebrows all peaky. "I'm loving nobody." How silly it had sounded even when *she* said it. And they made it sound more ridiculous when they mocked it, rumbling it, roaring it, rolling their heads like the

MGM lion. It made them laugh and laugh. Gales of laughter doubled them over. They almost wet their pants. They only had to pull that face, any one of them, and another would shout it out. "I'm loving nobody." Hah! Tell that to the marines, sister.

She did Nils's little boxes with him, she made her body calm in his arms, but it wasn't long before she was searching through the crowd for the stranger, and when she found him he was already looking right at her.

"Elena," Nils said.

"Oh. Yes?"

Mr. and Mrs. Gustafson pounded by with Mr. Gustafson's beard between them. Mrs. Gustafson reached out and gave Elena's arm a damp, approving pat.

"Where were you?" Nils asked.

"Here," she said.

"I don't think so. You looked like you were across the room."

She squeezed his hand. "No, no."

He said her name again when the music ended, with the same tone of impatience and frustration. He was, although half-unconsciously, a proprietary young man. He believed he had it in him to command others if only they would listen. But the orchestra, hardly taking a breath, started up, and Elena was already swaying. The lady at the piano was already bawling out "Shine On, Harvest Moon." About a guy and his gal. Okay, Nils thought. If it was going to be that kind of night – and all the songs were going to be prophetic – victory would go to the decisive one. He already had his hand on her arm. He opened his mouth to take charge, and then – as if nothing in the world had meaning – the stranger cut in, cut in and took her, just like that, out from under him, swept her away and danced her off to the middle of the room. And Elena didn't look back.

"You haven't asked my name," he said.

She said, "Nor have you asked mine."

He took her coolness for the light form of mockery he recognized as a prelude to flirtation. He dipped her and twirled her. He pulled her in close and murmured in her ear, "Can I take you home tonight?" He expected something arch in return, as arch as her previous response had seemed to him. But she stopped dancing and turned, wordless, towards the open door. She actually left him behind and he had to quicken his step to catch up to her. He hadn't meant they should leave at that very moment. The night was still early. But what the hell. Country girls, he thought; their naïveté was refreshing.

In a corner at the back of the hall, lolling with some other kids on a heap of sweaters and light coats – because an August evening can get chilly – Ingrid Gustafson sighed. At that masculine arm at that slender waist. At those wide, manly shoulders and beside them that wavy, honey-coloured hair. And at the sky past the door, that glassy, cobalt blue. One of the girls said, "I want hair just like that when I grow up." Ingrid ignored her. She bent her head and held her hands up close to her face with the thumbnails facing towards her. She whispered the things they would say to one another. Slowly she turned both thumbs so they faced each other, touching all the way down. Peter went looking for some boys he could tell his story to.

The band went on playing, but no one was dancing. The men were leaving, following Nils. The married women flocked to

Maria Gustafson and told her they'd always considered Elena Huhtala a modest girl, becomingly willing to hide her physical attributes. The girls who'd gathered around her earlier followed Lillian to the open door to see Nils stalk across the yard and down the road towards the fancy gold convertible. Lillian said she pitied the guy when Nils caught up to them, but nothing came of it. The stranger opened the door and Elena sat herself inside and they drove away before Nils reached them. Everyone stood watching their dust boil up and trail behind them. It was that clear navy-blue time of evening you'd like to bottle up and keep, it's so beautiful, and the dust looked white against it – like a wedding veil, Aggie thought, but she didn't mention it to anyone.

At least the girls still had Lillian to gather around. They still had Nils's broken heart to discuss, and after a while they dredged up a few practical suggestions for how it could be mended. Doris Knutson volunteered to take Elena's place that very night, but Lillian thought it could wait. They tutted over Elena a bit, too, but not much more than they usually did. Hadn't they always figured she was headed for disaster?

Lillian had once said that if only Elena Huhtala could be seen in black and white, her face sculpted by shadows as Garbo's was on the screen, they would all have to hold their breath in her presence. Until that Saturday night, Lillian had always said kind things about Elena. She was plain, herself, with a nose she considered to belong on a bigger person, and therefore she was in no danger of disgracing herself the way Elena had begun to do, and when she'd talked about the likeness, she'd meant the Garbo they liked best, not so much the one who'd shown that rangy body and rough side in *Anna Christie*, although they all knew even beautiful women could have their off days, times when they got tired of their beauty and sneered at it and looked as if they'd toss it in a trash can if they could.

Aggie didn't know exactly what Elena Huhtala was up to, but she knew she had it in her to do something the rest of them wouldn't. Doris Knutson said, "I can't imagine what she'll do next." But she could. They all could when they thought about it. They fell silent and imagined her grainy, flickery, all sleepy-eyed and music-laden, like someone who had forgotten who she was or didn't care, a girl slipping like a length of live silk from the arms of one man to another, looking sadder and sadder as she went on. None of the girls said a thing about it. None of them admitted they yearned to be her, physically yearned, the blood thrumming through their bodies at the very thought.

◇◇◇◇◇

In the Lincoln, he reached his arm out and she slid over the leather seat to nestle close to him. "Bill Longmore," he said, glancing down at her. "Pleased to meet you."

"Elena Huhtala," she said. *El*-ena *Hooh*-ta-la was the way she pronounced it, with the accent on the first syllables and making a lot more of the *h*'s than he would ever be able to do.

The stars weren't out yet although the sky was clear. The air was as warm as bathwater flowing over their skin. She never said she was hungry and he didn't have food on his mind. He stayed outside while she went into the house. That was her idea; she said she wouldn't be long and she wasn't. She came out with one small bag, an old black leather thing, the size and style of a doctor's bag, and threw it in the back. He gave her a last look at what she was leaving behind, sweeping the big headlights in a full circle so the homestead flashed by, the puny windbreak poplars, the unpainted farmhouse, the weed-riddled, drought-starved garden, the empty barn, the granaries that held no grain, and the dugout that had dried to crackled, khaki-coloured mud.

When they got to the road, he stopped the car and turned to her. "So, *El*ena *Huh*tala," he said, exaggerating her pronunciation, "Where do you want to go?"

She didn't comment, just gave him a look that seemed to say he wasn't as tall as she'd first thought. "Anywhere," was what she said.

◇◇◇◇◇

Nils Larson got drunk for the first time in his life that night, but he was such a nice young man drink didn't affect him much. He only made some rash statements about following Elena and bringing her back where she belonged, and then forgot why he was alive and stared stupidly at nothing for a while and then passed out.

Peter Gustafson told the boys more details about Mr. Huhtala's final days in the cellar of his own home with his daughter walking around above him while he yelled and swore and banged on the trap door. Quite a few people older than Peter, but no wiser, cobbled inventive stories together from the few discernible facts they could garner, and went around saying they'd heard she'd as good as confessed on the way to the dance. Their speculations were so enjoyable, they didn't ask Henrik or Maria Gustafson to verify them. They were just entertaining themselves, saying you could believe anything of her after the brazen way she'd waltzed out the door with that fellow's arm around her.

Aggie Lindquist decided that whatever Mr. Huhtala had done with himself, Elena was better off without him. On her own, now, she didn't have to care what she did. A father's what ties you down, Aggie thought. Without one, you'd be free. And then she had to stop thinking because Henrik Gustafson asked her to dance, feeling sorry for her, she figured – she'd known him since she was five – but as it turned out that wasn't the reason.

"Little Agatha," he said in a hot gust into her ear while they stomped out some tune or other. None of the music was memorable now, and everything irritated her, even though you could say she'd got her wish, what with Elena Huhtala going off with the stranger and thereby escaping the expected.

"I hate my name," she said.

"Oh you must not," Mr. Gustafson said. His yellow beard puffed up against her chin and that was irritating, too, all dry and scratchy. "It's a good name," he said. "Why, don't you know it's the name of a famous author?"

"Is it?" she said. Mr. Gustafson was known for being a reader of the kinds of books others didn't have time for. Some people mocked him – behind his back, of course – for growing a beard to look like Walt Whitman. Walt Whitman was a famous author; they'd had his poems in their school readers. Aggie had never memorized any of his; some of them seemed just nonsense. She had heard of this Agatha. People told her about her every chance they got, as if the idea of them having the same name would impress her and she'd give up living and take up writing books instead. She'd learned it was more flattering to a man if he thought he was original, though, so she didn't let on he wasn't the first to mention it. "There's no movie stars with the name," she said. And for good reason, she was thinking, because it has a throat-clearing kind of sound. *Agatha*.

"I have several of her books," he said, hot in her ear.

"You don't say?"

He squeezed her waist and let his hand drift down to graze her bum. A thrill went through her and she thought: You old goat, what are you up to? He'd always looked to her as if he'd been caught in the act of teaching Sunday School and had just said something nice about Jesus to the children. But she kept the polite look on her face, and in the meantime they were stomping away at the dance floor as much as he ever did with his wife.

"Say, how be I bring you one sometime and you can have a read of it, yeah?" He panted into her ear. "They're detective stories, you know. Light reading." He ran his hand down her spine, all the way to the bottom, though he didn't linger there. Right away he put it back where it belonged, and Aggie had to wish she had the guts to ask him to do it again. But the dance was over. He gave her a push on the waist as they trotted off that she figured was meant to be a reminder, in case she had liked the stroking and wished for more.

"I'd like to read one of those books," she said with a bold look into his eyes before they parted. It felt as if she was practising. An old fellow like him – as old as her father – he'd be safe to practise on. Safe but exciting, too, in a way that was too dirty to think about. She leaned against the wall again and bent to pick up her *Photoplay*. It should have been on the floor among the shoes that had been kicked off, but it was nowhere to be seen. She scanned the hall for a sight of Doris – she was sure Doris stole things – and saw Henrik (she thought she'd call him that, now) over by the door. She tried to catch his eye, but he didn't look her way again, and then he was asking Doris to dance. She remembered the odd expression she'd caught on Doris's face earlier. That was a guilty look if she'd ever seen one. Doris had probably hidden the magazine away somewhere safe where she could retrieve it later. She'd never admit it, though. That *Photoplay* was gone for good.

The whole time Doris danced with Henrik, Aggie leaned against the wall, watching. After a while she recalled what he'd said about Elena Huhtala at the last church social. If she told the girls they'd laugh and laugh. But she wasn't going to tell them.

"A face to launch ships," he'd said. And him a thousand miles from any ocean.

◇◇◇◇◇

Ten minutes out of Trevna the children fell asleep on the wagon floor, and before long Maria's head was nodding. Henrik half-dozed, too, until Bess and Basket picked up their pace, knowing they were nearing home, and then he sat up, blinking, in time to see the black shapes of the Huhtala farm pass by, the swing barely visible, hanging lifeless. No sign of the Lincoln roadster. He figured she'd sent the fellow packing and was sleeping as they passed, safe in her bed. But perhaps no longer a virgin.

They creaked and clopped along. The night was beautiful with stars and cool air and grassy smells. No one whistled. A breeze rippled over them and behind them the swing moved. He was sure it moved. The ropes groaned against the wood. Ahead, the road shimmered in the weak starlight. The fields Henrik owned went on and on until they melted into the darkness. He groped under Maria's dress for her knee, for the feel of naked flesh in his hand. When he found it, however, some reproof from the vast yielding softness of her inner thigh travelled through his fingers, and he was shocked by a gust of remorse, and worse than remorse, dread.

◇◇◇◇◇

Aggie Lindquist dreamed the writer woman came to supper at their house, Agatha What's-her-name. She looked like a writer, with glasses worn low on her nose, and she sat down opposite Aggie at the table, but right away Aggie thought there was something funny about her. She couldn't settle properly on her chair; she kept on slipping and sliding to one side or the other. Aggie didn't like to draw attention to it by asking what was wrong, so she stood up and peered over the table, and then she saw what it was. The woman was a mermaid. Her whole bottom half was a fish's tail and couldn't stop squirming.

ADDISON

Merv Badger, proprietor of the Addison Hotel of Addison, Saskatchewan, was petting the cat. Under the terms of his marriage contract (some thirty years old this summer), he was allowed to pet the cat, but the contract was unwritten, unspoken, and changed more often than the weather – way more often than the recent weather, which had been nothing but hot and dry. Merv cringed when Pansy entered the bedroom, in case it was a stupid thing to be doing this late in the evening before bed, sitting in his underwear indulging an animal that responded to him with indifference unless he was actively giving it pleasure. The cat took the moment of Pansy's arrival to begin purring like a lawn mower, sending vibrations down Merv's knees all the way to his bony bare feet. Involuntarily, he shivered and his toes splayed against the floor boards. Pansy ignored him and the cat. She sat down on her side of the bed, facing him as if facing the wall, and unbuttoned her blouse.

Pansy Badger was built to be a laundress; she'd said that to Merv the first time he'd watched her undress. It was her idea of a joke, but it was true. Her ribs were what you noticed. "You could use me for a scrub board," she said. Her tiny breasts the size of walnuts. She tossed her blouse to the rocking chair beside Merv and raised her arms to let down her hair. She'd cut it the year before, but every night she raised her arms the same, right after throwing her blouse on the chair. Merv glanced up through his eyelashes to her armpits.

She stretched her back. "*Christ*, I'm tired," she said.

"*You're* tired," he said.

"Oh, you," she said and yawned big enough to swallow him and the cat.

He'd never told her the sight of her underarms, with their own version of her fine, straight hair, aroused him. He could feel the old worm stir, although they rarely had sex anymore, it was too much work.

Pansy rummaged under her pillow for her nightgown. "This place'll be the death of me," she said.

"We should've bought fire insurance."

"Jesus Christ, Merv."

"I know."

"Why bring it up? Why go on about it? It's too late now. We couldn't pay the first month's premium."

They'd bought the hotel for the proverbial song during Prohibition and for a few years after repeal they'd managed to think they'd made a solid investment. When the Depression hit, they'd had to lay off the young girl and the old man they'd employed to do the work. Merv and Pansy were in their fifties by then and firm in their opinion that management was more their style than labour.

Pansy pulled her worn old nightie over her head and poked her arms into it.

"I think you're thinner," Merv said. He could still see quite a bit of her through the greyed fabric with its once-perky sprigs of some unknown flower.

"Thinner than what? You? *Christ*. That would be something."

They had both lost weight as the years went on. Neither of them liked to cook and when it came to meals, as in many other instances, they'd fallen into the habit of waiting one another out. Neither ever wanted to be the first to make a move. They ingested their fair share of baloney, trimming off the green when it got rather old.

Pansy shimmied out of her skirt under the nightie's tent. She fumbled at her waist to unpin her underpants, and half-stood. The elastic was so shot they slid to her ankles and landed at her feet, licking at her feet in a pale puddle Merv knew would be warm. Then she had the pin in her mouth, open, between her teeth. Silver colour, one end hooded, the other straight and sharp. Merv held his breath until she reached down and refastened the thing in the pants to be there ready the next morning.

"I wonder what Old Jock and Old Caldwell had for supper," he said. It was a game she liked as it gave fair scope for sarcasm. The cat rolled in his lap and bared its belly, then grabbed at his hand with its claws-out paws when he stroked it. Scared of what it wanted. Could only take it for a minute, and then rolled back again to feel his hand from the fine bones of its head down its bumpy length and along its tail. Liked its tail pulled. Wouldn't we all? Merv thought, lazily.

"Steak and onions," Pansy said. "Ham and scalloped potatoes. Pork chops and — some goddamn *entrée*. Seeing they can afford to eat out." Jock and Caldwell were the two old bachelors who made their home at the hotel. The skirt and the underpants joined the blouse on the rocker, and she fell back on top of the bed.

"Jesus. This room is stifling," she said. It was his fault, like everything else, and she meant to bring to his mind all the other rooms she might have found herself in, and didn't and couldn't, because of him. "And that cat is making the most annoying sound."

"Ah yes," he said. "The sound of contentment."

He could still make her laugh. She always acted surprised, as if he'd just developed a sense of humour as a gift for her. And when she laughed she looked right into his eyes. He made her laugh as often as he could. It took the two of them right out of time, right away from that place. It was like being immortal, for a second, or at least not the owners of the Addison Hotel.

He got up and let the cat out. Pansy refused to sleep with it in the room; she'd refused even to give it a name. He lowered the lamp wick and the room went dark. He crawled onto the bed. The two of them lay flat on their backs on top of the sheets, gazing at the shadowed ceiling, waiting for oblivion.

One thing Merv didn't like about getting older was the worrying. He didn't recall worrying so much when he was young, and about things that hadn't happened and were unlikely at that. Some nights it was tough to get the picture of her swallowing that pin out of his mind.

◇◇◇◇◇

Bill said it would be hard to get a room if they left it too late. Elena said she'd never been inside a hotel.

"These small-town hotels are mostly excuses for beer parlours," he said.

"I've never been in one of them, either," she said.

"You couldn't. No women allowed. You don't get out much, do you, kid?" She was still snuggled up to him, and he rubbed her arm to show her he felt warm towards her.

They pulled into Addison, one of the villages every seven

miles or so along the rail line – seven miles reputedly being the distance a crew could lay track before needing a bed for the night, back when they were building the railroad. "This look like anywhere?" Bill asked, pulling up in front of the one hotel.

"It sure does," she said.

He went ahead to make the arrangements, in other words to wake the owners up, since every window in the false-fronted box was dark and the whole of Main Street, which was almost the whole of Addison, was deserted.

If there was one thing that could remind Merv and Pansy who they were and where they were, if not why, it was a rap on the front door after they'd locked up for the night. Neither of them moved except to stop breathing. A little while passed and whoever it was knocked again, louder this time. Pansy groaned.

"I'm not going," Merv said.

"Well I'm not," Pansy said.

Down the hall, in the minuscule rooms they rented by the year, Old Jock Macklin and Old Caldwell Kurtz pulled their pillows over their heads. They knew the owners, if the poor sod outside didn't.

Elena waited in the roadster with the top down and the night around her. Bill looked up at the stars while he waited for someone to come and answer the door.

"Ever think about those things?" she called to him.

"All the time," he said. About a billion of them had pricked through by now, clustering in constellations he felt he should be able to name. He knocked on the door again, and turned back to see her sitting in the open convertible, her face moonlight-pale. He lit a cigarette and took a long drag that was like drinking her in. The night was still warm but with that rim of coolness where it met his skin. He backed away from the door and looked up at the hotel and saw a man's narrow face disappear from the middle window on the second floor and the curtain drop. He heard someone on the stairs – the walls were thin enough to allow that, he noted – and got his semi-apologetic smile ready.

The room wasn't as clean as it might have been, but it didn't matter so much because the globe on the one lamp was so smoky it hardly let out light. The water in the two pitchers on the dresser had sat there for several days, the drinking water covered with a cloth that said "Addison Hotel" in some kind of nubby pink cross-stitch, or actually "Addis Hote"; the last letters had been picked out or fallen off. The wash water had drowned an unfortunate pair of houseflies who floated on it, belly up, each of them with his brittle black legs tangled in his last struggle against his fate. The commode down the hall had been fully appreciated by Old Jock and Old Caldwell.

Bill passed her his flask after he'd taken a swig, but she wouldn't have any. Just as well, he thought, gauging how much was left by the heft. He'd drunk quite a bit of it before going into the dance hall, as he usually did.

In those days a double bed was smaller than it is now, and this one swayed to the middle, so when they were both in it, they were almost necessarily touching. He slid his arms around her and nuzzled and kissed the back of her neck. She hadn't taken her dress off, had only slipped out of her shoes, and his lips nudged at her collar and bumped along the curved vertebrae and vibrated over the fine hairs there. He moaned. It was a quiet, involuntary, yet satisfying moan. It had welled all the way up from his groin. He thought it reached out to her, the articulation of his desire. She didn't respond. He moaned again, more communicatively this time.

"I feel I do not know you well," she murmured.

He laughed. That was involuntary, too.

When he didn't move away, she said, "I am quite serious."

"Elena," he said.

She gave a little, foreign-sounding half-laugh.

"What's so funny? Eh?"

"Men."

"Men? What do you know about men? Come on, I'd like to know. And then I'll tell you what I know about women. Especially women that are cockteasers, eh? Lead a fellow on and then turn prim. I ain't used to that, baby." He stretched back against the meagre pillow with his hands behind his head. There were occasions when a guy had to lay it on the line. He gazed up at the dark ceiling and recalled her asking if he ever thought about the stars. He was pleased he'd answered, "All the time." It seemed a strangely sophisticated exchange to have with a country girl. He remembered asking if he could take her home, and her turning right away to the door.

"Hey, Elena!" He tugged on her shoulder. But she was asleep. He couldn't believe it. Fast asleep, in the old meaning of fast, like a locked-up vault. He shook her and she didn't wake up. He needed another belt from the flask after that. In fact, he drained it, and then he lay down beside her and made retributive plans to dump her in the morning.

Being deeply suspicious of strangers, Pansy Badger wasn't suited to running a hotel. She kept Merv awake with her quizzing.

"A young man and wife," Merv said.

What did they look like? What did they talk like? Had they been drinking? Were they really married? Arriving at this time of night? Merv didn't know. He pulled the sheet up to his shoulder and turned his back on her.

"It's too hot for a sheet," she said. "Where did they come from?"

"Trevna."

"Trevna? If they were married, they wouldn't need a room here. Merv, I said, if they were married they'd have their own place in Trevna. It's just down the road, for Christ's sake."

"Look, they paid for the room."

"I won't aid and abet that kind of thing."

"I'm asleep," Merv said.

She thought for a minute. "Tell me about the girl," she said. But he was asleep. He was already snoring. She could only stay awake and listen for any sounds that might indicate there was trouble down the hall.

During the night Bill made a trip to the toilet to relieve himself of the effects of trying to sleep beside the girl. When he came out of the bathroom, shuddering from the smell he'd labelled *eau de commode*, a crazy woman poked her head out, two doors down. Her chopped grey hair stuck out all over her head, and her face and neck strained out the doorway, the muscles all strung as taut as kite string, as if some cranky wind had yanked her out of her room. Her eyes bored into his.

"What?" he said. As a kid he'd sleepwalk now and then, and get caught outside in his pyjamas. He felt like that, like a kid in a place where he shouldn't be – and right now he didn't even have pyjamas on; he had nothing but the dim light clothing him. She pulled her head back in, left him shaking his, watching her door slowly almost close. He'd bet she still had an eyeball up against it. As he turned back to his room he swaggered a bit – since he was young, after all, and buck-naked.

Bill woke up to discover the girl still dead to the world, and started rehearsing what he was going to do. He was going to get out of bed and get dressed and take off – leave her there for Scrawny to find her and make a royal fuss when he found out she hadn't a cent to her name, which Bill was pretty sure was the case. But the rest of him wasn't listening to the plan, and he reached out and put his hand on the curve of her shoulder, where it fit so well he thought he'd remember it for the rest of his life, the bone so strangely solid through the thin fabric, and warm against his palm. His fingers curled over into the hollow between her shoulder and her collarbone, and she stirred. Almost immediately she turned and slid right into him, the full length of her.

"You awake?" he said. It came out like a croak, being his first utterance of the day.

She nodded and whispered something too low for him to hear that sounded strangely matter-of-fact for the situation. Her breath smelled odd, not bad exactly, but different. He noticed it but ignored it. He didn't know that a sharp, chemical smell is a sign a person is actually starving, and when he did learn it, later, he was still inclined to ask himself how anyone could have expected him to know. Her body was hot against him, pressed against him; her toes arched against his. The silky fine cotton between them slid against his bare skin. He didn't have to think to peel it off. He did, however, have a policy of using a prophylactic. It didn't help in these circumstances since it created more friction than he wanted, and there was that knotty little flesh gate to fight past. And sometimes girls would be embarrassed by the condom, preferring to think you'd had no prior intentions and were just overcome by a sudden unstoppable desire for them and them alone, a desire that would later easily be translated into love. (Elena was the third girl he'd had intercourse with, so he was able to employ this sort of generalization.) Anyway, he wasn't going to have any little gal or her old man tracking him down, coming after him with a carrot-topped claim against him, so he soldiered ahead with the rubber on his dick and the look of thinking of England on her face.

Afterwards, with the remembrance of the tepid Christmas mornings of his childhood floating through his mind, he reached for his cigarettes. You could still get them in flat tin boxes in those days; these were Black Cats, in a yellow tin with an appropriate picture of a black cat on it, kind of grinning at you. Bad-luck cat. A new thought occurred to him. "So, I guess you got to know me overnight, eh?"

She didn't answer right away but finally, in the formal way she had, she said, "Yes, I guess I did."

A little sunny-morning clarity trickled through the grimy windowpane across the room. "Ah, I respected you," he said.

She laughed, that foreign-sounding laugh again, with the bitter edge. Went on quite long this time, so he offered her a cigarette. She hadn't wanted one the night before but this time she accepted it, slid it from the package with her small fingers and took it in her mouth. Waited for him to light it for her. The match cracked to life at the first stroke, but he wasn't any too steady holding it for her, and when she inhaled, the flame went out. The thin paper stuck to her swollen lips, pulling them out a bit when she drew it from her mouth, and then she poked out her little pink tongue and plucked a curl of tobacco off it, and he was on top of her again. This time it was way more like Santa Claus had come to town.

When he rolled off her, she sat up, blinking as if the lights had brightened. She gathered the sheet to her, then seemed to change her mind and got up. She hadn't taken two steps before she staggered and fell to the floor. Just crumpled while he watched. He lay propped up on one elbow, staring at her. "Hey!" he called, in case there was any possibility she was kidding around, teasing him for some reason he couldn't understand but could accept if it would mean there wasn't something really the matter. She didn't move, just lay there in a naked heap. He started shaking so badly he could hardly crawl over the bed and down to the floor and when he did, sitting beside her on the cool linoleum, he only stared at her white face. He couldn't believe it. He couldn't believe his eyes. He'd never seen a face so white.

He wouldn't look down at her body. He expected he'd see a pool of blood down there and more blood seeping or gushing out. And whose fault would that be? She'd bled a little after the first time, but that was only natural. He prodded her breastbone a couple of times. Nothing. And no, he couldn't look down. He picked up her hand and started chafing it and whispering to her. "Elena, Elena," he hissed, over and over, staring into her face.

When she opened her eyes they weren't focussed. He could tell she wasn't seeing. He said her name again and she said something, a word he couldn't understand, the same word a few times, in some foreign language. Then her eyes cleared and she looked at him and smiled as if she understood his distress, knew it was more for himself than for her, and pitied him.

"Man and wife," Pansy said with a snort. "When's the last time you seen a man and wife order breakfast sent to their Christly room?" She'd agreed to toast and coffee. If they wanted anything more, they could drive themselves someplace else. They wouldn't get it in Addison on a Sunday morning. But she helped Merv carry it up, not having seen them the night before, or at least not having seen the girl. She'd had an eyeful of the guy, thank you very much. Merv had the tray with toast, jam, cups and cutlery. She carried the coffee pot. Caldwell Kurtz heard them on the stairs and poked his fuzzy old pelican head out his door. Pansy shooed him back into his room.

And there they were, the two of them, sitting up in bed, as downy-headed as a pair of pelicans themselves, and glowing like two light bulbs, side by side. There was nowhere to put the tray. The young man patted the small space between their bodies and Merv leaned over him and set it down.

The girl thanked him. She was wearing a dress, although it might as well have been a nightgown; it was wrinkled and clung to her breasts.

"I'll settle up later," the young man said, a smart-assed look on his face, as well there might have been, with Merv practically bowing out of the room so as not to have to take his eyes off the girl.

As soon as the Badgers left the room, Bill and Elena fell on the toast. Make extra, Bill had told Merv, but there were only four dry slices. He offered to let her have it all, but she said it wouldn't be good for her to have too much at once. She'd finally told him she hadn't eaten in quite a while. It came out when he'd asked her what foreign language she spoke.

"Finnish," she said. "But only a little. Did I say something? I don't recall."

He said it was *Eeesa*. When she'd come to, she'd said, "Eeesa."

"Oh," she said. "*Isä*. It means father. I always think it's my father, when I hear someone calling my name."

Bill wasn't all that interested in her old man. He kept asking her if she was okay, and after she'd told him a dozen times that she was, and finally that it was only that she needed food, he'd gone downstairs and got Scrawny moving on some breakfast.

She was so adorable and weak while they waited. He was fascinated by her weakness. He held her hand and she put her head on his shoulder. It seemed to him this was more than physical closeness; he'd earned this weight on his shoulder. He'd stood by her. He'd done the right thing. He was good to her. And that was why a bond was forming between them – he was sure it was, he could feel it – while they lay propped against the thin, folded-over pillows, waiting for their breakfast. She was different from other girls. She was intelligent in a way he hadn't encountered before, and he liked that about her. She said things you could make a smart answer to and feel pretty good about, like did you ever think about stars. If only she didn't laugh sometimes when things weren't funny, and other times gaze at him as if she had him up against a wall with a measuring stick.

"I could have used bacon and eggs," he said after he'd devoured the last of his toast. "God, I can see those eggs swimming in bacon grease. I can just about smell that bacon."

"Baked beans on the side," she said.

"Pancakes."

"Mmm. Dripping with syrup."

He leaned over and kissed her jammy mouth. She stuck an end of her toast into his. "You put me through hell, you know," he whispered into her ear. She didn't know the half of it – how scared he'd been that he'd killed her – and he wasn't going to tell her.

"I thought you were going to back out of the room, bowing all the way," Pansy said. "You couldn't take your eyes off the girl. She isn't that pretty, you know. It's that tousled look, that used-but-ready-for-more look that got you going. Not to mention the *Christly* smell of sex in the room. Don't look at me like that. It's unmistakable. Huh! If I had ten cents to spare, I'd bet it on feeling your hand on my arse before the day's over."

"Aw, you're too hard on the kids," Merv said. "I mean the girl, the way she was looking at you, she just wanted a little womanly sympathy. You know, motherly."

"If I have any *womanly, motherly* sympathy to spare," Pansy said, "I'm gonna spend it on myself, thank you very much. I seen her signalling, by the way, with that little pale face. I don't know why she couldn't see I don't have an ounce of maternal spirit in me. And if I did, I'm damned if I'd squander it on a heedless kid in a smelly bed." That seemed to be her last word.

They drove out of town, past the dozen or so vehicles gathered outside a white clapboard building, a Lutheran chapel, small as a family dwelling, marked with just a cross instead of a spire. She turned to watch it get smaller. She'd never gone to church; her father had never gone and when, pressured by neighbours, she'd asked him why, he hadn't explained. He never did explain about anything. Maybe the note he'd left for her on the kitchen table was the most explaining he'd ever done, saying she was old enough now to look after herself.

"Everything okay?" Bill asked.

"Yeah, sure."

"Sure?" They were coming up to the highway, and he turned and glanced at her as they rolled towards a stop.

"Yeah. Sure."

"Swell."

"That woman at the hotel," she said. "Wasn't she strange? The way she glared at us with the coffee pot in her hands. For a minute I thought she was going to dump it on us. Her husband seemed kind."

Bill was grinning to himself. He was only half-listening to what she was saying. It was the low, weighty sound of her words that he liked. That cute, serious hint of accent, the *w* almost turned into a *v*.

"I wonder what she's doing now." *I vonder.*

"Damned if I know. Or care." He stretched out his arm and drew her in. "Maybe she'll clean that room. It could use it. Huh. You can tell neither one of them do bugger-all. They've got nerve charging for a bed in that flea hole."

She was standing at the open second-floor window of the room they'd just left, noticing that it was windy, as usual, and already hot. She saw the big roadster driving away, flashy thing, as long as some houses, beautiful, really, all gleaming gold. She watched it roll past the church and pull up at the highway and stop.

"What are you doing?" Merv wanted to know.

He'd watched her strip the bed. She leaned out the window and shook the folds and the smell of sex out of the bottom sheet. The dust smell came up with the heat from the street below to mingle. The sun browsed along her arms and she turned her face up to feel it. "You could take that tray downstairs," she said.

"No, really, what are you doing, eh?"

She lowered the sash so the chunk of wood that held the frame up also held the sheet waving outside from the sill. Merv was still sitting on the bed, watching her do it, watching her bony arse twitch.

"Pansy."

"I'm going to let the sun bleach it."

"You'd have to rinse the stain out first."

"You just like to make work," she said. She plopped down on the bed beside him.

"I hope you're not trying to prove something."

"I hope you're taking that tray with you when you go downstairs."

"I'm not going downstairs," he said, leaning towards her.

She gave him a look that would have stopped a quicker man, but Merv was deliberate as well as slow, and she gave in and lay back on the bare mattress.

"You look fetching against ticking, my little lotus blossom," he said.

She laughed, but she said, "I already seen you looking at who looked fetching against ticking, remember?"

"Wasn't ticking until now you took the sheets off."

"You know what I mean, you bastard."

"Don't."

"Do."

He stretched her arms up over her head and pinned them. She was wearing cap sleeves. He could see her delicate hair, dampened by her window exertion, clinging to the vulnerable cave of her armpit, and caught a whiff of her personal smell. A gentle, dusty, summer breeze wafted over them, and the contrast of its light touch and the heaviness between them made a ripple of pure pleasure run through him.

The cat nudged the door open and padded in with the bossy air of a creature with work to do. They didn't see it or hear it until it jumped up on the bed (they felt its silent thump on the mattress). It rubbed its head against Merv's shoulder. It stared at Pansy with its slitted, empty eyes. *"Christ!"* she said, and rolled away. The cat hopped down. Landed on all four dainty feet. Left the door ajar.

It was only minutes until both of them drifted off to sleep. Old Jock and Old Caldwell saw them there on the way to their rooms, snoring lightly side by side, their mouths fluttering, their thin chests rising in unison.

"Tough night for the Badgers," Caldwell said.

Jock shrugged. He'd got so in tune with the establishment, most of the time he couldn't be bothered talking.

The wind picked up as the morning progressed, and the sheet blew out from the Addison Hotel window like a cheeky flag. On their various ways home from church, several of the Lutheran congregation, as well as the few who'd gathered in a living room for an Anglican service, observed it. Some of them pointed; some said the reeve should do something about Pansy Badger; others pretended it wasn't there, just pursed their lips and refused to comment. One woman said, "Oh, that's an old story." She was walking home, away from the hotel at the time, with two friends. All three of them were pretty women, still young, with young families they were rearing as best they could on limited funds. Two of them were pushing baby carriages, which required some effort on the dirt path. "They used to do it to prove virginity," the first young woman went on.

"What does it prove now?"

"Another one down."

They cackled all the way home, and even the one who didn't have a husband, who'd "got herself pregnant," experienced an unusual happy sense of belonging in her world.

◇◇◇◇◇

"I wonder how you know which way to go," she said when he turned onto the highway.

"Regina's east. I'm just driving towards the sun, sweetheart."

The wheels crackled against the gravel and then whirred as they sped up. Democratic yellow flowers nodded at them from the ditches and windswept clouds swirled across the baby-blue sky. Her hair blew back from her face. She started humming.

"What is that?" he asked. Before she answered, he was humming along. It was "Let Me Call You Sweetheart." They looked right at one another for a split second, and then immediately looked at the road ahead. They both tried not to smile.

The roads in Saskatchewan were poor in those days, many weren't even gravelled yet, and the big Lincoln bounced along in the ruts and out of them. People who would never know them stopped whatever they were doing and watched them when they passed by farms and rocketed through little towns. It was like being in a movie starring themselves. Elena Huhtala was no heiress, as she would have been in most of the movies of those years, but she rode with her right arm resting on top of the door ready to wave at anyone. Bill tooted the horn. After a couple of hours of this, they quieted down, and Bill admitted he liked a woman who didn't have to talk much. Eventually, he began telling her some of his thoughts and opinions, and as that is gratifying to anyone, the day continued as delightfully as he could ever have hoped it would – or that was how it was going until he tried to explain what he did for a living. He'd been prepared for her to ask, although she wasn't a very curious girl. He told her he bought and sold things. "I buy 'em low and sell 'em high," he said, and in case she got the wrong idea, he said, "I'm not a salesman, don't get me wrong. I'm no salesman."

"You sell things. But you are not a salesman," she said. Her eyebrows lifted like a schoolteacher's.

"I'm a trader, sweetheart," he said. "Both sides of every bargain." She didn't appear impressed. "I work out of Calgary," he added, but that seemed to mean little to her. He knew he sounded confident, and Calgary was a bigger city than she'd ever been to, but maybe that was the problem; she didn't know enough to be impressed.

"What do you trade?" she asked.

"Anything. Everything. Bought this Lincoln last week. When I see something I like better, I'll sell it. Trade up." He stretched back in his seat. "You see, it's a matter of knowing the value of things, eh? And knowing people."

"Do you own a house in Calgary?"

That came out of left field, but what the heck. "I own a few," he said. "Real estate's one profitable thing to trade in."

"But one you live in? A house that's yours? That you come home to?"

"Hey. Are you asking if I'm married?"

"No. You're not, are you?" She seemed genuinely shocked.

"No fear. I don't like the idea of tying myself down."

"Me neither." She sat up then, apart from him.

"You're a strange girl," he said. "Do you know that? I mean, you're different from other girls I've met." He had to say it; the idea had been nagging at him.

"I see myself as forward-looking," she said. She was sitting forward in her seat, too, watching the long, narrow road rolling towards them.

"Forward-looking? You're kidding."

"No," she said. "I'm serious."

They drove along for a while thinking their own thoughts and all the time she sat on the edge of her seat as if that was going to make the world come at her faster.

"Forward-looking," Bill said again, with a half-laugh. "You sure that's not just an excuse you dreamed up for taking off with me?"

She tilted her face up to him, serious as ever. "Teach me to drive," she said. She might as well have said teach me to fornicate. There's something about a girl asking to be taught anything at all, just gets to a guy. He pulled to a stop right then and there on the side of the road, and turned the ignition off. They were in the middle of nowhere, anyway; they hadn't seen another vehicle for an hour. "Come sit on my knee," he said. "Come on, I mean it. You'll fit, skinny kid like you."

She swung her legs over his and hoisted herself onto him. The steering wheel pressed into her belly, so he pulled her back and his penis lifted to fit between her legs like it was built to be there, but he went through the motions, put her hand to the key, swamped in his. "Set your feet on mine," he directed, and she did. She depressed the clutch with her left foot when he did, and moved the right, with his, from the brake to the gas as the ignition caught, but neither of them was fast enough and the Lincoln jumped forward, stalled.

"What now?" she said.

He turned the key backwards and put his hands on her breasts.

"We won't go far like this," she said dryly. And it's true they were stopped for some time. They'd made such a late start that morning, the sky was getting dark by the time they got back driving again.

"I think Charlesville's a bigger centre," he said, seeing the sign at the side of the road. "I sure hope we're not too late to get supper somewhere. I'm famished."

"Me, too, Bill," she said. "I could eat a horse." It was the first time she'd said his name, and he liked hearing it from her. In fact, he thought he'd like to hear her say it again, and often. You might say it was the most intimate thing she'd done, just say his name like that, like they were friends. After that, he felt bad for lying to her, earlier, about being a trader. But it didn't matter, he decided, and he was from Calgary, so part of it was true.

CHARLESVILLE

Night fell on Charlesville, the biggest town in a hundred miles, a little later than it fell on the small villages and farms surrounding it. That, and the few specialized shops it boasted, was the extent of its distinction. The hotel beverage rooms stayed open later in Charlesville than elsewhere and light still flared in a few windows after ten o'clock. And they had street lamps to dull the glitter of the stars overhead and take the edge off the darkness, and here and there a few trees to look blacker than the night.

Down a side street, in one of those small bungalows that look as if they were built for a spinster (picket-fenced, huddled to the ground, window in the door to peer through), Albert Earle, the district's one paid fireman, was visiting Peg Golden in her bed. Her bed had brass railings at head and foot and the mattress rested on metal springs, although it wasn't resting right now; it was shifting and squeaking and Peg was moaning so loud Albert was afraid her neighbours, whose house was only a few feet away, would come over and complain that they couldn't sleep. They had made a fuss once before when Albert and Peg had shared a bottle of rye whisky and got to singing. The neighbours were an old couple, seventy at least, and it seemed they required a full eight hours in spite of having no jobs to go to or family dependent on them. Such as Albert had, he reminded himself. He went to work on Peg, two fingers deep inside her, his arm like a piston thrusting while she rose to meet him and he stared into the wall, thinking only that he really needed to get home and get his own rest.

"Albert," she said, pulling back, although not completely away. She had a deep voice for a tiny woman, and could make him jump when she said his name.

"Sorry."

"I'm not a machine."

"Sorry."

"And stop apologizing, for heaven's sake."

"Okay, okay."

"How do you think it makes me feel?"

He ducked his head down between her legs and gave her his full attention, knowing fairly well how that made her feel. A few minutes later, she said goodbye to him cheerily, standing at the open door in a flowered silk dressing gown that dragged on the floor because she hadn't taken the time to hem it. She watched him slink along the sidewalk through the shadows of the sleeping houses, as if anyone cared if they did see him. He was a substantial man, not very good at slinking. He had nice, square hands; she'd liked that first about him. His hands were always warm. And he was a calm person, that was something she needed – and kind.

Charlesville was big enough only half the population knew everything about everybody else, and Peg was a newcomer; she'd lived there only four years. So even though she owned and managed the one ladies' wear store in the district, she knew only about a quarter of all there was to know about the townsfolk.

As soon as the rumours had started about Albert dropping by her house late in the evening, there had been an increase in window-shopping, and a few of her so-called customers – in case she didn't have enough information to judge him – went further than gawking and filled her in. They let her know that as a boy he'd been so good-natured and so kind-hearted and so bad at all team sports, his nickname in the schoolyard had been Girlie. And of course they had to tell her that he had a wife, although she was, each one of them said, as good as dead. Peg didn't ask why that was, but they told her. His wife was incarcerated. Betty Earle; it would be years before she'd be home, if she survived prison. She'd killed their baby daughter, born with so many deformities you'd think she couldn't have lived. Smothered her with a pillow. Just a bundle of pain, that's all she was, the women said. Someone had come up with that description, and it had evidently impressed them all. They'd each intoned it as if the phrase had popped into their heads that moment. Then they looked down at their dusty shoes and their dusty wrinkled ankles (since they all wore dreadful beige cotton stockings they got cheap at the Red and White store), and shook their heads. And that was how easy it was for them to rid themselves of the child's little life and Betty Earle's dilemma, once it had been reduced to those just-right words, those words that implied pity without the effort of forgiveness.

Albert had been left to absorb the pain that couldn't be assuaged by an apt expression. And look after the five kids left at home. And relieve just a bit of the awfulness with Peg, who'd thought herself too good for the boys she'd grown up with, and now had no one.

She went to her dressing table and began sectioning her hair, dipping her tail comb into the glass of water, coiling the sections into pin curls. She always thought of the Van Gogh painting while she did her hair up. *Starry Night*. She'd seen it in a *Life* magazine and ripped the page out. Couldn't find it now, but she thought of it every night, even pictured the page's ragged edges. Crazy painting, like the world was crazy. Just like. Spiralling out of control every time you figured you had a handle on it. She opened each bobby pin with her teeth, speared each curl. She was meant for better. That was the other thing she thought every night. She leaned closer to the mirror and examined the lines between her eyebrows, two sharp lines in a V over her nose, getting sharper every day.

On the way home, Albert thought about her face in the doorway. He couldn't quite decide what it was about her face, what showed in her face that put people off, put men off, anyway, even though she was still pretty. It was too confident or too knowing, or maybe it was too sexy. You could tell, just looking at her, that she liked it. She knew she scared most men away. It was good for him that she did.

He checked on the kids when he got in, the three boys lying across their bed on top of the rumpled sheets, even the oldest, at fifteen, flush-faced, sweet-faced in sleep, and the little girls spooned together on their bed. He raised his hand over each in turn, could almost feel them in the air between. Thought of Betty, last thing, as always. Kind of strange, how that was. He didn't imagine her, where she was now, or call to mind the image of her any time along their lives together. He thought of her being, her essence, the thing in the world that was her, and that was still tied to him.

◇◇◇◇◇

The Royal George at Charlesville, a three-storey brick box with the third floor closed off since the beginning of the Depression, boasted hallways wide enough to allow motor traffic. It really did boast about them, or the owners did; and they also extolled the fir woodwork and doors and floors, which were stained dark and varnished thickly, and the walls, which were calcimined a chalky mauve they thought looked regal. A bare light bulb hung in the centre of Bill and Elena's ceiling, the first electricity Bill had seen since Calgary. There were cloths draped over both the chamber pot and the drinking water. There were two young kids called chambermaids who twice a day lugged water up from the kitchen pump and carried slops down to empty into the septic tank. They knocked on the doors with fresh hot water in the morning. The girl who entered Bill and Elena's room blushed while she poured the water into the pitcher, and turned almost inside out when Bill tossed her a nickel from the bed.

That morning Elena felt a bit sore here and there, while Bill appeared to have grown taller, stronger, and even happier. And he showed considerable efficiency, getting them up and going earlier than they had the morning before.

"What is that for?" she wanted to know while she was dressing. She pointed to the rope coiled on the floor under the window. It was attached to the windowsill by a ring screwed into the wood.

"For you. It's easier than letting down your hair to a – lover," he said. "Rapunzel," he added when she didn't respond.

"Ah," she said, still back on the word *lover*, liking him for his hesitation.

"Fire regulations," he said. "It's easier on you than jumping, too."

He held his hand out to help her rise from the bed. He had excellent, natural manners, so natural he was probably unaware how agreeable it was to have doors held open for her, to have someone inquire in the morning how she was. She wondered if he knew he made people happy. Since she'd been with him, whole hours had gone by when she'd felt she could be any girl, living an ordinary life.

They had breakfast at the Monarch Dining Room, situated at the front of the Royal George, just past the large rotunda. She asked if she could borrow some money to buy a few things. He fanned through his wallet and handed her a five-dollar bill.

"That's too much. I don't need so much."

"Let's go shopping," he said, with that smile of his that made his eyes brighter. Then he was paying the bill, chatting with the waitress, making her laugh.

At the Red and White store she bought toothpaste, a jar of Mum's cream deodorant, a face-powder compact, and a lipstick. She showed it all to him afterwards, trying not to act excited. He could tell she was pleased about it, though. He'd have bet she'd never bought a thing for herself before. While she was in the store he'd smoked outside, leaning against the angle-parked Lincoln and nodding at all who stared – and that was everyone. Then he walked her down the sidewalk, past the bakery and the bank and the hardware store, in and out of those rectangular blocks of cool shade, heading for Peg's Style House, where Peg's name had been painted over somebody else's. Elena fell behind and he turned to see why. His heart kind of skipped when he saw her standing alone on the sidewalk of that big, wide Main Street, with a mile of sky over her head, and looking shy for the first time, clutching her paper bag that she'd rolled at the top the way a kid would have. She was gazing across the street to the Capitol Theatre. She was peering at the poster in the window, trying to read it. He came back and took her elbow and guided her across the street, stopping the traffic – one farmer in an old truck – as if he represented the Red Sea in Charlesville today.

It was a handsome couple, lying back, embracing, in a slice of yellow moon.

"Clark Gable and Claudette Colbert," she read aloud.

"Col-*bear*," Bill corrected. She only smiled. "How do you think I'd look with a moustache?" he said, and she smiled again, her standard almost-smile that he wouldn't have registered as a smile at all until he'd got to know her.

"*It Happened One Night*," she read. "Just like us, eh? It happened one night."

"*It*?"

"Yeah. It. It happened."

The way she spoke, with the accent not always where you expected it, and her voice falling softly in odd places, it seemed to Bill as if the words were melting and sinking down somewhere way below him. He knew what she meant, *it* was what people said in those days so they didn't have to say the word *sex* out loud, but he hadn't thought of the euphemism in connection with this motion picture and he said so.

"You didn't?"

"No."

"I wonder if they did, the ones who made the movie. They must be smart, to make a movie. You'd think they could dream up a title that would say two things at once." She reached out and touched the glass over Clark Gable's face and traced his moustache. "Does *it* happen between these two, do you know?"

"Listen, why don't we stay over tonight and find out?"

"Yeah?"

"Yeah."

"All right," she said. "I don't mind if I do."

Peg hated herself for perking up when they walked in – a guy with money and a gal who could make any dress look like you wish you'd shopped at Peg's. But you can't stop hope once it jumps up and knocks against your breastbone.

He picked out a couple of flashy numbers. The girl didn't say no, but she kept on looking along the racks. Finally she pulled one out and held up the hanger.

He said, "Brown? You've already got a brown dress."

She smiled, a secret half-smile. She knew herself and she was getting to know him – that's what the smile said. The dress she held up was a light tan, and a whole lot more stylish than the faded old thing she was wearing. It was a demure little summer model, classy, with great lines, short sleeves, and a V-necked collar that would have looked too cute on the wrong girl.

He strolled outside for a smoke while she tried it on. Peg held the curtain for her and she ducked into the little back room. "Call me," Peg said. She had the shoes to match if only she had her size in stock, two-tone beige spectator pumps.

The dress was perfect, as she'd known it would be. Peg joined her at the mirror and handed her the shoes. "Oh," the girl said, and they fit like a pair of glass slippers. She was smooth as glass under the dress, too, wasn't wearing any undergarments, and Peg didn't suggest any. Even the guy she was with would understand the beauty of that dress was its modest cling.

She said, "I might like to work in a place like this." Peg was standing back, behind her, and she was talking to her through the mirror.

"You got experience?" Not that it mattered one iota.

"No, I haven't worked before. I have my grade twelve," she said.

She saw Peg's opinion of that in the mirror. If she'd looked either haughty or cowed, Peg would have left it there, but she looked sympathetic, and Peg really didn't need sympathy from a raw kid. "Good luck getting a job of any kind, anywhere," she told her. "Especially with no experience. Do you know what the wage is, for a woman, right now? One dollar a week. One dollar. And even at that I can't afford a clerk."

"Oh," she said again. Not so enchanted with the whole business, now. Looking at herself, now, instead of at Peg, and looking pretty young and useless, too. A lot of good that did Peg, her own dream staring her in the face, the dream of getting out of Charlesville ever since she'd arrived, and setting up somewhere else, in some bigger centre where her ambition and her eye for the figure flaws of others could make her a decent living.

Once they were back in the Monarch Dining Room, having their supper amid the tables of single salesmen, Bill talked about the importance of not getting taken. He went over the example of Peg, who had expected to make an unreasonable profit off that ridiculously priced dress Elena had chosen, and the shoes, too. She was asking way more than they were worth. He'd simply said they'd take both the dress and the shoes for half the price she'd named. She'd opened her mouth and closed it, and wrapped up Elena's old things because she wore the new ones out of the shop. "You gotta know how people tick," he said.

"I wonder how she can make a living," Elena said. Peg's stock had been picked over and was outmoded, and she'd brightened too much when Bill and Elena walked in. She'd called Elena "Dear." It hadn't sounded natural.

"That doesn't take me in, that hangdog look, the whine in the voice," Bill said. "It's commerce. You shouldn't be in it if you don't know how to deal. Hell, most people don't have a clue how the world works. Why, everyone trades for a profit. She still made some money, just not as much as she thought she could take me for. You don't know people, living in isolation, where you were. You gotta look out for yourself."

Elena nodded. Bill paid for the meal and sent his compliments to the cook. The pork chops had been just the way he liked them.

◇◇◇◇◇

Clark Gable says she'll never get away with it. He's the big city reporter; she's the heiress who ran away from her old man. The movies know what you like to hear. Even back then they knew, maybe especially back then. But running away, it appeals at any time. Elena snuggled down in her seat, her mouth open like a kid.

Claudette Colbert says she wants to be alone, but everyone knows she doesn't. She just hasn't found the right man yet. In the meantime, her rich daddy has got everyone in the whole United States of America looking for her, and here she is – on a bus.

Clark Gable calls her a spoiled brat. The slimy guy on the make calls her "Sister." She falls asleep on Clark Gable's shoulder. Pretty soon he's looking after her, and it's a good thing; she keeps forgetting she has no money. He tells her she's on a budget, acting like he's her husband. When they have to share a room overnight, the walls of Jericho go up – a blanket on a rope Clark Gable strings between the twin beds. He tells her not to worry; he has no trumpet. Hah! Take that one two ways.

Off comes her nice little suit to reveal her pretty, lacy slip, the lace as delicate as the icy edge of a spring puddle. It suddenly occurs to her to ask his name. From behind the woollen wall. In the meantime, her rich father is in a plane, flying overhead. He's employed a detective agency. No expense will be spared to find her. No expense. That's how much he loves her. That's how much a father is supposed to love a daughter.

It's time for Clark Gable to establish some male superiority. He'll cook and he'll press her clothes, but in return she has to do what he says. She's fine with that. It's give and take, isn't it? And right then three detectives barge in, searching every room in the world, apparently, and why not, when money is no object? And now Clark and Claudette (a.k.a. Peter and Ellie) start acting a parody of a lower-class couple, haranguing one another in a lower-class way. That fools the dicks. Everyone knows an heiress wouldn't have such a shrill, unpleasant voice, or fight with her man in public.

Her father offers a $10,000 reward. Her picture appears on all the front pages. The whole bus sings "The Daring Young Man on the Flying Trapeze."

"I know who she looks like. Betty Boop," Bill whispers. Elena doesn't know who Betty Boop is. He squeezes her. He has his arm around her. "Is this the first movie you've seen?" he asks. Somebody behind them leans forward and says, "Shhh!"

Now they're walking by a stream. Moonlight on water, you've never seen a stream sparkle like this, and he picks her up like baggage and carries her over his shoulder across the sparkling stream, the sound of wading beautiful under their banter. She's such a brat, he gives her a spank on the bum. Bill laughs so hard he has to take his arm back for a bit. All the men in the audience are laughing with him. They've all been thinking she's just too sassy for her own good, this little gal.

Then it's morning and he tells her they'll have to hitch and she asks when the hitching comes in. Just like a woman, thinking of marriage because they've spent the night together, even if *it* hasn't happened. She started out the movie on a hunger strike and now she knows what it is to be hungry. After a day without food, she's so hungry she's finally eating a raw carrot, which she turned her pretty nose up at before.

It's another night and up go the walls of Jericho again. "It's not everybody who travels with rope," Bill says and Elena laughs. Even the woman behind them laughs.

Through the woollen wall, he tells her what he wants is someone who's real, who's alive, a girl who loves the moon and the stars and water. She says she loves him. But *it* can't happen yet. Her father arrives with a police escort, sirens wailing, and takes her away. Hobos wave from a train, happy to be poor. The front pages say "Love Triumphs," and after a while it does. In the nick of time, she bolts from the wrong man to the arms of the right one, her white veil flying out behind her.

The walls of Jericho tumble, the trumpet blares. Bill squeezes her again.

Walking back to the hotel afterwards, going over the movie's highlights in his mind, Bill said, "We'll have to get you a slip, sweetheart."

She just smiled, the way she did automatically, to get out of talking.

"Funny old Peg didn't sell you one today." He waited. "I said, 'Funny she didn't sell you one today.'"

"Oh," she said. "Yes."

She might be walking alongside him, but she was in her own world, that was clear. He slipped his arm around her. When he thought about it, he was glad she was quiet; he had time to imagine the kind of conversation he'd like the two of them to have, him talking to her the way Clark Gable talked about the moon and stars and water and the kind of woman – yeah, the kind of woman – he wanted to share all that with him. Love-talk, the likes of which he could only imagine saying in a dream.

◇◇◇◇◇

Sometimes a terrible depression fell on Peg. Albert had seen it before. There she sat, on her sofa, not even pretending she could go on. He'd passed her shop after work and saw that she'd closed up early, so he'd stopped in at the house instead of going to his mother's to collect the girls. On the way up the path to her door, he'd considered picking one of her own petunias and presenting it to her, hoping to make her smile. He was too much of a coward to do it. Someone might have seen him, and Peg herself might have thought it foolish.

He sat beside her, smoothing her springy hair back from her forehead, and she didn't shake him off. Then he took one of her hands in both of his. She nestled her head against him.

She found herself thinking of telling him what she was going to do, but in the past tense, as if she had already done it, saying "I thought I'd put the kettle on and make a pot of tea," imagining she'd already stood up and moved to the kitchen. But she hadn't moved, she wasn't moving; her head still rested on his shoulder. And she wasn't standing at the counter with a can opener saying he must be hungry, because he had to go home and get supper for his kids.

"You need to go. You need to pick up the girls at your mother's," she said.

"She won't mind if I'm late once in a while."

"No, go." It sounded brusque, rude. She didn't care. He had a mother, the kids. She stood up, a formality, the only way to make him go now that she'd decided she wanted to be alone. She could already hear herself telling him, the next evening, "I went straight to bed after you left." Saw him nod his head. Thought about banging hers against the bedroom wall.

"It's not enough," she said aloud. It just slipped out. She was starting down the hall towards her bedroom, thinking he'd already gone. He hadn't gone; he was standing by the sofa, watching her, but she turned away.

VIRGINIA VALLEY

Bill said she didn't understand motion pictures. And there was nothing wrong with being rich.

She said, "Well, there's nothing so good about being poor, that's for sure."

"Nothing interesting about it, either. That's why nobody wants to see it when they go out for an evening."

"I don't know why not. It's a challenge just getting through the day when you have no money," she said in her deliberate way, as if she'd figured it out like an arithmetic problem, and this was the solution. "And people have to co-operate, not just look out for themselves."

He didn't bother pointing out that co-operation wasn't exactly the engine of high drama. He wondered if she was going to turn out to have a great many opinions, and decided to try her trick and not bother answering at all. Just enjoy driving along with her beside him. That was what he liked, just having her beside him like she was, lolling back in the soft leather seat, her bare feet up on the dashboard. She was wearing his fedora to keep the sun off her face. With her tawny blonde hair she fit perfectly inside the gold Lincoln.

"Liberty Hall, for example," she went on, "would not have been built if everybody in the district had not pitched in."

"It was in their interest, that's why," he said. "And you can bet your bottom dollar somebody made some cash on the side, in the Liberty Hall deal and in every other instance you could name. Sweetheart, people are born selfish and they die selfish and in between they want what's best for themselves."

"If people have what they need, they don't have to take from others."

"Don't you believe it. Say, is your old man a Commie? That's Commie stuff you're spouting. You can get yourself arrested for that. Don't be talking like that in public, or we'll have the Mounties tailing us." He patted her knee. "Stick with me, kid," he said. He smiled to himself. She'd liked that shopping, yesterday. She was happy stepping out of the shop wearing her new high-heeled dancing shoes and her new togs. Funny dress to pick, though; brown, and it practically covered up all her assets. He'd teased her a bit about it and told her he'd have to help her out when they shopped again in the city.

"What's your old man like?" she asked.

"Oh, hell, I don't want to talk about him." He scowled down the length of the hood, at the chrome ornament at the end, a greyhound pawing the air. The greyhound was supposed to look fast, he supposed, but what it really looked was eager, and it wasn't ever a good idea to look too eager, especially with a girl. He put his foot down and the roadster responded right away. He wondered what she'd think if she knew his father had bought the car for him, had sent him on this road trip, a present for passing his final exams, getting his degree – or that was the official version. It was only coincidental that his father had planned to go away, himself, for the summer, and had taken his secretary with him.

There was a fair amount of prejudice against the rich, Bill knew, and especially when a lot more people than usual were poor. He didn't buy that gab in the picture show about values and what was important in life, but he wasn't going to advertise his situation, either. On the other hand, he was feeling a bit guilty over Peg – but he had thought Elena would be impressed. Every time he thought about trying to impress her, he found himself shaking his head. He couldn't figure her out. But he knew the thing to do was not let on you were ruffled, let it look like you were amused, put nonchalance on your face, like Clark Gable did. Whistle a little tune. He wondered if he might go into the newspaper business. He didn't have a clue what to do when he got back home in the fall, and he was getting good at telling lies.

A yellow wagon popped into his mind. He'd seen a Rawleigh salesman with a yellow wagon a few miles out of Rosseton and it came to him he could use the man for his father. "Now, there was a salesman for you," he said, liking the sound of that past tense, making it seem, even to himself, that his father was dead. No one he had to think about. No one who had any influence over him. "He sold Rawleigh, hawked Rawleigh products in a boxed-in, horse-drawn wagon. Painted yellow, for God's sake. Yellow, so the farmwives could see it coming and get excited." She was listening, her head tilted attentively. He knew she could see it, too, parked on the country road. "That damn yellow box. That's all I can think of when I think of him. The poor bugger. Bright yellow, colour of a kid's crayon. Yup, every couple years he'd slap on another coat, keep it looking fresh. Spent his life with his head in that damn yellow box. No kidding. I've seen him lean into it, looking for some tincture of something or other, and damn-near disappear inside it, tip right in so his feet went up in the air. Legs sticking out like some kind of frog being tortured."

"Tortured?"

Whoa, he'd got carried away. "Kids. You know they do that," he explained. "I don't know how I got started on all this." And he thought: Truer words were never spoken.

"It's not how you want to be, like him," she said.

"It's not how I am, sweetheart."

"That's true, Bill," she said.

"My head's in no box. It's not in the clouds, either. No sir, my head's square on these two shoulders." She was looking at him as if he was bleeding or something. "Christ," he said, "I need a drink. You go along, there's a goddamn town every seven goddamn miles, and when you need one, where is it?"

"Is your father dead?" she asked.

It was kind of shocking to have her say it like that, right out. "Ah, yeah," he said.

She said, "My father is also dead."

"I'm sorry." He was going to say more, he was going to say both of them having dead fathers gave them something in common, but he was glad he hadn't when she said, "No need to apologize. There is nothing at all to be sorry about." She sounded more cross about it than sad and since he was already mad at himself for going on and on about a yellow wagon he'd seen once on a road in the middle of nowhere, he let the subject drop.

She was quiet after that, too. She sat up straight and leaned forward, watching the road ahead. Forward-looking. Sometimes he didn't know if she was the most frustrating person he'd ever met, or if there was something wrong with him that he couldn't make it easy between them. He was used to easiness; it came naturally to him to find the right thing to say, the right attitude to fit a person and a situation. He hardly ever encountered an awkwardness that needed smoothing over – until with her.

It was a few miles later that she said, almost as if she was thinking aloud, "You know, I thought that movie was about what kind of man makes a good husband, but now I wonder if it was also about who makes a good father."

"Oh, who cares?" Bill said.

She looked at him as if she was going to say, "You do." But she didn't.

Virginia Valley had two hotels. Bill drove past them both so they could read their signs. The Balmoral advertised itself as "A Home Away from Home, Home Cooking, We Employ White Help Only."

"It means the other place is run by Chinamen," Bill said. "And it won't have a bar. They don't license chinks to sell liquor."

"Well, we can stay there and you can go to this one for a drink. I can't go into the bar with you anyway. And I've never seen a Chinaman."

He grinned at her. "You're gonna see a whole lot you've never seen before this trip is over," he told her.

The Windsor Hotel was cleaner than the norm. Somebody had laid wet cloths along all the windowsills to keep out the dust that was constantly blowing ever since spring thaw, even down in the valley. Bill moseyed over to the Balmoral for a few drinks and got his flask filled while Elena washed up, and then they had supper in the hotel restaurant, where she was able to observe two Chinamen taking orders, filling coffee cups, and distributing heaping platters of greasy food. She was disappointed neither of them had pigtails, which somewhere along the way she'd been told they would. And she was surprised they were dressed like other people. They talked like Chinamen, though. As Bill pointed out, they murdered the English language, if you could call their lingo English at all.

They had what he called a good time in the restaurant, but when they got back to the room, she sat down on the side of the bed, looking like some kind of orphan alone in the world. At first that annoyed Bill, and then it occurred to him that her name was almost the same as the girl in the picture show. He went up to her and ruffled her hair. "Ellie," he said, softly. "I just realized you have the same name, sort of. And you're running away, too, aren't you?"

She got under the covers and pulled them up to her chin. He crawled in beside her. "What you and I need to do is find us a beach somewhere," he said. "Yeah, we need ourselves an island." When she didn't answer, he poked her. "Hey? Don't you have any romance in you?"

She sat up. "Sock her once in a while. Whether she asks for it or not. That's what the father says Ellie's husband ought to do to straighten her out. And it's what Peter says he will do when they're married."

"They're kidding!"

"Kidding?"

"Don't you know kidding when you hear it?"

"I guess not," she said.

If that wasn't enough to flummox him, after a good minute of staring at the wall, all of a sudden she told him he was a good person. At first he laughed, but then he felt sad, so sad, in fact, he had to clear his throat and ask her something that had popped into his head the same time she was saying it. It was if her father had beaten her. He had to ask.

She seemed surprised. "No, no," she said. "He would never do that."

"He was a good person, too?"

"I don't know," she said.

After a while he said it was hard for him to believe they'd watched the same show. "It's a comedy, for God's sake," he said. "It's about a guy looking for the right kind of girl for him, and a girl finding the right kind of guy for her. That's all it's about." He said she made too much of it. "It's like you went to the restaurant downstairs in this burg, and asked for filet mignon. And all you're gonna get is fee and chee."

"What is fee and chee, anyway?" she asked.

"Fish and chips."

"Fish and chips?"

"Fee and chee!" He got her smiling, then. "Missie likee fee and chee? Eh? Eh? What Missie likee tonight, eh?" She laughed out loud. It was as if she forgot everything they'd been talking about. It was so gratifying, and led to such surprisingly satisfying love-making, that he fell asleep with a smile on his face.

She'd meant it when she said Bill was a good person, and not just because of his good-natured smile and the way his eyes smiled, too – that everything's-okay-here-isn't-it-sweetheart brightening of colour in his nice blue eyes that made him appealing to women, that made it easy for any woman to like him – and not just because of that bit of swagger that had its own attraction. Already she felt comfortable with him. She liked the way he touched her and how pleased he was with everything she would do for him. She liked the way she could see inside him to the person he really was.

A few hours after she fell asleep, she sat right up. She couldn't see into the black void that surrounded her, and she didn't have a clue where she was. She'd been dreaming; she'd thought she'd heard her father's voice calling her, first as if he stood at the door to the room, and then as if he were standing right over the bed. She'd opened her eyes and he wasn't there. There had only been his voice, getting nearer and nearer. Saying her name. He'd sounded urgent. "Elena, Elena. Wake up, girl." He was trying to warn her about some disaster that was going to befall her.

She remembered she was in a hotel and peered about as her eyes grew accustomed to the darkness. She still couldn't see far into the room, but the door seemed to be closed. She couldn't hear anything but Bill's even breathing. She thought of fire, maybe that was the disaster, but she couldn't smell smoke. They'd fallen asleep with the window closed and the air was stuffy. She thought about getting up, opening it. She imagined the fresh air in her face, but fear crept up from her toes. She lay back down, carefully, as if to move too fast would alert some lurking creature or fate, thinking maybe she did hear something down the hall.

In his back room, Jerry Wong was mopping up the glass of water he'd knocked over. Water was running off his bedside table and streaming over the slanted floorboards, and he saw himself, a ridiculous figure, chasing it. Waddling like a duck on his haunches. He could hardly keep up to it, sop it up with his pillowcase. It was stupid that he had a pillow, anyway, when he didn't use it, that he put a glass of water by his bed and seldom drank it, that he did a thousand things he thought he should do in order to seem to himself like somebody he wasn't. And then he ended up standing outside himself, watching himself – there was no one else to watch or care.

He'd flung his arm out in his sleep. His body had tried to imitate his mind. He'd been dreaming about his wife. How is business? his wife asked in each of her letters. He hadn't seen her for over ten years. They wrote to one another every month and on their birthdays they sent photos of themselves. He looked younger in his than he really did, and he expected it was the same with her, although in fact she didn't look young at all any-more. And didn't bother smiling, as she had in the first ones she'd mailed to him, or signing them on the back, as she had before, with her full name.

His son would soon be ten. His only son. Jerry had never seen him except in pictures. And he'd thought he was so smart, coming to Canada, his great escape. He'd been back just once, to get his wife pregnant. There had been no money to return a second time and she wasn't allowed into the country. He could speak English as well as an Englishman, and what good did it do him?

On the other hand, he was spared her constant presence. It had been an arranged marriage; there had never been any ques-tion of love between them, and now there was only the business, which she had never seen. And the son he'd never seen. But he had a son, that was the main thing, a fine youngster, studious and obedient, his wife assured him, and so he appeared in his photographs and in the short, careful letters Jerry received.

A big gust rattled his windowpane, but he didn't go to look outside. It was always windy, always dusty and dry and hot. He would see nothing out his window he hadn't seen a thousand times before. He hung the wet pillowcase over the railing in the hallway and went downstairs to his office and took out his accounts book. Industry was the only cure for middle-of-the-night self-ridicule. He would pore over the numbers until he fell asleep in his chair, and when his neighbour's rooster crowed, he'd jump up as if the night had never been, and make coffee and rouse his brother-in-law, and they would start cooking and cleaning and joking with one another and the customers.

The smell of fresh-baked bread woke Elena up in the morning. Bill had already risen and was getting washed. The room was lit so brilliantly she thought the sun must be sitting on the window-sill. Cool air wafted over the bed. She sat up, let the sheet fall off. "What's this?" she said, examining the bruises on her stomach. It looked as if she'd been punched. It looked like a thunderstorm brewing black and blue and brown across her navel.

"The steering wheel, sweetie. The other day?"

She didn't have to ask about the ache low down inside her pelvis; she knew where that came from. She wondered what you did with a man when your monthlies started. She was glad she'd thought to pack her rag pads the night she took off. It was unusual for her to feel grateful for those things, or to Maria Gustafson for giving them to her, four of them, neatly sewn of flannelette rags, to tie around you and protect you on those days, to rinse and wring nightly (shuddering) and hang up to dry.

And here was Bill, whistling like the first bird of spring, as if he'd just invented morning. Soaping himself in front of the dresser, watching himself in its mirror. Lovingly, he caressed his sturdy body with the soapy cloth, flinging suds around him. Iridescent bits flew off him in the sunlight, and when he got to that thing of his, well, lovingly only half-described it. He drew on it until it stood up like a separate being with the word *thrust* on its mind. The heaviness in her pelvis increased and then sharpened as she watched his hand follow its upward slant. He closed his eyes, turned his face up to the sun. "Baby, come here," he whispered.

After breakfast the coffee crowd arrived. One of the reasons Jerry Wong didn't have money to return to China was that he insisted on donating from their small profits to local initiatives. His brother-in-law understood; their generosity brought the coffee crowd to their restaurant and that was just about the margin that kept them in business. It was more than that, though, for Jerry; it was part of his idea of who he should be, the place he should establish for himself in the community for the time his son could join him.

Most mornings he didn't stop to think. You had to keep the cups full. You had to say something about the weather and at least one other thing that would make them laugh. But that morning – maybe it was the after-effect of spilling his glass of water in the night – he found himself a couple of times staring at nothing, with the coffee pot in limbo between where he was and wherever he was headed. He found himself wondering where his wife was at that precise moment, what she was doing. Sleeping, perhaps, on the other side of the world. It was best to picture her sleeping, his son, too, in a safe bed. Best not to concern himself with troubled times. When were there not troubled times in China? He tried to remember the stroll they'd taken one day through the gardens near her house, tried to picture his wife under the round red lanterns that hung from the trees, tried to believe his life would be different if he never saw her again.

On one of these time outs, he stood at the window, unseeing, and then realized he was looking at a magnificent automobile. He set the coffee pot down and went outside just as the car pulled away. It was the handsome young couple. He hadn't seen them arrive, and now they were driving down the hill to the ferry. He pulled off his apron and hung it on the fence post down at the sidewalk. He followed the huge gold roadster down to the water, and when he got there, he stood chatting with the town blacksmith, who was loitering there, too, watching while the car drove onto the barge and it chugged off onto the river. The day was warm, the sun like hands on his shoulders, like a wife's hands would be, a kind of benediction as she stood behind him, approving all he did. But it wouldn't be his wife's hands. She expected so much of him and she didn't understand goodwill. Every month she wanted an accounting. She wanted to know why he was poor in such a rich country.

◇◇◇◇◇

"Can we get out of the car?" she asked.

"We sure can," he said. He waited for her to come around to his side of the barge, and noticed her bag behind the seat. This morning it was bulging. He'd filled it with gifts back in Charlesville, that's why.

"We'll have to get you a new bag," he said, pleased with himself.

"Yes, I have hardly room for the things I brought," she said.

He put his arm around her and gave her a squeeze.

"I've never seen a river like this. So wide," she said. They leaned into the railing, watching the water make deep patterns out of itself while they chugged over it on the big ropes.

"I told you, stick with me, kid," he said. Their bodies gently lifted and fell, side by side, and he imagined her saying, "I might. If you're good, I might stick with you." And then he would say, "You're a flirt, you know that?" And she would say, "Sure I am. What girl isn't? On a beautiful morning with her sweetheart beside her." It was a beautiful morning. He'd never seen a sky so blue, clouds so white, the sun so strong.

They moved out towards the middle of the river. The barge tilted and he looked to her, worried she might lose her balance. But she hadn't seemed to notice the shift. Or she'd simply accommodated to it. She was staring into the distance, pensive, as if she were all alone. Well, he consoled himself, at least she didn't always have to share her thoughts. And he forgave her for the times she did. It was kind of cute, anyway, how earnest she could get. And hadn't he read her right from the start? She'd proved to have exactly what he'd divined: a great desire to be desirable, that he'd hardly had to encourage. Why, just this morning, look how sweet she'd been.

Elena saw him grinning. "What are you thinking about?" she asked.

"*Vaut* am I thinking about?"

She stood up straighter. She looked past him out over the choppy wake to the shore they'd left behind as if she could still see the two men who had stood there, getting smaller.

"Hey, don't get all huffy," he said. "Your accent's cute."

"I don't have an accent," she said carefully.

"Oh, yeah?"

"Yeah."

"*It duss sseem tat you do haff a liddle accent.* Hey, I told you, it's cute. I'm kidding you. I'm exaggerating." The boat lurched and his feet skidded. He had to grab hold of the rail. She was already holding onto it, and only swayed, staring at him. "I'm *kidding*. Anyway, I like it," he said. "I like the way you say, '*I vonder.*' Hah! You're always *vondering.*" He laughed and reached out and stroked her arm. "I was thinking about the Trianon. You're going to love it." This was the ballroom he'd told her about, where the orchestras were hot. Bands from all over North America came there. She hadn't heard nothin' yet. And dance – she'd never danced till she'd danced to one of them; real swing was what they played.

She didn't say anything more and she had no expression at all on her face, but he knew she was thinking and was not pleased. He turned away and watched the water. God, it looked deep. It must be deeper here. The further down you looked, the blacker it got. You couldn't see anywhere near the bottom, and both shores were far away now. He could have driven north, they'd told him that in Charlesville; somewhere north there was a bridge across the river. It wasn't that much out of the way. He didn't know why he'd opted for the ferry. You shouldn't put yourself into situations where you could end up feeling helpless. It was the same with women; you shouldn't do or say anything that would give them a leg up; they'd start to remind you of your mother.

He stood back from the railing, restless, but there was nowhere to go. The grinding of the ferry straining on its course was getting on his nerves. The noise hemmed him in. And Elena was looking at him as if she'd stepped inside him and was inspecting the inside of his skull. He knew a whole lot more about the world than she did, but that didn't seem to count for much, not when she searched inside him with those eyes.

It was just the ferry making him uneasy, that's all it was, the noise and the motion of the water heaving under him. He'd be glad when they reached the shore and he could get into his car again and drive off onto solid ground. But he wished he hadn't told her anything about himself. He wished he'd never mentioned his father. But at the same time he wanted desperately to ask her to marry him.

◇◇◇◇◇

He seemed more himself when they got back on the road. Mostly they drove in silence, with Bill explicating once in a while the ways of the city they would reach before nightfall and peripherally discussing himself and his ideas, and with Elena saying little, or, as she now supposed, *liddle*.

She drifted into thinking about learning, about the many things she'd like to learn, subjects that school hadn't touched upon, such as learning itself. It would be interesting to study how the human brain worked, how people figured things out and made decisions, why they thought the way they did, also what it was that made some things funny and others not very amusing at all. On the ferry, the shifting, shiftless sensation, that uncontrolled swaying, had got right into her blood. Standing at the railing, her dream had come back to her. Her father calling her. Calling her name, over and over. Insistent. Some disaster was heading her way. Maybe the ferry was going to sink, she thought. And what if it did? She looked across the boat and imagined a couple standing at the opposite railing, a sophisticated man and a woman in white gloves. The white gloves especially drew her attention. They were short, came only to the woman's wrists, and on the inside of each wrist, they had a row of three tiny buttons like seed pearls. But then Bill had distracted her, with that grin all over his face, and she'd made the mistake of asking him what he was thinking. She wondered if the unsettling feeling of the river under their feet was what had sent him into such a bad mood, or if it was only that she hadn't appreciated him mocking her.

All the time she was musing on these things, Bill was talking. "I like to take things as they come," she heard him say, and she thought: Especially when they come so easy. Well, what did it matter? She leaned back in her seat and let the hot wind handle her. She closed her eyes so that in her mind's eye she could see the buttons on those gloves. Something refined about them spelled assurance, a certain carefree ease, a way of being that needed money behind it, and made her think of her father's worthless land and the empty buildings, the way she'd last seen them flashing past in the wide circle lit by Bill's headlights.

Bill was talking about the city and she had an image in her mind of the road ending suddenly in tall buildings and traffic. "I would like some gloves," she said.

"Sure you would." He laughed excitedly. "Sure you would," he said again.

Stick with me, kid. "Thank you, Bill," she said.

"Come here," he said. "Come on over here." He held out his arm and she moved in closer. He draped his arm around her and absent-mindedly fondled her loose right breast inside the soft cotton of her dress. She'd heard boys say anything more than a handful is a waste, but she was pleased she had a good handful. He'd said she had nice little bullet nipples. She started to sink into the seat and he pinched the nipple between his thumb and forefinger, and she moaned. Actually, it was more of a whimper – her breasts were swollen and sore.

"Oh, *girl*," he said in a sort of deep growl.

At first he thought she was crying. Her chest heaved and she pulled out from under his arm and turned her head away. Her shoulders shook. She was still turned away from him but there was no doubt, now – she was laughing. She was laughing so hard she was choking.

"What's so funny?" he asked.

She shook her head, her hand clutched to her mouth. He'd like to know what was so goddamn funny – just when he was thinking how sweet she was, leaning against him, just when he was imagining one of these days she was going to turn to him and tell him she loved him – but then they hit a patch of washboard and he had to focus his attention on the road and use both hands on the wheel. They'd hardly seen another vehicle for miles, and now came up fast on a plume of dust. It was a farm truck, braking ahead of them, the driver signalling with a crooked blue-shirted arm out his window, taking his time turning onto a side road. Bill had to slow right down. Elena was still laughing and still looking away from him, watching the truck as it headed towards a little town down the narrow dirt road.

Then she said, "Stop," just as he was accelerating. It sounded so urgent, he hit the brakes hard, and they fishtailed in the loose gravel. The car jerked and stalled, stranding them sideways across the highway. They'd stirred up so much dust they couldn't see a thing until it started settling, sifting down on the roadster to coat its long hood and fenders. "Gilroy," the sign right in front of them said, when the dust cleared. From the highway, it looked a lot like every other town they'd passed. No sign of life except for a young girl, about eleven or twelve, out walking along the railway tracks, a kid on her own, dragging her feet.

"Elena?" He reached for her as she opened her door. His hand grazed her hair, but she was already hopping down from the running board, she was walking into the battered weeds at the verge of the road. For a few seconds she stood there, plucking at the thin material of her dress that clung damply to her thighs, and then she took off. She took off down the highway, towards the intersection they'd just passed. She was walking away. For a few seconds, he just stared at her. He couldn't believe his eyes. She was walking away, just walking away, like a person in a dream that you had no voice to call to, walking off down the road into the hazy white sky. And it was so white, that sky, it was like it wasn't real, so he thought: This isn't really happening. He wiped his arm across his eyes and she was still walking away. He lunged across the passenger seat and smacked her door shut, half-thinking the sound would bring her to her senses, although his hand moved naturally after-wards to the key at the ignition. He'd get the hell out of there, that's what he'd do, he thought, with his hand at the ignition. But he turned around in his seat to watch her.

She got to the intersection and made the turn and went on down the narrower dirt road. Either side of her the fields of wheat were almost motionless. The truck that had slowed them down had pulled into town; the girl she'd seen out walking by herself had disappeared over a little rise past the grain elevators, and nothing was moving in the whole landscape except for grasshoppers. They arced over the road, sometimes as many as twenty or thirty in her path at once. Their whirring fluttered the air, filled it with a sound that was so like being stroked by them, she shuddered, but she walked through them with her head up, pretending they couldn't hit her with their brittle, horrid bodies, leaving her spotted with their tobacco-coloured stain.

She wasn't laughing anymore; her second thoughts were any-thing but funny. It was hot, godawful hot, and what in the world was she doing? She'd left her bag behind and that ache inside her pelvis was getting critical. And she didn't have a cent in the world. She'd need money soon; without her rag pads she'd have to buy napkins and a belt. She didn't look back, but she started walking slower. She tried to think Bill might turn the car around and follow her. He hadn't started the engine yet; maybe he was con-sidering it. Maybe he'd come after her.

He was still watching her. He'd made fun of her dress, the brown colour, its modesty, but she didn't have a thing on under that dress and he knew it. Just watching her, thinking about her melting out there in the heat, he was growing hard. She liked that power she had over him, and he liked that about her. She had her faults. She laughed at the wrong times. It was disconcerting. One minute she was asking him for gloves and the next she was walking away. But he'd wait for her, if she stopped and turned back. He'd wait for her.

He did sit there for a bit longer, but she went on as if her feet were taking her mindlessly down the road, further and further down the road into the white sky. He half-noticed, then, that the whiteness was increasing, that it was actually billowing, like a cloud or like fog rolling in, as it might have, rolling towards her like this in some other place. But he wasn't interested in the sky or any other natural phenomena; he was only interested in her and in what she was doing, leaving him. He couldn't figure it out; she was walking slower than she had before, but there was only one direction she was going, and that was the one in front of her face. Tears prickled his eyes.

When he was a little guy, his mother would sometimes say to him, "You're happy now." He would look up from whatever he was doing and try to catch the expression on her face. It was always just fading. He never knew exactly what she meant. He assumed his happiness was a source of satisfaction to her, but a hint of musing in her voice caught him up each time and made him remember the other times she'd said it. He thought of them now, not the individual times, but the glint of them, stretched like beads through his childhood. He remembered Elena's pale face gleaming from the Lincoln that first night, in Addison, while they waited for the hotel owner to open the door. That was happiness, that girl in his car. He felt as if someone had snatched his life away. He started the Lincoln, shaking his head to clear his vision. He looked back a last time. She wasn't walking fast, couldn't, he realized, in the pumps he'd bought her, of soft light brown leather with a strap near the ankle, shoes that fit her like a glove. She was ruining those shoes by walking on gravel. That was one thing she hadn't considered. He didn't notice she'd forgotten her bag, or he would have heaved it out into the ditch.

She heard him gun the motor and take off, and turned to watch him go. The empty feeling, which he'd dispelled during their few days together, came back, familiar and almost comforting. Soon she couldn't see the car anymore, only the trail of dust it left behind, and when the dust from his leaving had died down, she was surprised to see that the sky above the highway continued hazy. A whole minute after he'd gone, she was still standing there staring at the spot where the roadster had stopped. Surely, the air held way more dust than one vehicle could have raised. It was unnaturally white dust, too, hovering like a low-hanging cloud over the road and the fields. Then she saw that the cloud hung all around her, and was all lit up, as if each particle was glowing from within. And when she turned to continue what she'd started, she saw that the little hamlet down the road, sitting pillowed in silvery grasses, knee-high foxtails and things like that, shimmered in it like a mirage.

GILROY

I was the one she saw. I was that girl walking along the railway tracks, looking lonely. I didn't see her arrive because I had
my back to Gilroy. It was such bad luck. I was facing away from
the intersection where Bill Longmore stopped his car and Elena
Huhtala got out and left him. I was trudging along between the
rails, inhaling the hot black creosote smell of the ties. I loved
that smell. Just thinking about it can make me feel like a kid
again, with summer all around me. That day I was mooching
along, wishing I could live in someone else's house – wasting my
time on wishing, when I might have been looking and seeing,
when I might have been experiencing what I could only, from
evidence painstakingly gathered later, imagine. And I have
often imagined it since; it was of such importance to me, the
moment of her arrival in Gilroy, that liquid droplet in that
pearly day, the car door opening, her wavy, honey-coloured
hair, one bare, tanned leg then another as she placed her feet on
the running board and looked up to find a pale sun in the sky,
the size of a coin tossed high. Her brown dress clinging to her

thighs as she stepped down to the gravel and the spurge at the side of the road.

As for my wishing, and the house I wanted to live in, that house existed. It had pictures on the walls and shelves full of books and other attributes I hadn't yet seen or guessed at. It was a small bungalow at the edge of town, where I thought I could have a room to myself, a cool, quiet room where I could be alone. I had chosen the house, but I hadn't been invited in.

Probably I was conscious of looking lonely, out there alone on the bare prairie, moseying along on a hot day when anyone with brains bigger than a grasshopper's would have found some shade; probably I was hoping to make the impression of loneliness if anyone went by and noticed me.

I'm sure it was the very moment Elena Huhtala stepped down from the car that I looked up in the opposite direction, and got stopped. I had to stop because way down at the end of the tracks, where they met at the horizon, a big whiteness was headed my way, a big, luminous, opaque whiteness. It looked almost as if an old-time steam engine was barrelling towards me, but whatever it was, it was bigger than a head of steam. It took up most of the horizon. For a few absurd seconds I thought snow was coming, but it was August, and so hot my clothes were drooping; it couldn't be snow. I didn't see how it could be dust either, on a day when, unusually, there was almost no wind. And it was much too white to be any dust I'd ever seen; it was the opposite of the dark billows we'd got used to in recent years that were our topsoil blowing away.

I thought I should run back to town and warn people. But warn them of what? I looked up into the sky, where the sun pulsed crazily, as if it wanted to break through, and couldn't, and I realized the white cloud was no longer in front of me; it had already enveloped me. The air all around me glittered with suspended phosphorescent dust.

It was a trek from the highway into Gilroy and the sun was getting stronger every minute. A pink strip appeared where Elena's wavy hair parted and along her pretty nose. The deodorant she wore went slick under her arms. Small rivers trickled down her ribs under her thin dress. And her poor young feet! Rubbed raw, especially at the heels where grit from the road met the moist skin.

The town was smaller than it looked from the highway. It was nothing more than a hamlet, just one row of false-fronted boxes along a wide main street and a few scattered, unpainted houses. The whole of Gilroy boasted four trees and none of them had grown yet much higher than Elena Huhtala's head. She could hear her own footsteps like whispers over the gravel, the kind of whispers gossips use. The place looked deserted. Almost everyone had gone inside to escape the afternoon heat as best they could. Then she saw that there were a couple of witnesses to her arrival. Two men stood in the open door of the garage opposite the general store – the only store in town – and smoked lip-wet roll-your-owns. They stood up a little straighter when Elena Huhtala appeared on the road that ran slantwise from the highway to meet up with Main Street. Men often stood up straighter when they saw her; it was simultaneously a sign of respect and disrespect, and it meant she had to walk without limping while avoiding looking their way. She stepped up to the wooden sidewalk in front of the store and stopped to take a breath. She put her hands up and shook out her hair. She wiped her face with her fingertips. The best she could hope for was to smudge the sweat, the powder, and the dust together. Ignoring the men, she peered down at herself, checking that the buttons on the front of her dress were done up, and snuck a look at the wet patches under her arms. She sat down on the bench in front of the store and brushed at her shoes.

The storekeeper in Gilroy was a tall man who stooped as much as he could to make up for having to look down on others. His name was Scott Dobie. He had a wife and two daughters, one of whom worked in the store, and a son named Leonard who farmed just out of town and helped him with any heavy jobs. Leonard happened to be stacking egg crates in the storeroom the day of Elena Huhtala's arrival, and when he heard the screen door squawk and then slam shut — a sound that was hardly unusual — he put his thumb through a shell. Usually a towel hung by his father's butchering apron, but his father had walked off with it less than a minute before, so Leonard came out, into the store, at the moment she walked in, blinking the way everyone did in the sudden dimness.

The Dobies' store was much like other stores of its kind. It had an oiled wood floor, and the penetrating smell of that oil mingled with the smell of the round of cheddar on the counter and the smell of brown paper and string. For a place designed to sell merchandise, it was subdued, and nothing about Elena Huhtala looked subdued. Her brown dress might have appeared modest on the hanger, but it didn't look modest now. Her hair might have been combed that morning, but it was messy in a most alluring manner now. No matter what she wore, or how she presented herself, Elena Huhtala was made to stand out in that store, and Leonard's eyes went right to her.

As soon as she saw him, she blushed. Her hand went up to her cheek and she lay the hot flesh against the cooler backs of her fingers. As if she'd read his mind. Because just looking at him, anyone could tell he was a serious person. He was a person whose regard you would want, whose esteem you would crave before you even thought about it. As for Leonard, he waited for some guy to follow her in, some city guy who was kicking his tires outside, or getting refuelled, or just sitting back in his car being glad he didn't live in this town, while she came in for whatever it was she needed. But he was wrong. When she reached the counter she asked if they might need a clerk.

Scott thought she looked about fifteen and he felt sorry for her. He had nothing for her, and there were no other businesses in the town that employed women except the café that was run by the Chows and the hotel that was run by the Ridges. Neither needed staff. He told her he didn't think she'd find work in Gilroy. She didn't say a word, just bowed her head.

Later, much later, Leonard admitted he would have crossed the store and knelt at her feet at that moment, if he could have acted according to his desire. He would have stroked the film of dust from her shoes. He would have laid his head against the modest brown dress and asked for her hand in marriage. He was the district's most eligible bachelor, the best pitcher in southern Saskatchewan, and one of the nicest guys you'd ever meet, and he would have knelt on the oiled boards in front of his father and declared his love and given all his worldly possessions to touch those shoes, that dress. In fact, he did nothing. Self-preservation kept him standing back, immobile, while she walked to the door.

Scott opened the flap that blocked off the counter from the rest of the store, and went to the window to look out. Leonard took up the towel and wiped off his thumb. He had to rub at the nail to get the clinging egg yolk off. He thought about going back to the storeroom and getting back to work, but he set the towel down where he'd found it, and went to join his father at the window. They stood there together with their arms crossed, the way they often did, waiting for something unusual to happen on Main Street. Now that something unusual had happened, they didn't know what they were waiting for.

Elena sat on the bench outside the store and wondered what she could possibly do next. The two men who'd been watching her from the garage across the street were still standing there. They didn't have much else to do, hardly anyone bought gas anymore. Most people who still owned a car had put it up on blocks. So they held up the walls except when one or the other of them went inside and brought out a mug of coffee or a dripping cup of water. Elena was thinking she'd have to go over and ask for some when one of the men, Walter Dunn, it was, started across the street with a cup in his hand, one of those shallow old speckled enamel cups that makes coffee cool quickly and water taste colder than it does in anything else. It was a wide, unevenly graded street that Walter Dunn had to cross, and it was quite a feat for him to get to her without spilling the water. He concentrated on doing it, partly because it wasn't easy and partly to keep from looking too anxious to make Elena Huhtala's acquaintance.

◇◇◇◇◇

If you were making a huge meringue and had gone overboard and beaten the egg whites dry, and then walked into the bowl – that would have been like the air that day, all glossy-dusty around us. Up above, the sun pulsed and pointed its long fingers down. It appeared to be trying to reach us and not with the intention of doing good. I wasn't the only one to notice that sun and find it scary. I passed Sammy Appleby's shack and the old bugger, as we always called him, was lying on his back on the sofa he'd dragged out into his front yard, staring up, and down the lane Aunt Lizzy Ridge was on her knees in her garden, looking up. Once you saw that sun trying to eat its way towards you, it was hard to stop looking at it. You couldn't see that sun without thinking something was going to happen.

Then I spied the stilts. I knew who they belonged to, Dutch Egan, and he'd dropped them in front of Jack Newton's house while he went in to see Harold. He wouldn't care if I used them. I'd have them back before he missed them, anyway. I grabbed the wooden poles in both hands and stepped up onto the blocks, first one foot, then the other, and then I teetered off wildly down the road. Well, who wouldn't? I'd had no opportunity to learn how to use them, and it was like having someone else's long legs grown under mine. And no feet to balance, either. I started at great speed and went faster as I went further. The little houses rocketed past, looking smaller than ever because I was taller. I fell off when I reached the corner.

I was doing better by the time I turned onto Main Street. I had the stilts almost under control and wasn't travelling quite so fast. I saw Walter Dunn a ways in front of me walking like an old man with a cup in his two hands, but then the sun broke all the way through the cloud cover and flared right into my eyes.

Walter saw me, too, coming straight for him, but he just naturally assumed I'd stop for him. And I would have stopped or at least swerved aside if the sun hadn't struck me in the face. There wasn't a kid in Gilroy who hadn't been taught to make way for an adult. And Walter was a man on a mission. He was also just about as solid as thirty years could make him, and I was an eleven-year-old girl. I flew off the stilts in one direction and my glasses flew in the other. The first thing I thought of was my glasses. If I knew anything for certain, it was that those glasses of mine were expensive. Not as expensive as the operation the doctor wanted me to have on my bad eye, but way more than my parents could afford to replace.

Walter made a big fuss. After all, he'd spilled the entire cup of water. If I'd been a boy, he'd have sworn at me. Since I wasn't, he bit his tongue, picked up my glasses, and helped me to my feet. My glasses were okay. They weren't even scratched. Walter didn't care. He started dusting me off, a bit roughly it seemed to me. I thought I might mention it to my mother; my mother wouldn't put up with anyone bothering her girls. But I forgot. I stopped thinking about Walter Dunn and my glasses and the stinging parts of me that had hit the gravel when I fell. Even the idea of my own importance, which was fairly constantly on my mind, fled right out of it, because just then I saw Elena Huhtala sitting on the bench in front of the store.

Shining. Oh yes, shining. Light curled in the waves of her hair; her bare limbs gleamed. I could hear Walter Dunn hustling back to the garage, behind me, for more water, and I could hear Bob Newton laughing at him. She didn't so much as smile. She acted as if none of it had anything to do with her, as if she was only sitting there as the first step to getting someplace else. But I'd grown up expecting maternal solicitude from anyone who'd graduated to woman-hood, and I went to her, holding out the hand I'd scraped when I fell, nursing the wound and trying to squeeze out a tear or two.

"Yes?" she said. She glanced from my hand to my face. Her eyes were the lightest hazel, with golden flecks that made them almost the same colour as her hair.

Walter came out of the garage then. I knew I didn't have much time. I shoved my hand at her. She took it lightly in both of her hands. She turned it this way and that and pulled the fingers back so the drops of blood swelled at the base of my palm and the stone chips embedded in the flesh stood up.

"I see accidents," she said. And she rose to receive Walter and his cup. I plunked myself down on the sidewalk at her feet, looking up in time to see her pass the cup back to him and wipe her mouth with the back of her wrist.

"You looked thirsty," Walter said. He looked gormless. That was an expression of my dad's, meaning dumb, and Walter surely fit the bill. Utterly besotted, and forgetful of the fact that he was overweight and still unmarried at thirty. Well, maybe not forgetful of that.

"Thank you," she said, like she might have been the Queen, or Wallis Simpson, even better. "I was thirsty." She had a charming way of talking, breaking up the words almost like she was singing.

"Well," Walter said. He looked down at the cup and turned it round and round. Suddenly he thrust out his hand. "Walter Dunn," he said.

"Elena Huhtala," she said. I remember it as if it were yesterday, exactly how she said it, the most exotic name I'd ever heard. She shook Walter's hand and he took it back and turned the cup around a few more times.

"I wonder," she said, and she said it earnestly, emphatically; she said it as if she really did wonder something about him. By this time he'd completely forgotten my existence and Bob Newton's, too, and he did what I suppose any young man would do faced with a young woman like Elena Huhtala, who seemed for no earthly reason to care about him. He swayed towards her, and his eyes went soft. He looked like Grandpa Hood's old Shep when you'd stepped on his paw and he had a right to expect you to pat him.

"I wonder," she repeated, "if you would like your palm read."

Walter cleared his throat. "You read palms?" he croaked.

She nodded. "Ten cents," she said.

"Ten cents." He fished in his pocket and jingled a few coins. That was a habit with Walter; the sound of his money usually kept him from spending it. "I guess you must be pretty good," he said.

"Well," she said. "You must be the judge of that."

He pulled out his change and poked through it and picked out a dime. A dime was quite a bit for a few minutes' entertainment, in those days. You could get into a movie for thirty-five cents, fifteen cents if you were a kid; a country dance would cost a quarter and last till after midnight. He looked at it for a few seconds before he handed it to her.

She didn't have a purse with her, and her dress had no pockets. She smiled at him suddenly. It was the first smile anyone in Gilroy had seen, and it was gone before you could blink. She bent down and slipped the dime into her left shoe, on the inside, at the arched instep of her foot. When she straightened she looked, just for a second, into my eyes, right into my eyes. She looked at me as if we shared a secret and as if I would know what the secret was.

That was how it began, the fortune-telling, I mean. I gave her the idea and she ran with it. She read the palms of half the people in town, her first day in Gilroy. The other half didn't go to her because they were afraid, not so much to know their futures as to have their hands held in hers. They said it was a cheap thing to do, anyway, setting yourself up like a gypsy, and what could a chit of a girl who'd landed in town alone, without a cent to her name, know about them?

It's true she started out a little rocky, with Walter being the first one. I guess she wanted to impress him with an official kind of palm-reading instead of following her intuition, and it got her into trouble, the way trying to impress people often does. Besides foretelling a general upsurge in the economy, she predicted a boom for garage owners who'd been smart enough to stick with the business. Then she found out she had the wrong man, that the other fellow lounging across the street owned the garage. Walter was the Rural Municipality administrator and just passed time helping Bob Newton keep an eye on Main Street. But she was a quick learner. She switched to talking about men who were wise enough to get an education, men who earned the respect of others by holding important, responsible public positions.

Mrs. Beggs came up to the bench while Walter was getting his palm read, and pretended she wanted to talk to him. Mrs. Beggs had a fluty British accent that made her one of the town's premiere ladies. It made her an organizer of teas and wedding showers and excused her from doing any of the actual work. The sun had come out in earnest by then and a lacy pattern of light and shade, thrown down by her straw garden hat, covered Mrs. Beggs's face and chest like a veil. She handed over a dime, too, which was not at all like her usual self.

Everyone who came to the store that afternoon either stopped to get their palm read or walked by, gawking, on their way in to pick up their groceries. Scott and Leonard watched at the window, arms folded identically, whenever the place was empty.

Like father, like son, that's what people said about Scott and Leonard, and with good reason. Leonard was twenty-one the summer Elena Huhtala came to Gilroy, and he had the scrubbed good looks and lean, feet-apart stance of a prairie hero. But he didn't know that, or he didn't care to know it. Like his father, he was a modest man. Humility was almost a flaw in both their characters, or so I believed in those days. As for Scott, before relief or official aid of any kind was available, he gave many of the people of our district (and that included my mother) unlimited credit, knowing it was all we had to live on. It was a hardship to him. He carried half the town through the Depression, and he didn't need a fortune teller to inform him that few would ever pay him back in full.

When I started grade one, a bit late because of eye problems, Leonard was taking his grade twelve; he was the oldest boy in our one-room school. The most wonderful thing he did was carry kids around on his shoulders at recess, and for eons I watched him, waiting for him to scoop me up and set me on high. But for some reason, maybe because I was a girl, or because I was shy in grade one, having to wear an eye patch that I feared made me look like a pirate, he never chose me. Finally one day I went to him and stood at his leg and looked up, kind of like a dog will do, kind of like old Shep, myself. Leonard was talking to some other kids at the time, but I didn't care; I couldn't wait another second. I remember he looked down – he'd felt me there beside him – and gave me that lopsided smile of his. You always felt he was smiling in spite of himself and because of you. I put my arms up and the next thing I knew, I was queen of the schoolyard. All the years of my young life, I believed I was going to marry Leonard Dobie one day, if he'd only wait for me.

Not long after Elena finished with Walter Dunn and got going on Mrs. Beggs, I caught sight of Leonard and his dad, the two of them, standing at the store window, and the idea came to me that they'd invented her, or they'd found her somewhere and placed her on their bench, and now they were watching to see how we'd all take it. I suppose that was because she was so foreign, so different from anyone who'd ever stepped into my world, it seemed she had to be a creation rather than a person who'd grown up higgledy-piggledy like the rest of us. But maybe it was more than that. Maybe I was already thinking she was made for Leonard, and if I couldn't have him, if he couldn't wait for me, she'd be just right for him.

As soon as I had her to myself again, I begged her to read my palm more seriously. There had to be more than she'd predicted in my future; she hadn't spent any time at all thinking about me. And the way she'd looked at me, earlier, when she'd put her first dime into her shoe – I kept thinking about that. She'd looked past the thick lenses of my glasses, right into my eyes. I was sure she meant that look to tell me she recognized we were alike. I was sure she meant it to tell me she saw the potential in me to be just like her.

"No," she said.

"Why not?"

She didn't sigh, the usual adult response to that question. She said she couldn't, I was too young, the lines on my palm would be unformed, and besides, my hand had been damaged and the reading wouldn't be clear.

"Do my left hand," I said.

But I wasn't left-handed. She said it wouldn't work.

"What if I only had one hand?" I asked.

"Then I'd feel sorry for you," she said. She didn't sound sorry, not in the least.

I said I'd get money, but nothing would move her. I had to watch everyone else step up and hear their fortunes. It was unusual and difficult for me to stand to the side. I was the oldest in my family and the caretaker of the six kids who'd been born to my mother and father since my birth, the most recent only weeks before Elena Huhtala came to town. I'd grown used to assuming responsibility and to being treated with some deference, although recently something had been happening to me. It seemed to be connected to the birth of my new sister, which had meant even more responsibility had fallen on me. In the midst of my busiest moments, which had formerly made me feel proud, my mind would fly away from my brothers and sisters, right out of the house or yard. I'd watch my hands wiping a nose or drying dishes as if they were someone else's hands and then I'd wish they were someone else's hands so I could slap that face, break that dish, and run. I'd started slipping away so my mother couldn't ask me to do the next chore. Instead of making me feel better, though, escaping made me feel worse. It was hard to go back and never be alone. It was hard to go back and find my mother angry because she'd needed me. I wanted to slip back into the house as I'd slipped out, unnoticed, and lie on an unshared bed in a cool, dark, empty room that was mine alone. And lately, more than ever, although I thought it was wrong of me, I wished I could live in that other house, the house at the edge of town, where I was sure I would find the solitude I needed if only I could get invited in.

Whenever I thought no one understood me, my mind went to my father. I didn't believe he understood me, either, but my mind went to him. My father was working that week for Jack Newton at the Pool grain elevator. I don't know what he was doing, fixing something maybe. Jack was Bob Newton's brother and all the time I lived in Gilroy he had the elevator. That's how people phrased it, and the elevator was a good thing to have. He had the telephone exchange and the post office too, or his wife did, so his kids got the music and elocution lessons, the ice cream, and the picture shows the rest of us didn't get. My father was a bricklayer, and if I tell you there wasn't a brick building within a hundred miles of Gilroy you'll understand what kind of provider he was. I don't know why he came to Saskatchewan except that one of his brothers lived nearby. His brother had a farm and my dad had a quarter-section, too, but he let Uncle Sid work it. He did odd jobs in town; people liked him and they had a lot of respect for my mother, so we got by.

While Aunt Lizzy Ridge got her palm read, I took off for the elevator. Aunt Lizzy was at least eighty; I figured I wouldn't miss much. I wasn't allowed inside the elevator but I climbed up the ramp and stood at the big open door and peered into the haze of grain dust until my father emerged from it with its ashiness clinging to his hat and his clothes.

"Ruthie," he said. I didn't often track him down wherever he was working, and he had a wary look in his eyes, figuring my mother had sent me, I suppose.

"A fortune teller's come to town," I blurted.

He scratched his ear and pulled a cigarette out of his shirt pocket. I'd rolled about a hundred of them for him only the night before so he could pluck one out of his shirt pocket like that and light it. I followed him along the platform to the edge, where he crouched down and lit his smoke, and I sat beside him, swinging my legs back and forth so my shoes brushed the tops of the foxtails growing there in clumps.

I told him she was young, she had honey-coloured hair, she was wearing a brown dress made of material so thin you could spit through it, and in my opinion she had nothing on under it. He pretended to be shocked and cross at me for talking like that. I started to explain that I'd sat right beside her and watched her closely. I knew he'd stop me before I could get into details, before I could tell him I'd seen the shadow of a breast through her dress and the round smooth roll of her thighs. He didn't need to hear the evidence. He listened and smoked, and when I was done and had nothing more to say except the things I couldn't say, and was waiting for what he would reply, he tapped me on the nose with his finger and stood up, dropped his cigarette and stepped on it, and went back to work.

I sat on, looking at my scraped right palm and then at my left. They were not quite mirror images of one another and idly I wondered why. The right palm had an extra line branching off from one of the main lines. Was it because my right hand did more work? I hadn't told my dad Elena Huhtala wouldn't read my palm; he would have thought I was whining. At least he'd tapped my nose. He never did that with the other kids. Sitting there, knocking the foxtails about, I allowed myself to feel sorry for my siblings, who weren't as important to him as I knew myself to be.

My father was a restless man, and although he'd said he couldn't get away just then to hear his fortune, I could see he was intrigued by what I'd told him, and I knew it wouldn't be long before he'd find an excuse to wander over to the store. He was just the opposite of the people who were afraid to have their hands held by a fortune teller.

I didn't have long to wait for my dad. I hadn't been back at my station on the sidewalk more than ten minutes before he showed up on Main Street. I can see him now, when I think of it, walking towards me. Looking like a movie star. My father was on the short side, maybe he was only five feet seven or eight, but he was lean, so he seemed taller. He cut a good figure, as people used to say, and even in dusty work clothes, in his shirt sleeves and suspenders, he walked with an effortless sort of elegance, the kind that can't be feigned. He wore his old felt fedora tipped back in a way that made him look as if he expected a happy outcome to any day, and he smoked his cigarette, and he looked at Elena Huhtala from way down the street, careless with the cigarette, careful with the look, like the leading man in a movie bound to bring them together.

Elena was reading Bob Newton's palm. She'd foretold (more accurately this time) a boom for garage owners who'd had the fortitude and wisdom to stick with the business. Bob Newton had a bright pink smudge across the top of both cheeks by the time my father strolled up and interrupted them. She ignored him, but Bob couldn't. With my father nearby, he started shuffling his feet and saying "uh." He hadn't minded me, sitting right there at his feet. Nobody had minded me, or even seemed to see me once their fortune teller had started making them feel they were part of the universe and its design.

In the few seconds before Bob Newton could mumble thanks and leave, and before Elena could turn her attention our way, I opened my mouth to say something to my father. He was standing over me. He put out his hand to stop my words, and I saw the lines etched in his palm and at the knuckles of his fingers, and I couldn't wait to hear what she would tell him. I shut my mouth and ducked my head, hoping to disappear from his vision. I didn't want to miss a word between my father and that girl.

I got to see a look pass between them while Bob Newton was backing off. At first I thought it was a look like a promise, but it wasn't. It was a recognition look. Neither Elena Huhtala nor my father were people for making promises, which was just as well, I suppose, since neither were people for keeping them. So I saw the look. But as for watching and listening and interpreting further looks, or hearing my father's future – that was denied me. Without taking his eyes off her, my father said, "Go home, Ruthie, your mother needs you."

I knew it would do me no good to wheedle. I inched further down the sidewalk, hoping he'd forget about me. A moment or two passed. Maybe he counted to ten. He once told me that when he got to be ancient and lost all his senses he'd still remember to count to ten if anyone mentioned my name. "Go," he said, and this time he reached back and picked up my collar. It was too much like being grabbed by the scruff of the neck for me to leave with dignity, but I jerked out of his grip. I was already crying when I started yelling at him for having so many kids and making me look after them. It was so outrageous a thing to say he laughed and shook his head, and for a minute I almost thought he was proud of me. I thought if he was, even Elena Huhtala might be impressed. But he stopped laughing, his face straightened, and he pointed the way home. I had to go.

I had to imagine what passed between the two of them after I left, and I couldn't even enjoy that because when I was walking away I heard them both laughing, the way two people laugh together when they think nobody else will get the joke.

◇◇◇◇◇

Although he was tolerant of indolence in other areas, my father never liked any laziness in speech. It irritated him when people said "well" when they didn't know what else to say. Whenever any of us kids said "well," my father would ask what kind of well we meant. He didn't interrupt his friends when they used the word, but I could always hear him thinking the question. And his friends said it all the time. They said "Well . . ." when they slapped their knees or stretched their arms up over their heads to show they'd just realized they'd stayed visiting too long. Or "Well . . ." with a warning sound after he'd said a thing too impudent or crazy for them to condone, even though they were at the moment laughing at the thought of it.

I always silently answered his question, whether he'd asked it or not. What kind of well? A wishing well, of course. Wishing is what the word contains. When they said "Well . . ." my dad's friends were wishing they could stay longer, or they were wishing they could believe him, wishing they could be carefree like him. They all knew better. He should not have been carefree, with a wife and seven children, but, well, that was the way he was. So I pictured the round stone circle, the ancient rope and wooden bucket I'd seen in storybooks, and observed his insouciant self-regard, his certainty that others liked and appreciated him. And I appreciate him, still, when I think about all the things he taught us and tried to teach us. Don't they show he cared about us?

It was the bad time of day, when I got home. Four o'clock. People blame it on low blood sugar now. Maybe it's just that you're tired; the day has worn thin. To counteract its effects the women of our town changed their clothes after lunch; they peeled off their aprons and old house dresses and put on their second-best, the one or two dresses that used to be for church, and they rolled stockings up their legs and went out to do errands between two and four of an afternoon. They picked up their mail at the post office, stopped in at the store, and, if they had an arm free or an extra kid with them on the way home, detoured to fill the pail they'd left at the town pump. Then they returned to their houses, renewed, and started getting supper ready. With a month-old baby and the rest of us like rungs on a ladder, my mother didn't get to what they called uptown very often. She didn't have much time for visiting, either, unless it was to exchange a few words with a neighbour when she was out in the garden. When people use the phrase about working your fingers to the bone, I see her chapped, big-knuckled hands that never were held by a fortune teller. She was a handsome woman, I think. She looked too capable to ever be called pretty. She was, and remained for the rest of her life, a model for the danger inherent, for women, in capability.

My brother Hal was playing marbles with some other boys in the empty lot by the curling rink when I passed it on the way home, but when I reached our yard none of the other kids was about. The sun was shedding a truly biblical light over Gilroy by then, looking down on us and shuddering. Yes, that's how it looked if you were fanciful and apt to anthropomorphize forces of nature, imagining the sun, for instance, as an entity that could have compassion for those in its power. But the state of the sky hardly affected me. I'd been banished to the house.

I smelled scorched cotton and lye soap when I opened the door. I wanted a drink of water and headed for the lean-to behind the kitchen where the crock was kept, but the ironing board blocked my way. The iron still stood upright on it, and the extra sad irons sat on top of the range though they were cool, the fire extinguished long ago. I forgot about my thirst. The dark house drew me in, into the living room where white sheets and pillow-cases, freshly pressed, lay across the sofa and tables, drying. Even the wooden high chair, perennially in use, with a yellow rose and a red rose painted on the backboard but nearly scoured off, was draped in tea towels. My father's spare shirts, the white for Sunday and the blue for work, hung over the backs of the chairs. My mother didn't believe in omens, but I wonder if she ever thought about their emptiness when she set those shirts on their chairs.

We were renting the little bungalow; it was too small for all of us, but it had a closed-in porch across the front where the boys slept in the summer. They used the fold-out couch in the living room during the winter. We girls shared one bedroom and the other was for our parents and the baby. That afternoon, as was not uncommon in our house, the door to the porch and the bedroom doors were closed. For a minute as I stood in the hall, I felt I might evaporate, if a person could do that, not disappear exactly but change my constitution, reduce to particles, float away. It was that quiet in the house. But I knew they were there.

I was an expert at turning our bedroom knob without rattling it. I pushed the door open a crack, fully expecting the heat that hit me. The blinds were pulled but in the south-facing room they only turned the light a murky green, as if the house lay at the bottom of a slough. My sister Vivian was sitting up in bed staring at me with that passive, patient expression she adopted when she wanted my sympathy. Viv was eight that summer, too old for afternoon naps. Marjorie, a year and a half younger, was sleeping beside her, mouth open, cheeks flushed, half-sitting up, and Dorothy, our toddler, lay sprawled across their laps. Sympathy was all I could give Vivian, and she knew it, so I nodded and backed away.

The floor squeaked when I passed my parents' room and the baby started up as if I'd jabbed her with a pin. *Waaa-waaa*. Just screaming, on and on and on, so I went in and plucked her hot little body out of the crib. She cried even harder and stiffened in my arms. Mother lay flat on her back on the bed, over her head a picture of Jesus standing in a dusky light, knocking on an old-fashioned door. It matched the one that hung on the dining room wall showing Jesus sitting in a dusky light, at his table with his disciples.

My mother didn't open her eyes. I took the facecloth off her forehead and dipped it into the basin on the washstand. I could have gotten colder water out of the stone crock in the room off the kitchen, but I had the baby wailing over my shoulder so she had to make do, and at least it was cooler than it had been before.

"Thank you, Ruth," she said, knowing it was me without opening her eyes, and I said she was welcome.

When I went out to the hall again, taking Louisa with me, my little brother Neil opened the porch door and waited silently for me to release him, his cheeks all pink and swollen from heat and sleep, his soft brown eyes hopeful. But I shook my head at him and he had to go back and wait. He'd forget, if he wasn't in his room, and start tearing around outside Mother's window pretending he was a wild pony or something. He was four years old and couldn't do a thing without making noise. Neither could Louisa, it appeared. In the few weeks we'd had her, she'd hardly slept. Mother said it was colic that made her draw her scrawny knees up and scream till her face looked about to explode. She told me much later, when she thought the information might be useful, I suppose, that she blamed Lou's colic on bottle feeding. She'd breastfed the rest of us, but people had started to look down on breastfeeding. It was for the lower classes, those who couldn't afford formula or milk or didn't know enough to feel dirty. Feeling dirty was a big deal in those days, in a small town, and we used the expression so often we'd shortened it to F.D. Embarrassment, or the threat of it, kept all of us in line. As for the lower classes, it was possible to be lower than we were and we knew how, in every degree. We might not have had much money, and we had to take relief and whatever else was offered, but our house and all of us were spotless, and our morals and manners were expected to be as immaculate as our faces.

The name Louisa was my idea. I'd harped on it for months before the baby was born. Mother had said it was too romantic, but then she capitulated; I never knew why. Anyway, she'd already started calling her Lou, this tiny thing. I didn't mind by that time; she was just one of us: Ruth, Hal (Harold but never called that), Viv, Marj, Neil, Dot, and Lou. I guess it was efficient when you had to call us for supper. My mother's name was Janet. I never heard it shortened. Dad's was Davy, as if he was the kid of the bunch. Davy McLaughlin.

I carried Louisa into the living room. She was still wailing and twisting her body like a fish that wants back in the water. There was nowhere to sit; all the furniture was shrouded in my mother's ironing. At the southwest window, light streamed in around the edges of the blind. You could imagine Jesus appearing and entering the house right there. I did try to imagine it. Really, I'd been thinking he might come for Louisa; it was hard to love her.

In the shed I laid her down on the floor and finally I had a long drink from the dipper. She practically had conniptions. I pulled up her nightie and trickled some drips on her chest. She startled and shut right up, and looked at me like a human being. "You're okay," I told her. She wasn't. She started up again.

I took her outside and sat down with her in the shade of the caragana hedge by the garden. It was too hot holding her. I stuck my legs out in front of me and laid her on them. It was weird to me to think my parents had made her, that she was a one-plus-one of them. She didn't cry so much as scream. You had to believe she was in torment. And there wasn't a thing you could do.

You can try not to think what you're thinking. It doesn't work. I was thinking Louisa was the natural result of my parents' fighting, that all their anger with one another – or more accurately, all my mother's anger at my father – was coming out in her little agonized body.

I grabbed one of her flailing hands and bent over it and examined the palm. The skin was so fine it let the pink flesh glow through as if lit from behind, as if inside Louisa was a clean, clear light, a rosy fire. The lines at her wrist, on her palm and at the knuckles, looked sweet, so new and so expected and unexpected at the same time. Why did she have them already? And so deeply indented. She'd hardly lived. I picked up her other hand. It was the same. Of course it was. But it seemed mysterious, that hands should fold in the same places, that her hands had the same lines as mine, that all our hands should fold almost identically.

A bumblebee came and hung itself in front of us. It looked too fat and clumsy and stupid to stay aloft in the air with nothing to support it. Louisa was watching it. She wasn't crying anymore.

There's something I didn't mention, something that happened earlier, just as I was leaving Main Street to head home. When I reached the curling rink, I turned around for one last look, and I was surprised to see that my dad and Elena Huhtala weren't alone. They sounded alone. But Leonard was standing on the sidewalk beyond them. He was standing near them but apart, staring in the opposite direction from them and me. I knew what he was doing while he looked down the road that came at Main Street slantwise from the train station and the elevators. He was standing guard for her. He was listening and noting what was going on, even though he was carefully giving the impression that he wasn't interested in the two of them and couldn't even hear their laughter.

Mother got up from her bed and threw a supper together, as usual. Viv and I set the table, slipping around as silently as possible, not even looking in her direction. I was pouring milk into glasses when she brought a dish of yellow beans to the table, and said, "*What* is this?" and ran her finger over the lip of the dark blue plate we'd used for the sliced cukes. She brought her finger up to her face and then waved it in mine. I didn't have to look at it; I'd seen the swiped-clean streak she'd left on the blue plate. "Dust."

It was the white dust, the same dust that had filled the air outside. Inside the house it sifted down like the powdered chalk that collects at the bottom rim of a blackboard. Viv's hand went out and dabbed along the lid of the dish Mother had just set down. She didn't show the results to us; she didn't have to — we could see the smear she'd left behind. The three of us looked up, but we couldn't see it falling down on us.

My mother peered at me. "Are you wearing face powder, Ruth?"

Of course I was not. I realized that my lips were dry, and when I licked them they tasted bitter.

Viv put her hand on my arm, in the way you might involuntarily touch royalty if they should stride into your presence. "You're shining," she whispered.

"Go and wash your face. And your neck," my mother said. "And clean those glasses. It's a wonder you can see a thing."

"Alkali dust," my father said when he came home. "It was worse north of town."

"I was north of town today," I said, and then regretted speaking. But my mother didn't say I shouldn't have wandered away. Sometimes she ignored things she didn't like.

"It blows in from Old Wives Lake," my father said, and I imagined witches, withered of face and bent of body, huddled around a steaming cauldron, muttering curses and brewing mischief and misfortune. That's the picture the words *old wives* stirred in almost everyone, those days. Women who'd been left behind and resented it. They had nothing to do with me.

We had sausages for supper and I knew Viv didn't like them. I hated it when she had to sit at the table long after the rest of us had left, over a plate of cold food. I put out my hand under the tablecloth and poked her thigh. She passed me half a sausage. I ate it with my usual finesse when Mother wasn't looking. Pleased with this bit of benevolence – I was such a good sister – I began to picture my shining self standing in front of Elena Huhtala, and her reaching for my hand.

Although I'd thought of nothing else since I'd left her, I didn't mention Elena Huhtala to Mother that evening. Dad didn't say anything about her either. She sat opposite him at the table and likely didn't know she had a frown on her face the whole time. We were supposed to converse at supper; it was considered rude to bolt your food in silence, so we talked about our day, each of us, and left out the most exciting thing that had happened in Gilroy all year. Hal, who was nine, kept looking from Dad to me. He knew we were deliberately not telling Mother about the fortune teller. He'd grown used to following my lead, especially when Mother had a headache, so I wasn't surprised he kept quiet. It wasn't a conspiracy, as I think it may have seemed to her later. I just knew, in a way I wouldn't have known the year before, how she'd feel hearing about a pretty young woman who'd set the town talking. When I remember she was only thirty herself and could have counted on her own two hands the months she'd gone without washing diapers since she was nineteen, I'm glad I understood at least enough to spare her my enthusiasm. But I was aware of having a secret, of my dad and me having a secret and her being left out – and in some way justifiably left out – because she was the steady one, the stern one, the one who scorned romance.

And romance personified sat on Main Street that evening while the air held its breath, and in the town's kitchens and backyards the women discussed what to do about her. She sat in the wide shade thrown by the store, and in front of her, but standing back a bit so as not to crowd her, was a line of eight or ten waiting to hear their fortune. When they were done, more came, some of them from the farms around town. The news of her talent had already spread. And it was one-good-rainfall country. One good rainfall would do wonders, that was the adage. And if she could predict it, maybe they could sleep tonight without visions of wind, drought, hail, and hoppers waking them up. If not, at least they were having fun. Elena Huhtala was as good as a whole town fair. It was a dusty, ragtag line of people that stood in front of her that evening, but they were laughing and joking with one another, guessing one another's fortune, ensuring everyone knew they didn't put much stock in anything a palm reader would tell them. When they reached her some of them turned sheepish, worried in case she'd overheard their joshing, or embarrassed (feeling dirty) to think the others might see them taking her seriously after all. Watching them move up one by one, I tried to picture my dad getting his palm read, and couldn't. He'd have laughed at the idea. I bet he just stood in front of her and chatted her up, charming her as much as she was charming him. It was a question I could never ask either of them, just one of the things I'd never know.

Oh yes, and the sky was still odd, still thickly radiant, the kind of ominous sky, coming near the end of a hot, airless day, that normally would have been the only topic of conversation. But now nobody cared; they'd all decided it was just alkali dust in the air and that when the wind changed they'd have their blue skies again. In fact, they'd completely stopped looking up at all, with Elena Huhtala drawing so much attention. I watched them going to her, saw my best friend Ivy Faulkner in line with most of her family, and my cousins Marion and Ginny Noble with some other teenagers, and among the girls and women there were a few men, they more than anyone trying to pretend this was just a lark, an evening's entertainment.

Ivy waited in line behind her mother and her sister, Annie, and her brother, Clifford, who was always called Boy. So by the time Elena got to her, she'd had a chance to understand what Ivy had to put up with. Marybelle Faulkner was not a woman I'd have wanted for a mother, and that's putting it mildly. The word *slovenly*, when I first encountered it, might have been invented for her. She wore a grimy ring around her fat neck that never got washed away and she never had a stitch of clothing that didn't strain to cover her and reek of her armpits. The dirty shack they lived in smelled the same. Ivy's older sister, Annie, was fat, too, and vicious, the family disciplinarian. Boy was the sensitive one; the teasing he endured because of it had turned him into a loner. Just looking at the gang of them, anyone would see the situation was hopeless.

You could buy a can of beans with ten cents. A loaf of bread, a pound of bananas, a container of ketchup. You could buy a pair of cheap stockings, if they were on sale. I had to wonder if the Faulkners were negotiating some kind of family rate. I could imagine what my mother would say if she heard about them all lining up tonight and likely not eating tomorrow.

Ivy came to sit with me after her fortune was told. At twelve she was the smartest student in our school, of any age, but most of the town girls avoided her because of her family. She had a little smirk on her face, of self-amusement. I watched her carry it to me. She was dressed in her brother's hand-me-downs because that's what she had, being neat in build and having a mother who never made anything over in her life. Marybelle could have made two dresses for Ivy out of any of her own, but Ivy wouldn't have wanted to wear them anyway. They went to Annie and likely contributed to her meanness. Ivy managed to make Boy's wide-leg trousers and shirts look stylish. She wore a men's tie with the shirt, an addition that emphasized the new little bumps on her chest and made her look, in every way, anything but boyish. Like the rest of the Faulkners, she was so blond her hair had been white until she was seven or eight and now it was yellow. Her skin and eyes were pale too, and her eyelashes were clear and iridescent.

I asked her what the fortune teller had seen in her hand. She pursed her lips as if to keep the knowledge in. "Come on," she said, and drew me away down Main Street towards the curling rink.

"Well?" I said when we were so far out of earshot no one in town could have heard her if she'd shouted. Even then she whispered. "I didn't tell her anything about me, not a thing, and you know what she told me?" She paused here, not for effect, just because what was coming was to her a big thing to say. "She told me she saw white – everything white around me."

Now, here's the strange thing; there was white everywhere, around us all. The sky was white, it had been white all day, and in spite of the gold glimmers of the lowering sun, it was still white that evening. But Ivy and I both knew that wasn't what Elena Huhtala had meant. She had meant a private whiteness.

Ivy grinned, after she told me, and gave me a sympathy push on the arm. She'd seen my face trying to be happy for her. And I was happy for her, seeing her like that, all lit up. But how could it have happened to her and not to me that Elena Huhtala had divined exactly what she wanted? She'd seen Ivy after meeting her family. She'd seen how dirty and coarse they were, and that Ivy was different from them. But this prediction went far beyond the things I'd heard her telling other people that afternoon. What she didn't know, because I was the only one who knew it, was that Ivy wanted to be a nurse. That's why the prediction meant so much to her. She took it as a sign it could happen; it was *going* to happen. In truth the likelihood of Ivy Faulkner finishing high school was slim. The dream of nurses' training was so remote it couldn't be spoken of after the once she'd confessed it to me. Now here she was, mocking herself a little to cover her embarrassment, but looking more decisive and determined than she'd ever looked before.

Elena couldn't have known Ivy wanted to be a nurse, but she'd been able to see why she would want that career. It wasn't just to help people or cure them of their illnesses; it was something more secret than that, something so secret it had almost been forgotten, I think, by Ivy herself. It was to have things clean. She wanted a clean, white room, just like I wanted a cool, dark, quiet room where I could be alone. But Elena hadn't seen my wish when she'd looked at me. She hadn't understood my secret desire and made me believe it could ever come true. "I see accidents"; that's what she said about me. Being flip. As if I was of no consequence at all. As if she'd never looked past my glasses right into my eyes and past my eyes right inside me. She was treating other people seriously. They were still lined up in front of the store, waiting to hear what she would tell them. And she was learning what they really wanted; she was starting to say it out loud.

After she'd told the last fortune, and everyone else had drifted away, Elena Huhtala continued to sit on the bench in front of the store. The store was closed, and Scott had locked up, but she showed no signs of leaving. The women of Gilroy couldn't allow a young woman to sleep on Main Street overnight. This was not a matter of her safety. The weather was warm and no one would harm her, but it wouldn't have been decent. There was the hotel; with all those dimes she could have paid for a room, but it wasn't an appropriate place for a girl on her own. The women of the town conferred and eventually they consulted Mrs. Knoblauch. Probably Mrs. Knoblauch was the only person in Gilroy who had remained unaware of Elena Huhtala's presence. She'd picked up her mail and the day's groceries in the morning, and sat in her backyard at the edge of town, in the shade of her caragana hedge, all the afternoon.

The women of the town liked to ask for Mrs. Knoblauch's opinions and advice; what she gave them was often unusual but useful. They knew almost nothing about her. She had come to Gilroy alone, in answer to the advertisement in a city newspaper of a house for sale. She'd bought Hugh Barclay's place, one of fewer than twenty houses in the town and the only one vacant because the town hadn't started to decline yet back then. They assumed, correctly as it turned out, that Mrs. Knoblauch was a widow. The most they knew of her in the way of biography they'd gleaned when they'd asked her, one morning in the post office, after a particularly philosophical discussion, if she agreed it was true that the difference between a happy woman and an unhappy woman was that the former had married a good man. Mrs. Knoblauch had said she didn't know how it could be true, when she herself had been happy most of her life.

The women of the town were surprised when Mrs. Knoblauch took the girl in. They were used to Mrs. Knoblauch surprising them, but they felt her offer to share her home was truly out of character. She hadn't invited any of them into her house for so much as a cup of tea. Although she was quite old, well over seventy, they didn't think she needed a housekeeper, yet sight unseen, and with no recommendation – because they knew so little to tell her – she welcomed the girl into her house. What they had been able to tell her was hardly enough for even a good churchgoing Christian (which Mrs. Knoblauch was not) to go on, which was one reason they had hesitated in offering her a place for the night themselves, although one of them would have done so if it had become neces- sary. The women wanted to fetch Elena and introduce her, but Mrs. Knoblauch said they were to send her along on her own and tell her to wait in the backyard.

That is how it happened that Elena Huhtala stood in a back- yard hedged with caraganas, bareheaded in her brown dress, and Mrs. Knoblauch watched her from a kitchen window, her strong old hand gripping the windowsill. The caragana pods were popping. They snapped and flew from the bushes. Elena flinched; one pod had hit her on the cheek. It left a red mark on her cheek. *Crack! Snap!* The pods shot from their branches. She stood still, surrounded on three sides by a hedge that assaulted her. Above her was the unnaturally hazy sky brightened by a setting sun, behind her a house she'd never entered, the house of an old woman she hadn't met.

Mrs. Knoblauch moved to her door. The screen was loosely tacked and blew a pulse inward every once in a while, although there didn't seem to be a breeze. A puff of dust rose each time the screen shifted. Elena Huhtala stood in the backyard, waiting for her future to catch up to her. She didn't realize she was waiting. She thought she was only stopping – here, now, in a strange yard in a strange town. But I was standing by Mrs. Knoblauch's gate, watching, and I knew better. I was remembering exactly what I'd said when I'd told my father about her. I was remembering saying, "Dad, she's just like honey," and how I blushed after I said it, not knowing why.

A quiet feeling came over me as I stood there, knowing they couldn't see me. It was almost as if no other time or place had ever existed. Or ever would. It was as close as I have come to the recollection of being unborn. Then the screened door opened with a squawk. She turned and faced the house – and colour. A row of hollyhocks grew against the back of the house, their leaves a luminous green, their flowers pink, wine red, maroon. Mrs. Knoblauch stood in front of the hollyhocks; the blossoms rose two feet higher than her white head.

In the west, the sky was mauve. The sun was falling fast. It happened to be sitting on Elena's head when she turned to the house, to the hollyhocks and the old woman standing in the doorway, and they were all brighter than life, lit to their very centres because the sun was sitting on her head. But for me, the sun turned into a blinding hole in the sky and I had to look away. For several seconds I saw green spots wherever I looked, and then the spots turned pink, and finally they faded when she came towards the house to find the cool, quiet room where she could be alone.

The sky turned wild with colour when that girl stepped up to meet Mrs. Knoblauch; it flared violet and apricot and cherry red and gold. They say nothing makes a better sunset than a lot of dust in the air and that evening proved it true. All the colours flushed upwards all around, and when the sun was about to slip under the horizon, the full bowl of the sky turned iridescent. It became a more tender sky than anyone in Gilroy had seen before. I always thought it was the coincidence of Mrs. Knoblauch inviting her and the sky being so tender that made Elena Huhtala decide to stay a while.

That sky. People talked about it the next day. How from morning on they'd thought we were sure to get hail, the biggest hailstorm we'd had in years, and nothing had come of it, nothing at all.

2

TREVNA

A transformation was scheduled to happen in the Knutsons' kitchen, and Aggie Lindquist had been invited to take part. Aggie was sixteen that summer but she felt younger than the other girls in more than years, and looked forward to anything that would change her. She headed out from her parents' house with a lipstick in the pocket of her skirt and a hot wind at her back that she owned too in a way that she would never admit to anyone, it would sound so dumb. Luckily, nobody else was around for miles, and that meant she could think of it as hers, her personal tempestuous wind. And the best part was that it was tireless; it would blow and blow and never give up. This was nine or ten days after Elena Huhtala had left Trevna for parts unknown, and the romance of her going was still crowding Aggie's mind and encouraging her to think more than usually interesting thoughts. A big gust shoved her along and she trotted easily for a few moments, like a colt towards some held-out carrot. Down the road the sky sagged in front of her, promising nothing, but the world in turmoil suited Aggie; she felt in her bones that at any moment — just give her the chance — she could do something heroic.

She stopped as she was about to turn onto the shortcut to the Knutsons' place, and pondered going the long way. Grit stung the backs of her calves while she stood there, hesitating, and her skirt belled, cooling her thighs. She'd caught sight of the Huhtala farm, the narrow, unpainted house, the glittering mud of the dugout, and the swing – actually swinging, lifting and twisting, all by itself in the wild wind, and making her feel so many sudden ways at once, she wasn't firmly sure she was herself.

She stopped again at the driveway and held her hair back off her face. The windows of the house glared at her. The Huhtalas had curtains, she knew (she'd been invited inside a couple of times), but no one had drawn them decently across, no one had seen the need. But the house wasn't Aggie's goal. She trudged down the long drive, at a cross purpose to the wind, to sit on Elena's swing, to sit where she'd sat and see what she'd seen. She settled herself on the old board and gripped the ropes and grinned out at the world. Dust swirled, the grass in the ditches rippled, the stubble shook, every single stalk of it. The wind wailed in her ears and filled her head as if it would scatter any wits she ever had, but she held on tight to them and peered forward, seeing herself like a figurehead on a ship, heading inspiringly into a storm.

Something moved at the upper edge of her vision. She turned to look at the house, at the upstairs window. It might have been just the play of the light. She stared and stared, keeping as motionless as she could in case one movement could cancel another. Nothing happened; she didn't see it again. She stood up and walked around to the door that faced the driveway, stepped up to the wooden stoop and tried the doorknob and it turned.

No one was in the kitchen and it was neat and bare; it was a kitchen no one had used for a while. Over by the window was the table, where everyone said Mr. Huhtala had left a note for Elena.

Aggie stared at it, waiting, straining to block out the wind and hear the inside sounds of the house. She swallowed, cleared her throat. "Elena?" she called. And then she called again, louder.

There were two chairs at the table. When she sat at the far one in the corner, she could see the whole small kitchen and the entrance to the living room. She had only ever been on the main floor, which was the two rooms. The girls would have called them mean if they'd seen them, to say they were not just poor but dirt poor, and that was exactly why none of them had ever been asked in, except for Aggie, because she didn't have to tell everything she knew.

Elena and her father had what they needed and no more. Besides the plain, handmade table and chairs, they had a wood stove, a cupboard, hooks for their coats and to hang up an axe, the dishpan, a towel, and a fly swatter. They had the one coal oil lamp, not lit, likely, until it was too dark to see your own hand in front of your face. The towel and the kitchen curtains were made from flour sacks that hadn't been dyed or embroidered. Nowhere was there what Aggie would have called a woman's touch. In the living room she remembered just two chairs and bookshelves, not many books. The stairs to the second floor. And the trap door leading to the cellar. Peter Gustafson's story came to her, the one about Elena pulling the chesterfield over the trap door and keeping her dad down there – and that was how much he knew. The Huhtalas didn't even have a chesterfield.

She couldn't tell, even listening hard, whether or not the place was inhabited. She looked up at the ceiling and felt none the wiser, but she began to imagine Elena up there in her room, staying as still as possible, waiting for whoever was lurking in her kitchen to leave her house. She wondered if Elena would think of it as her house, now, rather than as her father's; it would be such a different way to think of it.

Bang! She jumped to her feet. Almost immediately she decided it was only the wind throwing some loose board or something against the side of the house, but her heart thumped. She gripped the back of the chair, listening twice as hard as before and gauging the distance across the linoleum to the door. Someone was upstairs. She was sure of it. She would go. Doris and Lillian were waiting for her at the Knutsons'.

She let go of the chair and stood marooned, trying not to be a coward. She had to think about Elena; if it was her upstairs, think about the way she was, the way she'd always kept herself apart from the other girls. And beyond that was the sadness. Aggie had seen it at the dance, that sadness like a shadow living inside her; it had been stronger in her that night, her father being gone. Maybe she'd come back home because she had nowhere else to go, because she was broke and alone and there was no one to help her. Maybe she was like her father, and right now she was lying on her bed in her room, thinking suicidal thoughts that went around and around in her head and would not stop until something put a stop to them.

Oh Aggie, she told herself in the tone the girls used when she was being stupid; but even so, at the bottom of the stairs, her voice all quavery, she called, "Elena? It's me. Aggie." She couldn't make herself call again. Slowly, she mounted the steps. Every one of them creaked. She waited on the top landing, feeling her heart beating. Nothing, no sound, no sign of life. She was at the window where she'd thought she'd seen movement; there was the swing, below, but she only glanced down, not wanting to turn her back on the two open doors. From the hallway she could peer only partway into the bedrooms; she would have to go in.

At the doorway of the nearest room she could see the bed, covered with a multicoloured fan quilt, and she felt better, recognizing the familiar, feminine pattern. The Ladies' Aid had given it to Elena, telling her she'd won it in a raffle, that somebody anonymous had entered her name. They thought saying that would save her pride. They gave her clothes, too, once in a while, over the years. She never wore them except for Thelma Svenson's old winter coat that Thelma had grown out of. She'd had to wear that, that and the rag pads Maria Gustafson had made her for her monthlies, that everyone knew about because Maria had come upon her one day, crying, not knowing what was happening to her, having no mother to prepare her. "How did she know that's why she was crying?" Aggie had asked when she heard about it. "Elena didn't tell her that, did she?" Oh, it was her age, the girls said. That's what you cry about, at that age.

The house was empty; Aggie sensed that now. She didn't have to be afraid. She thought about lying down on the bed, gazing up at the ceiling, as Elena would have done more times than you could count. She didn't lie down on the bed. She turned to the bookshelf, ran a hand along the dozen or so spines. Among the books written by men everyone had heard of were two by Charlotte Brontë and one by Edith Wharton, so she was right; it had to be Elena's room. Mr. Huhtala wouldn't have bothered reading books by women. The other bedroom would be his.

What if it was *him*? Him she'd seen at the window and thought she'd heard when she was downstairs. Him, waiting all this time for her to leave. What if he hadn't killed himself? She didn't know him; she didn't know at all what kind of man he was. She hadn't met him when she was here visiting Elena; he'd stayed outside, working. People said he was distant, unfriendly; they said he'd been desperate, at the end. He must have been desperate, to go off with his rifle like that.

She stepped into the hall and told herself, the way her mother would have, to be sensible. She stayed there a few moments, weighing the air, and then she crossed the hall to the open door. The second room was unoccupied, as she'd assured herself it would be, but she went all trembly because the bed was unmade. She felt like she was floating, floating in the silence in the room, even though she could hear the wind outside, battling its way past the walls of the house. She tried to calm herself, to think whether or not Elena would have left the bed like that, him being gone those weeks before she took off. The rest of the house was tidy. She didn't think Elena would have left it unmade. And there – propped in the corner by his washstand – was his rifle, that everyone said he'd taken with him.

The stairs were steep and every one of them cracked with a sound like a gunshot as she plunged down. She was out the door so fast she couldn't remember how she'd got there or whether she'd shut it behind her, and then she was wading across the wind. Dust surged around her and obscured the road, but she squinted her eyes and kept going. Not until she'd turned out of the drive-way and backtracked to the shortcut and felt certain she was out of sight of that upstairs hall window did she slow down and catch her breath, and even then it wasn't long before she picked up her pace again, her mind racing faster than her feet.

By the time she reached the Knutsons' farm, so much excite-ment filled her chest, it was as if the wind had inflated her. He was alive, he was back – and she was the first to know. But he didn't have to worry; she hoped he knew that. His secret would be safe with her.

◇◇◇◇◇

You couldn't make Doris Knutson look like Greta Garbo; it might have been a mistake to try. Her hair was dark and bushy, her eyebrows like caterpillars, and a slight moustache shadowed the corners of her mouth. Aggie found the lip hair sexy but said nothing and Lillian went after it first. To her mind it must have been the most offensive. Doris winced a lot and occasionally jerked in her chair, but she didn't ask Lillian to stop or go easy with the tweezers. Whichever spot Lillian had finished with swelled and flamed turkey-wattle red and Aggie began to worry Doris would be mad when she saw her face in the mirror.

Aggie was operating on the sidelines; Doris didn't trust her with this kind of delicate procedure, so she had time to muse on Mr. Huhtala's return. She was going to call him the prodigal father, after the bible story of the son who came back and was fed the fatted calf. She didn't suppose he'd been prodigal and there wouldn't have been any feast on his return, but he was the kind of person who belonged in that kind of story. Maybe it was a different one she was really thinking of, where someone went into the desert for many days and was changed when he returned. She wondered if Mr. Huhtala had come back changed. She wondered what he'd thought when he found his house empty. He must have thought his daughter would be there with open arms to greet him, the father that was dead and then alive again, was lost and then was found.

"Aggie," Lillian said for the second time. She had her hand held out and she wasn't pleased when Aggie didn't know what she wanted and she had to scrabble for it herself. On the table were their pooled powder, rouge, eyebrow pencil, mascara, and lipstick, most of it supplied by Doris. It was their idea of a beauty makeover. They were guided by a *Modern Screen* that Lillian had bought ages ago and usually didn't take out of her house, the April issue with Garbo on the cover, her face slantwise across the page and that multiplication-table look in her eyes. Aggie still suspected Doris of swiping her *Photoplay*, but she couldn't accuse her and remain friends.

Her parents being absent – her father off to town on an errand and her mother out feeding the chickens or weeding the garden or husking old corn for the pigs, because she was shy even of Doris's friends – Doris was telling the girls about dancing with Henrik Gustafson at Liberty Hall the night Elena took off with the stranger. "Right away," Doris said, "he tries out the grope."

"Really?" Lillian said, with an air of one concentrating on bigger things. She had moved up to an eyebrow.

"Really?" said Aggie, sounding even to herself like one who has no idea what a grope could be, although she could remember very well the stroking she'd received from Henrik.

"Oh, yeah. Christ, he had his hand on my bum." Doris liked to swear when her parents weren't around, and she was forgetting to whisper.

Lillian stopped tweezing."What did you do?"

"Well, at first I ignored it," Doris said. "But finally I said, 'Mr. Gustafson!'"

"It was Elena Huhtala," Aggie said.

"What? What are you talking about? This has nothing to do with her."

"Oh yes it does," Aggie said, and she knew she was right. "The Gustafsons were the ones who brought her to the dance. She rode with them all the way in the wagon and I bet you anything she got him all hot and bothered."

"Aggie, really," Lillian said. She applied herself to Doris's eyebrow once more.

"You think everything is about Elena Huhtala," Doris said, darting out from behind Lillian and the tweezers. "Well, it's not. The rest of us have lives, too, you know. And I could get Mr. Gustafson hot and bothered on my own, for Christ's sake."

"Of course you could," Lillian said soothingly.

"I expect anyone could," Aggie said. "Did you dance with him again?"

"A few times."

"Doris. Did you really?" Lillian asked.

"Why not? Most of the men around here are limp if you ask me. I met him out behind the hall, too."

"What?" Lillian stood back and looked right into Doris's face, thus getting her first clear picture of her eyes. The left one appeared to have migrated to a lower plane on her face. The brow swelled in a red lump above it, like a fleshy king's-ransom ruby, with only a wavering line of hair remaining that still wasn't arched anywhere near high enough.

It was in that still moment that Olie Knutson barged in, yelling, "I heard enough!" He'd returned from town without them noticing and had been listening for a few minutes in the shed off the kitchen. He strode over to the girls – and he was a round little man with short little peg legs who found striding difficult except in times of high emotion. When he got to them, he raised his fist. Aggie and Lillian fell back. But he didn't hit his daughter. Wonder hit him first.

"Why, you look like –"

Aggie could have told him she looked like a painting by Picasso – her *Photoplay* issue had offered a full two-page spread on Art and its effect on Hollywood – but Olie Knutson hadn't ever read *Photoplay* and he had no comparison ready. In the pause that occurred while he sputtered, Lillian tried to slide the tweezers into her pocket, but ignorant as he might be on art, he was up on girls and their sly movements, and he grabbed them from her hand and flung them across the room. He was aiming at the window. As it was closed, they clattered against the pane and fell to the counter where they lay looking less than lethal but also leggily less than innocent. One sweep of his hand had the makeup on the floor. "Out!" he bawled, and Aggie and Lillian scattered.

At the roadside, as they parted, Aggie said, "You'll never see that *Modern Screen* again."

Lillian said she didn't care. She was still shaking. Her own father didn't use violence, but she had an imagination.

"He'd better not pitch my lipstick," Aggie said. That was as much bravado as she could muster as she set out to walk the hour home. The lipstick was all she'd had to contribute to the pile, all her parents allowed her to buy. She didn't believe Doris had really gone behind the hall with Henrik Gustafson. That was just showing off. Wasn't it?

The incident with Olie Knutson had rubbed the gloss off the secret about Mr. Huhtala. When Aggie came to the shortcut she took it, although she was picturing the empty swing at the farm and could almost feel herself sitting on it.

Some days even the shortcut seemed a long way to walk. The wind had moderated and the sky had turned sulky and stretched out all over the place. Was the world showing its bigness, its lack of ends and edges, or was it just the opposite – was she too big and pushed and bumped out corners? Whichever, the fit was wrong now.

She wondered if he'd seen her there, earlier, from the house or from the yard somewhere, seen her sitting on the swing and for a moment thought it was Elena. How his heart would have leapt, to think it was *her* sitting there.

◇◇◇◇◇

Maria Gustafson didn't drop the jelly bag when she heard the authoritarian knock at her door; it didn't plummet to the floor and splat open, spraying pink crabapple mush up the cupboards and the legs of the table and chairs. But she was caught, incapacitated, her hands to the wrists rosy red and slick with syrup. She'd just wrung the juice out of the bag, not having the patience to let it drip until it could drip no more. A strand of her hair, impatient, too, fell over her nose and stuck there. That morning she'd made up a batch of setting lotion from flax seed and with her head saturated, she'd dragged her comb back and forth, pinching each ridge with a metal clamp. So here she was, in the middle of swinging the jelly bag over to the sink, with a sweating head that looked as if it could electrify the nation, and someone who felt important was banging on her door.

"Come in," she yelled. "It's open, yeah."

In walked Olie Knutson and Mrs. Knutson, dragging Doris between them. Doris had been crying. Her eyes were little pink holes in her swollen face. One look at that face and Maria knew why they were here. It had come, at last, as she'd always known it would: a reckoning, judgement and punishment rolled into one. She pursed her lips and turned her back on them. She stood at the sink with her hands dripping onto the jelly bag, and thought how much like a breast or a cow's udder the bag was, so soft and warm and female – and now vulnerable-looking flattened against the unforgiving porcelain.

"Sit down," she sighed, not turning around. No need for politeness when it came to this kind of conversation. Perspiration ran down her neck into her limp collar. Well, it was hot in the kitchen. The sink was next to the wood stove and the roast was already in the oven because men need meat, even on the hottest days. She wasn't sure where Henrik was. He'd taken Peter and

Ingrid to the Svensons, to a birthday party for one of their children. If she was lucky, he was still there and would remain for an hour or two. Best if she handled this herself.

One of the wave clamps slid down the back of her head and landed on the floor. She looked down to where it lay on the linoleum by her foot. She nudged at the pump with her forearm and forced a trickle of water to rinse her hands. She shoved the coffee pot onto the fire – reheated would be good enough for this little visit – and then she was out of tasks because the cream and sugar were already sitting on the table along with a glass full of spoons. She turned to look at the Knutsons. "Well," she said. All three of them stared at her hands. A bright, almost shocking stain still extended well over the drape of flesh at her wrists; the nails were rimmed in red and all the wrinkles at her knuckles were outlined, too.

"Well?" she said again, more quietly this time. Doris dropped her face into her hands. Mrs. Knutson moaned. Olie pulled out his handkerchief and snorted into it. Maria stood over them, waiting for some momentum to gather, the event to play out however it had to. Then everything changed because Henrik came home.

"Maria!" he called from the open door. She recognized that tone; it was the sing-song way he said her name when he was pleased with himself. And in he walked with Mr. Huhtala.

In the brief chaos that ensued, Olie Knutson jumped to his feet. His wife shouted, "You!" At first Maria thought she meant Mr. Huhtala. She could have shouted at the man herself, she was so amazed to see him walk in, back from as good as the grave. But of course Mrs. Knutson's finger was pointed at Henrik.

It was always hard to tell what Henrik was thinking under the flowing moustache and the yellow beard, and he'd so long practised making his eyes benevolent, even now they beamed a general, latent goodwill that hardly seemed suitable for the occasion, as if, even now, he could not grasp that he'd ever done wrong. Maybe it was the very inappropriateness of his gaze that drove Olie Knutson to leap for his throat. As for Matti Huhtala, he stepped neatly out of the way, as far from the others as the walls would allow.

The scuffle didn't last long. Henrik was taller, meatier, and tougher-minded than his opponent. He soon put his arm around poor Olie and led him outside as if to impart a piece of older-brother advice.

"Sit down, Mr. Huhtala," Maria said. "I will bring you some coffee."

Mr. Huhtala did go and sit, nodding briefly, first, to Doris and Mrs. Knutson, who were standing together, staring at him as if he'd grown a second head. Poor man, Maria thought, he must be wishing he was anyplace else right now. His entire body and even his soul – for she thought she could discern it – expressed resignation. But of course. He had rejoined the land of the living and had to play by their rules. Oh yes, she understood him very well. She brought him a cup and sat down with him. "So," she said. "You have come back."

Olie Knutson returned just then, leaned into the kitchen and bellowed, "Doris! Mother!" and the women came to life and went to the door he held open for them. It seemed they would drift out and away, but at the last moment Doris turned to Matti Huhtala and set her hands on her hips. "So. You have come back," she said, sounding exactly like Maria. Then she laughed, looking at all their surprised faces. She laughed louder and longer than was necessary and not as if anything was very funny.

"Tsk, tsk," Maria said. She rose from the table and scooped a dipper full of water out of the stone crock that sat near the door. She was an efficient person, always, and didn't spill a drop. The entire contents went into Doris's face and then quite naturally down the front of her dress. Mrs. Knutson and Olie stalked off, but Doris only laughed a real laugh and wiped her face on the hem of her skirt, not caring if anyone saw her underpants, and then she left, too.

Maria returned to the table, for once at a loss for words. The entire incident with the Knutsons had been unseemly and Mr. Huhtala was always so reserved. Even today, in his old clothes that had bleached to grey from being outside a long time under a harsh sun, he maintained his dignity. He was famous all around Trevna for his composure, but resented, too, for keeping to himself. People who liked him, men who had worked with him even once and women who had felt his charm – because he had charm, although he didn't use it – explained it away, saying that the Finnish were odd to begin with, and none odder than Matti Huhtala, the only Finn in the world, probably, who hadn't built a sauna on his property, hadn't wanted anything to do with his homeland. Henrik had explained it differently. Where there has been a civil war, he said, even as short as the one in Finland, bitterness endures for decades. And Matti Huhtala had fought on the losing side.

"Crabapple jelly," she said, noticing him staring at her hands. He nodded solemnly; she might have confided a dread disease.

If it was difficult to walk back into the kitchen, Henrik would not show it. "I brought Mr. Huhtala to talk to you," he said to her. He was still wearing his elderly, brotherly demeanour. He got his own coffee before he sat down. "We met in the road, as I was on my way back from the Svensons'." He coughed, a single, only slightly apologetic cough, such as might have erupted from the throat of a poet or a philosopher or a statesman, and then both men examined the embroidery on the tablecloth. It was a piece Ingrid had worked on and you couldn't decipher the rabbits and mice and other small creatures she'd intended.

Maria thought about Mr. Huhtala losing his wife – to the Spanish flu, she'd heard, or was it typhoid? She'd died in prison, it was said, after their civil war. So he had lost a great deal. But how handsome the man was, still, in his close-shaven, undernourished way. And in spite of the grey droop of his shoulders, so alive. She wanted him to look at her. She could tell, even when he wasn't looking at her, that he had something for her, even for her, with her fat body packed into a housedress. She remembered the clips all over her hair and pulled out a few at her forehead. The waves fell, lank and heavy and still a bit damp, onto her cheeks. As for Henrik, sitting there avoiding her eyes, he could not hide forever behind that beard and moustache.

"Mr. Huhtala got home a few days ago to find his house empty. I told him you could tell him more than I could. About his girl," Henrik said ponderously.

Exasperation hit her, like something from outside. Why should she do the explaining? Were there not a few things Mr. Huhtala could tell *them*? Such as why he'd gone off without telling his daughter where he was going, taking nothing but a rifle, leading everyone to think the worst. He'd upset the whole community and driven his daughter away. But you wouldn't ask him. Not right out. Not like that. You'd get nowhere that way, battering him with questions. Instead, making herself quiet, she said, "We don't know where she is, you know." He nodded without looking at her and she turned to Henrik. "How long is it since she went, Henrik?"

"Not long," Henrik said. He perked up. "Well, it was a Saturday night, of course, and what is this? Tuesday? Wednesday. So a week and a few days."

They both turned to the man, the neighbour they didn't know. "I blame myself," Maria said.

She did not really blame herself for the girl's leaving, Henrik knew that; it was Matti Huhtala she blamed, but she went on as an incentive to him. "If we hadn't stopped that Saturday night," she said, "and persuaded her to come to the dance, she might have been in your house when you got home."

"Your girl came with us to the dance at Trevna," Henrik said.

Maria was wiping the backs of her fingers across her forehead the way she did when she was anxious. It made him impatient with Huhtala. Sitting there saying nothing, knowing full well she was itching to ask him where he'd been all this time and what the hell he'd thought he was doing, going off the way he did.

"I'll never forget seeing her on that old swing that evening, as still as a picture," she was saying, all the time watching for the man to lift his face. "She looked that forlorn, I said to Henrik, we have to stop and get her to come to the dance. A young girl like that, all by herself on a Saturday night. No one had seen her for weeks. I don't know if she'd spoken to a soul for days. It isn't good for a person, you know, especially a young person. They mope." She waited to see if Matti Huhtala would raise his head at that and when he didn't, she went on as if she hadn't noticed. "She'd said no. I'd called on her the day before to say we'd pick her up and she said no, but when we stopped that evening, she seemed happy to see us. She jumped up right away. We had the wagon, not liking to take the car with the price of gas, and it was a lovely evening, wasn't it, Henrik?"

She turned to him and he saw that she hadn't for a moment forgotten what he'd done. He would have to face her once Huhtala had gone. He couldn't imagine what he would say.

"The dance hall was packed," she said, turning back to the man. She brushed at her forehead again and encountered the hanks of hair that fell near her face. She held a strand out in front of her eyes and he remembered how she was as a girl, before they'd got married. He said, "She left with a young man, Mr. Huhtala."

"No one knew who he was."

"*She* might have known him before," Henrik said.

"That's true," Maria said. "We said so afterwards. Just because he was a stranger to the rest of us doesn't mean she hadn't met him before. She danced with him a few times. He danced with some of the other girls, too. You can ask them about him, if you like. They seemed to think he was a gentleman." A hush fell among the three of them; something about the way she'd said the word *gentleman* brought it down, until Maria went on. "Aggie Lindquist was one he danced with, I know."

"Your likeliest lead will be his car," Henrik said.

Huhtala didn't look up or move at all, let alone speak, and Henrik wondered if the man didn't intend to pursue his daughter. But surely he couldn't just accept what she'd done. "A late model Lincoln convertible roadster," he went on. "Not too many of them around. People will remember it."

"Painted gold. I didn't see it myself," Maria said. "And he had red hair. Goodness, we almost forgot to tell you that. He said his name was Bill. Longman, wasn't it? Something like that."

She talked and talked and Matti Huhtala just sat there, nodding once in a while. Henrik couldn't tell if he was even listening.

Finally, Maria said, "Now, Mr. Huhtala. Why don't you stay and have supper with us? I have a roast in the oven. I'm sure you have nothing at home."

Mr. Huhtala only shook his head, but not rudely; if anything, politely, humbly.

"Won't you stay? You have to eat sometime. If you don't eat now, you'll be hungry later and maybe have to pay for your meal."

That polite head shake again. He'd joined the living again, she thought, but he wasn't playing their rules, not any more than he could help. "If you won't stop," she said, "I'll make you a lunch to take with you." She was already at the oven, opening the door, releasing the roasted meat smell into the coffee and apple smells. "I can have a slice of beef between bread before you finish your coffee," she said, heaving the roast to the top of the range. Then she was sharpening the carving knife. Perspiration ran down her temples. "Can you eat walnuts? Some people can't. They just destroy the inside of Peter's mouth. I always make a batch without them. Hermits, I'm putting some in your lunch."

Mr. Huhtala looked up. He said, "Hermits. That's the cookie for me, Mrs. Gustafson."

"Well," she said, the knife stilled, she was so surprised and pleased. He'd spoken so ruefully. He'd reached out to her. At the same time, she could feel Henrik's embarrassment over the comment; he was always discomfited when people revealed themselves, even to such an extent. Oh, and look how *he'd* revealed himself! Anger welled up in her. At both of them. Asking her to understand them. And whatever did the man mean by calling himself a hermit? Did he mean to use that as an excuse? That he was too averse to meeting people to go after his daughter? "She thought you'd killed yourself," she blurted. "We all did."

Matti Huhtala had a face that knew how to be as blank as a face can be, but Maria did not mistake that blankness for a lack of pain, and as soon as she could muster herself, she rushed to cover her crime. "I expect she will have wanted to go to Edmonton," she said. "To look for work, you know. Or Calgary. Or maybe Regina, I suppose, if he was headed that way." She stopped, realizing they were in different directions. "She's a good, sensible girl, Mr. Huhtala," she said. "I've said so to everyone. If she went off with a man, it was because he could give her a ride to the city. What good was her grade twelve to her here?"

As if he was speaking to her alone and for her, to relieve her, very quietly Mr. Huhtala said, "I will find her." He rose from the table and shook Henrik's hand. He came over to the counter, where Maria was tying string around the lunch package she'd made for him. He thanked her and shook her hand, too.

"Courtly," she said afterwards, staring at the hand he'd shaken, the nails red-rimmed and all the wrinkles stained. "That's the word for his manners." They were standing together in the kitchen, just the two of them.

"I fear Thelma Svenson is right," Maria said softly. "I should mind my own business, and then if tragedy happens, it's at least not my fault."

"No tragedy has happened."

"A man has lost his daughter."

"He should have looked after her better."

Maria set her head to one side and gave him a long look and he knew she was wondering what she should say to him. He could deal with a man, as he had with Olie Knutson. He'd calmed Olie down soon enough; he'd made it clear to him that his daughter was hysterical and prone to fantasies. Convincing Maria would be a different matter. He went and sat down, feeling a bit weak in the knees.

She said, "Do you think the RCMP was after him and he was in hiding? That's what some said when he disappeared, that he was afraid they were going to put him in jail. Or deport him. They've deported some of them."

Henrik was more than content to follow her lead. "Huhtala's not a socialist," he said. "He doesn't care that much for his Fellow Man."

"But they must think he is. Even a Communist. Being Finnish."

"I guess after all we don't know much about him. Or about anyone," he added, in spite of himself. It was a time for truth, however inconvenient, and he had to speak it, even if as a consequence he betrayed himself. At the thought, his entire chest deflated and he looked up at Maria with naked eyes.

She set the knife down on the counter top. She'd forgotten she was holding it. She raised her hands to the remaining wave clamps and one by one released their grip on her head. "Henrik," she said. "The beard. The moustache, too. Why don't you shave? You're still young, you know."

◇◇◇◇◇

Doris said she was taking off. "I've had enough," she said to Aggie one day not long after her father had thrown all her makeup away and made her visit the Gustafsons to face Henrik with her accusation. "You won't see me again," she said.

Aggie asked her how she thought she'd pay her way if she was going to light out on her own; there'd be train fare and rent and food to pay for, and that was just to start. "You won't be crying over makeup and such, if you run out of money," Aggie said. "I suppose you think you'll pick up a man at the next dance."

Doris got a look on her face, her gaze sliding away to the corner of the room, and Aggie said, "It was you took my *Photoplay*, wasn't it? At the dance at Liberty Hall."

Doris got so mad she forgot herself. "I don't give a damn about your old *Photoplay* for God's sake!" she yelled.

"What's that guilty look on your face for, then?" Aggie said.

Doris said there wasn't any kind of look at all on her face. But there was. Oh, there definitely was. It wasn't guilt anymore, though.

It was a sharp look, cool and slitty-eyed; those green eyes had a glint in them, and Aggie knew Doris was busting to tell her what it was for. She waited, didn't say a thing, just waited, observing Doris as if from afar, as if she was getting a bit bored, and might walk off if Doris didn't get it over with pretty soon, and Doris threw back her head and said, "I have money."

Aggie rolled her eyes. She knew about how much money Doris could have scraped up, even if she'd stolen from her parents. The eye roll was enough. She didn't have to ask.

"I found it one day on a kitchen table."

Aggie could tell Doris was getting scared by this time and chickening out of telling her the whole story, but at the same time still wanting her to know.

"Left behind," Doris said, "by somebody who didn't need it anymore."

And Aggie knew. The look on Doris's face told her. Only one person caused Doris that particular kind of anguish. "Elena's father left her some money. When he took off. Didn't he? And you took it."

Doris tossed her head in her haughtiest manner. "What if I did? You don't need to look at me like that. I went there one day to be nice to her and she was out walking. I could see her a ways away, coming towards me on the road. As soon as she caught sight of me, do you know what she did? She turned around and walked back the way she'd come. So I went to the house. Walked inside to wait for her. It was the day her dad walked out on her, but how was I to know that? I'd seen him leave the house before I saw her on the road. He took off the other way, over the pasture behind his barn. I told the Mounties about it afterwards. He had his rifle with him; I didn't think anything of it at the time. I was just glad the house was empty so I could wait for her, see what she'd say, see if she'd admit to seeing me and turning her back on me, or what kind of story she'd make up to excuse herself, and there it was on the kitchen table with a note saying she could look after herself now. And I said to myself: 'We'll see about that.'"

Aggie didn't tell anyone about Doris stealing the money. Before she left the district, Doris made her promise not to tell, but Aggie didn't keep quiet because of that. It would only have upset Mr. Huhtala to find out. He must have sold something precious like his wedding ring or a family heirloom, the last thing he had of any value, to get the money. (Aggie envisioned a wad of worn bills, tightly rolled, that could be carried, hidden, in a man's hand, although Doris hadn't told her that.) And it was nobody else's business. Elena was the only person the information would have helped. It would have made a difference to her to know her dad hadn't taken off and left her with nothing to keep her. But Elena was gone and it didn't look as if she would ever return.

ADDISON

Only the cat could rouse Merv Badger from his easy chair in the office, and even then he paused a moment to sigh before he hoisted himself to vertical. But it had to be. The creature was in the hotel on impermanent sufferance, and anything it might leave in its wake, such as hairballs, piss, shit, vomit, dead mice, and dead birds, had better not be trod on by Pansy. When it started squawking, Merv moved. He scooped it up by the belly, intending to toss it out the front door, but its ribs contracted under his hand, and then its body started convulsing. It jerked and jerked and then, more frighteningly, stiffened. The gagging stopped. Merv moved faster. It wasn't making a sound, it wasn't moving, and flecks of white foam dropped from its mouth. Out on the steps, Merv held it up level with his eyes, and made himself look. The darn thing had a toad stuck in its throat; you could see the ropy back legs twitching. Merv had to reach in past the sharp little fangs and grab hold of the struggling toad; he had to do it before he thought twice. It was almost as bad as the time he'd had to deliver a baby. They hadn't let pregnant women stay in the hotel after that experience. She'd been alone, and they'd agreed afterwards they should have turned her away when they saw the size of her stomach. The doctor came two days late. Pansy had fainted.

He didn't see whether or not the toad came out whole, but enough of it did scrape free to let the cat breathe again. The cat gasped and shuddered and went slack in his hands. He dropped it, shuddering himself, and it ran off under the steps. He could hear it retching, could feel the gorge in his own throat as he bent and wiped off his hand in the long grass by the sidewalk. But at least he could tell himself later it was because of the cat he was able to head off the posse.

He was getting to his feet when he saw them coming, the reeve and two councillors. They were wearing hats, all three of them, and right away that gave them an advantage, since he was hatless, having just involuntarily stepped outside. But at least he was outside. At least. Whole slabs of his life could be listed under that heading, he thought, watching the men stride towards him. *At least* was his life, his foundation – or at least his propulsion. It got him up in the morning (at least the night is over), made the coffee (at least the coffee will wake me up), et cetera, et cetera. A constant round of consolation, if not compensation, was his lot. He tried to pretend he didn't know the men were on their way to see him. He began to whistle, with a look in his eyes that tried to say he hadn't a thought in his head, and in particular he had no thoughts at all about a certain sheet that was still hanging from a certain bedroom window. No, he was out here in the dirt beside the hotel for a quick trill or two, and wasn't it a nice day? It was a usual day for that summer, nothing more; a hot, cloudless sky backed the three advancing fedoras. He'd never been able to carry a tune and his whistle petered out before they reached him.

"Hello, Merv," the reeve said and the councillors nodded. The reeve put one foot up on the lowest hotel step and leaned forward in a way that could be friendly or could be threatening and was meant to look as if it could be either. The cat scooted out under his leg and streaked across the road. Merv backed up. His mouth had gone dry and he barely managed to croak out the reeve's name.

"Merv, Merv, Merv," the reeve said. The three men chuckled. The reeve knocked his hat back as if he needed more light to get a good look at the miserable creature cowering in front of him.

Merv knew better than to try to chuckle with them, or to attempt any hint of bravado. He didn't ask what he could do for them today. He could feel his shoulders getting narrower, his chest hollowing. His fingers felt sticky and he shuddered inside, thinking of the toad slime he hadn't quite wiped off still clinging between them.

"When's that sheet coming down, eh?" the reeve asked. "Or should we appeal to the little woman?"

"Today," Merv said. He cleared his throat and repeated the traitorous word so it was audible.

The reeve clapped him hard on the back. "Good man."

"I'd ask you in for coffee," Merv whispered, his throat even drier, now. "But the wife's not too well."

"Not up to it, eh?" The reeve said and the councillors nodded sagely, as if confirming Merv's untutored opinion. The reeve clapped his back again in a manner that suggested he'd just passed a death sentence on him, and Merv should be glad it wasn't worse, and the councillors, in unison, uttered a sound that was so sympathetic it was almost a moan. Then they left Merv to gird his loins and sigh his feckless sighs and go sneaking up the stairs to do his dirty work.

◇◇◇◇◇

The cat, fully recovered and as unrepentant as any animal that doesn't learn from its mistakes, bounded across the floor and batted a grasshopper a good one. The hopper landed in Pansy's lap, where it sat on a slightly vibrating fold of her skirt, unblinking while she observed its presence. If looks could kill, it would be dead, but nothing, not even the evil eye from Pansy Badger, could kill a hopper, nothing but a big foot coming down hard from whatever constituted grasshopper heaven.

"They're actually locusts, eh?" Merv was asking the solemn man from the Trevna area, who had volunteered that information and not much else.

"They're a Christly plague, whatever you call them," Pansy said. She hated it when Merv lowered himself to someone he figured had more education, or more status, whatever it was this Scandinavian guy had. "Merv's on the district committee," she told the man. "The reeve put him on."

"It's got Pansy worried," Merv told him. "Access to arsenic, eh?"

Merv's jokes weren't all lame, but when he sounded nervous starting to tell one, she got nervous, herself. And when they fell flat, nobody ever knew what to say afterwards. They all looked at the hopper, still sitting on Pansy's skirt, its feelers quivering.

"Heard the word," Merv said.

Pansy swatted it away. Its hard-cased body smacked against the wall. It sat on the floor after it fell, staring back at all three of them at once from the gleaming obsidian eyes on the sides of its alien head.

"They come up from the States," Merv said. "We're seventy per cent infested this year, around here. Cripes, they'll eat the armpits out of your shirt out there in the fields."

Pansy wanted to swat *him*. Going on and on like that. As if the man hadn't said he farmed north of here. He'd know as much if not more as Merv about hoppers or anything else.

The man looked down at the open hotel register one more time. It lay splayed across the desk, a book of such optimistic size it was able to go back the twenty years of the hotel's existence and still leave ample room for future guests. The man hadn't liked the look of the last new signature, enrolling Mr. and Mrs. Smith forever in the annals of Addison Hotel history. Wasn't the first thing he'd encountered in his life he hadn't liked. He had disappointment written all over his face; even when he was only talking about locusts, that face of his was just waiting to fall into those hardship lines again. Well, he'd asked if he could see it, and he'd got what he asked for. As for Pansy, it was the book's last, blank pages she didn't appreciate.

They sat on in the hot office after he left, and Merv started paging through the register. She knew what he was looking for and what he'd be pretending to find.

"Mr. and Mrs. Shaw," he murmured.

Grudgingly, she said, "And their son, Rick."

"Mr. and Mrs. Wire."

"And their daughter, Barb." She felt in her skirt pocket for the tube of lipstick she'd found under the dresser in those kids' room after they'd left. "He was the girl's father, obviously. She must of run away and he come after her," she said. After a minute, she said, "He must of done something or she wouldn't of run away."

Merv didn't know why Pansy was always so hard on men, why she always thought women needed defending against them. She frightened herself into believing it. He said, "I wondered if she wasn't looking to you for help. Remember, I said so that morning. She was watching you that morning, I told you so."

"Oh I know, with that limp look," she said, tossing it off. "Christ, if I'd had sex all night I'd be limp, too. And you'd be dead."

"That's right, my sweet one. I'd be in paradise."

"God, you're awful," she said, but she laughed.

"Mr. and Mrs. Coddle," he said.

"Molly?"

"Right you are."

She slipped her hand into her pocket and fingered the metal lipstick tube again.

"Ride," he said.

"Joy."

"Ruff."

"Ruff? Come on."

"Dan." He hid his grin. "Dan-ruff?"

She took the lipstick out, pulled the lid off and twisted the tube so the ruby red spiralled upward. She sniffed it. The smell was really nice, flowery. As if she was talking to the lipstick, she said, "Maybe I shouldn't of told her father which way they turned at the highway. But all the time he was here, I kept thinking about that sheet, flapping out the window. Hell, he must of seen it when he come to the door, the poor bugger."

Merv twitched. He could not tell her she needn't fear the man had seen the sheet.

Pansy sniffed the lipstick again. This time she held it too close to her nose. "Access to arsenic. Hah, hah, hah," she said. "Makes you wonder why there aren't more murders, when every farmer in the province can get his hands on it. Maybe there are more; maybe there's been a whole rash of murders, wives dropping dead at the kitchen sink. Husbands, too, eh? And the authorities are hushing it up."

Merv tried not to look at the red daub over her right nostril. "They mix the arsenic with sawdust," he said. "You couldn't eat enough sawdust. If you did, it alone would kill you."

"Maybe you could pick the arsenic out, like Vi Lunt, eh? Picking the mouse turds out of the tea." She put the lipstick back into her pocket and stretched her legs out and crossed them at the ankles.

"She didn't really?"

"She did. I asked her. Bert Thorpe paid her to do it, so he could sell the tea. Old Mrs. Wainwright said she'd buy it from him if he got the turds out."

"You couldn't pay me."

"That goes without saying."

"I seen Wilf Stone died," he said, leaping through an association of acquaintances and feeling almost nimble at this conversation, which was keeping well clear of the sheet, now a sheet no more, now ashes in the burning barrel.

"By his own hand," Pansy said, sounding satisfied.

"Took a while."

"Wasn't the best shot in the world, was he? Maybe we should try picking the arsenic out. The way things are going. Can you see it in the sawdust?"

"I don't know. I never handled it," he said. "I just do the paperwork. Anyway, I've got a better plan."

"Well?"

"No. It's my plan." He didn't actually have anything figured out that they could turn to if the situation got more dire, but he was happy to keep her on a topic that interested her.

"Jesus Christ, you better tell me about it," she said. "Any plan of yours. There's likely to be something drastically wrong with it you haven't thought of. And what if I want to go with you?"

He pretended to consider it, as if he really had a strategy all thought out and she really could have a part in it. "Waste of a human being," he said magnanimously.

"I'd be a waste and you wouldn't?" The cat, she noticed, was writhing immodestly on the linoleum.

"The hotel can support one."

"Are you kidding? One person do all this work? How would you like to be the one left? The laundry alone would have you weeping. We'd better go together or not at all. Let that cat out, will you? It looks like it's going to be sick."

He got to his feet and scooped the cat up and tossed it out the front door, thinking its days were numbered if it was going to pull him to his feet twice in twenty-four hours.

"What is it?" she asked when he came back.

"What is what?" He thought she must have seen him looking at her nose.

"Your way to do it."

"I'll tell you when the time comes."

"It's probably something dumb like jumping off the Pool elevator. Hah! That was it, wasn't it? You couldn't be sure of dying, you know. You could linger on for weeks, like Wilf Stone, in agony. You can put that out of your mind."

"If it was ever in it."

"I know that's what you were thinking."

"We could hitchhike to the coast."

That comment led Pansy to take the Lord's name in vain and to wish she had a dollar for every time Merv tried to end a conversation by saying they could hitch a ride to the coast. "I can see us here in this same room in thirty years, having this same goddamn conversation," she said.

"At least we have each other," Merv said.

"And Old Caldwell and Old Jock."

"We'll outlive them."

"And the cat."

"We'll outlive it, too."

"There's a happy thought," she said. "I seen you."

He knew it. He knew all along she'd seen him or heard him or somehow divined what he'd done with her sheet. At least the suspense was over. Now he just had to wait for the sentence to be passed, justice to be meted out, whatever Pansy decided it was to be.

"At least it wasn't me who had to give in to the bastards," she said.

At least, he thought. Whole slabs of her life, too. He reached over awkwardly and rubbed at her nose, trying to make it look like some new form of endearment.

"Did I get that Christly lipstick on my nose?" she said. "I thought I kept smelling it. I found it under the dresser in their room. Course, there's no way of knowing if it was his daughter's. Could of been there a year."

They were a lot alike, he thought — maybe from living together so long and making do with getting nowhere. She'd have the same picture in her mind, thinking of the bedroom upstairs and the open, empty window that seemed to promise some kind of possible escape.

CHARLESVILLE

Charlesville was big enough it took a few hours before everyone in town knew a stranger was making the rounds, asking questions. Albert Earle saw him loping down the sidewalk from the Red and White, heading for Peg's shop. Albert had been sitting outside the fire hall, soaking in some sunshine, as he usually did mid-afternoon of a pretty nice day. He had the volunteer roster out with him, a pencil tied to the clip, so he could look busy if need be. Just about everyone who went by stopped and passed what they called the time of day with him, so he knew the man was looking for the couple in the gold Lincoln, the kids who'd bilked Peg out of her profit that day. She'd been down ever since, as if she'd been hit a knockout punch and she still wasn't right in the head, even after she was back on her feet again. It was odd, Albert thought, that they'd had such an effect on her. She'd thought so, herself. She said, "Hitler's made himself *Führer* of Germany, we're in a major depression, the whole world is shite, and I'm fretting over losing some money from a sale."

She'd told him about the young couple so he wouldn't think it was something he'd done. Or failed to do. Most likely the latter. Crimes of omission, Albert Earle's specialty, passivity his stock in trade, "Whatever you think" his answer to any question. What had he ever done in his life but try to slip out from under whatever was going on? Now, of course, his thinking led him to Betty, always there to be thought about, to be remembered, hanging over his life like some gigantic Somebody's sword. He tried to think if Betty wasn't in prison, if it was her running that shop, he'd be over there right now, making sure that fellow wasn't annoying her. He took up the pencil dangling from his clipboard and started doodling, trying to draw an upright sword with the handle and all. It looked like a failed attempt at a penis with a scrawny pair of balls. Better than no balls at all.

A dust devil twirled up the street towards him, a little one that expanded when it got to him and threw a gust full of grit in his face. He sneezed and rubbed his eyes. He was getting tired of Betty's life sentence being his.

Peg Golden had taken the bell off her door. The thing had driven her crazy; you couldn't help identifying that two-stage, hell-o ring with hope, and not real hope, the other kind, the kind that leaves you with a tinny taste in your mouth and not enough air in your lungs, that puts a whine in your voice and makes you hate the day you were born. Anyway, she didn't need a bell on the door, she was always in the store; if she wasn't out front, she was in the back room eating her lunch or piddling in her pot, and she could hear a customer in the shop as clearly by their footsteps, even their breathing, as any bell. Sometimes, on a day like this, if the mosquitoes weren't bad, she'd have the door propped open, but these days the grasshoppers were as thick on Main Street as they'd usually be outside town, so no matter how hot the shop got, the door stayed closed. She sat facing it, listening attentively to the one sound in the stifling room, thinking that she was the one making the sound and that it would end if she stopped filing her nails into perfect moons, each a half-inch from her fingertips.

The man who came in was impressive. Space seemed to increase around him; the walls with their racks of ladies' wear fell back. He was tall, lean, dignified, with grey hair, but not at all elderly. His hair sprang up like a rooster's comb. His face was long and weathered, with deep grooves down his cheeks that made him look as if he'd repressed some bitterness most people were lucky enough to have been spared. His grey eyes held hers, something dulled in them, yet fierce. The standard line was "Can I help you?" But she only raised her eyebrows, and he came right to the point. His daughter. Yes, she could see the resemblance, not so much in face or form as in that intelligent expression in the eyes, that way of looking at you as if they already knew you well and understood every one of your troubles.

"Oh, yes, I remember her," she said. "She was with a red-haired young man. Bought a dress and shoes." He waited. "She talked about looking for work." Still he waited, his patient, knowing eyes looking into hers, and she thought: Take me with you when you go. He looked down at the floor, then. She didn't care; she wasn't embarrassed, any more than he was. She'd be one of many he'd encountered over the years. "They were heading for Virginia Valley. She said she'd never been on a ferry."

He nodded, said thanks, a momentary flash of something extra in his glance – she was going to call it pity. He left a vacuum behind him that wasn't going to be filled. She went directly to the back room, to the mirror, but instead of looking at herself as she'd intended, she stood as she always did, to the side, where she didn't have to see her own image, but could observe the woman, whatever woman it was who needed to view her body transformed by a garment off the racks. The mirror was empty; only the cramped room, filled with last season's clothes, was reflected in it, but she could almost conjure the girl – the daughter. The silvery reflection aged the brown dress, the tawny wavy hair, and exaggerated the resemblance to her father. But no, she wasn't there. No one was there, so Peg stepped forward herself.

She was too short to wear clothes really well, although she was stylish enough. Her skin was too sallow, and those lines between the eyes – way too much frowning, and somehow the wrong kind of bitterness. Ah, yes, a *woman's* resentment, aging and not alluring. She pinched her cheeks. Observed the effect. Pinched again until pink blotched the skin.

Next to the mirror was a dresser where she kept odds and ends – scarves and belts and beads to perk up an outfit or disguise the lumps and bumps women didn't want to see. She rummaged in the top drawer and came up with a pot of rouge. She dabbed some on each cheek and blended it in with a fingertip. "Takes years from you, dear," she said to the Peg in the mirror.

She heard the door and a hesitant step.

"Peg?"

She gave it a few seconds before she called, "In here."

She had a curtain over the doorway to the back room, a nice voluminous length of finely woven paisley fabric that could be swept aside if you knew what you were doing, or could entangle you if you didn't. Albert came through it like a duck through a weed patch and she had to laugh at the expression on his face when he saw her. She'd already chucked her dress and had her arms at her back, struggling with her brassiere. "Help?" she said, turning.

He ran his hands over her body. She sensed a hesitation. He was a man who put duty first. "I know it's the middle of the afternoon," she said.

"So do I." He undid the clasp with ease, practised at it, and her breasts tumbled free.

◇◇◇◇◇

The hot wind that had sent the dust devil in Albert's direction, earlier, started blowing in earnest by mid-afternoon. Clouds of dust boiled up as high as the third storeys of the highest buildings in town and cleared the streets of anyone who didn't have to be somewhere. In the Royal George Hotel, a few of the business travellers who figured they'd managed to get enough done to call it a day decided to go up to their rooms to take a nap. The maids were resting, too, the dining room being closed until supper time, the tables having already been set. The cook was sweating over pastry in the kitchen while a huge sirloin roast made its way towards overdone in the oven. His helper was peeling potatoes into a basin of water. In the living quarters at the back of the hotel, the owner, Mr. Macklin, was reading the *Charlesville Gazette*, a task made difficult by the fact that it lay across his face. Mrs. Macklin had completely given up the day as she did most days, calling herself an invalid even if the town's doctor didn't, and slept in the darkened bedroom next door to him. No one sat in the rotunda, as usually no one did, and no one manned the front desk because no one needed to man it. A bell sat on it, adequately visible, which could be rung to summon Mr. Macklin from his reading if anyone needed to register or complain about something. Not too far from the desk was a wood stove, which in the winter months supplemented the hotel's steam boiler heating system and made at least the lobby bearable, and close to that was a wood box where wood was stored in the wintertime and where, in summer, all kinds of unwanted things were tossed. On this particular day, one of those things happened to be a cigarette butt a young salesman named Emil Prendergast thought he'd pinched out.

As for Mr. Huhtala, he'd grabbed hold of the back of an empty grain car on a freight train rattling out of town and was miles away by the time the cook's helper finally smelled smoke and dropped his paring knife to go and investigate. The cook's helper, whose name was Roy Wah, and who happened to be only sixteen, returned to the kitchen for a pail of water after seeing the flames juggling each other over the wood box. The cook came with him when he went back to the rotunda, so there were two pails of water. By that time, they weren't enough.

The Charlesville Fire Department had one motorized fire truck, a pumper bought from the city of Winnipeg, and Albert kept its red paint and all its chrome waxed and polished. He kept it full of gas and in checked and ready-to-go-any-moment condition. Once a month he drove it around town, sometimes in a parade, if there was one. Twice a month he held drills for the volunteers under him. The list of their party-line phone numbers was posted by the fire hall telephone. The fire hall door, while Albert was absent, was closed but not locked.

Roy Wah was a shy young man, anxious about his manners. He knocked on the door and got no answer. He'd run from the hotel, feeling some degree of panic, having witnessed the cook pounding up the stairs to the second floor, screaming, "Fire!" So he opened the fire hall door, but when he saw no one inside, he was flummoxed. He went next door to the post office and asked the post office clerk what he should do. That turned out to be an intelligent choice since she also ran the telephone exchange, and with some foresight Albert had given her the list of volunteers' names.

The Royal George, in keeping with its pretensions, had a false front that extended down both sides, and behind the false front it had a flat tarpaper roof. When the first two volunteers, remembered now only as Beasley and Conrad, arrived on the scene, they could see smoke billowing out the front door, and they could see two scared-stiff salesmen shinnying down ropes from their second-floor rooms, but they could not see that flames were already eating at the roof. In spite of the appeals of the cook, the young chambermaids, and several self-important Charlesville businessmen, Beasley and Conrad decided not to get the truck out, but to investigate first. "Mr. Macklin, Mr. Macklin," the cook called as they went through the door. "And Mrs. Macklin, she in there." But the roar of the fire drowned him out.

The truck's siren alerted Albert, when finally one of the later-arriving volunteers revved it up and drove it out on the street. The sound pierced the curtain veiling the back room at the Style House, and for a second he froze, unbelieving. Peg fell back when he lurched to his feet. How his hands shook at those buttons, how white his face went, only she would know. Before his head had cleared, he was racing down Main Street, passing by a new model Chevrolet he didn't see, a Chevrolet driven by one Emil Prendergast on his way out of Charlesville somewhat earlier than he'd expected to leave.

Albert met the truck in front of the hotel. His men were already rolling out the hose, sweating and swearing with the effort.

"Who's in there?" Albert asked the cook, seeing him at the forefront of the crowd that had gathered.

"Nobody upstairs," said the cook, who was wiser and more efficient at disseminating wisdom than anyone had yet given him credit for. "Macklins in back and two men went in the front."

"Four," Albert said. Just then a shape like a whirling dervish, almost identical to the dust devil that had assaulted him earlier, but much bigger, appeared on the roof line. This one was made of flames, flaring crimson against the black smoke that was pouring into the sky. The flames twisted and then spiralled upward and outward as if whatever it was had suddenly grown wings. Sparks blew out from it. "Oh, God," someone said. The thing teetered on the edge of the false front.

It was for him. A sign. A promise. Retribution. The fast fall of the sword. It hung on the lip of the false front. It bowed to him. His chest hurt. He willed it to fall. Watched it plummet. Then it was writhing and fluttering and coiling at his feet, and he saw it was only a long swatch of tarpaper. Another was lifting off the roof, when he looked up again, and flying over to the pool hall. Then another, flaming, curled upward until the wind took it and deposited it two doors down, on the roof of Milt's Pawn Shop.

Running up Main Street, Peg saw the glittering tarpaper strips spiralling off the roof into the dense black smoke and thought her magazine picture had come to life. *Starry Night*, mid-afternoon in Charlesville. She arrived at the hotel in time to see Albert tying his handkerchief over his nose and mouth and going in. He wasn't entering that inferno as a hero. He was going in to be punished; she knew that by the way he bowed his head.

It was hell he walked into, and he didn't believe he'd walk out. Yet it was a slow-motion hell, almost peaceful in its own, inevitable way. The centre of the hotel was gone. Emptied, a black, black hole. Once, he'd seen a shotgun wound, a man who'd been hit in the chest, hollowed out. He thought of that. The staircase skeleton hung like a flimsy ladder leaning into space. Reminded him of himself. Any moment it could fall. And still the fire made a sucking sound as the flames ran up against the remaining structure. And every few seconds something fell from above; chunks of plaster fell, smouldering furniture fell, whole timbers fell. Ashes fell. Hot tar fell. The flames themselves fell. Calmly, he advanced.

You couldn't tell him, afterwards, that he was a hero, although he got the four out of the hotel alive, dragged them out, unconscious, Beasley and Conrad out the front and the Macklins out the back. It was possible to do that because of the wind. The updraft it created had sucked the worst of the smoke up and out the collapsed roof so that by the time Albert was in, he could breathe. Of course, at the same time, it spread the fire, and most of the south side of Main Street – the hotel, the pool hall, Milt's Pawn Shop, the Ambassador Café, Verna's Beauty Salon, and the Capitol Theatre – burned down.

"The burns will heal. The throat – I'm not sure, the next few hours will tell," the doctor said. "Sometimes the swelling increases and then – well. We'll do all we can for the pain."

But he was okay; the critical hours passed. Peg visited him in the hospital and found his mother and his two little girls standing by his bed. His mother gathered the girls like chicks when Peg walked into the ward, and herded them out of harm's way.

"Don't go," Albert whispered, when Peg backed off. "Mother!" he hissed. "Bring the girls here. I want them to meet Peg."

The little girls hung back by their grandmother, twisting their bodies identically towards her, but she looked her son calmly in the eye, and pushed them forward. They were around eight or nine, only a year apart. They didn't say a word when Peg said hello. They ducked their heads, their lips shut tight against saying a word, and then their grandmother took them away.

Peg sat down on the chair by Albert's bed. His nice square hands were thickly bandaged. The side of his face looked as if he had a bad sunburn. His eyebrows and lashes were gone and chunks of his hair were missing. Little black craters peppered his head where cinders and bits of burning tar had dropped on him. He wasn't wearing a shirt, to let air onto the burns that looked like polka dots on his shoulders and down his chest. Beasley and Conrad had the next beds and Mr. Macklin the fourth in the ward. Mr. Macklin was fitfully sleeping; the other two watched Albert and Peg through a dull, drugged haze, ready to hear whatever they had to say to one another. They didn't say much although Peg stayed for an hour, while Mr. Macklin whimpered and Beasley or Conrad, she didn't know which, fell asleep and cried out without waking.

Albert closed his eyes after a while; it was to let her go, she knew. She said, "You don't have to be polite." He lifted his lids slowly, like a comedian expressing staged surprise. "We've gone past that," she said.

"How do you know?"

She just looked at him. "I'll do my best to make your girls like me," she said.

"The boys'll be easier, except Garth, maybe. He's the oldest," he whispered.

"It's hard to talk, isn't it? It hurts?"

"Tiring."

"You rest. I'll talk." She went on, quieter. "I've been thinking. We're not going to waste time on guilt over this. Neither one of us. Responsibility is one thing, guilt's another. You've done your time in that department, and I never was any good at it. Maybe they'll fire you. Or they'll make you a hero. Likely they will, because it'll make them feel good about themselves to have a hero among them. It won't matter to us what they do or what they say."

Albert nodded. She touched his shoulder, finding an unhurt spot, felt the soft layer of flesh over the muscles, and capitulated. Knew the second it happened. Like a kid crying uncle after fighting an unfair arm-wrestle, knowing it had to end that way. "I love you," she said.

"Hear, hear," came from the next bed. She'd spoken louder than she'd intended. She looked up, flustered. But then she laughed.

"Sorry," Beasley or Conrad muttered.

"Not at all," she said.

"I'll introduce you two another day," Albert rasped.

"I'm going now," Peg said. "You all need to sleep."

A nurse came in right then and tapped her watch, although she must have heard what Peg had said. Maybe she hoped for an exasperated sigh or some sign of irritation, but Peg turned to her with a soft, incongruous smile, the kind of smile you just didn't expect from this short, dark piston of a woman. Some of the starch went out of the nurse; it was almost as if only her stiff uniform held her back from embracing the little woman, even though she knew the gossip about her and believed it.

VIRGINIA VALLEY

The talk in Virginia Valley was all about the Royal George in Charlesville. Gossip about the event had spread as fast as any fire, and everyone was free in speculating the cause and even the results, as if those were variable and unverifiable, too. Jerry Wong heard at least six different versions of what had happened.

In those days you would seldom come across a silent person. It was deemed unfriendly, perhaps suspicious, to keep your thoughts to yourself. People would accuse you of moping, if they knew you, and of being stuck-up if they didn't. So the man who'd arrived in town stood out. He would have been noteworthy on a day when there was no news. Even for a stranger, he was taciturn. Jerry's brother-in-law remarked on him and Jerry glanced out the window they'd cut into the wall between the restaurant and the kitchen so people could watch them cook and see that no stray cats went into the chop suey. The man was eating with a quiet solemnity that could have been copied by other clientele, in Jerry's opinion. He was a tall, dry man, looked as if he didn't sweat, and if so, he was the only one in the valley who wasn't, today.

A blistering sun had set itself up over them; it must have been a hundred degrees in the shade. He'd ordered a Denver sandwich, the cheapest thing on the menu. No coffee, just a glass of water – meant he couldn't afford the coffee. Jerry picked up the pot. Cups and saucers were always left on the tables.

"On the house," he said.

The man tipped his head politely. His grey hair flared silver in the light coming in from the window. In the few seconds after those eyes looked up, they looked alarmed, and that surprised Jerry. He would have thought this was a man you couldn't easily rattle. He turned to see what was going on behind him. Nothing in the restaurant was different from before, but outside a vehicle had pulled up in front of the hotel. Two Mounties were climbing out.

"Ah," Jerry said. In a second he made up his mind. "Come." He pointed the way to the door tucked behind the screen; it was the door that led from the restaurant to the back of the hotel. He walked behind the man, as if his smaller body could hide him from the Mounties' eyes if they came in before he and the man had made their exit. He led the man up to a vacant bedroom and left him there.

He was back downstairs in less than a minute. He didn't worry about appearing out of breath. Chinamen were always hurrying, bustling around, trying to give the best service. It was one of the things, he thought, that made them ridiculous.

They ordered lemon meringue pie and coffee, their faces wet and raw-beef-red above their tight collars. Jerry's brother-in-law watched him deal with them, and said nothing. Just before they'd arrived, the informal afternoon men's group, ranging anywhere from three mostly old geezers to eight or nine of all ages, had departed. The man was lucky, there. The only other occupied table was two girls, teenagers who'd made their Cokes last a long time. Their pop bottles were drained, the paper straws sagging over their glasses. Before he brought the pie and coffee out, Jerry got his brother-in-law to go to the girls' table and take their bottles and glasses away. Then he glided up to the Mounties with the pie in two plates along his left arm and the pot in his right hand. He heard the girls' chairs scrape. He apologized for the pie as he set it down. "Too hot for meringue," he said. "It so weepy it got golden teardrops." He often found it useful to speak as people expected him to. He knew the men, although not by name. They were from the detachment in Charlesville. Probably they were the whole detachment. They didn't stop the girls from leaving. They asked him if he'd seen any strangers yesterday or today.

"Tall old man," he said. "Earlier." He wasn't going to get into any trouble if he could avoid it, and they'd be sure to find out the man had been in Virginia Valley as soon as they asked around.

"We're investigating the fire, you'll have heard of it? At the hotel in Charlesville. Following up on suspicious persons. You'll let us know if you see him again."

He backed away from the table as obsequiously as he knew how, thinking of himself as if he were in a movie, one of those stupid characters who aids the villain against the honourable Mounted Police – and against all reason, because in the movies the Mounties always got their man. Those stupid characters could get themselves killed; the villain might find it advantageous to get them out of the way, or they could get caught in the crossfire during a shootout. Theirs was a useless, foolish, laughable nobility. Jerry didn't concern himself with that. He knew people. He might not always spot a villain, but he knew a good man when he saw one.

"I have no money to spare," the man said when Jerry went to tell him he'd better stay overnight and maybe wait a few days, not take the ferry any too soon because the Mounties could be there, waiting for him at the river.

"It's okay," Jerry said. "Every once in a while I do something for nothing."

The man inclined his head. His shoulders sagged. He said, "I'm looking for my daughter."

"The one in the gold car, eh?" Jerry said, realizing who the man looked like.

Mr. Huhtala stayed at the Windsor two nights. There was no problem about a room; they hadn't used the No Vacancy sign for years. If not for the restaurant, the hotel would have failed long ago. Jerry got to know the Mounties pretty well in that time. He fed them their every meal, although they slept at the Balmoral. Maybe they were spreading the bounty around. He got a kick out of them. The older was about forty; the other, nearer twenty and still the earnest young recruit, didn't know the older fellow was baiting him, setting him up for his own amusement as they discussed "the case." The younger guy had explained their theory that the hotel fire had been deliberately set by Communist agitators. The older Mountie had sat back in his chair and picked at a pimple on his chin and said the truth was they were just hanging around Virginia Valley because nobody for miles around made better pie.

Jerry knew that by holding out on them, he was going against what would have been his wife's wishes. If she'd been here, she'd have wanted him to turn the man in. She was a timid woman, always anxious to stay out of trouble, always seeing danger around every corner. If she'd been here, she'd have begged him to think of his reputation; she'd have called him reckless. Of course, she'd lived through worse times in China than he had here, the last dozen years, and he supposed she had a right to worry he was risking the business. She wouldn't have understood he was adding to his own private stature, or she wouldn't have cared about that.

He didn't get to know Mr. Huhtala very well, and he hadn't expected he would. He wasn't a man you'd question. On the third day, the Mounties didn't appear at noon. Jerry asked around and found out they'd been called back to Charlesville, to a shooting accident. A woman, apparently unused to handling a rifle, had shot herself and was dying. Mr. Huhtala asked who she was, but Jerry didn't know. The name hadn't been released yet.

"You can take the afternoon ferry," Jerry said.

"Mr. Wong," he said, "I will pay you back, some day, for your kindness. I'm sorry I can spare nothing now. I have about enough for the ferry."

It was awkward to offer to lend him money, but Jerry did offer, then.

"No, my friend. I'll hitchhike after that. I can pick up odd jobs along the way. It's what I've been doing the past weeks." He went to the window. "I believe a young fellow who drives a Lincoln will be heading for the city," he said.

By the time they walked down to the water for the five o'clock departure, word of the shooting incident in Charlesville had spread all over the southwest part of the province, and Jerry was able to tell Mr. Huhtala the name of the woman who had killed herself. Amy Sparrow, a housewife who'd thought she'd clean her husband's rifle, or that was the official story.

Mr. Huhtala bowed his head. "I shouldn't be relieved," he said. "But I am."

"You were worried about someone you knew," Jerry said.

"It wasn't someone I knew well."

"People are gossiping," Jerry said. "They say there was trouble between this Mrs. Sparrow and her husband, over another woman. They say she did it to show them." He hesitated. "Do you think that's what makes a person —?" It was impossible to go on and yet he was sure Mr. Huhtala knew the answer.

"To cause pain? To show them? No, my friend, I think it is just hopelessness, you know?" For a moment, he looked as if he might say more, even as if he might reach out a hand and lay it on Jerry's arm, but he didn't.

Jerry nodded slowly, judiciously. He'd noticed himself using Mr. Huhtala's gestures, his tone of voice and even his rhythms. He felt he was thinking like the man. He wanted to say, "I hope you find your daughter," but Mr. Huhtala would not have said that.

He watched as Mr. Huhtala stepped onto the ferry and nodded to the ferryman and handed him his ticket money. He wasn't as old as he'd first seemed. For a second Jerry saw the pretty daughter standing at the railing, looking out to the far shore; then she was gone.

He thought about his wife and the pleasure he'd had in doing a thing she would have disapproved of. Maybe there are times, he thought, when it is best for men to be alone. The thought did not lighten his steps as he trudged back up the hill to the Windsor. Some of Mr. Huhtala's gravity had rubbed off on him, that was certain.

REGINA

If you'd told Bill Longmore he would some day be old, he wouldn't have believed you; he would not have believed he'd ever look like a deflated balloon, thin-skinned and puffy and wrinkled at every edge like the pie-eyed old coot who'd stopped him in the street. "Say, ain't you the fella I seen with that fancy gold Lincoln in front of the Hotel Saskatchewan?"

"Sold it," Bill said.

"There's someone looking for you."

"Well, I sold it."

"Not about the car."

"A woman?" He heard his voice rise ludicrously. He could have punched the old fart in the face.

"No, sir. Maybe her father," the old guy said slyly.

Bill started walking away, and the old man cackled behind him as if he'd made a joke anyone around would share. Forgetting he was in the city now, Bill stepped off the curb without looking and a Ford truck blasted past, its horn blaring. He had to back up on the curb and then decided to cross the other way. He didn't care what direction he was going, anyway; he couldn't remember why he'd left the hotel. Out for a smoke, he thought, as if he had to answer to himself, for Christ's sake, but even so he lit one. The Lincoln, that's what this would be about, somebody half-interested in the car. Or it might be the owner of the Cadillac he'd been sniffing around, come to see if he could drum up a better offer. Good luck on that. The guy needed to sell that Caddy a whole lot more than he needed to buy it. All he'd needed was to dump the Lincoln. He couldn't stand driving around with that empty seat beside him, imagining her sitting there, snuggling back into the soft amber leather like the whole goddamn car had been manufactured with her in mind. He'd kept her bag. All the way to Regina, he'd thought about ditching it, and he hadn't been able to do it. He'd kept thinking he was going to see her again. He still couldn't believe he'd never see her again. He'd hung around Regina a couple of weeks, now, in case she changed her mind and showed up. He'd kept the roadster parked out front so she'd know where to find him. What a big, dumb sap. She'd taken him for a ride. He stopped and pitched his cigarette and laughed at himself. A kid was watching him, an Indian girl about fifteen, lounging in a café doorway, kind of cute. He gave her a look and she giggled and covered her mouth with her hand. More like twelve. He passed her by. He'd head back to Calgary right today, he figured, and was already speeding down the highway in his mind.

"Hey. Mister." It was the kid from the doorway. Saucy little nose and an overbite that was going to make guys want to kiss her hard in a couple of years.

He kept walking. She hastened up beside him.

"Hey. Hey," she said, gesturing to him to bend so she could whisper in his ear.

Keep walking, he told himself, but he couldn't get that soft upper lip off his mind. It made him feel mean. He bent down to hear what she had to say. Her breath was hot on his neck, her lips fluttered into his ear, and then he realized it was a kiss – she was kissing him – and he yanked his head back.

She laughed and laughed, still trying to keep up with him as he strode away.

By the time he reached the broad steps of the hotel, he was feeling so sorry for himself, he had to give her credit. Just a kid, but she'd seen through him, recognized him right away for the asshole he was. He passed by the uniformed doorman, hating him and his oily smile.

He knew who it was as soon as he saw the man. He looked like Elena, or it would be the other way around, he supposed; she looked like him. The same arrogance, that's how he labelled it, and it stopped him from asking how in hell he'd tracked him down. There were no introductions, nothing like that, just, "I'm looking for my daughter."

"Well, I don't have her," Bill said. He crossed his arms and rocked back on his heels.

The man nodded as if this was not unexpected news. "Do you know where she is?" he asked, so quiet he could barely be heard, as if in spite of his faded old farmer togs, he belonged in a fancy hotel lobby where the plush upholstery swallowed up your words and the deep carpets left your footprints behind you.

He almost refused to say. He had that bit of power – to refuse – and he didn't know which option would be a favour to her or how that would help him decide if he did know. He didn't take the time to speculate. He picked the one that seemed likeliest to get her off his mind for good. "I have an idea, yeah. I dropped her off along the way. She took a fancy to a little town, I guess, or an aversion to me."

Mr. Huhtala waited with a prodding kind of presence, patient and impatient at the same time, and Bill remembered the man was supposed to be dead. Elena had said her father was dead. This came to him late, he figured, because the man had such a strong presence, or maybe it was a strong need. A twinge of sympathy didn't stop him from thinking he'd like to say it out loud. Say, your daughter told me you were dead, mister.

"Place called Gilroy," he said. "On the highway between the river and here." For some reason he was ashamed he'd remembered the name of the town; he wished he hadn't. He wished he'd walked away as soon as he'd caught sight of the man. He had the feeling he was being played, and played for a sucker. "You're happy now," he heard his mother say, and she sounded spiteful, like she was on their side, the side of everyone against him. She sounded old and bossy and angry, and he wondered if that was the fate of every woman, so that in the end they were all unlovable.

"But who knows if she's still there," he added over his shoulder as he walked to the desk to retrieve his key. Then he stopped. "Wait," he said. "Wait there, okay? I have something of hers you might as well take."

In his room he hated himself for feeling like crying. He picked up the bedside lamp and cracked the porcelain base into pieces over his knee, and then hated himself for fussing that he should have unplugged the goddamn thing first. He could hear Elena laughing at him. Or was it the kid? Both of them, together.

Her father was standing by the reception desk, looking at the upside-down register, when Bill returned and handed Elena's bag over.

"Thank you," the man said with a formal nod of his head that was like his daughter's way of acknowledging the slightest debt. "It was her mother's."

Bill shrugged in an effort to indicate how little he cared for her parentage of any gender, this girl he intended to never think about again.

GILROY

The pumphouse was a little wooden hut built over the town well, with a hand pump to bring up the water and splash it into your buckets so you could take it home to drink and cook and wash your dishes and clothes. Every pail did triple duty; you'd reuse the dishwater to bath the baby and then dribble it along your puny carrots. You'd fill the pails no fuller than you could carry. Every drop spilled was a drop lost; you'd watch it hit the dirt and puff up, bead up, and then soak a star on the path.

I was leaving with a pail in each hand, balanced. I looked up and into the distance before I set out. When I saw Mr. Huhtala, I set the pails down. He was walking into town on the slantwise road from the train station. He was carrying a dusty old bag. He was tall and had a long stride, but he was staring down at the road in front of him, and so he looked humble, or more precisely, he looked humbled. I thought of Jesus. No beard, no halo, but that same sad and annoying air of ineffectiveness. Whatever he hoped he was going to do, he'd already figured it wasn't going to be enough.

It was an ordinary day, meaning the sky was a pale blue, with the usual number of innocuous clouds; the fields were heat-bleached, nearly the same colour as the road. He looked like Elena. Even from that distance I knew he was her father. He had come to take her home with him, to take her back where she belonged.

"Hah!" I said, right out loud, because he was too late. Her little time with us was over.

Mr. Huhtala went to Dobies' store first, as a person would, knowing nobody in town. That morning Scott and Mrs. Dobie had motored to Charlesville – as the *Charlesville Gazette* would no doubt record for posterity – where their oldest daughter lived. She'd just had her first baby, a feat that would also be memorialized in the newspaper. Their youngest daughter, Franny, had gone with them for a glimpse of maternity, so Leonard was minding the store. Mr. Huhtala didn't even have to open his mouth; Leonard knew at once who he was.

"I'm afraid I can't be much help," he said. "She took the train east yesterday afternoon, but I don't know where she was heading." He didn't tell her father she'd gone off with a married man. He didn't say he'd seen her walking to the station a good hour before the train was due, she was that happy to be doing what she was doing. He didn't mention that he'd gone to the station, himself, afterwards, and asked about her destination, and had been told she'd paid her way to Toronto. Mr. Huhtala could find that out for himself. He could go to Toronto and good luck finding her, if she was still living there, if they hadn't moved on by the time he got there.

"You could talk to Mrs. Knoblauch," he said. "She stayed with her a while." He took Mr. Huhtala out on the sidewalk, and in the gap between the store and the post office, he pointed out Mrs. Knoblauch's bungalow at the far southwest corner of town.

When he turned back to go into the store, there was the bench without her on it.

◇◇◇◇◇

Elena Huhtala didn't know a thing about telling fortunes. She'd had her palm read at a fair that had gone the rounds of some of the bigger towns the summer before, only because the woman had called her over and offered her a free reading. She hadn't paid attention to it; she hadn't believed a word of it and couldn't have repeated any of it two days later. She knew there were lines that were supposed to mean things; she thought she remembered a heart line and a life line, although she couldn't recall which was which. But it didn't matter. She was a big success those few days she sat on the bench in front of the store because she had the right approach. She sat straight and relaxed and did not smile at people. She took them more seriously than they took themselves.

And she knew these people. They were citizens of a town not more than twenty years old. They had no history behind them other than the culture and geography they'd given up in order to settle here. They'd had high hopes at first, the way people do, starting out, and they'd never been afraid of hard work, but work was supposed to bring rewards; it was supposed to make their children's lives better than theirs had been. And when their crops failed year after year, and the price of wheat fell, they got disappointed in themselves.

She knew about disappointment. She didn't tell them: You will die at a good age, you will have six children, a handsome stranger will change your life. She let them talk. At the fair a fortune teller would have a tent you could go into, apart from everyone else, so your meeting with her was private. You could hardly get more public than a store bench on Main Street, so she tried to create a space around each person who came up. You can do that with silences, by taking more time than would be usual with the hesitations in conversation. There was no hurry. I think she honestly hoped to give them something worth ten cents.

Of course they all wondered how she dreamed up her predictions – if you could call what she told them predictions – as if she conjured words from air, as if that was the mystery about her. Something made them feel stronger when she let go of their hands; they didn't know how to label what it was. Her body was unusually present to them and that confused them. It wasn't just sex, even though most people understood, without even thinking about it, that they were being seduced.

In those days people kept photos in their wallets; I kept a picture in my mind: Elena Huhtala walking barefoot through the dark, barely moonlit streets of our town, carrying her pretty shoes, piled high with silver dimes. On her way to Mrs. Knoblauch's house. It wasn't a true picture, but I held onto it, even though it was common knowledge that her first day in Gilroy, Elena had gone into Dobies' store and bought herself a purse.

I remember watching her bend to slip the dimes into her shoes, that first day she came to town. I remember how she looked at me, as if we had a secret, and how much that look meant to me. Later on, she eased her shoes off, one at a time, and gathered the dimes from inside them. She had to wriggle her feet to get the tight pumps back on, and then stood up with the coins in both of her hands. When she came into the store, blinking, Leonard stood back and let his sister Franny ask if she could help her.

She said she needed to buy a handbag. "Perhaps something a bit large."

"A *bit* large?" Franny said. There was something about Elena Huhtala that made everyone, even other women, flirtatious.

"Oh, yes, that sounds odd, doesn't it?" she said. Friendly.

Franny took her to the handbags. "Not a big selection, I'm afraid. We don't sell many. Everyone here has the same handbag they were born with."

"Ah yes, I know what you mean," Elena said.

"Here. Five to choose from," Franny said. "Hmmm. They skip from small to huge, don't they? And the only one in-between is ugly. Well, I guess they're all pretty ugly."

"Pretty ugly?" Elena said.

"Hey, good for you," Franny said, with a wide grin.

She bought a few more items and Franny tucked them into the handbag for her because they were women's things, and at the same time whispered something to her that made her laugh. Franny Dobie had fat arms and liked cats, but she had no intention of ending up an old maid, or of ever acting like one.

"You're a funny girl," Elena said.

"I'll take that as a compliment," Franny said.

"Of course."

"We can't be friends, though," Franny said. "You're too beautiful."

"Oh, go on with you," Elena Huhtala said, as if she were an ordinary person.

It's amusing, watching people enjoy themselves. To stand back, watching them. Those first few days that summer, when Elena Huhtala was in her heyday, the people of Gilroy looked different from the way they'd looked before. The women looked as if they'd pressed their cotton dresses that very morning, and the men looked as if they'd just polished their shoes. You'd have thought a public holiday had been announced for Gilroy and district, you'd have thought they'd gone past individual happiness and were headed for some kind of communal blue ribbon. All up and down that wide street, on the post office steps, at the garage door, down at the corner in the shade of the hotel, people were out chatting with their neighbours. They joked, they laughed out loud, tossing their heads back. In a manner previously unknown on the streets of Gilroy, they flirted with one another.

The sky was still white, those first days, and the alkali dust infiltrated everywhere. Some people found it irritated their eyes and some developed dry coughs, but they stayed happy anyway. Their fortune teller was back on the store bench, looking prettier than ever, and the hail that had threatened us with disaster had struck someplace else.

Ivy and I sat on the butcher shop steps so we could keep an eye on people arriving on Main Street, lining up and handing over their dimes. We were sharp observers, or thought we were, and sat back commenting on the women who arrived wearing lipstick, and the men who turned up freshly shaven. More than once we were asked if we didn't have something better to do. It pleased us to think we were being obnoxious.

And then the sky cleared, the women wiped down their furniture and swept the ashes-like dust off their floors and out the door, and everyone forgot about the alkaline storm.

One day Anna Quinn came to our house to see how much we knew. Anna Quinn was fair and plump and Scottish. She looked as if her skin from her hairline down had been scrubbed with Ajax cleanser, and everything she said sounded like indignation. She was sitting in our kitchen complaining about Elena Huhtala. She said, "Why doesn't she set up shop in Mrs. Knoblauch's house, and then we wouldn't have to look at her on Main Street."

My mother said she didn't think Mrs. Knoblauch would want people *traipsing* through her house. Traipsing is a word you rarely hear anymore, so I don't know if it's usually said with that derogatory slant. My mother often expressed her opinions about other people in that indirect way, allowing herself the pleasure of one critical word.

The days got hotter and windier and drier, but that was all right; it was the weather the farmers wanted. The grain heads were filling out and hope was expanding with them; even the cautious couldn't help thinking this year there just might be a crop. Hope grew so big in some people's minds that summer that when a bank of dark clouds came rolling straight for Gilroy, at first almost everyone declared it was only the usual dust, somebody else's topsoil blowing our way. A minute later we figured on hail, our turn to get flattened. But it was neither, it was hoppers, so many hoppers they blacked out the sun. By the time we knew what they were, they were on us.

You could hear them smack against the outside walls and the windows. We had about a hundred in the house within seconds of their descent. "How are they getting in?" my mother yelled, as if I could give her an answer. They came in through windows we hadn't had time to close, through the door when the kids who were outside rushed in.

She'd grabbed a broom but she stood paralyzed in the middle of the dining room. "What should I do?" I asked her, peering at her out of the tent I'd made of my hands to protect my face. She didn't answer. She stood in the middle of the room and stared at me, and I could only watch while they flew at her. The air was full of them. They hit her. They hit me, too, but it was different, watching them hit her. She didn't protect herself; she didn't even flinch. In seconds they were eating the bread on the table, swarming over the spills on the high chair. You could hear them munching. They were eating the tablecloth. Then she started swacking. The broom came down on the table, on the chairs, on the high chair. Half the time she missed. She didn't care. She worked silently, furiously, her jaws clenched, her hair wet with sweat. Plates cracked and smashed. The loaf of bread bounced up off the table, covered in them, and bounded across the floor. The little kids screamed. They flailed at the hoppers. I picked up a cushion from the couch and started beating the furniture.

I beat those hoppers and stamped on them and nothing I did could kill them. They were just about impossible to finish off. You'd think you'd squashed one, you'd hear it crunch under your shoe — and you'd move your foot and it would jump right at you, those creepy, malevolent eyes glistening. They knew they disgusted us.

Finally, they gave up. If they didn't die, they crawled about on the floor and on the furniture, crippled and waiting to be dead. The battle was over. I stopped beating and stamping. But my mother didn't stop. She didn't slow that frantic broom, not for a second. She raised it again and knocked the high chair over. She raised it again and swept the tablecloth and the remaining dishes on it off the table. Sugar sprayed across the room. The bowl smashed against the wall. The creamer thudded and rolled under the couch. It was the willow pattern set that had been her own mother's. She swept the thing out from under the couch and brought the broom down on top of it. She darted into the corners and swept the broken china and the sugar up with the corpses, piling them in the middle of the room. We all stood back now, so quiet that when at last she stopped and leaned on her broom and glared at us, her words rang out. "Of course your father is nowhere to be found."

They were still hitting the side of the house now and then, with enough force we could hear them. The windowpanes were smeared as if with molasses. We'd never heard her voice her criticism of our dad, not once ever before, although it had for some months been evident. Viv and I exchanged glances. We knew he'd gone to the pool hall to play cards. She saw us. Maybe she thought we knew more than that, way more than we actually knew. She let the broom fall. It crashed to the floor and she turned and went into her room and shut the door.

"What's wrong?" Viv whispered. The other kids all looked at me.

"Well, what do you think? This mess," I said. "Come on, let's get it cleaned up." I picked up the broom. Hal got the dustpan. As the male representative in the house, his father's son and heir, he was at a disadvantage. Neil was no help; he was too young and overwhelmed and crouched in the corner, sobbing. Marj held Lou on her lap. Dot was sitting on the floor, where the ruined cloth lay littered with their bodies, taking a hopper apart quite scientifically. I gritted my teeth and started sweeping, then something about the way Hal stooped with the dustpan got to me. I don't know, maybe he looked like our dad. I started crying. Then we were all wailing, the whole bunch of us. I looked around and there wasn't one of us who wasn't making the most godawful fuss until Dot said, "Ruthie? Why are we crying?" So then we all had to laugh.

My father liked to laugh. He had that relaxed kind of laugh, that take-a-minute-to-sit-back-and-enjoy-life kind of laugh, that makes you feel you're in the middle of things, in a circle of friends, you're right where you belong. And he liked to make others laugh. I could find him anywhere in town if I heard people having a good time. He'd be there in the thick of it. We were meant to find pleasure in life, that was my father's philosophy, and he said our very name proclaimed it.

"Our name has 'laugh' in it," I remember telling Mrs. Knoblauch one day not long after I'd learned to read and had mastered the difficulty of spelling McLaughlin. My father had pointed out the hidden word I could use as a reminder. "But you say it lock," I added. "Just like your name. Both our names say lock, only yours has the knob too."

"That's right," she said. After that, we were friends. Or she took an interest in me, that would be the better way to put it. But she never invited me into her house.

No one blamed Elena Huhtala for the fact that every crop in the district was eaten to the ground. They didn't think they had any right to feel disillusioned. It had only been a game, after all, just a way to pass the time, and after the years of drought, disaster was only what they'd expected. But they stopped coming to her to learn any more about their futures. They could see their futures in front of their eyes.

"People are talking," Ivy said carefully one day. We were lounging on the butcher shop steps. Elena Huhtala was sitting on the store bench, but no one was lining up to get their palm read or even to talk to her.

I said it was because they were ashamed. Feeling dirty. All of them. F.D.ing all over the place. They knew they couldn't afford to give her their dimes; they should have saved them for pencils and schoolbooks and shoes for their kids. Ivy looked embarrassed and I rushed on. I wasn't saying anything that couldn't be corroborated. Half the population of Gilroy was on relief. They got their groceries with coupons and they put everything else – from kerosene to tobacco – on their tabs with Scott Dobie. I said you had to wonder how he'd felt, watching them line up – and not just once but for a second and third time – and hand her their money.

All the time I was talking, trying to express my utter disdain for every one of those people who'd wasted their time and their money on a palm reader, in the back of my mind was the image of my father coming up to her the first day she appeared on the bench in front of the store. I was seeing them as if they would always be there, like a photograph in an album exists whether you ever open it or not; I was seeing the way the two of them had looked at each other, as if in some other life they'd met before.

Mrs. Beggs went over to Mrs. Knoblauch at the post office and asked her right out in her most garden-party voice what was going on with Elena Huhtala. Mrs. Knoblauch looked taken aback and answered that nothing was going on.

"We're worried about her," Mrs. Beggs said. She meant the whole town was worried. She squared her shoulders to carry the weight of the town and to indicate beyond a doubt that her question arose from an impersonal and charitable concern for Elena Huhtala's welfare.

Old Mrs. Knoblauch had two letters in her hand and she examined the handwriting on them until Mrs. Beggs thought she was being rude. She described the conversation to several others later, putting a British emphasis on the word *rude*.

And one day when Dobies' store was empty, Leonard asked Franny what she thought was wrong. He'd come into town, although Scott hadn't asked for him, and he was mostly in Franny's way. She knew he was there because of Elena. He'd tried to talk to the girl; he'd taken her a Coke and she'd thanked him and then looked at it in her hand as if she wasn't sure what to do with it. She'd acted so distant, he'd given up.

"You know, Franny," Leonard said, "that kid looks so down, you'd think she'd discovered some terrible secret about the whole human race."

"Oh, Leonard," Franny said. "Don't you know what's going on? Can't you see?"

I didn't see her looking depressed. That was Leonard's memory of her last days in Gilroy. I remember something my mother said one morning as I went out the door. She'd overheard me telling Viv about a few minutes I'd managed to spend with Elena. This was earlier, when I still had hope she would come to understand the kind of person I was and befriend me. "I don't want you hanging around that girl," Mother said. "She's pandering to people's weaknesses."

My mother didn't usually give reasons for her decrees; it was a testament to the strength of her disapproval that she couldn't stop herself from speaking it out loud. Pandering to people's weaknesses. Did she think I was weak?

A few days later, on my way out of town, taking the back way to avoid meeting people, I saw my father and Elena Huhtala talking beside the lumber office. That office had been closed for a couple of years, and nobody lived nearby, so there was no reason for them to be there. I turned aside before they caught sight of me, and cut across the empty lot behind the Egans' house.

My mother's language came back to me with that glimpse of them. It described them as they stood there, laughing. The word *pandering* was Elena Huhtala, up against the lumber office wall, with the heels of her pumps planted in the sod and her calves caressed by the long grass. And weakness was my father, in front of her.

I overheard a conversation, one day, between Marj and Viv. Marj said, "Why is Mum so mad all the time?" and Viv said, "Because Dad's so stupid."

◇◇◇◇◇

Mrs. Knoblauch was standing at her kitchen window, looking out over her backyard, and when she heard the knock at the front door, her heart jumped in her chest. She'd been remembering the evening Elena Huhtala had come to her, how she'd watched her standing in the backyard looking out to the prairie. And the caragana pods were shooting off the bushes. Now piles of them lay spent on the ground all along the hedges, glittering a rich brown that belied their emptiness. She went to the front door remembering the many-coloured sunset, the sky so tender and the young girl waiting. She knew before she opened the door it wouldn't be Elena standing there.

She didn't offer Mr. Huhtala coffee or tea or anything to eat. She didn't ask him to come in and sit down. She wasn't disposed to like him. He also seemed slightly antagonistic towards her, or perhaps he was just impatient. She had no compunctions about letting him know what was what. "There's one person in Gilroy who might know where they went, and that's Mrs. Janet McLaughlin," she said. "If he told her. Which I doubt."

She didn't point out the way to him and he didn't ask if she would. He could ask anyone he met in any street in town.

My mother never set eyes on Elena Huhtala. As soon as she heard about her, she avoided going uptown. She sent us kids to the store and the post office instead of going herself. She often did that, anyway, but she made sure of it in those days, as if she knew in advance the girl would be trouble for her. Some things aren't hard to predict.

She only referred to her once to anyone outside the family, and that was the day Anna Quinn visited.

"Everyone says she's so pretty," Anna said that day. "But I canna see it."

A momentary startle in my mother's eyes turned to amusement. She even laughed, letting Anna laugh too. The statement had been so staunch and ridiculous.

You might think she wouldn't have given Mr. Huhtala the time of day. After all, she must have been in shock over my father's leaving. Betrayal was one thing; abandonment had some bigger repercussions for a woman with seven children. You might imagine she'd be so bitter about it, her bitterness would spill over in such a situation, but she put the coffee on and fed the man.

My mother knew when a person needed to talk. She brought the coffee and the simple meal and sat across from him, rocking Louisa in her arms and crooning to her so it wouldn't seem as if she was waiting for anything from him. I was doing some work, pasting in my scrapbook at the table, and she didn't tell me to leave. He started slowly and it took a while before he warmed up. Maybe even more than the food and her quietness it was his sympathy for her that drew him out. He had a thoughtful way of explaining that seemed to thank her for her kindness.

He told us of his travels. He said he'd talked to his neighbours and to people in Addison and Charlesville. He'd stayed a while in Virginia Valley; he didn't say why. He'd figured the fellow his daughter had been travelling with would head for Regina, so he'd gone right there and had tracked him down. It wasn't hard, he said, because of the car the guy was driving, a big gold roadster that people had remembered seeing on the road. Bill Longmore was the guy's name. A young man from Calgary. He told Mr. Huhtala she'd left him here, at this little place called Gilroy. He didn't have a clue why. She just got out of the car and took off down the road, he said.

Before then, any time in my life before then, I'd have interrupted. I'd have hopped up and down and waved my arms if I had to, until they let me speak. Because I knew why. I knew why she'd stopped the car and got out and come to our town. But I didn't say anything. I let them go on talking, not even speculating, either one of them – as if it didn't matter why a person did a thing. They just went on in their calm voices, following Mr. Huhtala's course to Gilroy, and skirting around the fact that my mother didn't know where my father had gone, and the fact that, therefore, it was unlikely Mr. Huhtala would ever find his daughter.

I suppose if I had spoken up, what I had to say wouldn't have mattered to either of them. It wouldn't have meant anything. To my mother's mind it would have been only another instance of me thinking I was important. But it was what Elena Huhtala had left behind for me, whether she'd wanted to or not.

She'd stopped the car and got out and come to Gilroy because she'd seen me. And something about me, I suppose the way I was trudging along the tracks, alone, reminded her of herself. I was right from the start. Even though she'd tried to deny it, even though she wouldn't admit we had anything in common and had tried to ignore me. She'd seen herself like me. She was riding in that open car, dreaming an open kind of dreaming, oh yes, imagining that the world was like the view from the passenger seat – endless, lying all before her. Until she saw me. A girl. And she'd lost her girlhood. I don't mean she thought she could get it back, not at all, in any way, but maybe she was reaching for some bit of herself she didn't want to travel on without.

My father once told me the stars had crossed my eyes. It was only to get me to wear my eye patch; I knew that at the time. He liked being fanciful. But I never forgot it, how he called me to sit on his knee, how I felt too big – my arms and legs draped over him – yet privileged. His favourite; I always thought so. My brother and sisters watched with their mouths hanging open, and my mother clattered the dishes to register her disapproval. He picked it up from the table and tied the hated thing around my head, and all the while he was telling me I had a special vision. A gift that I must develop.

I'd already suffered a little, knowing I was different from other children, and I took to the idea of specialness with fervour. I wore the patch. It didn't make much difference, otherwise, in my life; it didn't incite any worse teasing than my wonky eye had. But the idea that I was important, not because the stars thought so, but because he did – a lot depended on that.

I believed that because of watching so much, I saw more than other people saw. I thought Mr Huhtala recognized that, even though his daughter hadn't. I thought that was the reason he talked to me when my mother took Louisa to the bedroom to change her. But it might have been just that he'd got started talking and then he couldn't stop.

Mr. Huhtala told me that Finnish people are supposed to be good at finding lost things and lost people. Finns pride themselves on seeing, he said. They think they have a special sense that enables them to find what they've lost, and also to know the future. "Especially when it concerns a death," he said. "They can predict their own demise, you know, sometimes so far in advance you have to think it's more inevitable than clairvoyant." He stopped there and smiled, I think the only time I saw him smile. I remember how I felt when he said that, with that melancholy smile, how strangely rewarded I felt, as if I had been admitted to a secret and incredibly select society. And so I told him about the picture I kept in my mind, of his daughter walking that first night through the streets of Gilroy, carrying her shoes full of dimes. And he told me the Finnish people did that at their wedding dances. The bride took off her shoes at the close of the evening and they were passed around so everyone could fill them with silver coins for good luck.

I didn't tell him I had one of her dimes, one she'd dropped, pasted into my scrapbook under the heading: "What a fortune costs." I didn't tell him I'd written down the things he'd told us earlier about Bill Longmore and the gold roadster he was driving and that he was from Calgary. I didn't tell him my father had once said I possessed a special vision. Speak a little, hear a lot, that's a Finnish proverb I would learn years later, but my mother had already taught me the concept.

Mr. Huhtala rose from our table and thanked my mother, standing over her.

"Wait," she said. She took up a pencil and opened her bible to the back page. "Give me your address, and if I hear I'll let you know."

So she wrote "Matti Huhtala, Trevna, Sask." into her bible,

and I surreptitiously noted it down in my scrapbook, in case the bible was ever lost.

I know that I, in the last stage of my childhood, reminded Mr. Huhtala of his daughter. I expect that's really why he talked to me and told me things he didn't tell my mother. I had the same sturdiness Elena had at that age, before she grew taller and more slender, the better to slip away from him. He told me more about being Finnish than he'd ever told her; why he did that was a mystery to him, I'm sure. My fanciful picture of those shoes full of dimes provoked it, perhaps. It was a long time since he'd thought of weddings in the old country.

Those days when Elena had been her more solid self, before privacy had become important to her – and naturally so; all adolescents must be reticent in order to protect themselves, he knew that – those were good times for the two of them. And when she changed, she still played cribbage with him, she still listened to the radio with him, maybe, curling up in her chair, next to his, in the living room. She did her homework at the kitchen table while he read the newspaper or pored over his bank statements or filled out government farm reports. They had learned English together at that table, he told me, studying her elementary readers. As she grew older, she took on more of the cleaning and cooking and gardening. The chickens became her job, the only animals they kept besides a dog to bark at foxes. He stayed away from everyone, and didn't think it harmed her.

From time to time during her last year of school, he worried about her future, but he didn't speak of it and she didn't, either. He didn't talk to her about the failure of the farm; it wasn't necessary; she had eyes to see. He didn't put a crop in that spring. She finished school and continued with her daily chores, which were not many since they had no animals anymore. She read all his books again, sat motionless on the swing he'd put up in the yard for her years before. He thought she was waiting for him to say what he was going to do for her, while every day went on like the day before.

He'd had to leave, he told me. The farm had failed. He couldn't provide for his daughter. All he could do for her was set her free. He was talking to himself, really, more than to me, telling himself again how it had been, the way you do when you think going over the steps you took will tell you why you made a decision. He'd left her some money, all the money he had in the world; he wanted me to know that. It wasn't much, he said, but it would have been enough to keep her until she could find a job. I didn't say she'd landed in town penniless; I opened my mouth to tell him and then the look on his face scared me. I don't know how to describe it. Like he was ready to do something desperate if he couldn't hold on to knowing he'd done that. He knew he'd frightened me and settled his features. I watched him do it. Then he told me some more about Finland. Maybe that was when he told me about Finnish people being good at finding lost things and lost people. So I wouldn't worry.

He went back to his farm when he left Gilroy. He didn't know what else to do. He had no money and no hope.

I don't know what it would be like to lose your daughter. Losing your father is like losing your footing. Your vision tilts. You say to yourself: Things are not what they seemed to be. And they never will again be what they seemed to be.

◇◇◇◇◇

My father called me to come sit on his knee. "Come here, Ruthie," he said, and patted his knee. We were at the table, finishing our supper. My little brother and my little sisters set their forks down to watch and I slid off my chair. I slid around the table, too, so as not to create too much fuss, and climbed up on his knee. My mother rose from her place and started gathering the dirty dishes, clattering. I giggled and clapped my hand over my mouth. Then I couldn't stop laughing even though it felt as if I'd grown extra arms and legs that hung too far over my father, and I pulled myself in as small as I could when my mother passed by.

My father was a man who did everything easily. He did everything as if he'd already half-forgotten what he'd intended to do, and it wouldn't matter much if he did forget, but after all, here he was, in this dinky little rented house, at this child-crowded table, with this what's-a-great-big-girl-like-you daughter on his knee, so he finished what he'd started; he reached over the mashed potatoes bowl and picked up my eye patch from the tablecloth where I'd thrown it down beside my plate. The hateful, homemade, black thing. I closed both eyes when I saw what he was going to do. His fingers fumbled with the strings at the back of my head, and some of my hair got caught in the knot and pulled. I opened my mouth to squawk. Too late. He was speaking. He was telling me the stars had crossed the sky the night I was born.

Every night in a small town that did not have electricity the sky was crammed with stars, banks of stars diminishing in size as they multiplied in numbers – presumably to infinity – but none of us had ever seen them move. The interest on my siblings' faces turned to awe. The baby drooled. My mother clacked plates and banged pots a few steps away in the kitchen. My father, who appreciated opposition, went on with pleasure lifting little eyebrows in his voice. His method was to toss out details as he would have tossed scraps to a dog too disciplined to beg at the table, if we'd had a dog, which we didn't because our mother said we needed to eat our scraps ourselves. In spite of the nonchalance, my dad couldn't hide the fact that he liked to tell a story. And he was apt to let it carry him away. In this case, not only had the stars swept from their usual, seemingly fixed spots in the firmament on the night of my birth, but their doing so had given me a special gift of seeing, which it was up to me to develop.

My father by now had spent enough time on me. Someone had asked to see him after supper. That meant a poker game and only the baby didn't know it. He stood up and I slipped off his lap as effortlessly as a crumb, just brushing my cheek against his cotton shirt before I lost contact. I adjusted the black patch more firmly over my eye, but I think he didn't notice. Maybe he was already out the door before I drifted around the table, picking up cutlery and stares and a noodle of warm saliva from the baby as I pried the spoon from his strangely appealing fingers. But it didn't matter that my father had left, or that my mother continued to slam things in the kitchen. Children will believe many things if you let them. Sometimes they will even believe that they are important, that you are important, that we're all so important something in the universe cares what we do. Just thinking about it, I gave the baby my little finger in place of the spoon. Neil was the baby then. His warm, wet fingers gripped my finger and tethered me.

"Ruth," my mother said. "You're daydreaming." She pulled Neil out of the high chair. He tried not to let go of my finger, but the suction was broken. I took the cutlery into the kitchen and began drying the dishes that lay piled on the wet tea towel. Although he was already gone, I pretended my father went by and tapped my nose on his way out for the evening. I vowed, as I watched him walk out the door (stooping as he went through, because he was always taller in my imagination), to wear my eye patch every waking hour of the day, to go around town with one eye covered and the other wandering until the bad eye learned to focus better and see further than the good eye ever had.

That night I couldn't sleep. I couldn't even lie down. I sat straight up in the bed I shared with my sisters until every single soul in the house except for me had fallen sleep, and then I slipped out of bed.

A clear night was waiting for me out in our yard. The stars were glinting like a million bucks. I lay down flat on my back on the damp grass and stared at them. I recalled the grand sweeping motion of my father's arm, as he'd indicated how they'd looked sweeping across the sky. I heard his voice again, and the background clashing of pots and pans. I lay there feeling the dew rise through my nightgown, and I thought about the stars falling, at the bottom of their arc, all of them plummeting down at once and landing on me like hoar frost, like a fairy-tale quilt, like a shroud fit for an important, astral kind of person. I thought it would be perfect to die right then.

3

GILROY

When the past returns, it doesn't give warning. It happens suddenly, like this: I didn't think I'd ever see her again, and then one morning, late in August, she drove into our yard. I know it was late in August, nearly September, because we'd started combining. *Com*-bining, we said. I don't know why we gave it that pronunciation, maybe to distinguish it from com*bine,* although the term must be derived from that verb, since a *com*-bine performs three harvesting activities at once: reaping, threshing, and winnowing. Yes, the combine is a wonderful machine; it cuts the grain, it separates the grain from the chaff, and it spews the chaff out the back. It's modelled on any animal eating, digesting the nutrients, and excreting the waste, but being a machine, it's noisier in the execution of its business than any animal would be, and lumbers and lurches over the land, and kills things unlucky enough to be living in its path.

Most of the time in the early years of our marriage I drove the grain truck, but once in a while Leonard let me take the combine, although never near the road where neighbours could see the shaky rows or the skips I left behind. And that was a shaky kind of happiness, sitting where he usually sat, vibrating on the loose seat, gripping the steering wheel, mesmerized by the whine of the auger and the clatter of the header, my eyes on the restless wheat ahead of me and the stalks flipping through the blades. The sun bore down on me, the wind whipped my hair, dust and fumes went up my nose, but it was glorious, driving the monster, gobbling up the wheat and the sky in front of me. All was gold and blue, like a Roman Catholic's idea of penitence (this a concept inherited from my Presbyterian mother) until I turned into the sun and saw what dust could do to it, transforming it to a fireball in front of my eyes.

But most of the time I drove the truck, rumbling over the field at the exact speed of the combine, while the grain poured out of the chute and the dust roiled over the cab, and the pile of wheat grew in the back, and I'd be sweaty and filthy and itchy by the end of the day, and I'd climb up the back of the truck and run my hands in the cool grain, cool as water to the hands.

This fall that I'm remembering, I wasn't needed much in the fields; our sons were old enough to drive, and it was left to me to provide the hefty meals they had to have, and I was grateful, or so I told myself. I had much to be grateful for.

My daughter saw her first and came slamming into the kitchen. "Mum, there's a lady in the driveway." A lady, I thought. I went to the door in time to see her getting out of her car. She did look like a lady, like a city woman, a fish out of water, a bit stunned by all the sudden oxygen. I knew it was her right away, though – she couldn't have been anyone else. Valerie stuck close to me. She was our youngest, thirteen that summer.

Elena Huhtala stood by her car in our typical bare prairie farmyard (one tractor tire filled with earth and spouting marigolds; otherwise no colour, anywhere), her hand still on the open car door, and with that vague, quizzical, city look on her face, she said, "I'm looking for Gilroy." As if there must be some joke, right? Because a whole town couldn't just vanish, could it?

"Elena Huhtala," I said.

"Yes?"

Valerie slid up against me so our sides were touching. I put my arm around her. I didn't speak right away, too much oxygen in the air for me, too, just then. But there was plenty of time, and I remembered that about Elena, how she always gave the impression she had plenty of time, and you had plenty of time, and even that the whole world was somehow timeless. She just waited, one hand on the top of the open car door. And what was it that hooked you into waiting with her? Her motionlessness, her silence? The fact that she would wait? Or was it just that she was so attractive, so appealingly symmetrical and slenderly graceful, so watchable. You would not be able to help yourself. Standing with your arms crossed (barricading that organ we consider tender), you'd be drawn to her.

"I like your dress," Valerie said, out of nowhere.

She was wearing a sleeveless shift dress with many colours in an unusual geometrical flower pattern. Her arms and legs were tanned.

"Come in," I said, and turned back to the kitchen. I threw some coffee into the percolator and she and Valerie sat down at the table. I kept my back turned towards them until my hands were as calm and still as hers were. When I joined them, I said, "I'm Ruth."

"Davy's girl," she said, nodding as if she'd already figured it out. I thought maybe she had. I still had to wear the thick-lensed glasses not too many have to wear.

"*Girl*," I said. I'd turned that perennial age: thirty-nine. Then I remembered that she was older.

She almost smiled that almost-smile that made her famous in Gilroy long ago, that sad-edged smile.

"So you didn't find the town."

"It can not have disappeared?" she asked in her slow way, separating the words so they had a strange, melodramatic weight.

"Off the face of the earth."

"There isn't a sign. Not even a sign."

"That's right. Nor a stick nor a stone. Anything that had any value got carted away, and everything else they burned to the ground." I looked into her face, trying to see more than the perfect bone structure, trying to see what it was that was different about her, besides the fact that she was older, and wondering if she was seeing the question I wasn't asking, the one about my father. If she saw it, she ignored it.

"The store," she said.

"Yeah, the store. Gone."

"Where did they go? The Dobies?"

"You remember the name." (And my father? I suppose you remember him?) But Valerie was squirming in her chair. She looked about to pump her hand in the air the way kids do in school to get the teacher's attention, and it occurred to me there would be parts of this conversation that would surprise her; she was still an age she could be surprised by adult behaviour. "I married Leonard," I said. I don't think I'd ever said that out loud before. I hadn't needed to say it; we lived in a place where everyone knew us. "This is our daughter, Valerie."

"Valerie," she said. "That's pretty."

"Val," Valerie said.

"And do you have other children?"

"Two boys. Older. They're in the field with their father. They just started combining." They were quite far from the house today, I remembered with some satisfaction.

"And his father and sister?" she asked, her head at a concerned angle.

Her hair was a lighter shade than it had been, I noticed, more ash than the former taffy colour, and it had been smoothed and styled. And that dress – it had been chosen to hide as well as to enhance. She'd become careful. Bad luck does that to women. Life does it. But we had a conversation to carry on, and it was so polite, so easy, this little social conversation, like a genteel game of badminton, played outdoors on the grass in a summer breeze, and I didn't care if she was sad, if her life had turned out badly, if disappointment had dogged her steps since the last time I set eyes on her. She meant nothing to me. "Oh, Scott moved down the road to Lawson," I said. "He runs the general store there. Franny lives in Winnipeg, married a bank inspector."

Valerie started humming "Heart of My Heart," an old song and an old family joke. She jumped up and went to the cupboards, still humming. She hadn't picked up on the undercurrents of the conversation. Yet. A grin fought at the corners of her mouth as she brought the mugs and cream and sugar to the table.

"You can have a cup, too, if you want," I said, and she blushed and stopped humming.

"Everett, Franny's fiancé, used to board with us," I tried to explain. "We moved into the manse after Dad left. The town council gave it to Mother, rented it to her for a dollar a year." I stopped there. *After Dad left.* So matter of fact, as if she'd had nothing to do with it. And then I was proud of that. It was old, old baggage, after all; it was a long time ago, and anyway, she could hear the steel under my words; I could tell by the wary way she watched me she'd feel the poke of the knife if I got it out. "The manse was empty, anyway," I went on. "The town never could afford a minister, and of course Mother couldn't pay the rent on the house we were in." That made her look away. No, she didn't want our eyes to meet over that little declaration. "They had to do something with us," I said. "Luckily, the manse was big enough she could take in boarders. The school teacher, the occasional salesman. And the bank inspector whenever he came to the district – Everett – even though we didn't have a bank in Gilroy. He liked Mother's cooking. He used to telegraph ahead. Called her Mrs. Gilroy and he'd telegraph he was coming and ask her to make stuffed heart. It was his favourite."

There was a little pause. I thought it was fitting.

"How is your mother?" she asked.

That took nerve, I figured, but I was up for the game. "Oh, fine, just fine," I said. "She has a nice little house in Lawson now, lives alone and I think she likes it."

"And Mrs. Knoblauch," she said. "I suppose she is no longer alive. She would be – well, over a hundred."

Oh, yes, well over a hundred. Stone cold dead and in the cold, cold ground. And I remembered Elena standing in Mrs. Knoblauch's backyard, and the sun setting, and the cool, quiet room that had been waiting for her, just for her alone. "Why are you here?" I asked. Valerie gasped. I'd spoken more harshly than I'd intended.

Elena didn't seem to mind. "I am on my way home," she said. "Well, hardly home." She blinked and cocked her head, as if she'd heard a tiny bell we couldn't hear. Maybe she was testing the idea of that word, *home*, wondering if she knew what it meant. "I had the idea I would like to see the farm where I grew up. I haven't been back since I left years ago – and on the way I decided to stop and see Gilroy. I was so astonished. It's on the map and I didn't see how I could have missed it. The land is so flat, you can see forever, but I drove up and down the grid roads, thinking it must be just over the next rise. I've been driving around here for an hour. And then I thought, when I saw your driveway, well, why not stop and ask."

"Well."

The conversation stalled for a moment. I thought now she might mention my father. I was pretty sure she was thinking the same thing; she was staring hard at the floor. But then Valerie spoke up. "You want to make sense of the past," she said, and it sounded so earnest, the way only a child's voice can sound, we both turned to her and she blushed again.

"When Elena was in Gilroy," I said, "she was in the business of telling the *future*."

"It was only a few weeks," Elena said, and then she stopped as if she'd lost the words she'd had in mind. "A few weeks I was here," she said at last.

"She read palms," I said.

"You did?"

She shrugged. "It was all I could think of to earn some money."

"Would you read my palm?"

"Oh, I am not good at it. I never was, and that was a long time ago."

Valerie held out her left hand and examined the palm. Elena reached across the table and took it. Slowly, she traced the lines with her forefinger. "I'd had my palm read once," she said. "But I'd forgotten what the lines were, what they were supposed to mean. I forgot about these ones going up the hand. They're faint, anyway. I concentrated on these two that run across." She drew her fingertip, twice, across Valerie's palm. "I thought of them as the life line and the love line. Do you see how they go, parallel to one another? Let me see your other hand. Yes," she said when Valerie obliged. "In your left palm they separate at either end. In your right, they come together, here at your pointer finger."

"What does it mean?"

"It means you have the same choice in life that everyone has. To love or not to love. It means love is possible for you." She smiled into Valerie's eyes and Valerie melted. Just melted. Of course she did, faced with that smile. "But also, there is much more, of course, in your future. I see intelligence. And caring. A sense of humour. Some impatience. You will have a life of adventure, I think. You will travel, you will go to school, to university. Your mother will be proud of you."

"Hah!" Valerie said. "What did you say when you read *her* palm? I bet you didn't tell her she'd end up a farmwife."

"She wouldn't read my palm," I said.

That made Valerie sit up.

"You were too skeptical," Elena said. "You knew it was all made up; I could have said anything to those people. You didn't for a minute believe. Like Val. She's not one to get taken in, either."

"You're wrong. I was taken in."

"Then I am sorry."

"And you didn't say just anything to people. Not back then. You didn't talk about love and adventure and travel. You knew about people. You understood them."

The kitchen clock started ticking loudly.

"I was younger then," she said.

"You had a gift."

"We all have gifts, when we're young."

Valerie peeked at me and then at Elena. When neither of us spoke, she asked, "So, how did you end up in Gilroy, anyway, back then?"

"Oh, it was — a stop along the way."

Like this little visit, I thought, just a stop along the way. "Did you know your father came here?" I asked her.

I could see she didn't know. "You are mistaken," she said.

"He came looking for you."

"No, it could not have been him."

She looked stricken. She looked like she'd stepped off a cliff. Valerie went and got a Kleenex and handed it to her.

"It was him," I said. "He tracked you down. Went from town to town, followed your trail, found the guy you were with – in Regina, I think it was, and he said he'd left you here, in Gilroy." I thought about her doing that, just getting out of Bill Longmore's car and walking away. I figured she was likely good at leaving people. I said, "It was your father. He came and talked to us."

She clapped her hand over her mouth. The tears that had been swimming in her eyes blinked out. "Maybe he is still alive," she said.

I didn't answer that. I chose that moment to ask Valerie to take her bike and find her dad and bring him to the house. She was reluctant to leave, but I knew once she was out on the road, scanning the fields for the combine, she'd be happy to think of telling him who was visiting and what was going on. She'd use the time on the way back to question him, try to worm some answers out of him. I didn't know what Leonard would think, but if I didn't let him know Elena was here, he would wonder why. He would think it silly of me to prefer to keep them apart. After all the years?

Elena asked to use the washroom so I sat alone in my kitchen and wondered if I would have to ask what I wanted to know. That was all I thought about those minutes, whether she would have the decency to tell me without my having to ask.

She returned with her makeup gone. I hadn't realized she was wearing it until then. She looked younger without it, but the dress clashed, too bright against the paler face. I thought likely she

wished she'd picked something else to wear that morning, something more subdued, like that brown dress she was wearing the
day she came to Gilroy. She avoided looking at me when she sat
down. It took her a minute, but finally she started talking ner-
vously. She told me she'd left my father long ago. They'd stayed
together only a year or so, and she'd lost track of him.

"Where?" I asked.

"We were in Fergus, Ontario, when I left him. An old friend of
his took us in for a while. I don't know where he went after that."

"Apparently no one does."

I went for the pot and poured us both more coffee.

"You haven't heard from him."

"No," I said when I sat down again. "No, I have no idea
where he is or how he is." She almost looked right at me then,
but it was too difficult, I suppose. She started talking about her
own father, instead. She said she'd always believed he'd killed
himself. She said he'd walked away one day with nothing but his
rifle. Left her with a note that had implied it was his intention
to take his own life.

I watched her while she talked, observed the consternation in
the forehead, the still-red eyelids, the leaky eyes, the lips trembling
before each word. She was upset, all right, but I didn't believe her.
Mr. Huhtala wouldn't have done that, not the Mr. Huhtala I knew.
I couldn't imagine him writing her a note and walking out on
her, leaving her to think he'd killed himself. He'd left her money,
I knew, and I noticed she somehow hadn't mentioned that. I wondered if this talk about suicide was a story she'd invented while she'd
washed her face, if she'd looked into the mirror and thought she
needed to be pitied. Or maybe she was trying to excuse herself for
taking off and never going home and not thinking about him.
Letting him worry all these years.

"That was wrong of him," I said, to see if she'd go on.

She dismissed it. "His life was hard."

"He had you to think of," I said. "But then, where would we all be if we were always thinking of others?"

She ignored my sarcasm, or accepted it. "Do you always think of others?" she asked.

"I was raised to. I resent it. Sometimes I think I'd be happier if I were more like my father."

"No," she said. "I don't think so."

"At least your father came looking for you," I said.

Her hand went to her mouth again, and she calmed herself. "All these years," she said, "I have raged at him."

It was after that announcement, every word given its melodramatic weight, that I remembered she'd had no money when she landed in Gilroy. She had no purse and no pockets. Maybe she'd lost it somewhere along the way. I wondered what she would say if I asked her. Mr. Huhtala had been insistent about it; I'd guessed that giving her that money had been a point of honour with him. And my father sure as hell hadn't given any to us. Right then she sat forward as if to say now we had come to the heart-to-heart.

"Your daughter reminds me of you," she said. "So serious. And at the age when – everything – " She stopped and looked around the kitchen for something she couldn't find, and ended up looking down at her hands. "I didn't want to read your palm that day, Ruth," she said. "I'm sorry, I don't know – truly, I don't remember why."

"Oh, I forgave you long ago," I said. "You were just being yourself."

"Maybe I was afraid you could make me be honest with myself. You see," she said with a little laugh, "you're doing it now."

"*I'm* doing nothing."

She laughed, then, really laughed, and I was glad because it made it easy to despise her.

When Leonard came in he was covered in dirt, every inch of him. Only his teeth and his eyes shone out. He met her with that lopsided smile of his, that slight stoop, the farmer's tan under the black grit, the white band of skin at the forehead when he took off his cap. She stood up. Held out her hand. But it was all right. He evaded her eyes.

"I am glad to see you again," she said formally.

He asked her how she'd been. When Leonard asked that question, people answered; he had that two-feet-firm-on-this-earth gravity that demanded more than an offhand response.

"Oh," she said. "I have been – peripatetic."

He smiled at that. Valerie looked to him for an explanation. "Wandering," he said.

"All over the place," she added, as if it was some kind of accomplishment.

I brought him a coffee. Valerie hung over his chair, her arms around his neck. Good girl, I thought, you hang onto your dad. It was small talk after that, Kleenex no longer required. She said she intended to head out soon, since she wanted to make the ferry to Virginia Valley by noon.

"Not much there anymore," Leonard told her. "You'll want to drive straight on to Charlesville. It has the only decent motel between here and Edmonton."

"I'm amazed," she said. "Gilroy – gone. It's nothing but farmers' fields. Just abandoned, Ruth said. As if no one had ever lived there."

"As if we'd never existed," Leonard said. He winked at me. "Oh, you two have been married a long time," she said.

He didn't mean to be disloyal. It was the furthest thing from his mind. He knew how complicated anything to do with Elena Huhtala would be, had to be, under the circumstances. He had no interest in the woman; it was only politeness to ask her to stay to lunch, and she declined, anyway. Not that the invitation was the problem. We could have sat through a meal with her, or had her stay overnight, for that matter, if it hadn't been for a momentary indiscretion. And momentary was all it was, but it was enough.

We didn't speak of it after she went; we acted as if nothing had happened. Well, not quite as if nothing had happened, but certainly as if nothing needed to be discussed. Valerie was full of questions, and we talked a long time about the summer my father left. I even got out my old scrapbook and showed it to her. Leonard ate his lunch and then went back to work. I think he thought we could ignore the incident, or at worst it would become like one of those bumps that grows under your skin, shows up one day and sits there, doesn't ever change, and doesn't go away. But just because you've got it there forever, you're a changed person. It was only a look. She'd been clutching that Kleenex and dropped it on the floor and bent to pick it up. And then she gave him that look, kind of under the table, but I saw it. The thing was, his response hadn't been automatic. He could have stopped himself from returning that look, and he didn't.

I kept seeing the look that had flashed between them; I saw it over and over again. I knew so well what it was. I'd seen it before; I'd seen it on Main Street thirty years before. Even then I knew what it meant, that two people have recognized each other, that they've identified the spark in one another's eyes and claimed it.

I figured this kind of exchange must be routine for Elena, almost mechanical: see a man you're attracted to, let him know. Any man would be flattered. You're overreacting, I told myself. Because of your father, because it was the same look she gave him. Doesn't mean it was the same thing.

"What does skeptical mean, really, Mum?" Valerie asked that day.

VIRGINIA VALLEY

Without resorting to landscape, it can be hard to think about the past. She had to drive by a cemetery just before the little town of Lawson, the last town that side of the river. She didn't stop, but slowed and glanced at the graveyard as she drove by. A couple of crooked, blasted trees; a few headstones ostentatious enough to see from the road, sticking up in the untended grass; three or four crows circling over the bare limbs of the trees. And all around, the harvested fields shone, the straw left behind in gold stripes, the bales scattered over them like gold bricks. Soon she was parking at the river, nosing in to the ferry landing, the only one around, watching the barge come towards her, crossing empty.

The young ferryman accepted her money. She couldn't remember how long it would take to get to the other side and almost asked him, but she didn't want to start a conversation. When she stood at the railing, staring into the black water, she thought about her father, or tried to think about him; her mind kept sliding away. The noise and the heaving barge under her feet lulled her. The rich fields under the bright sky were imprinted on her mind, the grey road, the green verge, the white, innocent clouds. She heard Ruth's words: *He had you to think of.* But he'd been weak, and he hadn't thought of her, not at all. The same could be said of Ruth's father. Again, she heard the sarcasm: *Where would we all be if we were always thinking of others?* No answer to that one.

The ferry motor droned, the water lapped against the boat. She was grateful for this spell of in-between, grateful, too, that she wouldn't be able to reach the farm today; there were a few hundred miles to go, miles that would give her time to gather herself. She should have told Ruth about Hattula. The thought struck her like a revelation. But why in the world think that? Ruth hadn't wanted to hear anything she had to say. And what she'd heard she hadn't believed.

She had gone to Finland in July. She couldn't have said why. It had been an impulsive decision; she knew before she went it would be like going to a completely foreign country. She was only six when her father brought her to Canada, and she couldn't trust her memories of those early years, the childhood years before they'd emigrated. Trees were what she thought of. Thinking of Finland had always led her eyes upwards through speckled light to the branches and leaves of trees that truly might have rooted anywhere.

She had spent a week there. In Helsinki, the first few days, she sat and sipped coffee in the outdoor cafés along the Esplanadi, content to be alone, listening to the babble of voices she didn't understand. The waiters were solicitous. A table in the shade? In the sun? A glass of water with your coffee? The purchase of one cup included a seat for hours, if you wished it, and she did; it felt like luxury. She brought a book she didn't read, a notepad she didn't open, a camera she didn't use. She sat with her hands in her lap, watching the people who walked past her. She saw her father in men who were her own age. Of course he'd been about that age the last time she'd seen him.

She'd been fine as long as she was sitting doing nothing, but when she left her favourite table and strolled through different parts of the little city, through streets of bland apartment buildings, or past the big ships at the harbour, she was overcome by a sick kind of restlessness. She hadn't realized how little there would be for her in Helsinki, how disconnected she would feel. The days were passing and she was only wandering – in her mind as well as physically. Her time was half gone and she didn't know why she'd come.

"You ought to go to Hattula," someone told her. "Your father's family might have originated there, given the name, after all. They say many people's names were changed, the spelling was changed, over the years."

It had been a chance remark, although in retrospect, as she knew well, what was luck, nothing more than luck, could come to seem like design. She'd booked a hotel in Hämeenlinna because she couldn't stay in Hattula; it was only a little village. But that had been fortunate, too. Yes, because there she'd met the desk clerk and her daughter. She pictured the two of them, as if they stood in front of her again, and once again the woman raised her hand to her daughter's brow in a tender, unnecessary gesture, brushing back hair that hadn't fallen.

She was far away when the ferryman strolled over and asked if she was from these parts. She'd known he would, sooner or later, only the two of them on the boat, after all. "Long ago, I was," she said, and she could hear the softness in her voice that came from remembering where she'd been. He leaned towards her, casual, but unmistakably interested, so she knew he'd heard it too and thought it was for him.

He said his name was Keith. He was quite young, or at least younger than she by a decade. He wore cowboy boots and jeans that had moulded to his thighs. He stayed beside her, leaning with his butt against the railing, and gave her a relaxed smile. "You got family here?"

"My father, north of here." She could have said no, put him off, but there was something about him she liked, and it was good, it was restful, to talk to a stranger.

"What's his name?"

"Oh, I don't think you'd know him. Matti Huhtala."

"No, can't say I know him."

"I am not sure he is alive."

It sounded odd; she knew that as soon as she said it. He broke out into a big grin. To hide it, although it was too late, he cupped his hand against the wind and lit a cigarette, then offered her one and lit it for her. He took a few appreciative drags, a meditative look in those blue eyes. Hey, you, his eyes said, as they had said fairly often before. *I'm doing nothing*, she heard Ruth say.

She tossed her cigarette into the river. "These are not good for me," she said.

"Yeah." He was a perceptive young man. He tossed his own smoke into the water where it bounced for a few seconds beside hers, and then he ambled off.

She watched him taking his time crossing the deck, and there was something almost like nostalgia in her feeling for his broad shoulders and long legs. A sharp pain ran through her. Confused, she called after him, "I wish you'd known my father."

He turned around, walking backwards away from her. "If I did, you'd know whether he was alive or not, eh?" He was only teasing her a little bit; he wasn't challenging her, even if it felt like that. He had kind eyes. He'd been hiding that, because they were unusually kind for a man of his age.

"I think he has been alive all this time," she said. She called it out to him and it was an idiotic thing to say, completely loony, really; she realized that as soon as the words came out of her mouth. But it didn't matter. It was all right; he'd already turned around, and anyway, he was too far away; her words were drowned out by the grinding of the cables and the motor. Past him, the shore was advancing, the gently pleated hills leading up to the plains, greener now than they used to be.

Keith came up to her open window before she drove off the ferry. He told her there was no hotel or restaurant anymore in Virginia Valley. There was a small café, but he couldn't recommend it. She said that was okay, she didn't need lunch; she was heading to Charlesville.

"They've got a new motel in Charlesville, right on the highway, on the way into town. You can't miss it."

She said she'd heard that. "Keith," she said. "Do you ever want to go down the river, instead of across?"

He looked bemused, then grinned at her. "I'd be up the river if I did it," he said.

She drove up the hill, through the little valley town, without stopping or even thinking.

CHARLESVILLE

Something got into Albert Earle that Friday night. It seemed to begin about six p.m. when a voluptuous light the exact colours of the new peaches in Dodds' store – and with a hint of their fuzziness – was flooding the countryside, but it probably began years before, maybe the day he was born. He'd been told he hadn't cried on that occasion until the midwife slapped him hard. He'd also been told that life catches up to you, and he certainly thought it had caught up to him.

The light at six o'clock that evening hit Charlesville at an angle that made even dull materials reflect it. The shiny corrugated tin siding on the Sports Complex that housed the curling rink and the swimming pool could not be viewed without pain and possibly lingering damage to the eyes. A recent structure, it blocked Albert's access to Main Street. Now to get to Main he had to exit his front yard. He had to walk around from the back of his house. (More than personal habit made that circumambulation necessary; custom dictated it. People in Charlesville did not use their front doors unless someone like the Queen came to town and knocked on them.) He had to take Railway Street to Main, and that meant he had to round the corner, passing the side and then the facade of the Jasper Hotel. But it had to be. He might have chosen to go the opposite way, turning left at his front gate (an old-fashioned, small-town wire gate with the metal on top scrolled into the shape of an imperfectly connected heart). He might then have taken a similar but opposite route, but his wife wouldn't countenance the extra steps it would have taken. She was annoyed enough just being prevented from walking as the crow flies, as you should be able to do in a small town. She would rather have lived in a smaller town. And the fire was decades ago, for God's sake.

They turned right. Beside their house was an empty lot, for which he was grateful. Knee-high grass and weeds and a lot of ironic clover flourished there, and Sanderson, who owned it, had parked his old half-ton at the back, the hood torn off, the motor torn out. The truck stood sideways across the back of the lot, but its front wheels were turned towards the street as if it would drive away if it could, as if it was embarrassed to be splayed open and found empty. If it could speak, Albert thought it would announce it was decomposing as fast and as decently as it could. Albert thought about dying quite often lately, because he was pretty sure he had throat cancer. He hadn't told his wife, or anyone else, his suspicion.

While the Royal George had been a three-storey brick building and sat foursquare on the corner of Railway and Main, the Jasper, half the size, was a white stuccoed box they'd tarted up with pale green trim, the colour of green Albert associated with hospitals. The paint was flaking off the crumbling foundation, it had gone chequered across the false front, and whole strips of it had lifted off the window frames. It had worn off most of the pitted cement front steps that led to the double doors (also painted pale green). In every way the Jasper was a far cry from the intended elegance of the old Royal George.

Of the Plains Hotel across the street, Albert wouldn't speak, because Stuart Flint, who owned it, wouldn't speak to him. The Plains had prospered by default, being for years the only place to stay in town. Albert had made Flint install fire escape doors at the back of the building, with two sets of iron stairs zigzagging down the wall. He'd had to fight to get him to do it. Now the hotel was up for sale because of the new Park City Motel out at the highway.

In back of the Plains, across the alley, was the RCMP detachment. You couldn't see it from Main Street, another thing for which Albert was grateful. Oh, he was full of gratitude for the small favours of happenstance, and as they passed between the Jasper and the Plains, heading south, strolling because his wife didn't walk fast unless she wanted to, he tried to gaze on Main Street without hatred.

It wasn't the changes he hated – many of them had occurred years ago – it was the optimism that lay behind the idea of change. He felt badly that he felt that way. He thought he shouldn't. The sun came bouncing off the bakery window and he shielded his eyes, but too late. Just a minute, he said, not out loud. She stopped, sighing, to wait for him to haul out his handkerchief and dab at his eyes. He looked back as he did, and the first thing he saw when his vision cleared was the corner of the Mounties' building in the gap between the bakery and Dodds' store. When he faced the street again, he decided it wasn't the optimism he hated, it was the ugliness: the squat, square, small buildings that seemed to him to advertise squat, square, small minds; the ridiculous false fronts; the tacky signs, the oily puddles in the rutted side streets; the cringing weeds along the sidewalks; the cracks in the cement; the two fire hydrants, stupidly painted to look like British policemen.

Why British? Why policemen? And the immodesty. The pretension. Would anyone believe that the Plains Hotel had a Banquet Room? That Boyles' Bakery made the best cheesecake this side of New York? That Shirl's Salon could advise the women of Charlesville on anything remotely close to the latest styles? The only properly named, properly advertised establishment in town was the new Pioneer Villa, and it was already housing the last of the *pioneers*. The great laugh was that the people who'd built it – people his age or younger – didn't realize they were next in line. They'd built it for the old folks without a thought that they were getting older every day themselves and that it would be their own last stop before they hit the cemetery out by the Park City Motel.

On their way down Main, the Earles had to nod and say something about the weather to a few people, or rather Albert had to, but they only slowed down, they never stopped, until Old Sally came rattling towards them pulling her wagon – a child's red-painted wagon full of jiggling, clinking, dirty-bottomed pop bottles and beer bottles she'd collected out by the drive-in and the cemetery, where the town kids liked to drink. She ploughed down the middle of the sidewalk, and they were obliged to stop and wait for her to pass. His wife insisted on saying hello to her and asking her if she needed anything. Old Sally said the same thing she always said. She said, "Hah!"

His wife picked up the pace after that, and he recalled they were late tonight, his fault. He'd cut himself shaving, a tiny scrape that had bled like the dickens. He'd walked around with a piece of toilet paper stuck to it for ten minutes, and it had bled again when he'd peeled it off. So now he had a Band-Aid on his chin. Not that it mattered. He was a sight, anyway, pockmarked all over his scalp, nose, and cheeks. Polka dots, Peg had called them. And there, kitty-corner across the street (that was filling up with angle-parked cars and trucks because they were later than usual), was Lynn's Style House, just where he'd known it would be, just where it always was, needing to be faced, needing to be passed by on the way to the Bluebird Café, and calling up, as it always did, the same *needling* question. Was it or was it not valid to consider the possibility that his having to face the Style House every Friday night was the reason Betty insisted on eating at the Bluebird? To make him, in her company, read Lynn's name imperfectly covering Peg's on that sign, to force him to pass that door he'd never open again, to remind him that he'd renounced Peg and their life together and taken her back, taken her back because she'd needed him, because he'd pledged till death do us part and he'd meant it, because he'd prized loyalty above all qualities. He was pretty sure it was part of her grand design to remind him on a weekly basis that he'd given up everything for her and had thought well of himself for doing it.

Soon they would make him retire. (He'd caught sight of the Fire Hall down the street.) The town would give him a gold watch and sentence him to spend the rest of his days in that little bunga-low by the railway tracks with Betty beside him. It was unbear-able. He said it right to her, if not aloud, while he held the screen door of the Bluebird open for her. "I can't bear it," he said, and she passed through.

◇◇◇◇◇

Charlesville's population had topped two thousand and it served a wider district than Virginia Valley had, but Jerry Wong knew just about every person who walked in the door of his café. Most of them sat at the same table every time they came in unless it was already occupied by someone who didn't know better, and most of them ordered the same meal every time. There was one "Chinese" dish on the menu and that was chop suey, which every one of them said with a sing-song intonation meant to amuse him. On this particular August evening, the Kulak brothers had been the first to arrive.

"Chop suey for me," Hermie Kulak had said before he'd balanced himself on the fourth stool in from the door.

"Fee and chee," Jacob Kulak had shouted from the door. He was holding it open while he scanned Main Street for a distant sight of girls. The brothers ate at the Bluebird every night. They were big-boned heavy eaters, farm boys who worked hard and hadn't washed behind their ears.

"You let in flies," Jerry had yelled at Jacob. He'd been feeding the two of them and yelling at them since he and Roy Wah opened the Bluebird in Charlesville. They didn't mind. They liked him bossing them around. They missed their parents. They still looked stunned whenever they spoke of the car accident. Their parents had been killed in a second-hand rattletrap the brothers had named "Fargo" because they'd had a bet about how far it would go before it would fall apart. Unfortunately for the elder Kulaks, the brakes had died before the engine, and it had happened at a busy intersection with the new Trans-Canada Highway. Jerry stood in for the parental guidance the brothers missed, although he was old enough to be their grandfather. He was old enough to be everyone's grandfather, now. His own family had remained in China. His wife still wrote almost monthly, and he mailed his letters to her like clockwork, since she remained concerned about his business. She could have joined him in Canada, but their son couldn't immigrate. He was always too old. When the Exclusion Act was repealed in 1947, allowing children under eighteen to join their parents, he was already twenty-four. The age limit went up over the years, but so did his son's age. Now he was teaching at Xi'an Jiaotong University and had his own family. Jerry had visited them once in thirty years and was not resigned to not seeing them again. One of these days, he told Roy, we're going to get it all repealed. Roy was a shy man and did not belong to the committees Jerry sat on, and he'd never been accused of being overly optimistic, but he'd extended himself to agree with Jerry on that.

"The usual?" Roy asked, stubbing out his cigarette as if it was his only joy when Jerry went back to the kitchen. While Jerry was a bustler, Roy, decades younger, perpetually drooped. His eyes drooped and his shoulders drooped and in the last few years he'd begun to sigh after the slightest effort. It suited him to stay in the kitchen and cook, but he liked to let everyone know he was the one carrying the workload while Jerry flitted around out front, socializing.

Jean Ross arrived right on time that evening, came in the back door grinning all over her flat, freckled face. She tied on her apron, noted the deep fryer releasing steam and stink and the blackened wok heating on top of the stove, and opened the swing door to the café an inch. "Oh God, look at the two of them on them stools," she muttered. "Like a pair of overfilled ice-cream cones." She wasn't exactly svelte herself. She was all horizontal planes, a spread of buck teeth and hips. "Why do they sit on them stools?" she said, but she knew why. It was so they could talk to her and Jerry. They were awkward young farmers, not easy with townsfolk.

Everybody liked Jean. She could get away with murder at the Bluebird and she knew it. Jerry and Roy both indulged her. She didn't care what anyone thought about her or said about her, a white woman working for Chinese. It was, in fact, against the law in the province, although few people knew that. Jean herself hadn't known until Jerry informed her the day she'd applied for the job. The Mounties ate in the café regularly. Jerry didn't know if they were ignorant of that law or if they'd decided it didn't concern them. Either way, Jean didn't give two hoots. She liked her work, and why shouldn't she? He and Roy were lenient with her, the patrons were grateful for a decent restaurant, and the place was cheerful, exactly what he'd been aiming for when he'd had the walls painted an airy blue and hung a few Chinese pictures among the posters of Elvis and Connie Francis and Sandra Dee and the ads for Coke and Doublemint gum. Cheerful was in his mind when he'd picked shiny turquoise for the Arborite counter and tabletops and the vinyl that covered the stools and chair cushions. The café could seat forty. It could have accommodated more, but people here had a low proximity limit and Jerry wanted them to feel comfortable. He'd had one business failure. (It had been no fault of his own, but tell his wife that.) He couldn't afford another.

Jean was setting two dripping Cokes in front of the Kulak brothers, and Jerry was polishing the far-end serviette holder when the woman walked in and turned an ordinary Friday into unusual. She was not from these parts, obviously, not in that stylish dress. Even her ash-blonde hair, with its fall and gleam and its casual upward flip, looked foreign to Charlesville, but her face was flushed from the stinging heat of the late-day sun on Main Street, or maybe from the four of them staring at her as she walked in, the brothers with their mouths gaping.

"You want table?" Jerry asked her, but she was already seating herself at the closest table but one, the corner table next to the window. He brought her a menu, battling with himself about asking her to move. She thanked him solemnly, her eyes momentarily looking into his, and he couldn't do it. She'd instinctively slipped to the most private spot they had, banked by the wall and the window and a row of snake plants in tall Chinese pots. He couldn't ask her to move. Jean gave him a meaningful look when he came back to the counter, but he shrugged it off. They didn't reserve tables at the Bluebird, no matter how regularly customers came, or how important that corner table was to them.

Jerry fussed a bit before he took the woman her water, giving her time to settle and read the menu, and while he was fussing, the Thompsons arrived, bringing with them their usual hubbub, just the two of them and the two little kids, so far, but you'd think there was a dozen of them. "God, don't tell me that bump in her blouse means another's on the way," Jean muttered as she hauled out the high chair for them and they ranged themselves near the back of the room. And then Dr. Pilgrim came in and drifted to his usual table, sitting facing the front so he wouldn't have to talk constantly to the Thompsons. Jerry watched his surprise when he glanced up to find a strange woman sitting in the corner. The doctor was a thin, tired, nervous man, but not unattractive to women, Jerry had observed. He blinked a lot. He was blinking when Jerry came over with the menu. He was one of the few who pretended he didn't know it by heart.

In their division of duties, Jean took the orders since she remembered better than Jerry. He didn't like hearing, "*Not* gravy, this time," and it made Roy mad to throw out even a scoop of mashed potatoes. Jerry preferred the greeting, the cheering, the delivery of menus and water, the pouring of endless cups of coffee – shuffling back and forth as if he wore slippers and a gown and a pigtail.

Besides the big table at the back that was meant for parties of eight or ten, there were now three tables open, all three in the exposed centre of the café, and when Albert Earle and his wife came in, a little later than their normal time, they stalled by the pop dispenser. Faltering, they made Jerry see them as they were going to look ten or twenty years from now. They were just sixty or so, but the smallest surprise could shock people into a kind of temporary old age. Jerry had observed that before. He'd noticed it in himself. And for people who relied on every day being much like every other day, maybe this wasn't such a little surprise. It certainly wasn't a pleasant one. Betty Earle, after that one look at the occupied corner table, seemed about to turn around and leave, but Albert cupped her elbow and guided her forward. She was a broad-backed woman, thick of shoulder and with almost no neck, and it was odd to see her being led anywhere, even across a room. Jean and Jerry stood back behind the counter and watched to see whether she'd sit beside the Thompsons or by Dr. Pilgrim. Either would pose a problem.

When she finally chose the table next to the doctor, she sat on the chair that faced away from him. She stared up at Jerry for a belligerent moment and then transferred her annoyance to Jean. Well, it wasn't the best seat in the house. Either side of Albert, she'd be looking at the Kulak brothers' backs as they bent over their plates, forks in constant motion.

"Betty Earle don't like it," Jean hissed in Jerry's ear as she went by on her way to the kitchen. It was a little joke and on two counts. One, because everyone in Charlesville called Betty Earle by both her names. You never heard her called Mrs. Earle or Betty. It was as if people wanted to impress themselves and everyone else with her identity. And two, because Betty Earle didn't like much that she came across and didn't hesitate to let the world know when she didn't. But it wasn't a funny joke, because she could scare the pants off you if it was you on the receiving end of her anger.

Jerry went over with the coffee pot. Right away, Albert Earle asked for the roast beef. "And veal cutlets?" Jerry asked Betty Earle. She was staring at the woman in the corner as if she knew her from a long time ago and had never liked her.

"Betty?" Albert said.

She looked down at the coffee in her cup and nodded.

"Hot one, today, Jerry," Albert said in his apologetic way.

Jerry flinched. He wished Albert wouldn't talk like that. He hovered over them, looking down on the man's broad, pitted skull. The scars from the dripping tar had never faded. You could see them through the hair; they'd created odd little whorls in his hair like some people had at the backs of their necks. His head and forehead and nose were sprinkled with the black dots, indented into the flesh like inside-out moles. Couldn't he see his wife's scars were just as visible? He didn't make things better by apologizing in advance for whatever she might do.

"How's it going?" Jean asked when he came back to the kitchen with the orders. She was catching a smoke while she could, leaning against the sink, watching Roy sling food around.

"Scary," Jerry said. "Mr. Earle apologizing already."

Jean popped a few smoke rings and watched them drift over the stove. "He can apologize for every word that comes out of her mouth," she said. "It don't make no difference."

"He's scared what she might do if anybody say something to set her off."

"Nobody around here's ever gonna speak two words to Betty Earle they don't have to."

"She hasn't hurt anybody," Roy said.

"Huh. You don't get life in prison for teaching Sunday School."

"There were extenuating circumstances, with a baby like that," Roy said. "You don't know what she was going through."

Jean blew three perfect, fat doughnuts.

"I gotta get out there," Jerry said.

"Don't get your shirt in a knot. I'm going. She likes it, you know. She likes it that we're scared of her."

Jerry thought she was right about that. Betty Earle seemed to want to frighten people. Sometimes Jerry thought she did it to punish Albert for living while she was in prison, or maybe she wanted to punish them all.

Stranded in the open middle of the Bluebird Café, Albert decided coffee must have been invented as a substitute for talking. In their usual corner, sheltered by the snake plants, nobody noticed that he and his wife didn't talk. They should have gone home, turned around and gone home. Betty had wanted to leave. He could have opened a can of soup (he could see the can opener and feel the key in his right hand; he could feel the tin's resistance while he twisted it). Why should he care if everyone in the café was staring at them, wondering what they were going to do?

The woman in the corner had his usual chair, facing the other tables, but she wasn't looking at anyone. She had a calm, composed manner, almost an aura. She'd be a peaceful person to know, he thought. Jean was setting her meal down on her table, now, and the woman was looking up and chatting with her in a friendly way. Dr. Pilgrim was watching them, too, his eyes blinking away. Betty wouldn't forget the doctor was behind her. He was new in Charlesville; he hadn't been around back when she went on trial, but just the fact of his being in the medical profession made his presence intolerable to her, and not only because of the baby. Angela. Involuntarily, Albert shook his head. He knew before he looked up he'd find Betty glaring at him. She didn't like head shaking. But Angela – the very thought of her demanded physical expression, just her name in his mind had to be shaken free, had to be gone as soon as he could make it go. At the trial they'd asked Betty who had chosen the name and why, and she'd said she'd picked it because she'd thought the baby wouldn't live long. Nothing but the truth, the stupid, stupid truth.

The café had quieted. It was because it had this tension at its centre, the tension Betty created wherever she went. Made it seem like everyone was holding their breath. One of the Thompson kids started chattering. Albert tried to think it was a good thing the young family was here tonight, otherwise the occasional whine from the overhead fan and Jerry's shuffling would be the only sounds to bridge them all. On the other hand, the children were sure to annoy Betty, and the louder they got, the more irritable she'd become. It wasn't that kids weren't afraid of her, but they'd forget she was nearby. Nobody else forgot her presence. He sure as hell didn't. A day hadn't gone by since her return that he hadn't borne her like a burden on his back.

People were staring at them and then trying not to stare. He should say something, anything. But what? Only misery words came to his mind. Drab. Dirty. Dull. Dumb. Well, he was certainly that in every way. He coughed. That earned him a glance of disdain. And then he couldn't stop coughing. His face was getting red, he could tell, but he had something in his throat and he could not quit hacking. Betty pushed his water glass towards him. He picked it up and put it down again because he was in danger of spilling it, he was coughing so hard. He pulled out his handkerchief and blew his nose. Sometimes that worked. He blew and cleared his throat and coughed. He was sweating now. Everyone was trying not to look at him.

Finally he got himself under control and was able to sip at his water. He coughed a lot lately. He often thought he had something caught in his throat. It reminded him of the days after the fire, when his larynx and bronchial tubes had swelled and he'd wheezed and gasped for breath and coughed up black phlegm full of soot and shreds of flesh from his seared lungs. Sometimes he thought he was losing his voice. He found himself speaking almost in a whisper, as he'd had to do right after the fire. He was pretty sure these were all symptoms of throat cancer. He did nothing about it, preferring to contemplate what people would say after he died, that he'd left it until it was too late.

This was the world in which Elena found herself, that pressed on her. She picked at her sandwich, telling herself she had to eat, and tried to ignore the coughing man's attempts to calm down. He'd been nearly beside himself, while the woman with him looked as if she was on a different planet, or wished she was. Elena could only sympathize with both of them. How many times had she watched couples like this, while she sat alone, quite sure she was less lonely than they were? Now the restaurant had gone so quiet she could hear her jaw click when she opened her mouth to take a bite.

She thought about her favourite café in Helsinki, and how she'd anchored herself there her first days in Finland. Quite a few people in the city spoke English, but she hadn't initiated any conversations, any more than she would do here, in Charlesville, and only the waiters and the hotel staff had talked to her. Once they'd got to know her a little, the question they all asked her was "Why did you come here?" They'd assumed, by her looks, that she'd come to visit relatives, yet she was obviously alone.

And then she'd gone to Hattula, where she'd found some peace. Once again, thinking about Hattula, she thought about Ruth. Ah, Ruth, sitting there the whole time with that disbelieving expression on her face. They shouldn't have talked about their fathers, about the past. *That was wrong of him*, Ruth said, but it was only to hear what she would answer.

She remembered walking through the cemetery beside Hattula Church, on her way back to her car. Tears had sprung up in her eyes for no reason. The headstones swam, the entire graveyard shimmered, broken into bits. It was just because they were all dead, all those once-upon-a-time people; it would make anyone cry.

"How are the cutlets coming?" Jerry asked.

"As you see," Roy said, pointing to the frying pan where syrupy pink blood was oozing on top of the meat.

"Can't be ready too soon," Jerry said. He should have told Roy to leave off his rule of cooking the orders strictly in sequence. Just this once you'd think he could have made an exception.

"Don't I know it," Roy said. After defending her earlier, he'd remembered how Betty Earle had once barged into the kitchen to tell him off when her meal had been late. "But you know, I don't think she's trying to scare us. I think she's the one who's scared."

Jerry threw his hands up. "I don't know why it's so bad tonight. We're losing business. People come in, they see Betty Earle, and they leave."

"Usually the Earles come earlier."

"I should have kept the corner table for them."

"Yup. Keep 'em hidden away."

The problem with dying of cancer was that it could be painful. He was pretty sure it had to be painful – that pain was the essence of cancer. Albert was afraid of pain. He assumed most people were, if they'd experienced it once or twice. Even thinking about it made his throat burn. Maybe he should be making an appointment with Pilgrim instead of wondering what to say to him in a friendly way when either one of them got up to leave.

Jean clattered out with fish and chips for the Thompson

kids and the shrill tang of vinegar wafted over the restaurant. A few minutes later the parents got their burgers and fries. The Kulaks asked for the apple pie à la mode, and Albert watched Jean dig out the ice cream while Jerry sliced the pie. Till death do us part, he thought. Betty rolled her eyes. He was sure she could read his thoughts. Just get us through supper and get us home, he prayed to the impersonal no one he prayed to.

Dr. Pilgrim got his meal. Betty turned to stare when Jean took it to him, but he wisely focussed on salting his omelette. The woman in the corner had finished her supper. She was trying to signal Jerry for the bill. Good. They could move to her table if she left before their food came. It wouldn't matter what anyone thought. They could simply get up and move to the corner table, and Betty could sit in her usual spot facing the snake plants, and eat her supper and it would all be fine, it would be like any other Friday night. They'd be home by seven, seven-thirty at the latest; they'd watch TV, they'd go to bed.

Something had changed in the room. For a few seconds he listened, conscious of the fan whirring above him, and then he realized that Jerry and Jean had gone to the kitchen. Both of them. They'd left the café at the same time, deserting them all, abandoning them to their little islands. *Whir, whir.* Nothing else. Not even the Thompson kids were talking. It was pathetic to be anxious just because Jerry and Jean weren't among them, moving around the room, ministering to their imagined needs, and how contemptuously Betty regarded him, reading his thoughts. Why would he care what these people thought? The Kulaks eating like pigs, Dr. Pilgrim blinking like an advertisement for medical incompetence, all of them small-town people with small-town minds. Except for the woman in the corner. She definitely had a sophistication that set her apart from them, an urban gloss. She had absolutely no eccentricities, not that he could see. She'd done nothing untoward or odd, and he thought she never would. She could sit in the corner, facing them, where he usually sat, without intruding on them, without making anyone uneasy, somehow even seeming to imply she liked them all. He felt that she liked him, or would like him if she knew him. But he wasn't going to spend any time looking at her. If Betty saw him – too late. She'd seen him. Oh no, now she had that cynical expression in her eyes, the one she got whenever anything made her think of Peg. His throat hurt. Maybe the pain wouldn't be so bad, not much worse than this. And it would make no difference if he lost his voice completely. And if he couldn't swallow, he'd heard starvation was not actually a bad death. He wondered if it would really take forty days. Not if he couldn't take water. That would be much faster, as long as he told no one it was happening so he wasn't put into the hospital. He would have to find some kind of personal ice floe, and then it would be a matter of days.

Finally the kitchen door swung back and Jerry came bearing roast beef and Jean came bearing veal cutlets. The Kulaks both turned around. Why did they turn around and stare, their big, wide faces open with wonder? Holding their forks aloft, dripping mangled pastry and soft, moist apples (dead apples – they had the discoloured and melting look of death, of decay and dissolution). Jerry and Jean set the plates down, one at either side of the table, and it was all happening as if it was a dream, or a dance; it was all choreographed with uncertain, unknowable meaning; and all the while he was seeing that, he was ticking each action off. There would only be the eating to get through. So move away, Jerry, don't hover. We don't need you now. See, Jean's already escaped to the kitchen. You go too, and leave us to get this over with. Then he saw the knife, where Jerry had left it after cutting the pie, a long, sharp knife, gleaming silver on the turquoise countertop. He saw it because Betty was staring at it. He thought if he turned his gaze and looked at her now, their eyes would meet.

His fingers found the Band-Aid on his chin and pressed, so he could feel the delicate pain that caused. He could smell his roast beef; it had a canned smell. His mother used to can beef. A nagging weight pulled his innards down. How could he eat? He couldn't eat. He was sick. She wasn't eating, either. They'd finally got their food and now they couldn't eat. He didn't know how much time had passed since their meals had arrived, or if any time had passed. Maybe he was in some dream state. Maybe she would do exactly what she was thinking. It would happen in slow motion. He wouldn't feel a thing.

It occurred to him, while time stretched and no one in the café moved or even breathed, and some part of him sat outside himself, ready to mock, that Betty's second trial would cause less public consternation than the first. The murder of a spouse would surely be at least understandable to most people. Just the experience of living with another person and putting up with their irritating peculiarities would be enough to elicit some basic comprehension of the act, and Betty had endured way more than that. People who knew them – or rather knew of them, because no one really knew them – would come up with all kinds of reasons for her behaviour, although they wouldn't be considered excuses. His betrayal of their marriage while she was incarcerated would form the domi-nant theory, and would be enough, in most minds, to explain her homicidal rage.

He found himself smiling over the phrase, actually smiling down at his plate, tenderly, as if one of his slabs of beef had sat up, separating itself from its gravy, and whispered the words aloud to amuse him. Homicidal rage – it sounded pretty grand for a stabbing at the Bluebird. But it didn't take a huge leap to think he might be able to provoke her to it. He'd seen anger close to it flare in her eyes after he'd done something as seemingly innocent as asking her to pass the salt when he could easily reach it himself, and nothing irritated her more than his attempts to smooth over her roughness with others. Funny, in her early life she'd wanted her edges smoothed; she'd wanted to be someone she wasn't. She'd tried to hide her background. She'd been ashamed of being Ukrainian, of coming from a big, rough, unhappy Ukrainian family. In fact, he figured it was entirely possible she'd married him to get a legal right to his solid Anglo-Saxon name, thinking Earle had an upper-class sound, too. He'd known her last name, of course, but he hadn't realized until the day of their wedding that her first name wasn't Betty. People in the Charlesville area hadn't known her identity until the newspapers published her birth name after her arraignment, and her old classmates, from the one-room country school she'd attended up to grade nine, realized that it was Oksana Pawluk – who'd been nicknamed (predictably if not affectionately) Ox – who was notorious.

She'd put her head down and was steadily eating. For a big woman, she ate with little enjoyment, the same way she drank herself most evenings into a stupor. A fly was buzzing around her head, but she didn't notice it. Of course she would plead insanity. Her lawyer would insist on it. Self-defence would be no defence in this case, given the number of witnesses to the act. At her trial for Angela's death, she'd refused a plea of temporary insanity, although people might have understood you could go crazy watching your child's constant, excruciating pain. She maintained it had been a sane thing to do, to end that suffering, the only sane thing to do. That got her some of the wrong kind of sympathy, from people who supported eugenics and viewed children like Angela as a drain on society. She'd hated that. Her own sister, who had been "a little slow" (especially, Betty said, when it came to running away from the boys who wanted to take advantage of her), had been institutionalized and sterilized after giving birth to an illegitimate baby.

He set his fork down. All this time he'd been holding it without eating. He wanted to put his head in his hands. Just that. Nothing more. But he couldn't do even that, sitting as he was in the middle of the café. If only he could believe she would pick up that knife and finish him off, end it all, here and now.

Little Tammy Thompson, seeing her parents absorbed in their burgers, slithered down from her high chair and toddled over to the Earles' table to see what they were having for supper. Albert saw her – and everything was still happening in slow motion – set her hand on Betty's knee. He saw Betty look down, not at the child but at the hand. He did a rehearsal in his mind, as Peg used to say she did when she got anxious about something she was going to do. With a mental pang, he saw, in a brief flash, her sharp-featured face and her dark, knowing eyes. At the same time, he was seeing what he was going to do. He was going to bend over – quickly – and pick up that little body in his two big hands before Betty could give her a shove or a slap or whatever would occur to her demented mind. And then he was doing it. He swooped down, he swooped up, and before he knew it, he was holding little Tammy Thompson in front of his face. He was watching her tiny face crumple, her eyes close, her mouth open. He was seeing all the way past her pearly little teeth to her spongy, rosy tonsils and uvula (he knew the right name from his research on throat cancer, and watched it vibrate with particular horror before a sound came out). It was a long moment, and then she wailed, she sobbed, she screamed for her mother. She screamed so loud, he held her out at arm's length, and that's when he noticed everyone in the café was staring at him, with shock on their faces. He scanned them all. They were all absolutely stunned. Of course they were. What in the world was he doing? And how could he be stopped?

He was grateful when her parents jumped to their feet. He was grateful when her dad crossed the room in two bounds and snatched her out of his hands. "What the hell do you think you're doing, Earle?" he said. But he didn't wait to hear what Albert thought he was doing. He took Tammy – still screaming as if she'd been defiled by Satan or one of his minions – back to her mother. Albert turned to Betty to tell her they should go home. He could see himself flapping around her like an old man, plucking at her sleeve. She wasn't there.

Elena had forgotten time; she'd been halfway between now and next. When the child toddled across the floor, she realized she probably didn't need the bill, that in a small place like this you just walked up to the cash register at the end of the counter when you finished your meal, and she was about to do that when the man in the centre of the café scooped the little girl up and set her screaming. Then the woman with him took up her purse from the floor by their table and stood. Elena thought she meant to leave, but she slid the purse to her forearm and picked up her plate and her cutlery and carried them over to Elena's table. She said, "You won't mind if I finish my supper here? This is my usual table." And when Elena said she would go, the woman asked her to stay.

Albert was still standing by their table, his feeble "Betty!" echoing in his own head. He wasn't sure whether or not he'd said it out loud. His life had gone from slow motion to stop, but he could see that others were carrying on. Betty was chatting with the woman in the corner. The Kulak brothers remained turned towards the rest of the café, both of them sucking on toothpicks. The Thompsons were packing up. Jean was helping them gather up all the bits and pieces they'd dropped. Tammy was hiccupping with the same dedication she'd given to screaming. Dr. Pilgrim had gone back to his omelette, and was chewing in a manner that implied professional dignity. Jerry came sliding up to Albert's elbow. "I get lady's bill," he whispered. Albert sank down onto his chair.

"You're not from here," the woman said. Betty, her husband had called her. "It's refreshing. And I like that dress you're wearing."

Elena thanked her.

"That's a different kind of dress, kind of a Jackie Kennedy dress, eh? Kind of thing *she* wears, eh? What's your name?"

Elena told her, putting on her patience, another kind of dress.

"Mine's Betty. Originally Oksana, Oksana Pawluk, but I changed it."

"Oksana is a pretty name."

"Not where I come from. Where'd you find a dress like that?"

"I got it in Finland, this summer. It's a Marimekko dress."

"You're kidding. What the heck is that?"

Elena explained it was a fabric and clothing store where she'd shopped in Helsinki. She told her it was a company run by women. She knew Betty would like that. She could always access useless insights about other people. Or maybe they weren't useless. Every day they slipped her past situations she wanted to avoid, eased her way.

"You know, you've got the craziest way of talking," Betty said. "You could put me in a trance."

Jerry approached with the bill. Betty glared at him while Elena paid, and when the transaction was over, she told him to get lost. Elena smiled at him and shook her head to let him know he didn't need to be concerned. "Okay, missie," he said, retreating backwards.

"You married?" Betty asked.

"No," Elena said.

"Why not?"

"Well, for some years I lived with a man who was married to someone else."

"And now?"

"I'm on my own."

Betty reached out and fingered the armhole of Elena's dress. "I'd say that dress would be a cinch to sew, not much to it, a couple of seams, a couple of darts. I worked as a seamstress in prison."

She turned around and surveyed the room. Everyone evaded her eyes and she turned back to Elena, who was starting to feel as if she was the one in a trance, glued to her chair by a woman who'd worked as a seamstress in prison.

"Just look at this crew, eh?" she said. "I mean, usually I sit here on a Friday night, right here in this chair, with a bird's eye view of the snake plants. So tonight was a bit different. They trained me as a seamstress. You have to do some kind of work. It turns out to be a useless trade here, where people know me. They don't want me around them with a pair of scissors. I'm good, I could smarten them up, but they don't care. My mum used to sew. Had to. She come here at seventeen. My dad brought her here through some ad in the papers. He was a widower with three little girls, eh? And then the two of them made more. She had no sense of style, poor thing. Style. There ain't none of that here. Look at them Kulak brothers, for instance. With their waistbands under their armpits. No fly on their pants. Suspenders. In this day and age. Their mother made those pants before she died, ended them above the ankles so they wouldn't trip. And take a gander at Roxanne Thompson. Look, quick, before she gets out the door. See that godawful excuse for a dress she's wearing? Thinking she's all dolled up for a Friday night at the Bluebird. If I had a nickel for every time I've overheard her say, "I made this myself." Hah! She might as well put *that* down the front instead of the fifty tiny buttons. Her husband, he's from my old district, I knew him when he was a little kid. My sister and me used to babysit him. Used to put his clothes on him backwards. The whole lot of them might as well wear their entire wardrobes like that, it would make no difference." She had turned a little to watch them go out the door, and set her elbow into her plate. She lifted it and stared at it, at the gravy dripping off of it. "I guess the guy you lived with must've been rich," she said, wiping it off.

"Well, there were a succession of men, and they tended to get richer."

"Hah! I'm gonna remember that line. I've only got the one. And I'm fed up, I gotta tell you. He's a bully, you know. Nobody realizes that, but he is. He drives me crazy. I mean it. I seen him watching you, ever since we come in. Looking at you with that *chivalrous* look on his face. You know what I mean? If only you had a suitcase he could carry for you, he'd be pleased to lug it anywhere. Or if you'd drop your serviette, he could fly to rescue it. Because here you are, clean and innocent and pretty as all get-out. While me – why, he's got to hide me as best he can." She stopped and shrugged her big shoulders.

"I must go," Elena said.

Betty picked up her purse and set it on her lap, but didn't rise. When Elena stood up, she said, "Just stand still a minute, will you? I want a look at how that dress is made."

Elena obliged. The husband watched from his table with the dullness of a man who has drunk enough to kill him.

As soon as she stepped out the door, she had a feeling of escape as visceral as any she'd ever experienced. Even her feet felt light, and she was glad of the few blocks she had to walk to the highway, glad she hadn't brought the car. It was good to feel cement under her shoes, air on her skin. She passed a drugstore and then a new, low building called Pioneer Villa. She smiled at the word *villa* for such a utilitarian structure. Next door to it was the Old-Timers' Museum. She laughed out loud. She was forty-six and intended not to grow old.

She didn't meet the old crone on her way back to the motel. She'd seen her earlier, dragging her clanking wagon behind her, a woman not likely as ancient as she looked, with candy-floss white hair and a sunken mouth where her teeth had once been, a rough old woman dressed in a man's pants held up with binder twine and a man's flannelette shirt. She'd released an awful gust of body odour when she'd passed by, and when Elena had turned to look at her, not being able to stop herself, the old bird had said, "Hah!"

When she slid between the strangely damp-feeling sheets on her bed that night, she thought about all the escapes she'd made in her life, and how she would escape that fate, too. She closed her eyes. The motel had installed a yard light, and you couldn't make the room dark. She tried to keep her eyes closed, but they opened on their own as soon as she forgot about them, and then she could see her clothes thrown over the one chair. She wore nothing to bed. She wished she could go about naked. Not have clothes at all. "Hah!" she said out loud. She hadn't been able to sit nude in the sauna, in Hattula, even though she was all by herself.

Why are you here? They'd all asked her that, in Finland. And Ruth had asked her, too. She thought about arriving at the room, earlier (it seemed a month ago), tired from the long day – the driving and the discoveries – and forcing herself to shower and change and make up her face. She closed her eyes and saw Ruth's plain face, her anxious eyes behind the thick lenses, and the daughter's face, glowing with misplaced admiration. *You were just being yourself*, Ruth said.

Clean and innocent and pretty, the woman at the cafe – Betty – said. Elena could hear the exact way she'd said it, as if every word was fact.

She climbed out of bed and walked around the room, watching her naked feet, feeling the cooling air move against her bare skin. The yard light bloomed behind the drapes. She threw up her arms as if explaining herself or giving up to someone, but all she let herself think was that she hated those goddamn Marimekko dresses – and she'd bought seven of them.

◇◇◇◇◇

Jerry was so tired after the Earles left, he let Jean send him home. He was dead tired, but once he'd crawled into bed he felt too sorry for himself to fall asleep. At his age he shouldn't have to watch the kind of suffering nobody wants to see. He shouldn't have to see people turned inside out. He thought about his hot water bottle, but he was too lazy to get up and fill it. He thought about his old wife, far away across the world, who would seem ancient to him now. Probably, if they were together, she'd want him to look after her. He'd be dragging himself out of bed to get a hot water bottle for *her*. Then (and he pictured a line of dawn at the bottom of the window he knew would be black) he thought how lucky he was to have been born with a proclivity to find his situation lucky, and he drifted for several minutes on that concept, along the edges of oblivion; but even though he knew it to be true – he was lucky enough to know he was lucky – the space was growing at his forehead, the cavity widening, a vacuum was ballooning. Only someone else's words could keep grief, once it had been roused (my son, my son), from rushing in and taking over there. He turned on the light. He rummaged in the hutch he used for a bedside table. Where a thunder bowl used to reside was a stack of pocket novels, detective stories, the covers softened with handling, pliable and comforting to his fingers. It didn't matter which he pulled from the pile. (My son, my son. No one could say what was really happening in China. The letters told nothing; he couldn't read between the lines.) It didn't matter where he opened the book. Tonight it was a John Dickson Carr, *The Case of the Chinaman's Rescue*. No, but they should all be called that.

◇◇◇◇◇

"That dress she was wearing was made by a women's company, started by a woman, run by women," Betty told Albert the next morning. "I'm gonna start my own just like it. I'm gonna make up a bunch of those dresses in a bunch of sizes and start out by selling them at your floozy's old shop."

He didn't doubt she could do it and told her so.

"That's the first bit of encouragement you ever gave me," she muttered, and some of her defiance deflated to an almost normal level, and she went on to say she would also start a society. She was going to call it something like The Society for Reasonable Clothes for Women. She looked almost happy, thinking about it.

For a whole minute after that, he flung thoughts out like a busy little worm arcing into new worlds, how she would make the dresses, how they'd sell at a profit, how she'd bank the money, and when she'd made a pile, how she'd pack up, clear out of here, set out for some bigger centre. But that only reminded him of Peg and the things she'd said to him and about him before she'd left town.

Ever the mind-reader, Betty said, "Maybe I'll get rich and leave you. Wouldn't that be nice?"

CALGARY

For years after Elena Huhtala dumped herself out of his car, Bill Longmore's mind turned to her on a regular basis. What had become of her? And was she, in some existential way, still laughing at him? He'd tried to stave off that kind of thinking with much more acceptable anger, told himself she'd taken him for a ride, no doubt about it. What a sucker he'd been; should have had his head examined. But however he framed the discussion with himself in those still-young years, it was her laughing he ended with. He believed she'd ruined his life with her laughing. Every woman he met after her seemed to conceal hidden mirth, no matter how deep within, every one of them like a pump that only had to be primed by him to gush. Even on first dates he watched for the signs of withheld hilarity, and he always thought he saw them: the taut jaws, the twitching lips, the watering eyes, the quick glance away.

He'd always shunned a tendency to be self-conscious. He'd liked knowing that his easiness with people made them happy. But how could he be easy or happy when he was constantly on guard? When every woman he dated reminded him of his mother in her enigmatic moods?

When he changed, gradually, over the span of a few years, he thought the difference was in the women. He didn't think he'd altered anything about himself. But the truth was, he'd learned a few things. He'd watched women so closely, he started to think about them as often as he thought about himself. He began to observe emotions that had more to do with them than with him, and to discern quite a few reactions other than enjoyment at his expense. Not long after that, he became interested enough in a serious young woman to try to provoke her to laughter, and she became interested enough in him to laugh with him, and they married and had three children.

On the day Ruth phoned him, he was alone again. His wife had died the year before, and his children, all grown up now, had settled into lives of their own. It had been months since he could recall even smiling.

He got to the phone on the fourth ring. He'd been in the shower. It was unusual to get a call so early and it set his heart pounding.

"It's Ruth."

"Ruth?"

"Sorry, did I alarm you? I just wanted to catch you before you left for work."

He brought his breathing back to normal. She always called like this, as if a couple of years hadn't passed since they'd last talked. "What's up, Ruth?"

He shivered while she talked; he had only the bath towel around his middle and the house was chilly. He pictured her shivering, too, he didn't know why, and standing in a dark room by herself. He'd never seen her in her house, had only met her once, and she was just a kid then, she was just around twenty. She'd contacted him, called out of the blue. It was nine or ten years after his ill-fated trip across Saskatchewan, when he was teaching at the Air Training School at Currie Field, getting young pilots ready to go overseas and see action he would never see. He was already married and two of the three kids had been born. It was a Saturday and he was home. His wife answered the phone and gave him a funny look when she passed the receiver over and that was why for a second he thought it could be Elena.

He asked how she'd found him. She said she was visiting in Calgary and had looked up his number in the phone book. That wasn't what he'd meant. He thought he'd travelled through Saskatchewan without leaving a trace. It was quite a surprise to find out his actions and his identity had been known and remembered.

"My father took off with Elena Huhtala after you left her at Gilroy," she said, almost as if it was his fault. "I'm trying to find him," she said.

He'd met her for coffee; his wife hadn't wanted to come. He'd already explained on the phone that he had no information for her – he'd never heard a word from Elena and didn't expect he would – but he felt sorry for the girl and curious, too, he couldn't deny it. He remembered driving past the little town of Gilroy on his way back to Calgary that summer and not letting himself turn in, and he felt a bit flattered now to think Elena had been talking about him. He'd forgotten about her father until Ruth brought him up. She said it was Mr. Huhtala who'd told them about him, about following him and the Lincoln to Regina. "I wrote down everything he told us," she said. She was a cute kid, wire-rimmed glasses and a pompadour kind of hairstyle she didn't quite pull off. She had some theories about why her father had never been in touch with his family, mainly to do with her mother's pride. She thought if she could locate him, she could let him know she understood. "Now that I'm older," she said.

"All I have to go on is what Mr. Huhtala told me," she went on, trying to act efficient, like a newspaper reporter tapping her pencil against her notebook just before she makes a discovery that will save some guy from the gallows. Mr. Huhtala had told her quite a few things, from the sound of it. They were things he'd never told his own daughter, she said with a secret smile, about Finland and the ideas Finnish people have.

The man had of course gone to Gilroy, looking for Elena. Right after they'd talked in the hotel lobby, he must have left. He'd arrived too late, as it turned out, too late for him and too late for Ruthie and her family. Ruthie, that's what she'd called herself when she first phoned him; it was only later that she'd changed to Ruth. She'd phoned a few times over the years, after that, just checking, she said, even though he assured her there was almost no chance Elena would ever get in touch with him. His wife said probably it gave the kid some comfort, having even such a slim connection with her dad. "I'll say it's slim," he said. He didn't mention that there was often a flirtatious edge to her conversation, and that he thought the phone calls gave her a bit of a thrill, and what they actually connected her to was that summer romance long ago.

This time was different. Ruth's voice alerted him right away, it was so tense and it got more strained the more she talked. "Is something wrong?" he asked, and then she gave him the news. Elena had returned; she'd shown up at Ruth's house the day before.

"Hey," he said. "That's – that's surprising." He tugged the towel tighter with his free hand and shivered.

"Thought you'd want to know," she said.

He thanked her. "It's kind of unreal, isn't it?" he asked. "How is she?"

"Fine," she said. "Herself."

"I bet you never expected her to turn up at your door," he said. "After all these years."

She didn't answer and he thought he understood. This was one momentous return. It almost obliterated the time in between. And now there was only one question. He looked out the living room picture window at the lawn and the linden tree framed by the drapes. He remembered planting that tree and the way doing it had made him feel permanent, planted here at this house, in this neighbourhood. "And what about your father?" he asked finally. From her tone he didn't expect any good news in that quarter, but he couldn't not ask.

"Oh, she lost touch with him long ago."

"I'm sorry." He paused. "Ruthie, I'm really sorry."

"Yeah, I know. She says she's going home."

"Home," he said. "Is her father still alive?"

"Yes. Well, as far as I know. He's so old . . ." Her voice faltered and she stopped and cleared her throat. "I guess anything could have happened to him since I last heard. We write back and forth a couple of times a year."

He remembered the way she'd talked about Elena's father, the day he'd met her for coffee, how she'd almost glowed with feeling special, talking about the things he'd told her.

"That's good, Ruthie," he said. "That's nice."

He could feel her shrug him off.

"I don't expect she'll stay with him long," she said. "She's not exactly stable. But I suppose she never was."

He asked what she meant by that, but she was vague about it and sounded distressed, and he didn't push her. After they said goodbye he set the receiver down gently into the cradle and stood a moment with his hand on the phone. "Poor kid," he said. He'd got so used to talking out loud to himself lately, half the time he didn't notice he'd done it. He was thinking about her writing back and forth with the old man all this time, and wondered what it would mean to her if Elena went home and stayed there. He hadn't asked her if she'd phoned Mr. Huhtala or if she was planning to let him know. Maybe she'd hold off on that. You could never tell what Elena would do; she might not make it all the way home. No use getting the old fellow's hopes up. He must be at least eighty by now. He would see her before he died or he wouldn't. Or maybe he'd passed away already, too late again.

He went to the bedroom and dressed automatically. Buckling his belt, tying his tie and then his shoes, he stared into the past as if it existed in the next room, as if it could explain itself if he walked through the door. He could recall a nebulous version of the face and form that had haunted him more than a few years after she'd left him, he could almost see her searching eyes, he could feel her watching him, and distantly, he could hear her laughing; he thought he could.

Ten minutes later he called his office and talked to his secretary. "Just postpone what you can't cancel," he asked her.

"Two weeks?" she said, incredulous.

"Maybe longer." He cut her questions short. "Nothing's wrong. I just need a vacation."

She was a good person but tended to get too solicitous. He apologized for being curt and made a joke about his age and the quest for the meaning of capital L life and was sorry when he heard her listening for more.

He packed a suitcase and thought of the day he handed Elena's bag over to her father in the lobby of the hotel in Regina. He could still remember the look on the man's face at that exact moment. And he had tried not to remember it. He'd tried to ignore it. There was some poem he'd read about hollow men or a hollow man that came to mind. No, he hadn't wanted to see that face. It had made his own pain look trivial, and he was holding onto that pain; it was all she'd left him with.

He went around the house snapping lights off, making sure nothing was running that shouldn't be, and it occurred to him that these actions were endings and that endings were supposed to be the precursors of beginnings. He had no clear idea what he wanted when he walked out the door and he felt disloyal when he locked it. In the car he felt better, as he always did. He had more of a sense of purpose when he was behind the wheel than any other time except when he was flying, which nowadays wasn't often. He backed out of the garage and drove down the lane into a sunny day. As usual he had the top down, and two young women who were waiting at the bus stop at the corner waved to him.

ADDISON

Merv wouldn't go for a walk in case the woman from Pioneer Villa phoned, so Pansy set out on her own. *Pioneer* was a word she detested, but she'd move in before you could say Jack, she'd move in whatever they called it, they could call it Shit Hotel and she'd haul her ass there with her glad rags on. The apartments were modern (running water, flush toilets), subsidized, and in Charlesville, three things that made them perfect. And supposedly she and Merv were next on the waiting list. Pansy couldn't take another winter in Addison. At least in the summer Bob Pearson's son lived in town while he farmed his dad's land and looked after his cattle. In the winter it was just the two of them, and the ghosts of people who'd always disapproved of her, hanging about their falling-down bungalows and gaping cellar holes. She didn't like walking on her own. Without Merv's company she was always seeing the others, picturing them wagging their fingers at her, wagging their tongues – but she liked her routine. We'll seize up if we don't move, she told Merv. Funny that she was the one, that he'd proved lazier than her, after all these years, looking for any excuse to avoid exercise.

She walked to the Pearsons' dugout at the edge of town. It wasn't as hot as it had been the day before, but that would be far enough. She stood on the road gazing at the churned mud where the cows had stepped around one another on their way to the water. About a hundred, no, about a thousand tiny toads were hopping on the mud. "Where the heck did you come from?" Pansy said out loud.

On the way home she thought about telling Merv about the toads. She decided she wouldn't. Just mention toads and he'd go on about the cat gagging on one. That was decades ago but it stuck in his memory the same way the goddamn toad had stuck in the cat's throat — as she'd pointed out to him more than once. And when he talked about it, he swallowed all the time, over and over. She hadn't pointed that out. She hated it. Swallowing like that, as if he was the one gagging. It made her scared he would gag. She stalked through the high weeds that grew up in the middle of the seldom-used dirt road, making towards the shortcut to the hotel. She could see his scrawny old face going purple in front of her. She could see his eyes bulging, the stubble sticking out on his chin. And what was gagging him? What made it so he couldn't speak and couldn't breathe? Was it her? Something she did to him? Something he couldn't tell her? What nonsense. She knew him like the back of her hand, like the ache in her back. And Christ, if there was a single thing he ever thought that didn't come out his mouth, she'd like to know it.

At the Vierlings' lot, she skirted the dent in the grass that marked where their outhouse had stood. At the bigger hollow, where their cellar had once stored their preserves and bacon and crocks of fermenting sauerkraut, she stopped. The grass rippled over the land, dipping into the ladle-like depression. Soon the earth would fill in and the grass would grow over everything.

She'd told herself a lie. There were things she didn't want to know about him. Or rather, if there was anything she didn't know, she was happy to protect that ignorance, thank you very much. She thought of the magazines she'd ferreted out occasionally through the years; but if he had secrets, they'd be bigger than that, harder than that to understand, and they would be his own secrets, belonging to him as hers belonged to her. She kept on trudging down the wreck of Main Street, and it came to her that if he had submerged some part of himself, it was so another part could be fulfilled. It was so he could love her. She took the few steps up to the door and stalled with her hand on the knob, stalled there so long she almost did seize up. It almost seemed her old hand and the knob were one, and then she turned it.

"Got the call," Merv said before the door closed behind her.

She sat down to change from her shoes into her slippers.

"We can move in the end of the month."

"Give me a hand, will you?" she said. He hauled her to her feet and kissed her. She shook her head. "Christ," she muttered. "Let's not go overboard."

"You see now the value of procrastination," he said.

"I do?"

"It makes you wonder, though, if we hung around here all these years because we're lazy, or because we're optimistic. Did we see a glimmer of this brighter future? Or was the past not as rotten as we thought it was? Which makes you wonder, which comes first, hope or fear?"

"Hope," Pansy said. "Babies are born with it. They learn fear."

But Merv said only one thing could end fear, and that was hope.

"It don't matter which comes first," Pansy said.

"*Egg*-sactly," Merv replied, darting his face in front of hers.

"Don't start that."

He followed her down the hall. "I'm agreeing with you. Don't you find it *egg*-citing? Oh dear, no response *egg*-cept a per-*egg*-nant pause?"

"Christ," she said over her shoulder.

"Ah, at last – an el-*egg*-ant *egg*-spletive."

"I notice you didn't pick the chicken to harp on."

"Oh, a challenge. A challenge from my loving wife. Chicken, chicken . . ."

"Hah! You're stumped."

"No, no, I'm slowed, I admit it, but I'm not giving up yet."

"Maybe you need to think quietly for a few hours," she said.

He laughed and laughed and told her she was witty.

◇◇◇◇◇

Elena woke up later than she'd intended and pulled on her clothes from the night before. She made instant coffee in her room and put on her makeup while she waited for it to cool. By the time she was done, a scum had formed across the cup; the coffee was tepid and bitter and she grimaced after downing it. She pulled the drapes and stood looking at the parking lot. It was completely irrational to think of going home.

She'd seen what happened to people who dwelt on the past. They stranded themselves between whatever had happened and whatever might have been. They tied themselves to people and places they should have long since left. She'd always refused to be one of them. Long ago, she'd stopped asking questions, pretending she didn't want answers, and now she really didn't want them. She wouldn't have thought of the fretful night before if it hadn't been that a newspaper was flopping from car to car across the parking lot, pasting itself briefly against a wheel of one and then the bumper of another, and it reminded her that she'd walked barefoot, back and forth for half an hour, without a thought of how soiled the carpet must be.

She went to the bathroom and brushed her teeth, staring into her own mascaraed eyes. The person in those eyes agreed with her. It made no sense to go home. And when that person tilted her head and started to look pensive, she turned impatiently away, packed up briskly, and checked out.

She decided she would drive straight through from Charlesville to the farm. That way, she'd arrive in late afternoon. If someone else lived there now, which was entirely possible, it would be a good time to stop. She'd ask if she could look around, as if that was why she'd come, to walk on a bit of ground she'd walked on before, gaze on a few spots she supposedly remembered. And if her father was there, if he could be there – well, that would be that, wouldn't it? And if the whole place was abandoned, the buildings gone, just some farmer's fields or more likely pasture, because that land had never been arable, she'd go on into Trevna; and if there wasn't a place to bed down in Trevna, she'd just keep driving. It wouldn't matter to her, then.

That was the plan, and she drove through the morning and into the afternoon with it firm in her mind. She drove fast, since the roads were nearly empty, and kept her eyes on the view out the windshield. The landscape held no surprises for her now that she was used to the idea of better crops and lusher ditches. The wheels skittered on the gravel, the car nearly floated, the road took her effortlessly onward. But then she had to slow to a crawl for a farmer moving his machinery, and then she saw the sign for Addison, and then she thought about Bill. It wasn't the first time he'd crossed her mind lately; she'd thought of him as soon as she'd decided to come to Saskatchewan, but this time there was a difference. Because they'd spent their first night here, she decided, that's why. But it was the morning she remembered, the morning they left here – setting out – the big roadster throbbing under them while they sat at the intersection, having no idea which way they would turn.

On the way into the little town she passed a car cemetery, half a dozen rusted-out shells abandoned beside the glittering pile of a nuisance ground. Her rented Ford was the only licensed, road-worthy vehicle in miles, but she angle-parked anyway in front of the Addison Hotel, one of the few buildings left standing on the main street. She turned the engine off and rolled her side window down and listened for any sound of life. She imagined a dog barking but didn't hear one. The smell of dust wafted into the car. She got out, leaving the door open. Nothing to see, up or down the wide street. She'd forgotten how small the buildings were in a prairie town. Even the false fronts on the two that sat across from the hotel, wide apart like a mouth missing teeth, barely reached the height of a normal one-story. One of them advertised itself as The Modern Department Store; neither had been painted for decades and the boards had silvered with age. Weeds grew right up to their doors. The two grain elevators beside the railway tracks appeared to be in operation, however, and telephone poles – or power poles, she didn't know which they were – marched down the street, stringing wires across the blue sky. Hadn't she gone far enough for one day?

She knew at once it was the same couple. They were nothing if not distinctive, might have been the two skinniest old people she'd ever seen. Between them, they had barely enough flesh to cover one set of bones. They came to the door together, and she knew it was because nobody had knocked for a long time. They leaned forward, sharp shoulder blades bent in permanent protection of their hollow chests, and peered at her. They said the hotel wasn't open. The man said he was sorry. She didn't have the heart to ask if they'd let her stay anyway, even though she suddenly felt she would be ill if she continued on. She forced herself to breathe slowly and deeply. It was only nerves; she knew that. The woman must have seen her distress; she asked if Elena wanted to use the bathroom.

"Oh, no," she said. She remembered the state of the bathroom the night she'd stayed here, and backed down a step. The old woman was staring at her. She looked at the old man instead. "I'm sorry for disturbing you," she went on quickly. "It was foolish of me. Obviously you're not open."

"We're leaving soon," the old woman said. She was staring, still, as if she would take something from her if she could. "End of the month," the old woman said. "We're packing up, moving out."

"This town is history," the old man said. The old woman squeezed his arm. Like a pair of skeletons, the two of them, pleased with themselves for breathing. They didn't recognize her, of course; she was only one of many girls and women who'd spent a night in one of their rooms and moved on. They waited in the open doorway while she went down the last steps. She turned when she reached the street and said, "I stayed here years ago." Blurted it out. They looked startled. They tipped their heads politely, but what was there to say? She shrugged her shoulders to acknowledge it and avoided looking at them before she drove away.

At the intersection she noted the time. It was just after three o'clock. She was right on schedule; if anything, she would arrive earlier than she'd intended.

You didn't find the town, Ruth said right into her ear when she turned the car in the direction of Trevna. She could see her standing in the middle of her kitchen, revelling in the moment. *Off the face of the earth*, she said, triumph in her voice. *Gone.*

"Odd kind of dress," Pansy said while they watched the car turn onto the highway. "Must be the new style."

It was possibly the first time Merv had heard the word "style" fall from Pansy's lips. He thought it was a good sign, a forward-looking trend potentially developing late in her life. And then he had a Eureka moment. "Yes," he drawled. "I'd say she's very chicken fashionable." He waited. "*Chic 'n* fashionable?"

Pansy pretended to be ignoring him. She pretended to be examining the length of Main Street and at its end the foundation stones of the torn-down Lutheran church.

"What?" he asked, slipping his arm around her. "You think I'm repre-*hen*-sible?" He chucked her under the chin. "C'mon my little sugar plum, admit it, I re-*coop*-erated."

"You slay me," she said.

He jumped back and regarded her with admiration. "Hey good for you, love. S-*lay*? We're back to the egg. *Egg*-squisite, isn't it?" He let her deliver a disdainful look. "Give me a kiss, dear, and I'll quit."

She kissed him. They both went and had a nap after that.

◇◇◇◇◇

Bill hadn't planned to stop anywhere along the way, but when he saw the sign for Addison, he couldn't resist turning in. He was pleased to see the hotel still there, slumped like an old cardboard box at the far end of their main street. He pulled up right where he'd parked almost thirty years before, and sat with his engine idling. He still had the top down and although the day was warm, he could feel the cool air of night around him. He remembered Elena had waited for him in the car when he'd gone to knock on the door. And then she'd asked him something about the stars.

He was about to drive away when a face appeared in the grimy downstairs window, the nose almost pressed to the pane. He couldn't believe it; he recognized her. It had to be the same cranky woman. Then the front door opened and there was Scrawny stepping out as cautiously as you might on a gangplank over a violent ocean.

"Merv," Pansy called, but he'd already gone out the door. And then the fellow got out of his car. Big, fancy car, the colour of blue old ladies liked to knit into baby booties, a convertible, no less. And of course Merv wouldn't have the sense to get rid of him. He was yakking away to him on the steps. Christ, now he was inviting him in.

"Two visitors in one day," he was saying, ushering the man into the office.

He came right over to her with his hand out so she had to shake it. Said his name. It meant nothing to her.

"Bill here stayed with us one night," Merv said.

It was on the tip of her tongue to say nobody ever stayed two, but she didn't like to talk to strangers.

"Have a seat," Merv said and the fellow took a chair.

"I was telling Bill not too many stop here in Addison, any-more," Merv said.

Pansy snorted.

"So it's quite the coincidence, having two in one day. I was telling him the lady who just come not an hour ago also said she stayed here one night. And then – see, I recognized him. I didn't know from when, but I knew he looked familiar, and then I thought, Jeez, that woman looked familiar, too. And then he says he stayed here with a young woman."

"It *was* a long time ago," the fellow said.

He must have seen the look on her face. If he'd lived with Merv all these years, he'd be looking the same. Merv could spout six reasons off the bat for whatever he was wishing, and he wasn't even trying to convince you it really happened so much as to make you wish along with him that the world really could unfold his way.

"I'm pretty sure it was her," Merv said. "People don't change that much you know, and I recall bringing the two of you breakfast in bed. We didn't do that often, here. It's hard to believe, though, isn't it? Cripes, the two of you must be on the same wavelength."

Pansy snorted again. All she could think about, and see in her mind's eye, was the two Berger kids who'd tried to talk to one another with two empty tin cans and a big long string. It had worked best when they shouted.

"No, really," Merv said, "I bet she started wondering about you, eh? And that's why she's here. I can tell you she doesn't live around here because she was driving a rental. A two-tone brown Ford, Bill," he added, looking significantly right at him.

"I guess that would be some fluke, eh?" the man said.

"No, it wouldn't," Pansy said. "She wouldn't think you'd be here. Nobody would think anybody would be *here*."

The fellow only laughed as if she'd made a pretty good joke and looked on her like he'd just remembered she was his favourite aunt. He was making himself at home, sprawling back in his chair like he'd grown up here, watching the business along with them since he was a freckle-faced kid. "Did she say where she was headed?" he asked.

"No," Pansy said so sharply it was clear they both expected her to say more. But she didn't.

"You didn't see which way she turned when she left?"

"No."

He sat back in his chair and smiled at her. "You don't still have a cat?" he asked.

"Imagine you remembering that," Merv said.

"Those Christly cats," Pansy said. "We're too old to look after anything but ourselves."

Let them think it was a coincidence, Bill thought. The old fellow was having fun with it. He went on chatting with them about their health and their upcoming move to Pioneer Villa – which might as well have been called Heaven on Earth, they were so happy to be going there – and all the while the old woman sat up straight in her chair with her arms crossed in front of her, clutching her own old elbows, reminding herself not to tell him which way Elena had turned. It didn't matter to him; he knew he'd find her. He had a map and now he knew the colour and make of her rented car. The old man was getting agitated, though, and finally after some hemming and hawing, he excused himself and pulled his wife out of the office, obviously to confer.

Bill leaned back in his chair and looked up to the ceiling and pictured the room upstairs, the way it was when they'd walked into it, the dim light, the cheap furniture, the small bed with the permanent gully down the middle. He remembered her beside him in the bed the next morning, how soft and weak she'd been. She hadn't wanted him to know it, was afraid to show it, he figured. He'd puzzled over her behaviour, taking everything she did and said to be a comment on him. He wondered if she could have been as beautiful as he remembered. His eyes had often followed women in the street, looking for her. Two or three years after she left him he was still doing it, and even once in a while after he was married he'd glimpse a slim figure like hers at the end of a block, turning the corner, maybe, walking out of sight, and he'd have the urge to go after the woman, just in case.

He could hear the old couple hissing to one another behind the closed door. Then the knob turned. "Wipe that grin off your face," his teachers used to say when he was a kid, and he remembered it in time to look neutral before they walked back in.

When he got to the intersection he knew which way to go, but he didn't know where the farm was, only that it was somewhere between Addison and Trevna. It would be an hour's drive. The map was spread out on the seat beside him, held down with his shaving kit, though he didn't need it anymore. He could ask at a house or two along the way until he found her. He was driving a Lincoln, this year's model, not as splendid a vehicle as the old roadster, but she'd see it coming. That's as far as he'd let himself think except to remember he was bald, nearly bald anyway, nothing but a rim of sandy hair left on his head. His wife had said it was okay; he had a good-shaped skull, she said, but he hadn't looked in a mirror for a day of his life, since it started thinning, that he didn't remember his mother saying (he must have been all of five years old at the time) that red-headed men lost their hair early.

LAWSON

My mother got it into her head that my dad was coming back. She wasn't senile. She was barely sixty and fully enjoying her life and she said it just like that. "I've got it into my head your father might be coming back." Something had made her think he was returning to Saskatchewan that very day. She thought other people knew about it and had decided they shouldn't tell her. "There's gossip going around," she said.

"Have you had a letter from your father?" she asked right away, as soon as I stopped by to visit before getting my groceries. We never talked about my father. She hadn't mentioned him to me once, not once since the day he left Gilroy. I was pretty sure she hadn't mentioned his existence to anyone on earth since that day, and I'd been proud of her for that. I had (privately, mutely) extolled her for that. Of all the qualities that made me look up to her, the first was that she was strong; nobody trifled with her.

"I have never had a letter from him."

"I have reason to believe he's going to show up today."

"Show up today? Today? Where?"

"Here."

"Why? Why would you think that?"

"On the five o'clock train," she said.

"It's been thirty years."

"Twenty-eight."

"Right. Okay. Really, Mother?"

"Of course I may be mistaken, but when old friends start getting evasive, I'll tell you, something's going on." She stood up and then, I suppose, didn't know why she had. An excess of emotional energy, likely, had brought her to her feet. "I don't know, Ruth, to be honest," she said. "But in case he is on that train . . ."

I thought I knew what was behind this, why her old friends had been acting evasive; they'd been talking about her behind her back. They'd heard about Elena Huhtala. It was only natural that Valerie would have told a friend or two, not only about the visit but about the story behind it, and gossip that provocative travels fast, and invariably gets embroidered on the way. I didn't intend to explain; nothing would have induced me to say a word about Elena Huhtala to my mother.

Lawson was not much bigger than Gilroy had been, but my mother's house wasn't near the train tracks, and there was no station, just a platform by the grain elevators. I didn't ask her how my father would know to get off here, how she thought he'd know where to find her if he did come back. I also wondered why she was so sure he was coming specifically to see her. He might, for example, have thought of returning to see me. But really, I didn't for one minute believe he was coming. It hadn't occurred to me for ages that he ever would.

"It's not likely, is it?" I said.

She didn't answer that, didn't like the question and didn't like me making my voice gentle when I said it. You would not call my mother a hopeful person. I don't think I ever saw her look as if she was anticipating something unless she was play-acting it to amuse a child, the way you do, pretending to expect one thing and then, when the opposite occurs, affecting great surprise. Sufficient to my mother was the moment she was in and the hand she was dealt. I really think she saw hope as an affront to her God and the reality He'd created. She was motivated by belief.

"I'll come back after I get my groceries," I said. "If you want me here." It would mean I'd be late getting home and late getting supper on the table, and she knew it and thanked me. I held back my sigh. It wasn't new between us that my mother expected much of me and I rose to her requirement. She had named me Ruth for a reason and I was every bit as loyal as my namesake, but when I thought of the biblical Ruth, I always pondered the fact that "ruth-less" is the word that has survived.

I shopped at Scott's, of course. The new store was bigger than the one in Gilroy had been, although not as big as the Co-op down the highway in Central Butte, where the majority got their groceries. Scott had to keep longer hours because of that, but it didn't bother him. The store was his life.

"How is your mother?" It was the first thing he said to me every time I came in, even if he'd seen her that morning. Then, no doubt, we'd have to go through the entire family, each brother and sister, since none of them had remained in the district and couldn't speak for themselves. I'd worked for Scott for several years and had clerked for him off and on since Leonard and I were married, too, when he'd needed extra help, and in spite of my fondness for him, his little tics irritated me. My mother used to say of Olive, his wife, that she thought she was one of the elite because she lived above the rest of us over the store (we called it The Emporium because of her), and Scott sometimes employed the same upper-class assumptions, in spite of his innate humility. Oh, how complicated we all are, I thought as I browsed the shelves for Corn Flakes and such. And Leonard was so much like him.

How was my mother? A good question, and not one I was going to answer out loud. Nor, apparently, was I going to think about it much, because Scott was alone in the store, and we had to chat about the crops and the harvest and the weather. I wondered, as we talked and I picked up canned baked beans and dish detergent and set them into the cardboard box beside the other necessities of life, if he didn't have any *under* things on his mind, any fires that ran underground and never stopped burning. I'd tried to put out one of those fires that morning. I'd called Bill Longmore. I wasn't at all sure of what I was doing and I hung up a couple of times before the phone started ringing. It was likely wrong to call him, even though I'd told him I would if I ever heard any news. I knew his wife had died after her long illness and he'd been alone for more than a year. I heard his voice get hopeful, and I wasn't doing it for him. I didn't ask him to do anything, but I let it sound as if she might need somebody and I could hear him thinking it might be him. He was the kind of guy who responded to other people's needs. If he thought he could be a help to her, he would try. All the time we were talking, I worried that if he did head out to find her, it would end badly for him. It had been on my conscience ever since and it made me feel like picking a fight. That wasn't going to happen; you didn't fight with your father-in-law, not in my world. I was saved from any confrontation, anyway, when the Milton brothers came in, gabbing nonstop, as they always did, as if they'd just accidentally bumped into one another on the street, and didn't see each other every hour of every day and (some said) sleep together at night. They did interrupt their conversation long enough to say, "Scott," in unison.

"Boys," he said.

They didn't get far into the store. They stopped by the window, gesticulating and spouting such wisdom as, "What goes round, comes round," and "History repeats itself." I wondered about this applying to my own situation. Could I take it as a sign that I was hearing such phrases said? But that was a dumb kind of logic; my father had never returned, he had never written to us, he had never shown the slightest interest in our existence – so if he did show up today, it wouldn't be a case of history repeating itself, it would be a case of a miracle occurring in Lawson, Saskatchewan. While I finished my foraging, the Miltons got well into their most recent theory that Khrushchev and Kennedy were going to start a third world war, and more than history was repeating itself.

And then Anna Quinn came in and her eyes bugged out so far when she spied me, they nearly spurted off her face. By the time she was breathing on me, I knew why. The gossip about Elena Huhtala wasn't only about my mother and father; there would have been talk about Leonard, too. I hadn't been the only one in Gilroy to think he was head over heels about her that summer, and it didn't matter that it had been long ago. Well, her visit had proved it didn't matter. Anna wasn't delicate when it came to dissecting relationships; she never had been back when she lived in Gilroy, and she was worse now. She was eager for fodder, happy to think of herself as the broadcaster of a bit of community scandal.

"Heard you had a visitor," she said.

I tried a simple, disdainful downward glance at her shabby shoes. Awful women always wear un-self-respecting shoes.

"That's what I heard," she said.

"When you've heard it all," I said, "try silence. Old World proverb."

She laughed as if I'd been good-natured and after that I only had to put up with Scott repacking my groceries and acting paternal, as he often did to compensate me for my fatherless youth, while allowing himself to mumble a little over the milk and butter and eggs that an industrious farmwife could have produced for herself if she didn't refuse to keep animals other than dogs and cats on the farm. "You're looking well, Ruth," he said before I left, and even that annoyed me.

I got back to Mother's about four o'clock and unpacked the box from the back of the truck, so the milk and butter and eggs could be hauled to the fridge. The first thing I saw when I went inside was that she had changed her clothes. She was wearing her good blue dress and her white high heels. She looked elegant but it was an outfit normally reserved for weddings and funerals, and I thought: All this for my father?

The first couple of years after my father left, I used to pretend he would drive up beside me as I walked home from school. Sometimes I stayed late on purpose, volunteered to erase the blackboard or help some kid who couldn't do his arithmetic, so I could walk home alone, so my dad would find me alone on the road and pick me up and take me home. I'd drag my heels the whole way. I'd pretend I could hear the motor half a mile behind me, getting nearer. Often this would be in winter, and walking along, shivering, I'd imagine the car pulling up beside me and think how warm it would be inside and how happy he would be to have a few minutes alone with me before he had to face the rest of the family.

When I was a teenager I used to imagine a kind of revenge scene in which he did what Elena Huhtala had done – drove around looking for a town that was gone from the face of the earth. Gilroy wasn't one hundred per cent abandoned, yet, in those years, but my mother had moved us away, to Lawson, and almost everyone else had left, too.

The terrible thing was that I'd tried to blame him for everything that had happened to us because of his leaving, but I knew in my heart I'd wanted Elena Huhtala to fall in love with him, and him with her. I'd even envisioned them leaving Gilroy so they could be together, but somehow in a crazy-kid way, I'd believed they'd take me with them. I'd even thought someday they'd send for me to join them. That was my other fantasy, that it wouldn't be my dad in the car; it would be some messenger he'd sent with money and a note telling me to board the next train east.

My mother made tea. I'd have liked to take it outside, but she had no patio, and you don't sit in the dirt in white heels. The minutes ticked by until she went to her bedroom around ten to five, and I went to stand on her front step to get some air. I thought about my conversation with Ivy, the day before. I'd been fussing over that look between Leonard and Elena. More than fussing. There was a big ache growing in me with nowhere to go. I needed someone to talk to, and then Ivy came. I was so glad to see her, I had to pretend I wasn't, or she would have thought something was wrong. She knew me so well.

She sat at our kitchen table, in the same place Elena Huhtala had sat that morning, but as I stood on my mother's doorstep I wasn't picturing her there; I was seeing her up in the sky, against the clouds, in her white uniform and the cap that looked like wings on her head. I was thinking about the fortune-telling that had predicted all that white and wondering if anyone else's future had come true or if Elena had made a special connection with Ivy when she was supposed to be connecting with me.

I quit school in grade ten, a straight-A student. My mother had arranged a job for me at Scott Dobie's new store in Lawson. She was excited when she told me; it was going to be such a help to the family. While I worked at the store and brought my pay-cheque home to my mother, Ivy kept on at school and got her grade twelve; I endured that by telling myself her family didn't care about being respectable. Then the war came and she went into training with a scholarship because nurses were needed. Now she was the matron at the small hospital in Central Butte. She'd been married twice, but had less success in that line. At forty, she was a compact, stylish person, as blond as Marilyn Monroe, and it didn't come out of a bottle.

I told her Leonard hadn't meant to be disloyal. I made sure to say that. But the more sympathetic she looked, the more sympathy I wanted. I wanted her to denounce him and stand up for me. "It's his knowing what it would mean to me," I said. "He had to know."

"Yes," she said.

"It's all tangled up with my father."

"Yes."

"He knows that."

"Of course he does."

Her consternation increased as I went on and I could feel paranoia leap in my bloodstream. "Do you know something more about him? With someone else?" I was wondering if it could even be her. She knew what I was thinking.

"No," she said. "Of course not."

"You looked so concerned."

"I am concerned," she said. "For you."

"It was only a look," I said. It sounded like a whimper.

She didn't reply, didn't have to. The whiteness that suited Ivy so well had something oddly virginal about it, and restrained, and I knew, too late, that she wouldn't have told me what I'd just told her. I had not protected myself, I had revealed too much, even to a best friend. She'd be watching me now, to see what I was going to do. She'd be expecting me to do something. Not nothing, not just let it go. I couldn't just let it go. I'd made myself the pitiable one, the always contemptible little wife. "Where's your pride?" my mother would say if she caught any of us kids snivelling over some slight we'd received in the schoolyard.

"Men," Ivy said.

"Yeah," I said. "They're disappointing." And wasn't that a nice way to think about it? Disappointing. So calm a word, so accepting, no rage in it, and not too much pain. Like a cup of weak, milky tea. And that very minute he could be betraying me. How did I know where he went when I couldn't see him? Maybe he'd gone to Charlesville. Maybe he was meeting her there, maybe she was waiting for him at the Bluebird Café, sitting alone at a side table, holding a cup of coffee in both hands, turning it sometimes in the saucer. People gawking at her when they came in. Jerry Wong shuffling up to her to talk about the weather. He'd recognize Leonard, standing a moment at the door, but only as a farmer from somewhere south of Charlesville.

And why was it Elena, waiting at the Bluebird for a lover? It could be me. I could be the one sitting at that side table, with my wrists resting on the turquoise Arborite (with the flying triangles, boomerangs; tiny coloured boomerangs flew across it), with my hands warming either side of that thick pottery cup, with my eyes down, but only temporarily, my eyes waiting to look up and see my lover standing in the doorway, the screened door with the Coca-Cola banner slapping shut behind him.

It was Leonard I pictured in the doorway. But it wasn't me in the cafe, it was Elena, looking cool in a fresh dress, looking serene, looking free – yes, free to do what she wanted – and happy to see him. A little anxious, maybe, just a little. She wouldn't have been sure he'd come. Pretty sure, though. There was the old attraction on top of the new one. There would be that moment at the door when he was free, too, when he could still turn away.

And I thought: How did I end up trapped in this life I didn't ask for?

After Ivy's visit, I went out for a drive, just drove around with no destination. I didn't want to talk to anyone, and it was the only way to guarantee I'd be alone. I took the old highway – it had become a back road, used only by the locals – and ended up at the Gilroy townsite. I got out of the truck and stood at the spot where the road into town once met the highway. It was the intersection where Elena got out of Bill's car and walked into Gilroy. I was still asking myself why she'd stopped the car, and why here. Was it really that she'd seen me mooching along the railway tracks, as I'd thought back then? Bill thought she'd just decided she didn't want to go on with him.

Maybe we were both wrong; maybe she'd intended to go back home. I stood there at the intersection as if I was her, all those years ago, facing a decision, to walk into this little town or to turn back and hitchhike home. I thought about her father, waiting all these years for her to return. I wondered if she'd make it home and what would happen when she got there. Mr. Huhtala and I had written back and forth for years but I hadn't seen him again. I tried to think what he'd look like so much older than before, and when I pictured his face, I was afraid for him, for what she'd do to him. I wasn't thinking, just then, what the reunion would do to her. If anything, I was simply jealous, imagining her walking in the door, and his face when he saw her.

The land where the town used to be was owned by a farmer, a neighbour of ours named Ted Evans. He hadn't started harvesting yet. I looked out over his shining fields of full-grown wheat, and as far as I could see, and I mean all the way to the horizon, those fields showed no memory of houses or of people. Not a shrub or a stone or a hollow remained to mark where we'd been. I felt my father standing beside me, as if he were there, as if he really could be standing next to me, seeing what had become of Gilroy. Seeing what had become of me. Oh, yes, looking me up and down, raising his eyebrows, nodding his head, telling me – as I was sure he would do – that it's best to remember the wider picture. Ruthie.

Leonard wasn't in the yard or in the house when I returned from my drive. The kids didn't know where he was. I was late coming home; they'd been too hungry to wait for me to make supper, and Valerie had fried up some grilled cheese sandwiches for everyone, which she'd burnt. The kitchen stunk; you could barely see across it for the greasy smoke. The boys were scraping the black crust off their bread into the sink when I walked in. They all had plans, they couldn't wait for a better supper, and were gone before I'd started cleaning up the mess.

I put everything away and still Leonard didn't appear. I went out to the front step and looked around the yard, to the garage and the granaries and the dugout, and down the driveway to the road. I thought maybe he really had gone after Elena. But I had replayed that little drama a few times, and I was too tired to revive it. I didn't even imagine something untoward had happened to him, some accident that would take him from me so I wouldn't have to make a decision. I really thought I might leave him and it was not, right at the time, a totally unattractive thought. I still had in me the vestiges of my old longing for a quiet room where I could be alone.

I went and sat down on the edge of the tractor tire that held the marigolds, those jolly, upright little flowers that will grow anywhere, under any conditions. Marigolds have a distinctive, herbaceous scent, more bitterness than sweet, a bit like the taste of marmalade, and even now, years later, decades later, remembering that evening, I think I can smell them.

Oh yes, he came along eventually. He'd been delivering the combine to Ted Evans, and then Ted dropped him off home. I'd forgotten all about that, I'd forgotten we'd agreed to rent our combine to him. I should have remembered; I'd been on his property that very afternoon. In fact, we'd planned that I would follow Leonard in the truck and bring him home myself. And then neither I nor the truck could be found when Leonard was ready to go. I didn't apologize and he didn't question or even mention my absence. He sat down with me on the tractor tire. I remember his body sitting there beside me, and my resistance to his tug on me.

After we'd sat there a while, I had to say something or hit him. I'd have preferred to hit him. It would have been quicker and more satisfying to flail at him with my fists, but I had to be civilized. Strange to remember how savage I felt, how savage a person can feel beside a bed of marigolds. "I've been thinking," I said. "Elena Huhtala didn't stop at our place by accident. She didn't just happen to pull into our farmyard to ask whoever might be around why she couldn't find Gilroy. It was deliberate. She asked around and found out where we lived."

He was supposed to ask, "Why would she do that?" He wouldn't, but I answered it, anyway. "She was looking for you."

"You're being ridiculous," he said. "Yeah, you are. You get an idea in your head and you stick to it no matter what." Then he said some other things. I was going to say he said something about my father, about how I'd always idolized him and how unfounded it was to care about him at all, but I wasn't listening and I don't really think Leonard would have said anything like that. More likely I was thinking it, reading it into whatever he said, just so at last we could fight. And soon we were on our feet, facing each other, and I was yelling at him. I was yelling so hard I made all the colour leave his face. I don't know what I said to him, but I remember what he answered. "Oh, no," he said. "You're getting confused. Don't confuse me with your father."

"Are you different? Are you any different? Can you answer that?"

"Yeah," he said. "I'm here."

My mother joined me on the step, wearing white gloves and with her good white purse hung neatly over her arm. I tried not to look surprised, but I'd thought we'd wait at her house for the train to uneventfully pass. I hadn't realized we were going to walk to the tracks. In a small town, it was an excessively public thing to do. What would she say when people asked her where she was going and why, and who she expected to be arriving on that train? What would I say? We were bound to meet someone on the way. And she was all dressed up. It was clear she'd made a special effort, and for what? For the arrival of a man who wasn't coming.

It's hard to explain my mother's strength of character, except to say that she tended to carry all before her, certainly to carry me along. Rather than have her go out on this fool's errand, maybe I should have tried to stop her, told her what I knew, or what I thought I knew: that this was all due to gossip about Elena Huhtala's visit. But to say that to my mother was beyond me. And there was something else. As she strode past me and I followed her along the path out of her yard, just as we set out, I took note of that straight back of hers ahead of me, and I understood the only thing that mattered. This was business she needed to transact. And she needed me, she needed me at her side, because there was no way he was on that train that every day passed by Lawson, that seldom stopped.

Miraculously, we met no one as we walked through town, avoiding Main Street, although I was aware we were being watched. I distinctly caught the glint of Anna Quinn's protuberant eyes behind her plastic lace curtains. Oh yes, there were noses pressed to windows in several of those little shops and houses, and soon we'd reach the road; we'd be fully exposed. We couldn't pretend we were simply out for a walk, not with my mother in her high heels. By the time we got to the road, a few of the watchers would have phoned a few more, people originally from Gilroy, who might be able to explain our behaviour. People tend to think you can do that.

We clacked along the wooden sidewalk towards the road that led to the tracks, and I started talking to my father in my head. I said, "There are two endings to this story, two possible endings, although one is so far-fetched as to be laughable. Either you're on that train or you are not, and neither one is happy." And then I thought about him standing beside me at the old Gilroy townsite, advising me to see the wider picture, and I had to wonder if he could ever have imagined, in his wildest, widest dreams, that my mother would come to meet him if he came home.

Then we were on the road with nothing but the open fields and the sky around us, and the earth was trembling under our feet, and the train was coming, yes, from Gilroy direction came a long, low whistle. We could hear the hustle and bustle of the wheels on the tracks, and an answering hustle and bustle rose in our blood.

We didn't walk all the way to the platform. We stopped on the road, side by side, and watched the train roar past, not even slowing as it sped past Lawson. Our eyes followed it out of sight, and then we stared at the place it had been, the fields bisected by the long rail line, the empty sky above.

"I'm sorry, Ruth," Mother said.

We didn't turn back right away. I think, like me, she wanted a few moments to picture him standing there alone on the platform, the train pulling away, leaving him behind. Just a few moments to imagine him turning and seeing us waiting for him, his wife and daughter, twenty-eight years after he'd left us.

Mother touched my arm and we began the trek back to her little house, past the gauntlet of unseen eyes. I emulated her, walking calmly, naturally, easily along. It wasn't long before we got quite a rhythm going as we strode over the springy boards, our bodies moving so freely I thought we must look almost cheerful.

The streets were still utterly deserted as we neared my mother's house. No figures stood in doorways or, visibly, in windows. If any of them came to their doors and windows and saw us, they must have retreated further inside. I figured they must have thought we were doing something so embarrassing, it would have embarrassed them to be seen watching us. I started laughing and of course Mother looked to me for an explanation.

I pointed around us, to the little shuttered houses. "They're all such cowards!"

She stopped and touched my arm again. I can see her now when I think of that moment, standing in front of her house, standing tall in her high heels. We all have truths we have to face, that's what her touch said.

Leonard's last word on the subject of Elena Huhtala was this: "If she came here on purpose, it was to see you." I felt a lifting inside me when he said that. It still makes me blush to think of it. I don't know if Leonard noticed; he'd tossed off the remark as we were walking back to the house. But he was one for tossing off remarks as if he didn't think twice about their significance. He was always good at that, letting me off the emotional hook, reassuring me without ever intruding. He had an exceptional instinct for respect. No wonder I loved him so.

But at the time I was ashamed. I'd made a great song and dance out of that look between him and Elena Huhtala, and I had been jealous, for sure, but I'd left something out, another thing that had stung as much. She'd looked at him instead of me.

TREVNA

Once you got a little further north, the countryside rippled and rolled more than in the south, and there were more shrubby dips and sloughs. Some people would call it prettier, since it had more variety, but Bill wasn't looking at the landscape; he was picturing his wife standing at the stove, her head on one side while she stirred some pot absent-mindedly. She'd been a great reader. In the early evenings, after he'd come home from work, he would read aloud to her from whatever book she'd left dog-eared or open on the kitchen counter while she finished preparing their supper. Whenever he barbecued or made pancakes for the whole family on a Sunday morning, she would read aloud to him. He'd liked that so much he'd developed a few more culinary specialties. It had been a good marriage and it made him wish for a second chance someday. She'd given him her blessing, in fact she'd urged it on him the last months they'd had together. She'd told him his hooking up again would be a compliment to her.

In some ways she'd been an antidote to his parents as much as to Elena. She'd seemed to understand his fear of his mother's disapproval and his shame at his father's eagerness, which he knew he'd inherited. She'd understood he loved them and needed to put those feelings about them behind him. The main reason he wanted to meet up with Elena again was to show her he'd put a whole lot behind him – and maybe that she'd been mistaken in her assessment of him in the first place. He didn't think anything more than that would come of it.

The old fellow at the Addison Hotel had reminisced about bringing the two of them breakfast in bed and Bill tried to think back again, to capture something concrete from that morning years ago. There were the things that had happened – the sex; her falling to the floor, utterly collapsed; the breakfast they'd shared afterwards – and then there was his experience of them. For a second, suspended in the moving car and at the same time in memory, he could recall exactly how he had felt back then, being him. But as soon as he fixed on the feeling, it vanished. He remembered standing in front of the movie poster in that bigger town they'd stopped at, how she'd thought the title was referring to sex. *It Happened One Night.* Maybe she'd thought that was all they'd had going on between them. But it was more than sex, a whole lot more than sex. For him it was. It was a kind of expansion beyond himself. That was about as close as he could come to nailing the feeling he knew he'd experienced with her body next to his as they sat up in bed that morning and ate the dry toast they'd been given for their breakfast; the heat that rose from her flesh had somehow expanded him. But that thought recalled to him the stronger warmth of his wife's body next to his over all the past years.

He should turn back. He should go home. He didn't know what he was doing, chasing after a woman he hadn't seen for decades. Yet for some reason, as soon as he doubted himself, he felt suddenly and unduly optimistic. This was only a lark, anyway, wasn't it? Hope for the best, expect the worst. Yup, and a well is a deep hole.

He began to whistle as he drove along the old road, loose stones pinging under his car and spurting out from the wheels. He glanced to the empty seat beside him and it seemed to him his wife's spirit was there, smiling on him.

◇◇◇◇◇

"And there you have it, hints from the hinterland. Thank you Mrs. Gustafson!"

The announcer had a voice that slid like melting lard over the air waves. Maria went back to chopping her onions, which was what she'd been doing when he'd called. Tears rained down her cheeks. It had gone well. Soon the phone would ring. Some would call her, others on the party line would call friends to ask if they'd caught her on the radio. The announcer's voice, not to mention the silly nature of the call, had made her feel witty. She was funny in her old age. Sixty-six, she thought. Well, thirty dollars' worth of cake mixes isn't to sneeze at, and I'll use them. Homemade is twice the work and it seems I'm the only one can tell the difference. She turned away from the onions and swiped at her eyes and cheeks with her sleeve. The phone rang, her number, and she went and received congratulations. "Ah, it was only how to fold fitted sheets," she said, but Britte said Maria had explained it so well, she'd gone to the linen closet for one of her own and tried it, and it had worked like a charm. "And you had me in stitches, Maria. You're so funny."

"I'm just myself," Maria said, as if that was being modest.

Two more called while she was caramelizing the onions and then Wendy, her daughter-in-law, ran across the farmyard to tell her she'd heard it, too. "All the way from the old house," Maria said out loud after she'd gone. "Quite the celebrity." Peter wouldn't like it, wouldn't approve. He'd never forgiven her for Henrik's obituary, though he knew what she'd written was a mistake. She was no writer. He should have composed the thing himself, but he was too shook up. She'd tried to tell him most people wouldn't have noticed, they'd have read it the way she intended, but Wendy had pointed it out to him and he'd thought everyone would be smirking. She'd simply said Henrik Carl Gustafson had waged a long and coura-geous battle with dignity. And then, when Peter had castigated her for it, months after Henrik's death – because he'd been unable to speak of it at the time – she'd laughed, compounding the error. When she saw the effect of her laughter on Peter's face, however, she regretted it, recalling how much he was his father's son.

She'd mixed the ground beef and pork with the onions by this time and somehow forming sticky meatballs wasn't conducive to deep thoughts. She began to sing "Zip-a-Dee-Doo-Dah." She was a celebrity, after all. She tapped herself on the shoulder and then shook her head. She'd left a knob of pale, fatty pork on her blouse. But she didn't stop singing and she didn't stop working. Every day she made up meals for Aggie Lindquist. Aggie ran a small busi-ness, although she didn't think of it as a business, only as a way of making money. She drove around the countryside cleaning house for bachelors and widowers who didn't have females to mop up after them. The district had prospered, and women – unless the men married them – would no longer work as live-in servants for their bed and board and the occasional new apron. The problem was that the men wanted meals and Aggie had never learned to cook, but the solution, the lucky solution, was that Maria loved it so much, nothing could make her happier than to think of her casseroles and stews, her salads and desserts, going out across the land. And every evening, when she brought the empties back, Aggie ate her supper with her.

The meatballs were simmering in their gravy when someone knocked on her door. She glanced at the clock. Too early for Aggie, who never knocked anyway. Nearly suppertime, an odd time to call.

It was a stranger, a salesman, she supposed. He had a salesman's smile. Unlike Aggie, who had every Rawleigh and Watson product known to man, Maria wasn't a sucker for anyone's patter. For a second she wondered if it could be her cake mixes, but of course it was much too soon for them to be delivered. The man went into a sorry-to-be-interrupting-you spiel. Nice-looking fellow, friendly-looking. Trying to find a person who used to live somewhere around here when she was a girl, he said. A woman called Elena Huhtala.

"Wait!" she said. "My potatoes are boiling over!"

While she was at the stove, she brushed at her shoulder in case the blob of meat was still there. Twenty minutes later, Bill Longmore was sitting with her in the dining room, telling her his hopes and his plans while he waited for his supper.

◇◇◇◇◇

What Elena thought about, while she drove to the place she still called home in her mind – which was definitely illogical since most of her life had not been lived there – was that her father would be an old man, if he was still alive. Also, that he was a person who had a life separate from hers. So he would be a stranger to her.

Fatherland. The word popped into her mind. She'd gone to his, and now wondered if she had one, if this was it, this landscape, these people. Her gaze travelled over the land and she saw a strange phenomenon. More like a fabric than light, a gold veil was floating at the same speed as the car, a long veil unrolling and unravelling. She began to rehearse what she would say if she found her father at the farm. It seemed as if her words lay on the veil and were borne across the fields. But they wouldn't be gifts if they reached him; they wouldn't be welcome. He would nod and glance up once into her face, or maybe he'd refuse to look at her.

"I went to Finland, to a little town called Hattula." That was how to start. No, she should tell him about arriving in Hämeenlinna and about the desk clerk and her daughter.

The desk clerk had seemed aggressive, at first. "Why don't you speak the language?" was practically the first thing she said. Of course, the woman was struggling to communicate in English.

It was a relief to escape to her room. Later, returning to the hotel after dinner, she was glad to see there were two of them behind the desk, the bossy woman and another who was about thirty, who had to be her daughter, she looked so much like her. The desk clerk nudged her daughter and shoved her forward. "My mother is nosy," the daughter said. "She wants to know who you are. You have a Finnish name."

"I was born here."

"In Hämeenlinna?"

"No. In Finland." In spite of herself, she added, "I don't know where."

"Why do you come here?" the mother interrupted.

She told them she'd come to see Hattula because of her name, because maybe the spelling of her last name had been changed and maybe her people had come from here. She didn't want to explain all this and was wondering if she could be rude and tell them to just hand over the key, when the woman, the mother, erupted and shouted, "No!" as if she'd been lying.

"There is a small village called *Huhtala*, where your people may come from, but it is far from here," the daughter said. She had put her hand on her mother's arm, apparently to stop her from bolting over the desk.

"North," the mother said.

"North of here," the daughter said.

The mother spewed something more in Finnish, her eyes fierce. The daughter still held her arm. She sighed. "It is in the northwest, Huhtala. Near Kokkola. You know where that is? On the coast, north of Vaasa." Her mother prodded her. "It's many of Swedish descent, that place. Huhtala, the name means woods or glade."

"Does it?"

"You are pleased. It is a nice name." Her mother's entire body expressed a counter-opinion. "The north was White; Vaasa was their capital," the daughter explained. "You know of our civil war? In 1918." She sighed again and glanced at her mother. "For years no one spoke of it. And now, oh, all these people are suddenly doing research into records, visiting prisons, battle sites. My mother thought you are one of them. This area was Red, the other side. Hämeenlinna had the biggest prison camp after the war."

"I didn't know."

"Little war, long memories." She went on to explain that her mother had been a soldier in a woman's unit. "She was later in prison, here. She has a grudge still."

"But my father fought with the Red Guard. I do know that."

The daughter spoke to her mother, then turned back. "I tell my mother you can't decide from a name." The mother interrupted with another flood, pushing at the air with her hand as if to sweep the words across the desk. "My mother says your father lived a hard time, you should know that. Maybe he fought here. A big battle was held in Hattula, in the cemetery there. The men they captured were executed. Many. Her fiancé. Her brothers. Shot down, between the graves where they stood. Thousands died also in the prison camps. It was merciless there. They starved to death, yes, or they got very sick and died."

"Typhoid. My mother died in a camp, of typhoid. She was a doctor."

The daughter told her mother this. For once the mother had nothing to say. "Maybe the same camp," the daughter said. "Maybe here. Who knows? You could find out in records, I think."

The mother was crying now.

"She isn't angry at you," the daughter said. "She was very young, just twenty. It's hard for her when people come wanting to find out what happened. You see, it's easy to ask, to look, to wonder. Different to live it. Some things you don't get over."

"Today you go to Hattula?" the daughter asked the next morning, when Elena dropped off her key.

"I suppose so. I've hired a car, and it's too far to drive to *Huhtala*." She said it as if it were a little joke. Surely it was para-doxical, that she should come all this way, cross the ocean, to land in the wrong place.

The daughter took it seriously. "Yes, much too far unless you have more time." Her mother interrupted. "My mother wants to know how old you were, when your mother was in prison."

"Oh. I would have been about two."

"What happened to you? Who looked after you? My mother says your father would have been in prison, too, or else in hiding. He would not be let to be with you."

"I don't know. It never occurred to me to wonder." They seemed surprised. "He didn't tell me," she said. "I didn't know."

The two women fell silent. Their concern was obvious and unsettling, and she felt the oddest leaning towards them, looking at their identical frowns, a leaning so strong in her that for a second she had the idea they were going to tell her it was them – or at least it was the mother – who had taken her in and cared for her all those years ago. For a second, she let herself think it could be. But then she realized that of course they were only imagining the toddler she would have been. That was all it was. The look on their faces was for the two-year-old, for any distressed two-year-old. The mother reached up to her daughter's hair and brushed at it as if it had fallen forward over her brow. The daughter handed Elena a note. It was the name and address of a sauna in Hattula, with a time and date marked on it: four o'clock that afternoon. "My mother says you take sauna today."

It was absurd to go to Hattula at all, but she had no time for much else; the next day she would return to Helsinki and board a plane for home. So she found herself in the quaint little church, Holy Cross Church, outside the village of Hattula, where every wall and ceiling, every arch and column, was decorated with frescoes. Monks centuries ago had painted them, every one to tell a story. She walked up and down the aisles, alone in the church. The soft colours, warm against the old plaster, and the simple scenes with their flattened perspectives soothed her. There was a patient kind of hope, strange to her, in the bland faces of the angels and devils and the men and women on the walls. There were many women. Her favourite was one with flowing gold hair down to her knees, who held a building in her hands. Probably it was a church, but she held it as if it was the entire world. She held it like a child holds a dollhouse she still believes in, and looked into its windows with deep, abiding interest.

As she was about to leave, she passed by a set of stocks that rested against the wall near the door. Punishment for misbehaviour in church, she assumed. Not wanting them to be her last impression of the place, she turned back to survey the paintings, to let her eyes sweep over the aqua, green, ochre colours; the awkward grace of the figures; the acceptance on the faces. One scene caught her eye. She stepped up to see it closer. A girl was lying in bed with a pillow under her shoulders and a rumpled green blanket up to her waist. She was holding an open book, and although one of her eyes was focussed on the pages, as if reading, the other was cast down, so you realized she was not seeing the words in front of her; she was thinking – or maybe not thinking, just musing. Yes, something in the book had made her sink away, into her mind. She held the book with one hand; the other hand was clasped protectively around her ribcage. She was unconsciously cradling herself. Three haloed women hovered over her bed. Two of them looked down at her, holding their hands out, ready to go to her aid. Her mother and her sister, Elena thought. The third was praying. Whoever she was, she had already given up hope. The squiggles and arabesques that decorated every otherwise bare surface, and linked the scenes throughout the church, swirled about them like a breeze, or like vines waiting to take over once these humans had played out their time.

Beside the church, on bucolic land leading down to a lake (there were low stone walls, buttercups blooming in calf-high grass), was the cemetery. She wandered for a while, reading names and dates. Not much more was incised on the stones, not many clues were provided to tell who these people had been, and the little information that had been given had eroded on the older stones and was unreadable. There were many buried here who had died in 1918, as her mother had. She strolled up and down the rows, wondering how she would feel if she found a headstone with that name on it.

The women at the hotel had told her about the battle that had taken place here, and she could see marks on some graves that might well be bullet holes, but it was impossible to imagine how it would have been, to fight here some sunny day like today. Boys and girls – the troops were mostly young, in their teens and twenties – running from one headstone to the next, ducking behind them, shooting from behind them, shooting at one another, the booming of the guns, the panting, the curses, with the lake glimmering in the background and the clouds floating by, oblivious, overhead. The dead below, oblivious. Impossible to feel how it would have been to stand among the graves, afterwards, waiting to be executed. Or to hide behind a headstone and witness what was happening. Perhaps her father had done that, right here, where she was standing; perhaps he'd crouched here, at the outside edge of these old graves, watching. She sank down, herself, her hand on an old stone for balance, and looked out from behind it. She shut her eyes and heard birds chirping, not gunfire, not cries, birds.

She walked down a country lane, alongside the lake, to the traditional smoke sauna, a little wood hut by the water. She reached it at four o'clock and found it ready for her. A note pinned on the door had her name on it and the time and the information that the bill had been paid by the hotel in Hämeenlinna. Inside was a towel and a switch made of birch twigs. More punishment, she thought, recalling the stocks, but she didn't feel she was being punished; just the opposite. She felt thankful. She stayed longer than she'd thought she could in the sauna, sweating in the extreme heat so encompassing that it blocked out all thinking.

After the sauna and a cold dip off the little dock, she sat under the trees, enervated. But it suited her to feel weak and tired and cleaned out and at the end of things. The tree branches lifted and fell, the shadows around her lifted and fell, the secretive leaves rustled. *The name means woods or glade*, she remembered. Maybe her father had been here; maybe after the battle in the cemetery, he'd run here and rested. She saw the very place for him to rest, in a hollow between two trees. It was a bright spot, covered in fine, dense, spongy-looking emerald green, dotted with yarrow and buttercups and ferns. She could see him lying there, the whole long length of him.

Her mind went back to the cemetery and she imagined herself standing over a grave marked with a simple cross, down near the lake, imagined it belonged to her mother, that her mother was lying there under the quiet grass. She almost knew how it would have felt to have found it, to get that close to her.

How beautiful this little woods. Above her was the speckled light she thought she remembered from childhood, the sun glinting through the branches of birch trees. Ah yes, they were birches. She sat for a long time at that spot. She thought about the quietness, about being alone. She sat with her hands lightly clasped and it seemed she'd completed the circle of herself.

GILROY

My daughter wanted to talk to me about our visitor. It was the evening of the day I walked to the railway tracks with my mother, and I wasn't at my most patient. We were doing the dishes together, so the conversation took place alongside the clacking of plates as she dried two at a time and the clinking of glasses as she shot them into their rows in the cupboard shelves. She wanted me to give Elena a label of some kind, call her strange or extraordinary, pin her down in some way that would put her in her place as neatly as the knives and forks in the silverware drawer. She didn't know that's what she wanted. She searched for the questions to ask, the ones that would lead me to define Elena for her, and in doing that define me, which would in turn supposedly tell her something about herself.

"She's not like anyone I ever met," Valerie said.

I nodded as if that had been my observation too, as if I'd always thought there was no one like Elena Huhtala.

"I wonder where she is now."

I wondered, too, where Elena was now, if she would have reached Trevna yet, if she would make it home. I had never been to that part of the province, but I could imagine the countryside; it wouldn't be much different from here, a long gravel road between unremarkable fields and then the driveway, the huddled farm buildings, and Mr. Huhtala waiting there. Or maybe not waiting there. It had been a few months since I'd heard from him, and he had talked about dying in his last letter, not in the roundabout way most people do, but right out, because it was on his mind.

Standing at the sink, I had my back to the table where Elena had sat the day before. I could feel her presence, still, in the room. "I did something wrong," I said.

Valerie stopped with a mixing bowl midair and looked at me over her shoulder. It was a somewhat unusual admission, I suppose. That was what the expression on her face said.

"I've been writing to her father for years and I had a letter from him only a few months ago. I should have told her that. I don't know why I didn't. I should have."

"It was a secret. You kept it even from us. I mean, you never talked about him."

I didn't know how to answer that. It seemed a pointless thing to have done. I didn't think I'd done it deliberately.

"It's okay, Mum," Valerie said.

"He was alone. All these years." I leaned against the sink. "I just thought it would be good for him to have someone keep in touch. I liked him very much, you know. I mean, I like him. He writes good letters; it's as if he's thinking out loud. Last time I heard from him he reminded me about something he told me long ago, about Finns who think they can predict their own demise. That's how he puts it – demise. The thing is, they predict it so far in advance, it's more . . . more inevitable than clairvoyant. But I think . . . well, it's been hard for him." I remembered Elena had said that. *His life was hard.* I hadn't wanted to believe her that he'd let her think he'd killed himself, but now I thought anything could happen; you could never tell what someone would do.

"Do you think she will go home?"

"I hope so."

We worked away quietly for a bit, the old routine taking over. I started thinking once again about my phone call to Bill that morning, worrying about meddling in somebody else's life, and reminding myself how unknowable Elena really was.

"I hope things turn out okay for her," Val said finally. She'd stopped drying and was watching my face for any telltale thoughts.

"It would be hard to know what okay would be, for her," I said. I don't think I meant it quite the way it came out. I'm afraid, since Valerie grinned so conspiratorially afterwards, it must have sounded sardonic. I remember it clearly, that moment – the intimate, approving smile, and how briskly she hung up her tea towel and turned to me.

"She'll get what she deserves, I guess," she said. As blithe as can be.

I have to say I was startled. For one thing, it wasn't how we talked about people; it wasn't what we believed, that people got what they deserved, or that they should, and I thought we would have to have a talk about the complicated feelings a person like Elena could evoke. But at the same time it made me happy, her saying that. She was so obviously – if a little wickedly – on my side.

She grinned again and gave me a little shove, her preferred method of showing affection lately, and then she was flying out the door, leaving me staring after her. Gone, I thought. I was still staring at the empty space in the screened window that had held her just a second before. The sun had set by then; beyond the door it was the time of evening called the gloaming in poetry and songs, not quite dark, a shadowy time, just right for thinking about people being gone.

Driving home on the old back road after leaving my mother that afternoon, I'd known I was going to stop at the Gilroy townsite again. I parked on the bit of intersection that remained, as I always did. I got down from the truck and walked the few feet to the ditch. The wind had picked up and Ted Evans's wheat came towards me in waves. It was quiet but for the usual sounds of the usual insects and the odd bird twittering the way they do, making it seem quieter than ever after they stop. I think I knew there was nothing for me there, but I stood for a few minutes watching the wheat heave like the ocean.

After that I drove home fast, conscious of being late and having groceries to unload and supper to get ready. By the time I pulled into the driveway, the sun was getting low, and I hurried to do all that. Now I stopped tidying my kitchen and imagined myself stepping out of the truck and standing a minute with my hand on the open door, looking at our house the way Elena did the day she showed up, as if I had all the time in the world. I didn't really see the house or the yard or the fields or the sky beyond, all of which would have been in the picture. I saw myself in the doorway with my daughter at my side. I saw it the way Elena would have seen it.

TREVNA

Now she was driving on a road she knew, a road she'd walked along many times as a girl. It hadn't been paved, and much of the gravel had worn away; the packed dirt surface had been gouged into tire tracks. Her car was coated with satiny dust. Some of the land on the south side had been irrigated and was growing a vegetable crop she couldn't identify; some of the fields were just pasture, divided from the ditches by sagging barbed wire. A green smell came in her open windows and she thought about the years when there had been no green, when the sparse grass had bleached to the colour of the hard clay underneath it, when the dried-out ground had split in long, deep cracks. She passed the Gustafsons' farm, if it was still the Gustafsons' farm, and remembered riding into Trevna with them, in their wagon. They'd had a little girl and a son; she'd sat in the back of the wagon, between them, not knowing she was on her way out of here.

She pulled over to the side of the road and stopped the car. Her father's land was just ahead, to the right. The house looked the same, the barn and outbuildings, the long driveway. The windbreak poplars had grown taller and some fir trees had been planted. The dugout was full of water that looked blue from this distance.

◇◇◇◇◇

He was sitting reading a book at the table in the window. Once in a while he scratched the side of his nose with his forefinger, and once in a while he appeared to look over at the old wood stove that gleamed across the kitchen, all shiny black iron and highly polished, curlicued chrome. Regularly, he turned a page. He was him, that's what she thought, he was him in some way she'd forgotten or perhaps had never understood. So much older, but still he was the him that was her father. He didn't know he was being watched. She was standing off to the side, but within his field of vision, and he would see her if he looked. Coming home from school, as a girl, she had done this. He'd be bent over some work and she'd sneak up on him, wherever he was, outside or in, to see the expression on his face when he looked up.

She backed away from the window. Now that I know, she thought, I could turn around and leave. She did turn; she thought about leaving. She looked at her rented car and pictured it driving away, got it as far as the road, and then the field in front of the house drew her attention. Every pebble and blade of grass, every stalk in the stubble was lit as if on fire by the western sun. She had seen a prairie fire as a child. She'd watched it from the Gustafsons' yard, where her father had left her while he went to help fight against it. The flames had raced over the neighbouring land, sounding like the wind. The men had worked for hours, digging trenches to confine it. Then all they could do was let it burn itself out. She'd had to stay past dark and even then she wouldn't go into the house, so Mrs. Gustafson had come outside and stood beside her, eating a slab of bread and butter.

The fire had almost died by then, but it still reeked; smoke and ashy flakes still drifted over them, and dozens of cow pies still smouldered in the blackened pastures. Like candles in the night, Mrs. Gustafson said, or like some of the stars had fallen. After a minute she tore off half of the bread and handed it over and Elena ate it.

He hadn't heard the whispers she'd overheard. *At least he didn't hang himself in his own barn.* Somebody had done that, some other farmer who hadn't been able to make a go of it, who couldn't watch his animals starve, his kids take charity. *They'll find him in a gully one of these days, with his gun beside him.* That was another. He hadn't seen the pictures those whispers summoned. She leaned her back against the ridged clapboard and closed her eyes for a moment. When she opened them, it was to survey the glowing fields beyond the farmyard. Her father's land had been harvested, so he must have had enough rain and sun this year to make up for the poor soil. Or maybe he'd amended it over time, growing pulse and things like that, as she knew he'd been advised to do. The garden was at the other side of the house, by the dugout. She supposed it would be doing well, if he'd kept it up. There would be vegetables to cook on that shiny stove.

The linoleum shone, too, she observed, when she walked in. He looked up from his book.

His long, deeply furrowed face expressed nothing. Maybe a mild surprise, at someone he didn't expect walking into his house. His eyes, enlarged behind the reading glasses, looked cloudy. He removed the glasses, but she still wasn't certain he could see well enough to recognize her, although he looked right at her and she was only a few feet away. She thought he must be getting deaf, or he would have heard her car pull up, the door open.

"Isä," she said. She sat down across from him. He put his glasses down on the table and gripped his book with both hands.

The book trembled with his old man's palsy. He stared at her, either unseeing or stunned, she couldn't tell. He'd always been good at hiding his feelings.

"It's Elena," she said.

He nodded. He closed his book and looked over at the stove, the way he might have looked to a friend to help him. She looked at the stove, too. It had sat there for as long as she could remember.

She turned back to him and said, "You look well."

He shook his head. She could see the side of his face, his mouth working. She thought he might cry and he would not want to cry, so she said, teasingly, "And the kitchen is very clean."

After a few moments, he said, "I have a housekeeper, these days." He faltered, but almost managed to speak in his old droll way, looking up at her just at the last moment. He was grateful to her, she could see it in his eyes, the glimmer of relief. The pattern he'd set long ago would hold, he could rely on that. It would keep him safe, the way it always had, slightly mocking everything to do with himself.

"Times have changed," she said, and when he looked uncertain, she explained, "A housekeeper, no less."

"Yeah." He sounded shy, as if it was an admission. Maybe he thought she was criticizing. There had been no hired help when she lived here.

"That clock is new," she said. It was a round disk embedded in a red plastic rooster.

"Aggie bought it."

"Aggie Lindquist?"

"Yeah."

"She's your housekeeper?"

"Yeah. Comes afternoons. Brings supper, cleans."

"She certainly does clean," Elena said.

He almost smiled. "What would people say if it wasn't spotless?"

A fly came to life and started attacking the ceiling light fixture, buzzing and bumping against it. The flyswatter hung by the screen door on a nail that had been pounded into that wall forty years before. It was a new swatter, though, of perforated red plastic. Elena was beginning to get an idea of Aggie's taste. And Aggie was slyer than she was sometimes given credit for, she decided; there was more than a bit of the rooster about her father, still. What would people say, indeed, if Aggie spent a few hours here, and the house didn't get cleaned? She took the swatter and waved it around a foot below the fly while her father watched her – how? As if she'd never left? As if he might not ever see her again? There was no telling. The fly retreated and crawled across the high ceiling, just far enough away to be unbothered by her. She followed it to the living room, which looked exactly as it had the day she left, sparsely furnished and uncomfortably overlaid with shadows. But sunlight splashed down the stairwell from the hall window above and in spite of Aggie's efforts, dust motes floated up and down in the lit space.

"Is it all right if I stay a few days?" she asked when she came back. He pointed at the squat refrigerator. It was new. Well, electricity was new, the sink and running water were new; the farm hardly looked prosperous, but the times had surely changed. The fly sat by the capital F at the beginning of Frigidaire. So he could see quite well out of those rheumy old eyes. She slapped the swatter hard and the thing dropped like a raisin to the floor.

◇◇◇◇◇

Driving east from the town of Trevna on her way to Maria's for supper, Aggie Lindquist started musing about death and how unbelievable it was to think that the sun would go on shining and lighting the harvest dust above the fields when she was no longer here to love the way it looked. She had lost one of her old bachelors recently, and in the past two years both her parents had died, but it was Matti Huhtala who had led her mind down this path. The things he said to her. Most of the men wouldn't talk about dying, but he, who spoke so little, had recently told her he was beginning to grieve for all he was going to lose. He hadn't said it quite like that though. He'd said, *A table lasts longer than the man who made it.* Watching the clock, he'd said, *It gets less before it's gone.* She was thinking how it would be, to feel like that. So she drove along, loving the occasional black-eyed Susans – they were easy to love – and then about twenty grackles flew over the road, dropping their shadows across the hood of her truck, and then she saw the car in Matti's driveway and slammed on the brakes. She backed up for a better look. If she'd been a different person, if she'd been Maria, for instance, she'd have turned in even though she'd cleaned for Matti earlier and had already left him his supper. If he'd been a different person, too.

It would be a salesman, she decided, insurance likely, since your ordinary Watson guy couldn't afford a new car. She drove on more soberly, glancing in her rear-view mirror from time to time and seeing nothing but an unphilosophical sun in her eyes. As soon as she gave up doing that, from way down the road she spotted the convertible parked in the Gustafson farmyard. She had lots of time, before her truck rattled and bumped to a standstill in front of Maria's house, to wonder who could be visiting. She pulled up right beside the car. It was longer than her truck. When she got out she wished her hands weren't full; she would have liked to touch its gleaming blue paint and the chrome along its headrests and the ribbed leather seats. If she could have been sure no one would see her, she would have loved to open the wide door and slide inside, settle her back against the seat and run her fingers over the knobs and buttons on the dashboard.

Maria shouted to come in. She sounded a bit breathless and was wiping her face against her sleeve. Aggie set the stack of empty casserole dishes and Tupperware down on the table and looked around the kitchen.

"We're eating in the dining room tonight," Maria said. "We have a guest." The word had wings attached. Up it flew to the ceiling while Maria led the way to the dining room. "This is Bill Longmore. And Bill, this is Aggie. You may remember dancing with her long ago."

"Aggie," he said, rising from his chair to shake her hand and look into her eyes. "I believe I do remember dancing with you."

"Pshaw!" she said, louder than she intended, and heat rose in a line she could feel from her chest all the way to her forehead. She plunked herself onto the chair he drew out for her, and then she knew who he was. She opened her mouth to say so, but Maria interrupted. "He's here looking for Elena Huhtala!" she said. Then she turned to Bill. "Tell her."

"I believe she's on her way home," he said. "She might be there already."

"There's a car in the driveway!" Aggie said.

"A rental, right?"

"I don't know. A new car."

"A two-tone brown Ford."

"Yes, I'm almost sure it was."

"That's what she's driving."

A pause followed that announcement while the three of them beamed at one another as if they'd orchestrated this miracle themselves. Then Maria suddenly said, "Eat, eat." She was so emphatic, she made Bill laugh. Aggie shook her head and laughed too. Maria could always relax you and put you in a good mood. Obligingly, they passed her dishes around the table. They tucked into the mashed potatoes in her blue bowl, the buttery garden green beans and carrots in the yellow one, and the cast-iron pot of Swedish meatballs, still simmering over the copper warmer. They ate and then ate more to please her, and talked very merrily all the while without too many expressions of wonder on Aggie's part or too many questions or explanations on Bill's. Maria did most of the talking, especially when it came to relating Matti Huhtala's sad story. "In this very house he said, 'I will find her,'" she told them. She rose to clear the plates and Aggie helped her and then they ate her famous Saskatoon pie (warm from the oven) with her fresh farm cream.

"How was it you ended up here, anyway, Bill, the night of that dance in Trevna?" Aggie asked while they were having their coffee.

He looked startled by the question, and stared across the room a few seconds before he answered. "My father gave me a new roadster as a gift for college graduation," he said. "My mother was going through a bad time, she had cancer and was in a clinic, and my father took off for a little break – or so he called it. Took his secretary with him. I wasn't supposed to know that, but he wasn't all that careful to hide it." He smiled at her. He must have noticed she'd flinched at that word *cancer*, a word most people didn't say out loud. He had one of the most appealing smiles she'd ever seen; it was as if he was asking something of her that he knew she wanted to give. Her approval, that's what he was asking for, or even her prior pardon for whatever he might do or say. She felt indulgent and privileged at the same time because of it.

"So there I was in the house alone," he went on, "with this big convertible sitting in the driveway. I cruised around the city for a few days, but my friends were mostly off on holidays or working through the summer. One night I drove out into the country, to a dancehall, had a good time. Went back home and packed a suitcase and set out. I thought I'd do a tour, you know, hit some more halls, spend my vacation that way. Hey, it was fun for a while," he added, seeing them listening to every word. "I was young then." He even looked young when he said it, Aggie thought.

It was Bill's intention to spend the night in Trevna and then to drive back and visit the Huhtala place in the morning. At the end of the evening, when they were standing at the door about to leave, Maria said to him, "Ask Elena if she'll come and see me."

Aggie said, "I'm not sure I want to meet Elena again." She'd spoken without thinking and laughed self-consciously when they turned to her for an explanation. "She's almost bound to disappoint me." Maybe she'd meant it for a warning. She didn't think so, but sometimes her mind went ahead of her, and she did like Bill an awful lot. He took it as a warning; she saw that. He turned serious, with something like second thoughts in his nice blue eyes.

Maria saw it too and before he left she tried to override it. "I always think of her sitting on that swing they had in their yard since she was a kid," she said. "She was sitting there the night we picked her up and took her to the dance at Liberty Hall – where she met up with you, Bill."

She smiled at him, her sharing smile. She wanted him to think what a happy accident it was that they'd picked Elena up, that she'd gone to the dance, that Bill had showed up the same evening. How lucky it all was. But Aggie thought a whole lot that wasn't so pleasant could also happen because of the simple sequence of time. "That swing's gone now," she said.

"That's right," Maria said. "Thelma Svenson asked Mr. Huhtala to take it down so her youngsters wouldn't bike over there to play." She touched Bill on the elbow. "But you don't care about that."

They were all amazed by the time, by the darkness that filled the sky when Bill opened the door. As he backed down the driveway in his impressive car, Maria said to Aggie, "I remember driving into Trevna with Elena that night in the wagon, and turning around to talk to her – she was sitting in the back with the children. I thought I'd never seen the like of her big, empty eyes."

"We used to think it was glamorous, that sadness," Aggie said.

They both lifted their arms and waved to Bill before he turned onto the road and drove off.

◇◇◇◇◇

While the last of the light pulled away from the yard and fields, Elena and her father sat in the dark house over their coffee. She'd suggested they move from the kitchen to the living room, where they could catch the cross-breeze from the two open doors, and he'd hobbled behind her. It took an effort for him to move from one chair to another, but he did it, he made the effort. They could barely see one another across the room.

They'd sat in the dark this way in the old days, each of them deep in private space. Not wanting to waste the coal oil by lighting the lamp, not having the coal oil to waste. It had been a comfortable, companionable quiet when she was a girl, but as she grew older, he'd become increasingly withdrawn. That last summer, they'd hardly spoken. It was true she'd wanted to go, she'd longed to get away from here, but she'd never said so. She wouldn't leave him when he was depressed. Now, looking back, she couldn't see how things had got to such a state, when surely she could have hitchhiked somewhere, found some kind of job, come home to visit once in a while. She didn't understand herself, let alone him. Somehow they'd got locked into a situation that only repeated itself.

When she'd gone upstairs earlier, she'd seen that he'd left her room unchanged. Three hand-me-down dresses still hung in the closet, along with Thelma Svenson's dusty, shapeless coat. She could ask him what he'd been doing those weeks after he left, while she waited every day for him to return, but she knew what he'd been doing. He'd been pretending to be dead. She'd searched their land and past it, those days, her legs scratched, her face and arms sunburnt, creeping into every copse and coulee in case she would find him there at her feet – and she hadn't found him. She'd woken up afraid, those mornings, like a kid waking up in a strange house, not knowing where she was. Hour after hour she'd sat out in the yard, unmoving on the swing, and all that time he was pretending to be dead.

She had thought she would tell him about Finland, about the woman and her daughter in the hotel, and about the church and the cemetery and the woods by the lake. But she didn't want to tell him now. *He keeps himself to himself, doesn't he?* That's what the neighbours said, and he always had; he'd kept his troubles and his sorrows to himself. And she had been expected to do the same.

"You knew I meant you to go," he said finally, his gruff voice travelling across the darkness as if he'd been listening to her mind. After a while, he said, "I am sorry the money wasn't much." His voice shook. "But it kept you till you were on your feet, I hope." He paused but she didn't speak. "It was so you could get out of here, make a life for yourself."

She was glad she couldn't see him. Making excuses. Or worse, remaking history. Is that what she had travelled all this way to hear? There had been no money. Where would money have come from, in those days?

"I didn't worry about you, Elena. You were always resourceful; I knew you'd do well."

It was a lie; he had worried about her and she knew it. He only said it to end the conversation, to make it possible to get up from his chair and go to bed. She stood up and went to the centre of the room and pulled the cord that hung there, turned the light on so she could see his face. She had meant to tell him what she thought, but she found she couldn't.

A car was passing on the road to Trevna. It was all she could see besides their reflections, the entire room's reflection, beyond the black window. Another living room seemed to exist there, out in the farmyard, in only a slightly spectral state. She couldn't see the road, only the headlights, but she watched them cut into the night beyond the reflection, and then she watched the red tail lights until they disappeared and all that was left was the two of them in the room that existed in the two places.

"You're right, Isä," she said before she went up to bed. "I was resourceful."

◇◇◇◇◇

From the kitchen window they could see the driveway, and as they sat at the table with their morning coffee, and heard the car approach – or Elena heard it and her father knew she had – they both lifted from their chairs the inch necessary to peer all the way down to the road. Neither of them recognized the vehicle as a Lincoln Continental. They saw that it was long and low and summer-sky blue outside and in, that it had expensive chrome detailing and four doors. The top was down and the driver wore a suit and a Frank Sinatra fedora that marked him as an older man in these modern times.

The convertible pulled up beside the rented car. "It's Bill," Elena said. "I believe it is. He had a gold convertible, last time."

"He's the one?"

"Oh, the one."

He was sitting in the car, looking at the house. He'd tilted his hat back, and yes, that's who it was. She felt completely resigned, not even surprised, since it was only justice that he should appear. Now he was getting out of the car. He wouldn't be able to see inside until he came to the door. She drew the blind down all the way to the sill. Her father glanced at her, but didn't ask her why. He looked tired to the marrow of his bones, this morning. His flesh seemed to have sunken and you could see his skull, the eye sockets more noticeable than his pale eyes.

Bill was knocking at the door. Only the screened door was closed; the other was propped open with a big stone, one they'd chosen for its dark mica flakes that sparkled in sunlight. She could remember the day they'd found it. "You go," she said. "Please. I don't want to talk to him."

He got to his feet and made his slow way to the door.

◇◇◇◇◇

It had been a typical start to a late August day, with the slight chill of autumn retreating as the sun gained strength. Nothing is like the feel of the sun when the air is cool; if he thought about his surroundings at all, it was about that delicate warmth. The farmyard was like every other farmyard, or maybe poorer than most. He hadn't really seen it as he'd pulled up to park beside the rental. He hadn't registered much more than the make of the car and the dingy white paint that was peeling on the siding of the house. He had an image in his mind of her coming to the door, appearing behind the screen, a hazy figure, but solid. Solid as houses, people used to say, he didn't know why, given their inclination to rot and fall down. And why was he thinking like that?

The old man came to the door, her father. He opened it half-way and stood in the gap, a tall old man, not much stooped in spite of his age – and the years had surely aged him since they'd last spoken. He filled the gap. You couldn't see past him. The light coming through the screen cast freckles all down him; even his faded old-farmer shirt and suspendered pants were dotted, and the effect was to soften him. But he stood his ground. "She won't see you," he said.

"She saw me drive up? She recognized me, then. She knows who I am."

The old man nodded, a curt nod that gave nothing away but acknowledgement.

Bill nodded, too. He'd seen her the night before. As he'd passed the farm on his way to Trevna, he'd slowed to look at the house and a light had come on in a window and he'd seen her standing in the middle of a room. Seeing her, he'd wanted to stop, not to go in and talk to her, not then, but just to keep looking at her. But he'd driven on; it wouldn't have been right to stop. He'd gone on into Trevna, thinking about her, because who knew how she was getting along with the old man. It was hard enough for anyone to come home. And now she didn't want to see him. She'd pulled the blind down when he got out of the car. She's afraid, he thought with a sudden instinct that he was right. He stepped forward and leaned his hand against the door frame. The old fellow maintained a calm detachment, as he had that day in the hotel lobby. It was a kind of nobility. "Tell her she has to see me," he said. "Please. That's all, just see me."

For the first time something showed on the bitterly weathered face and in the clouded grey eyes, something that looked like an emotion. But it was only a flicker, and it was gone so fast you couldn't tell what it was he'd been thinking.

"Would you tell her that?" Bill said. "Okay? I'm not leaving."

The old man wavered, then. "Wait here," he said. He closed the door.

Elena had heard the exchange at the door and neither of them spoke of it when her father returned. He sat down again at the table and stared at the stove. Well, she had nothing to say. So they would sit in silence, waiting. This was how they were together, always waiting, and for what?

He reached across the table and put his hand on hers, a surprise. The hand trembled and the shiny skin looked too thin and tired to hold bones together much longer. But she wasn't going to weaken just because he was an old man. Or because he'd tried to explain. Saying he'd left her money. No doubt it was convenient to remember it that way. But what difference did it make? He'd let her think he was going to kill himself and then he'd let her think he was dead. Why should she put up with his hand on hers, as if all was forgiven?

He was shaking his head now, so he was thinking something or other, trying to drum up something to say, likely, more justification for what he'd done. His eyelids flared red, tears brimmed. She wasn't going to save him this time. Why couldn't he speak? Here they were, after all these years, and he could not simply say he was sorry.

She turned to look out the window, forgetting she'd pulled down the blind, and ended up staring at the white rectangle that blocked her view. Bill was still sitting out there, she thought; he must be or she would have heard the car leave. She remembered her father had followed their trail across the province that summer. Ruth had told her he'd done that. A feeling of plodding, hopeless and dreadful, came over her as she thought about him walking miles, hardly eating, hitching rides when he could. She saw him standing at the side of the highway with his thumb out, a tall man, resolutely alone, the wind battering him, cars and trucks passing him by. She thought about him going all the way to the city and then backtracking to Gilroy and talking to people there, speaking to Ruth and her mother in case they might be able to tell him where she'd gone. Knowing who she'd gone with.

She leaned back against the hard ribs of her chair and saw Ruth's face again, as it had looked when they'd talked about their fathers. *At least your father came looking for you.* A childish thing to say, really, the kind of thing the girl, Ruthie, would have said. She could see her on the main street of Gilroy, she could see her clearly, without even trying, as if that little town would always exist and Ruthie would always be there. She was holding her glasses – they had fallen off – and she was staring from the middle of the street, with one intent eye. The other eye, meanwhile, gazed off in its own direction until she put the glasses on and came forward with her scraped hand out.

"Ruthie," she said out loud. She sat very still, trying to sort out her thinking.

"Ruthie," her father said, a tenderness in his voice. He was speaking of a child. "She writes to me once in a while. Since that summer."

"Oh," she said. "All that time. All those years." She spoke automatically, not really paying attention to him because she was thinking and because the girl was still in front of her, walking towards her with her hand held out. She was seeing that saucy face and those impudent eyes behind the thick lenses. She was seeing expectation in those eyes. All the kid wanted was a little sympathy. But she was so certain she'd get it, that was the thing.

She was so sure that was the way the world worked. It was natural to want to deny her, and it wouldn't have hurt her a bit. But then something else, something more, had presented itself, something she'd found irresistible, a love affair that struck her now as a disturbing, unintentional kind of revenge. She hadn't thought it out at the time, she hadn't let herself think about it at all, certainly not the way she was thinking about it now. Why hurt a child the way you've been hurt? It made no sense, but she did it.

And how useless it is to be sorry, she thought, how utterly, unforgivably useless.

Her father was patting her hand. She looked down. Why was he doing that? Pat, pat, over and over, like an old man. She wondered if he knew he was doing it, and which of them he was trying to console. He was staring at the stove again. Tears were running down the long creases of his cheeks. And all the time he was patting her hand. There, there. There, there. She saw that she would have to do something, say something, and as soon as possible. They couldn't go on like this.

"Isä," she said, turning to him.

◇◇◇◇◇

Bill didn't knock again. He didn't try to peer through the screen. After a while, he sat down on the wooden stoop, settled his seat on the warm boards and stretched his legs out into the powdery dirt. The morning sunshine was playing across the driveway, driven into patterns by some shifting clouds. The patterns were meaningless, he figured, just like the movement of clouds was meaningless. Except for their effect on the weather. He supposed you'd have to consider that; he supposed rain, hail, sleet, and snow might just contradict that idle thought. So not exactly meaningless. He stirred some of the dust at his feet with his pant leg, and it rose as he'd predicted it would into its own small cloud, and he smiled as he brushed the fabric off. It was helpful to have this feeling of things being connected when you were a bit at loose ends.

He couldn't remember being here the night he'd brought Elena to pick up her things; he tried to picture it and failed. He wondered where the swing had been. He placed it improbably far out in the field by the road, and imagined her walking towards it in her bare feet, wearing the faded brown dress she'd worn when he first set eyes on her. Why bare feet? He didn't know. Maybe he was just being nostalgic, trying to make the past sweeter, softer, than it had been. She'd been a starving kid, and would have bolted with anyone who'd take her away from here. But it hadn't been anyone; it had been him. And what was she thinking, now? She must be wondering what to do about him, and maybe changing her mind a few times. Maybe just by sitting here, waiting for her, he was showing her something she didn't know. Daring her to find out.

A whole lot of maybes going on, he thought. Maybe that ruler-straight road beyond the driveway – running parallel with the horizon as far as he could see in either direction – spanned the entire country, maybe he'd find that out, maybe he'd drive that road as far as it would take him. But he wasn't in any hurry. He could sit here all day. Till the sun went down. Nothing like the sun's warm touch, he thought; it could be his wife's hands on his shoulders.

He looked up at the house behind him, at the blind pulled down to the windowsill. She doesn't know I had a life all the time she was gone, he thought. She's afraid of making the same mistakes she made before. The more he thought about it, the more he was sure he was right. There were times in a life that mistakes could start to seem like crimes. Well, he was guessing. But it could be why she'd come home. *No more we'll go a roving.* He'd read that in a novel, a character had thought it, a woman who barely noticed what she was thinking; one of those fragments of a poem, it had slipped like a breeze through her mind. *So we'll go no more a roving. By the light of the moon.* He wanted to tell Elena he understood, give her something to lean against, even if it was only for ten minutes on the doorstep. She might not need anyone; she might be better off on her own. We're not all alike, he thought.

In the quiet of the farmyard, he heard a soft shushing sound he hadn't heard before, that might have been the earth sighing. Or maybe he'd sighed, himself, he couldn't tell. If so, it wasn't because he was getting melancholy; it was a sigh of contentment, and why not? He had time, he had plenty to spare, and Elena would have to come out, sooner or later. She'd have to come out if only to deal with that rental car, but she'd come out, anyway, because she wasn't a house kind of person. And then they were going to talk. He wasn't at the end of this, and she wasn't either. No, she was no house kind of person; she was a woman who belonged outdoors and preferably in a car, a big, fast, luxury convertible with the top down, open to the sky. He'd ask her where she wanted to go, and she'd say anywhere. He laughed. The old fellow would be on his side, he could tell.

Later, he began to whistle, an airy tune that sounded lonely to those inside the house.

ACKNOWLEDGEMENTS

While I was researching and writing this novel, I often consulted my father about life on the prairies during the thirties, and I would like to thank him for his help. My mother's letters also guided me. I found the local histories compiled by various communities to be as valuable as the history texts I read, and a wide range of material available on the Internet was useful. A special thanks to historian Joan Champ whose blog, *Railway & Main*, provided an intriguing amount of detail on small-town hotels.

I would like to acknowledge a grant from the Saskatchewan Arts Board during the writing of this book and an award from the City of Regina at its inception.

Many thanks to my editor and publisher, Ellen Seligman, and to my agent, Dean Cooke, and to my first readers: Joanne Lyons, Marlis Wesseler, Joan Givner, and Dianne Warren. And a special thank you to Chris Hatley for driving me around Finland.

And to Gordon Gault, for all the years of support and encouragement, my lasting gratitude.